ARDA

A TALE OF MIZ

ARDA
A TALE OF MIZ

BY
E.C. PRATHER

Cover and interior design by Masha Shubin | Inkwater.com
Cover Images (BigStockPhoto.com): Mountain Sunset Landscape © SpicyTruffel;
King With Sword © Cattallina; Clouds © foxeel.

This is a work of fiction. The events described here are imaginary. The settings and characters are fictitious or used in a fictitious manner and do not represent specific places or living or dead people. Any resemblance is entirely coincidental.

Paperback ISBN-13 978-1-7359206-0-3
eBook   ISBN-13 978-1-7359206-1-0

1 3 5 7 9 10 8 6 4 2

For my parents, partner, friends, and brother.
Without his persistent support this
book may never have happened.
So blame him.

CONTENTS

Prologue. xi
Repercussions 1
The Disappearance of the Wizards 6
A Growing Stream. 11
A Single Droplet 16
Ultimatum. 26
Stale Beer. 31
Subterranean Schemes. 36
The Brothers Arda. 38
Momentary Respite 46
"Prisoners". 48
Butterson's Beers 51
Family Reunion. 56
A Newfound Path 62
The Hall of Heroes 65
A Storm Breaks 71
Across the Great Divide. 75
Vandra. 81
An Unlikely Alliance. 87
The Followers. 100
Beauty and the Beast. 105
Fireside Tales 112

Sabotage 118
Disaster 121
A Change in the Wind. 124
The Right Thing 127
Golden Apples 132
The Oethyrlands 134
Hunted 138
The Wolf and the Ram 140
The Eleventh Hour 144
Riddleston's Goat. 147
The Sanctum. 157
Riddleston in the Dark 167
To the Waypoint 172
An Unwelcome Guest 184
Preparations. 194
Between a G'rok and a Hard Place. 197
Growing Shadows 202
The Cost 207
Flight 213
The Canyonlands. 216
Assurances. 221
Behind Bars. 225
Dark Dreams 232
Contact 238
A Wizard's Tale 247
Calm 253
The Signal 258
An Invitation. 264
Special Delivery. 267
A Toast to the Fallen 270
Darkening Skies. 273
A Flag Unfurls 277
The Gallows. 279
The Color of Peace. 282

Revelations. 285
The Trial of Heldan Port .292
The Best of Friends 300
A Reckoning 303
The Western Wall 304
Desperate Times 309
Proof 315
Once More. 320
Into the Fray 323
Aves Ex Machina 328
Urban Legends. 333
Darkness 342
Absolute Power 351
Nightfall. 353
Singularity. 357
A Second Droplet. 361
A Promise Kept 364
Honor the Dead. 367
A Familiar Path 370
From the Desk of Sylvus Riddleston 372
Just Reward 375
Chapter One 378
Epilogue. 383

PROLOGUE

Vandra sat by her window, dreaming of a world beyond the woods. A fire blazed in the hearth at her back, its lambent glow spilling into the cascading darkness outside. The raven-haired young girl rested her forehead against the glass. The deep forest pressed near to the cottage, unfathomable and boundless, the serried ranks of pine black in the storm. She returned to her book and read on by the shifting firelight.

It was one of Father's oldest tomes, a dusty account of Mizian history compiled by the wandering poet, Yfron. She idly flipped through the pages, scanning the yellowed maps, noting with pangs of curious desire the locations of the great northern capitals. But there was nothing here about magic. She rubbed her eyes and put aside her studies. Her gaze was drawn back to the window. It was a moonless night, the trees an indistinguishable mass that shivered in the wind. The rain was lessening.

She could hear Mother and Father shuffling about the tiny

kitchen, their laughter accompanied by the tantalizing aromas of dinner. Her dark eyes strayed to the door and her cloak hanging alongside. She hadn't been able to play outside all day because of the storm, and they would be preoccupied for some time yet. With a smile, she stealthily unlocked the iron bolt and eased the door open before slipping into the night.

As Vandra strode into the clearing, she imagined the creatures from Father's stories, the exciting ones about magic and adventure, emerging from the forest. Over the treetops flew an eldritch dragon, its gaping maw spewing fire as it rushed her through the blackness. With a wave of her hand, she sent the wyrm crashing to the ground, flames extinguished. But now came a horde of goblins with greedy eyes and ragged claws. She twirled her cloak and drove the goblins into the trees, squeaking with fear. She spun round the clearing, sending foe after imaginary foe fleeing from her powers. Dizzy and giggling, she slumped into the wet grass. Mother might chastise her for soaking her clothes, but Father would laugh and hang them to dry.

As she sat catching her breath, she realized the woods had fallen silent. The rain had abated, and the needled branches were still. A pale mist wended its way through the trees, faintly illuminated by the firelight playing through the windows. She knocked the toes of her boots together. The spring storms were common, but she couldn't remember there ever being mist in the deep woods. Tendrils of the fog crept along the ground with unnerving certainty, followed by a haze of gray that consumed the woods as it came.

"Vandra, you better not be getting your new dress filthy!"

She jumped at the call from Mother and sprinted for the door. It opened as she approached and flickering light poured from within, but it was Father's silhouette that greeted her. He knelt in the doorway and laid a calloused hand on her shoulder.

"What have we told you about playing outside?" he asked.

She lowered her head and stuck out her lip. "Never go outside without telling you first."

"And why is that?"

"'Cause I can't defend myself without magic."

He gave her shoulder a gentle squeeze. "That's right, V. Magic is *dangerous*. You need to be more responsible if you wish to learn. Magic must always be respected."

She stomped her foot in the mud. "You said magic is a gift! I want to use it to help people! Like the heroes in your stories. I won't hurt anyone."

Father's beard twitched with a quick smile. "You don't know that." She opened her mouth to protest but he held up a hand. "Accidents happen, V. When you come of age, you must treasure the gift and never take it for granted or abuse its power. Can you do that for me?" She nodded sullenly and Father broke into a warm smile. "That's my little mage. Now, what did you battle tonight? Any dragons?"

Vandra perked up and nodded eagerly. "This one was bigger than last time, too!"

"Excellent! Werewolves?"

"Just one."

"Were you bit? Because if you were bit we'd have to lock you in the goat pen and feed you scraps from the table."

"No!"

He examined her in mock scrutiny. "If you say so, but I'll be keeping an eye on you during the next full moon. Now, let's get you into some dry clothes before Mother catches you. And-" He was looking past her, his eyes widening. Vandra spun about and whimpered.

The mist had completely encircled the clearing. It stood like a great mercurial wall, writhing and coiling, as if indecisive about whether to proceed. To Vandra, it felt as though the silent gray radiated an otherworldly anger and malice.

It felt as though some atavistic presence was watching them through the ether.

"Everything is fine, V," said Father. "It's just mist. Mist isn't scary!" He was trying to sound nonchalant, but she could hear the trepidation in his voice, could see the tightness in his jaw. They watched the mist for several minutes, neither saying a word.

Footsteps approached from the kitchen and Mother joined them in the doorway. "What in the world? Why I, I've never seen anything like it." She wrung her apron. "Just a spot of weather, isn't that so, dear?" Father remained silent, dark eyes scanning the gloom. Mother took Vandra by the hand, hers clammy to the touch. "Nothing to worry about. Come now, before supper gets co-"

A hulking shape moved beyond the twisting veil, then dissolved back into the gray.

Father squeezed Vandra's shoulder so tightly she almost cried out. "Inside now!" he ordered. They tumbled over the threshold and he bolted the door. Vandra ran to her alcove by the window and peered into the darkness. Huge shadows were stalking back and forth like caged beasts, never stepping beyond the wall of mist. And still more were coming.

Mother and Father joined her at the window. His voice was a hoarse whisper. "V, if I tell you to hide, you must lock yourself in the crawlspace under the pantry. Don't make a sound, no matter what happens. No matter what you hear. Can you do that for me?" She nodded, heart pounding in her ears. "That's my little mage." He kissed the top of her head.

Hundreds of shadows now paced frenetically back and forth in the mist. It was as if a pack of hounds was preparing for the hunt. The shapes clambered over one another in their eagerness. Guttural howls rent the night, filling the girl with a dread so terrible she felt paralyzed. And then the shadows froze. The howling faltered. They remained motionless beyond the wall of mist. Total silence fell upon the clearing. Vandra stifled a sob.

A single figure stepped forward, taller than the rest. It stalked to the edge of the clearing and paused. Then, with singular deliberateness, it stepped from the mist. Yellow eyes blazed through the gloom, bright as twin stars.

The figure raised a hand and pointed at the house. It was as if a fire had ignited in the woods. Everywhere, pairs of crimson eyes burned from the shadows, luminous and full of an inhuman hunger. The howling began anew and the shapes rushed at the house with terrible speed.

Vandra was vaguely aware of Father shouting at her to hide. As if in a dream, she ran to the pantry, opened the cellar door, and crawled under the floorboards. She covered her ears but couldn't prevent the sounds from above; the windows shattering; the door exploding under an unrelenting barrage of shuddering blows; her parents screaming incantations. Magic illuminated the house in a kaleidoscope of colors that lanced through the gaps in the boards. She buried her face in the cool dirt, tears wetting the soil, and listened to her parents fall to the shadows.

As she fought to control her breathing, the world began to spin. Slowly, it faded to nothing at all.

She awoke, not knowing how much time had passed. The house was utterly silent. Cautiously, she pushed open the door. The fire had been extinguished in the hearth and total blackness ensued. She felt her way along the familiar walls, crying quietly, and stumbled over something on the floor. She knelt beside the mass and felt Father's coarse beard, Mother's silken hair.

A floorboard creaked behind her. Vandra spun and was lifted into the air. She struggled against an iron grip but was too weak to break free.

From the darkness, yellow eyes gleamed down at her.

REPERCUSSIONS

Tanduil dipped below the chiseled skyline of Heldan Port. The dying sun basked the capital in an amber glow, trapped in an evening haze rising from the Westerly Seas. The city teemed with life, despite the hour. Cries from peddlers selling their wares rose over the crowds in the Merchant District and Cralenson Square. Blacksmiths' hammers clinked endlessly in the Craftsman's Borough, the smiths' fires belching lazy plumes of smoke into the sky. Drunken singing and laughter echoed from the taverns sprawled across the city. Underneath it all, the rhythmic susurrus of waves breaking against the docks and shipyard drifted over the great city walls, as though the capital itself was alive and breathing. And in a way it was, for Heldan Port was thriving, and in no small part thanks to Sylvus Riddleston.

Sylvus Riddleston, Highest Hat of the Occult Sanctum of Wizards, looked down on the city from his office. He was nestled at the peak of the Sanctum's tallest tower. The

1

entirety of the capital sprawled before him like some great map. He threw open his windows. A cool breeze washed over him, smelling of salt and smoke, beer and sewage, people and horses. The wind ruffled his waist-length beard and billowed his robes about him. He smiled, imagining the figure he must strike. So much poise, so much control, so much power over the city that lay at his feet.

An overly enthusiastic knock sounded behind him. He started and tripped over a pile of scrolls before righting himself against his desk. A smirking gnome stood in the doorway. Riddleston composed himself, and attempted to straighten his extremely tall hat in the most dignified manner possible.

"Damn you, Gefwyn," he grumbled. "Why can't you ever knock like a normal person?"

The gnome's smirk grew wider. "Pardon me, yer Hattiness, but yer were doin' it again."

Riddleston tented his bushy eyebrows. "Doing what, precisely?"

"That thing where yer stare off into the distance and act all mysterious-like. Broodin', some might call it. Not me, of course."

Riddleston coughed. "Yes, well, never mind that. Is everyone here?" The gnome nodded. "Then I shall be down presently." Gefwyn bowed and closed the door behind him.

Riddleston turned back to the city and sighed. Today, the wizards of his Sanctum would vote on Chancellor Marstarrow's latest proposition for increased magical restrictions. The sanctions were less stiff than those previously proposed, but Riddleston had no doubt the measures would fail to pass. The capital relied too heavily on his wizards to preclude their practicing magic. Without the Sanctum, the surrounding infrastructure would undoubtedly crumble. Chancellor Marstarrow's propositions to reduce dependence on magic were grudgingly admirable, but foolhardy. Yet it was important to maintain open discussion. Or at least the pretense of open discussion.

Riddleston checked his reflection in an ornate mirror. The collars of his robes stood as straight as attending men of arms, but he tugged at them all the same. Adopting an important expression, he descended the spiraling staircase into the heart of the Sanctum and made for the auditorium. With a wave of his hand, he slammed open the heavy oaken doors. He noted, with more than a touch of self-appreciation, the resounding *BOOMS* that echoed off the vaulted ceiling. Any wizard worth his hat respected a grand entrance. Conversations died as hundreds of eyes followed his approach to the raised podium at the front of the room.

Riddleston cleared his voice and raised his hands. "Gentlemen, thank you all for coming today. An unfortunate use of our time, but necessary." He rummaged through a sheaf of parchments, selected one, and scanned its contents. "Ah, here we are. Marstarrow proposes a ten percent blanket reduction for all industrial, commercial, and residential services the Sanctum offers here in Heldan Port." Laughter and hisses echoed around the auditorium, and one particularly loud *'BOO'!* Riddleston looked at the wizards over the top of his crescent spectacles. "Borneus, I know that was you. One more word and you've got yourself latrine duty for a month."

"Sod off. What's the despot mean by 'blanket' reductions?"

Riddleston sniffed and sifted through the papers. "Restrictions would target our involvement in shipping, mining, harvesting pertaining to both agriculture and lumber, and masonry, in addition to the menial tasks we perform on a day-to-day basis." More jeers greeted this pronouncement.

"What's our motivation for passing these measures?" someone called.

Riddleston sighed and removed his glasses. "Tiberion Marstarrow believes it essential Heldan Port reduce its dependence on our magic to function. In return for our cooperation, he promises a substantial annual monetary stipend to supplement our Departments of Research and Theory."

"So, move us off the streets and stick us in the library where we can't practice magic," said another.

Riddleston set aside the parchments and came out from the podium. "Essentially. Am I correct in assuming that our collective opinion on the matter hasn't changed?" Shouts of agreement followed. "Then let's put the matter to a vote and be done with it."

Suddenly, a tremendous explosion rocked the entrance to the auditorium. The oaken doors shattered, as if made from brittle glass. Splinters flew in all directions, and wizards dove behind benches to avoid the shrapnel. Riddleston was momentarily stunned. He and the rest of the wizards looked to the ruined archway.

A figure stepped into the auditorium, face obscured by a black hood. Despite himself, Riddleston marveled at the stranger's power. *That* was how you made a grand entrance. He composed himself as the rest of the wizards struggled to their feet. Magical light flickered as spells were primed, and the room hummed with power. The stranger appeared not to notice and sauntered up to the podium.

Riddleston swelled to his full height and jabbed a finger at the intruder. "That's quite far enough! It is forbidden for an outsider to enter the Sanctum!"

The stranger paused, face still shrouded by the cloak. "You have failed for the last time, gentlemen." The voice that spilled forth was distorted and sonorous. Alien.

Indignant magic flared up Riddleston's arm. "Failed? What do you mean? Why are you here?" The wizards pressed warily closer, magic crackling in their hands.

The awful voice was deathly calm. "I am here to cleanse the capitals."

"Cleanse... cleanse how?" Riddleston was ashamed at the tremor in his voice.

"By removing every last one of you from power."

There was a moment of resentful silence, and then everything started happening at once. With shouted incantations and spells, the wizards launched their assault. Dazzling lights illuminated the auditorium and powerful detonations rent the air as magic met magic. Riddleston joined the onslaught. A cloud of magical smoke and blinding light consumed the intruder. The attack lasted for less than a minute.

Breathlessly, Riddleston waited for the haze to clear. His ample stomach heaved with the exertion of battle. But as the last plumes of magical residue dissipated, the intruder emerged, still standing. There were shouts of amazement and fear throughout the auditorium.

Riddleston recoiled from the podium. "Impossible!"

"My turn," said the voice. A nova of crimson magic exploded from the intruder and boiled over the auditorium. Riddleston's arms and legs snapped to his sides when it struck him. A crushing tightness enveloped his entire body, as if some great hand had seized him about the chest. He fought to free himself, but to no avail. He vaguely noticed his fellow wizards falling, one by one, their bodies rigid.

The pressure increased. Riddleston couldn't concentrate. He couldn't breathe. He couldn't even think. He couldn't exist. With a faint *pop*, Sylvus Riddleston, Highest Hat of the Occult Sanctum of Wizards, disappeared from the world, leaving behind an extremely tall, wide-brimmed hat, and a miasma of swirling colors.

THE DISAPPEARANCE
OF THE WIZARDS

Lundel Figgens sighed and adjusted his spectacles. His City Clerk office within the chancellor's keep had been filled with indignant Heldan Portians since dawn. A queue had now formed that stretched into the neighboring corridor. The clamor was deafening as people shouted overtop one another.

"One of dem wizard fellers were supposed to help us in the mines this mornin'!" bemoaned a dwarf, his beard caked with grime. "Lost a whole vein of good ore 'cause he didn't show. Who's gonna pay for that?"

"Maybe you dwarves should actually think before you dig," said a farmer, with skin like boiled leather. "It's your fault for relying on the wizards to remedy your negligence. But, Mr. Figgens, my wheat's come down with blight. I need their magic to cleanse my stores or I'll lose the entire harvest!"

The dwarf smirked and folded his corded arms. "Ha!

Serves yer right, you hippercrit. Preachin' about others relyin' on wizards... bah."

Lundel stood on his chair, though he was still shorter than most of the room's occupants. "A moment, please, if everyone would just listen to me!"

An elderly woman pushed forward and shoved a bedraggled cat in his face. "Those wretched animals have escaped the wizards' menagerie! My poor Mr. Whiskies was nearly killed by a dachshund with bat wings." Mr. Whiskies took the opportunity to hiss and claw Lundel's nose. "He refuses to eat his liver and will need therapy again! Come to think of it, I may need therapy. That thing was an abomination."

"Oi, lady!" someone called from the recesses of the anonymous throng. "I'm a professional pet psychic-ologist, take my card! And you's wearing a sweater with a cat stitched on it, so you's definitely the one needing help. Talk about an abomination."

The tanned farmer scrunched up his face and managed to produce a few dirty tears. "How will I feed my family? The profit from that grain was supposed to last us the winter."

The dwarf let out a cackle. "Don't lie. Yer don't have a family. Nobody likes you."

Lundel threw up his hands and waved them crazily about like a man unwittingly set on fire. "Ladies and gentlemen, please take up your concerns with the Sanctum's Public Relations Forum, just down the hall! Highest Hat Riddleston will see to your problems directly. And get off of my desk!"

The man in question obeyed, but left behind a pair of muddy boot prints. "But Beardie's not in his office, is 'e? Well on my pop's grave, those wizards were supposed to 'elp with my demon infestation! Little bastards won't get out of the eaves and are eatin' all my apples. You tell me, 'ow am I supposed to be rid of 'em now?"

"Butterson's Beers, at your service!" A plump, ruddy-faced

man, his beard as full and wild as a blackberry thicket, shoved to the front of the crowd. "An open cask of Evernut Ale placed directly under the nest should do the trick! The terrors will be sleeping fitfully in the stuff before the hour."

"Heh, unless I get there first," said the dwarf.

Lundel shouted so forcefully that his spectacles dangled from one ear. "Everyone be quiet! Vile man wiping your filthy boots on my new carpet, yes *you*! Did you say Riddleston was absent from the forum?"

"Aye, 'im and all the rest of 'is filthy lot. The door's sealed tight. And there's not been a wizard coming or going from that wretched Sanctum. On my pop's life, I swear they've gone and left the city."

"But you said your pops was dead!" observed the dwarf. "Oi! Butterson, I could use some of them brews, how much for a pint?"

"Well for your ed-if-ick-ay-shun, I 'ad two pops and no mum and one's still alive. So bugger off!"

The man called Butterson hoisted a tankard into the air for all to see. "Two copper for a pint. Tell your friends! 'Butterson's Beers; because Sobriety is Shi-'"

Lundel tore at the precious little hair still clinging to his sweaty pate. "Stop selling things in my office! Everyone out! I don't have time for this!" He steered the crowd toward the door. "Please send a letter to the chancellor's office outlining your grievance and the issue will be dealt with at the next available opportunity. Thank you! No, Ms. Tiddle, I don't care about your cat's eating disorder, please get out. Thank you."

He slumped against the door as the echoes of the furious mob steadily quieted. The distant tolling of Heldan Port's great clock tower announced ten o'clock's coming and going. He closed his eyes and rubbed his temples where a dull throbbing had begun. "Leave it to the bloody wizards," he grumbled, to no one in particular.

Another knock sounded at the door, accompanied by the muffled voice of Lundel's assistant. "Been a rush of angry letters arriving via the post, Mr. Figgens. They're overwhelming the mailroom workers. Care to advise?"

Lundel clenched a fist and drew himself up to his full and inconsiderable height. He glared at the door, as though it was personally responsible for his current ordeal. "I would *advise* them that their time would be best spent in the frivolous pursuit, location, and retrieval of Sylvus Riddleston, his having no doubt absconded from his duties in favor of an annual "Essential Sanctum Retreat," which, despite his assurances to the contrary, I know to be a transparent excuse to get drunk and invoke magical mayhem in the surrounding countryside with his cohort of bearded and geriatric miscreants, all the while depositing their foul and innumerous responsibilities on *my* doorstep!"

This outburst was greeted with a moment's silence, then, "Erm, so I'll just tell them to get on with it?"

Lundel shook his fist at the door. "You do that! And while you're at it, draft a strongly worded letter to the chancellor regarding these latest transgressions! The Sanctum's gifts are not worth these adolescent rampages, I'll have him know." He waited, but there was no response. "And, and," he bellowed, clinging to the momentum of his indignation, "and tell the chancellor that I am going on a much deserved and needed vacation! Yes, a damned vacation, you hear me? I am bound for Angoma this very evening! Let us see how the indomitable Tiberion Marstarrow functions in my absence!" The door remained impassively silent. Lundel deflated and pushed his glasses up his nose. "I'll do it! I'll leave this very moment and don't think I won't! Nothing you or he can do to stop me!" He fidgeted in the ensuing silence. "Erm, maybe don't use those *exact* words, per se, but, but, but my message is clear. Defiant and resolute in the face of such abusive negligence." A line of sweat dampened his collar as he considered the door. "Erm, the chancellor isn't out there at this very moment, is he?"

"No, sir," said the door.

Lundel collapsed onto his desk. "Very well. This changes nothing, mind you. My sentiment remains the same."

"Of course, sir."

"My disapproval shall be noted?"

"It shall be made abundantly clear, sir."

"Very well." Lundel slumped into his chair and turned to the stack of grievances littering his desk. He idly leafed through the pages. Then he buried his head in his hands. "Please inform the chancellor I'll see to everything."

"By your leave, sir," said the door.

A GROWING STREAM

Rain drummed a fierce staccato against the soot-encrusted glass of Chancellor Tiberion Marstarrow's window. He rose from his seat and examined the pane in the failing light of evening. The droplets coalesced into streaming rivulets that twisted and forked across the glass, gaining momentum as they plunged past his field of view. He watched as they disappeared into a blanket of mist that obscured the base of his keep far below. "Fascinating," he mused, "how a well-placed droplet can alter the course of an entire stream."

He turned and settled into an ancient straight-backed chair. It creaked morosely. The only other piece of furniture in the room was an equally aged desk, bare, apart from a lone candle and partially furled scroll. The room was austerely uncomfortable in the wavering light, the only movement the soft shadows that dipped and swayed in accordance with the flame.

Marstarrow sat completely still, his body rigid. He stared at the paper. A message had been hastily scrawled in red ink with an untidy hand:

'Wizards gone. Somethin' must've took 'em. Somethin' must've got into the Sanctum. No idea how: tis impossible.
-Gefwyn, Steward of the Sanctum

The chancellor collected the paper and held it to the candle. "Impossible," he said aloud, considering the smoldering words. "Yet here we stand." The charred fragments fluttered to his desk. He swept aside the ashes and raised his voice. "Mr. Figgens! Please attend, if you would be so kind."

His door swung open and the bespectacled clerk peered in, sweat beaded at his temples. "Yes, Chancellor?" Marstarrow considered his clerk and allowed the silence to grow like fingers of ice across a pond. Lundel gulped and adjusted his glasses. "Chancellor Marstarrow, please forgive my, erm, *misgivings* regarding the Sanctum and your, erm, *capabilities* in my hypothetical absence. It has been a trying week, sir."

Marstarrow cocked an eyebrow and the pond snap froze.

Lundel whimpered and sidled as far behind the door as was possible while still remaining inside the room. "I was simply overwhelmed, you see, and, erm, and, well I-"

"Have there been responses to my inquiries?"

The little man perked up at the change of topic. "Yes, sir! And they were done quietly sir, per your instructions. Ravens from Angoma and the Frozen Steppes returned this afternoon. Neither claims knowledge of Heldan Port's current, erm, predicament, or at least they're not letting on if they do. Nothing of note to report on those fronts, apart from a bout of nasty storms off the Blacklock's coast. Afraid shipping routes to the north may be delayed for the time being."

Marstarrow stood and resumed staring over the rooftops of his city. "And what from my ealdormen in the Lowlands?"

"No sign of Riddleston or his men, sir. Haven't been seen coming or going from Heldan Port. And no damage to report from the hamlets that would indicate their traveling incognito."

The knuckles on Marstarrow's hands shone white as he braced himself against the windowsill, though he took care to shield this from Lundel. "And what of Dinh? How does the baroness respond?"

Lundel fidgeted. "Erm, well she hasn't, sir."

The frozen silence returned. "And she is the only not to do so?"

"Yes, sir."

Marstarrow slammed a fist against the wall. Lundel squeaked and scrambled behind the door. The chancellor turned and strode to his desk. He wrenched open a drawer, collected a pile of stationary and quills, and shoved them into Lundel's arms. "Write her again. I will flood Dinh with ravens, if that is required."

Lundel cleared his throat and grimaced. "Erm, pardon my saying, sir, but reliable dispatch to Dinh has proven impossible for centuries, thanks to the Wilds. Maybe she simply hasn't received your letters? And if that's the case, is all of this really necessary..." He trailed off, avoiding the chancellor's eye.

Marstarrow stared down at him, unblinking. "Consider this, Mr. Figgens. The Wilds are awakening. Tales reach my ear of strange forces haunting the southern reaches. And now, coincidentally, my capital stands on the verge of falling into civil and political disarray as industries and citizens inevitably seek viable replacement for the Sanctum's supports. And now, coincidentally in the Sanctum's absence, the cowardice of my people shall blossom like a spring rosebud. My city stands ripe for the taking."

Lundel cowered against the door. "I thought you don't believe in coincidence, sir."

"I do not. So consider also, Mr. Figgens, that no message from Dinh, might be, in itself, a very pointed message." Marstarrow leaned closer. "One with teeth."

The little clerk blanched and dabbed his forehead with a sleeve. "But, sir, the capitals have been at peace for decades!"

Marstarrow swept to the window. "Peace endures only until it does not, Mr. Figgens. I *must* learn where Dinh stands." And then, only to himself, "Or uncover confirmation of culpability."

His gaze passed over the Lowlands surrounding the city walls and alit on the eastern woods and the rolling mountains beyond, near blue from distance: the Gateway to the Wilds.

And then he smiled. Not a smile of happiness or contentment, but a smile of grim realization. For there were those who did not fear the Wilds. There were those who might be persuaded to ride for Dinh, if pressured with the proper finesse. There were those small droplets of water that might alter the course of an entire stream, if one only knew how to guide them into critical position.

"Change of plans, Mr. Figgens." He relieved Lundel of his burden and steered him into the corridor.

"Sir?"

"Fetch Captain Whitney."

Lundel bowed. "Yes, sir. Anything else, sir?"

Marstarrow laid a hand on Lundel's shoulder. The clerk flinched at the touch. Marstarrow softened his expression. "After you have sent for the captain, the remainder of the night is your own. You have performed admirably this week."

Lundel beamed and straightened up. "Yes, sir! Thank you, sir. Won't disappoint you, sir. I'm your man, sir, and-"

"Mr. Figgens," said Marstarrow patiently.

"Sir?"

"Get going."

"Right away, sir."

Marstarrow waited until his clerk had disappeared down the stairwell before returning to his office. He stood at the window, unmoving, silently considering the vast expanse known as the Gateway to the Wilds.

A SINGLE DROPLET

Sten Bregon strolled down the narrow, cobblestoned streets of Heldan Port's Merchant District. The sidewalks bustled with activity as vendors rushed to set up their stalls before the morning crowds arrived. It was a radiant summer day and Tanduil was just beginning to crest the capital's ramparts. Exotic aromas from spices, meats, and perfumes battled for aerial supremacy.

Whistling a happy tune, he dodged around a trundling cartful of fine silks, ignoring the curses from its driver. He nimbly skewered an apple with his knife and flipped a coin to the seller.

"Good morning, *Lord* Bregon!" cackled an old woman from the interior of her makeshift shop. "Will you be having some of my finest salt pork today?"

Sten flinched at the emphasized title, though his stomach rumbled at the delicious smells. He shook his head ruefully.

"Not today, I'm afraid. I'm on an important mission you see, top secret." He touched the side of his nose with a wink.

The woman's civility vanished alongside the prospect of a sale. "Bah, the day you have something meaningful to do with your life is the day I die. Looks like Heldan Port found its first immortal butcher. Lucky me." She dismissed Sten with a wave of her cleaver.

"Always a pleasure." He continued on his way.

A gaily-decorated wagon dominated a nearby street corner, surrounded by a whispering crowd. Sten paused and glanced at the capital's distant clock tower. He still had several minutes to spare, so he pushed himself into the eager throng. With a flourish, a piebald sheet was thrown back from the wagon's bed to reveal a puppet's stage. An Angoman man dressed in shimmering velvets leapt spritely into the wagon. Bowing, he took his place behind the stage. The crowd applauded and gushed, then fell hastily silent as a miniature curtain was drawn back.

The stage came to life in a whir of hidden gadgetry. The puppeteer launched into his story in a singsong, melodious tenor. "Gather round, gather round! Pray hear the Sensational Mamaoi! Miz dangles from his fingertips, for he is the keeper of her soul, the teller of her stories. You may weep at what is to come, but do not despair. You may laugh at the world's follies, for they are many. But most importantly, you may line this storyteller's coffer, for he is hungry." A straw puppet pointed demandingly to a felt hat at the wagon's rear. The clink of coins was accompanied by scattered laughter.

The puppeteer forged on. "Today is a tale of history. For without history, we are nothing but yoked oxen, looking only forward down the road of life. This I say true." A white sheet thumped down as a backdrop, adorned with steel-gray mountains. "Three continents Miz has nurtured over the eons, so three tales I shall tell." The storyteller dramatically lowered his voice. "The first lies atop the world. The Frozen Steppes. A barren, pitiless wasteland, home to an extremely proud, extremely resilient, and extremely cold peoples. The Hammerstone Mountains extend along its entirety, north to south, a backbone of ice, snow, and rock that serves as a bridge to the Heartlands." Children oohed and aahed as Mamaoi nimbly danced his puppets across the painted mountains.

"Far to the south reside the isles of Angoma. My homeland." Another sheet draped into place, all sunlight, sand, and aquamarine waters. "There you shall find white-sand beaches, blistering heat, and floral libations. The islands are a sanctuary for the ingenious and the progressive, those folk so ahead of their time that total isolation is essential for unlocking their full potential. And, due to an utter lack of social skills and self-awareness, essential to avoid getting murdered by annoyed common folk." More laughter accompanied a clatter of coin.

A third sheet descended, this one a motley assortment of colors. Two pinpoints of light twinkled at either end. "And nestled at the center of Miz, stretching for thousands of miles in all directions, lie the Heartlands. Awesome in size and beauty, the Heartlands dominate Miz. They serve as the cultural hub of the world, a veritable melting pot of sentient beings, magical or not, thrust together and forced to live in harmony. Initially, this harmony was complete and pure, and as a result, Miz flourished." The puppets paraded happily across the stage, trading embraces. But then came a harsh rattle of metal from somewhere in the wagon's hidden recesses. The crowd flinched away.

Mamaoi let the wary silence build before speaking. "Then came the capitals. Two self-proclaimed capitals of Miz were born, Heldan Port of the west, and Dinh of the slightly more east." The lights on the backdrop glowed as he said this, first the left, then the right. "Positioned at opposite ends of the

Heartlands, both cities believed themselves the epitome of Mizian politics and civility, and both refused to recognize the accomplishments of the other.

"In the early years of the two cities' founding, there was conflict. The rulers of the capitals were incredulous that another faction had the gall to assume lordship over their lands. It was clearly their sovereign right to impose their will over every other creature on Miz, and anyone who challenged this mindset was a filthy heathen."

A blood-red vista lowered behind the puppets. The crowd shuffled forward eagerly. Sten allowed himself to be carried along, smiling good-naturedly.

"War became inevitable. Barrel-chested humans, dwarves, elves, orcs, and every other race of Miz donned impossibly shiny suits of armor. Monstrous warhorses were corralled and outfitted with deadly harnesses. Smiths' fires spewed endless streams of black smoke into the sky as thousands of weapons and shields were forged. Soldiers reeked of self-righteous honor, and encouraging phrases like, 'Fight for King and Country!' were bandied about. Some were downright excited at the opportunity to lay down their lives for a chance at glory, honor, or if they died in a particularly gruesome manner, an inspiring footnote in the annals of history." The puppets briefly disappeared to reemerge in battle regalia. The crowd whistled.

"Yes, yes, cheer for the advent of bloodshed!" Mamaoi chuckled darkly, and positioned the puppets on opposite sides of the stage. "For the capitals were preparing for war, and everyone was blissfully unaware of the implications." Another thump and the sky of blood was replaced by a land of mountains and trees and rivers. "Fortunately, the Mizian Wilds split the Heartlands atwain. A vast expanse of forests, deserts, plains, and ice-capped mountains, with a smattering of dangerous flora and fauna thrown in for good measure, the Wilds exist for the sole reason of eradicating anyone foolish enough to enter its depths. This storyteller names the Wilds a lethal litmus test for intelligence."

Sten let out a guffaw and hastily stifled his laughter at the confused glances. Again he looked to the clock tower. He had time yet to finish the story.

"The first war of Miz consisted of the two armies marching headlong into the heart of the Wilds and promptly performing an about-face." The puppets strode confidently across the stage, then abruptly turned to flee as painted beasts and plants rose to meet them. Mamaoi waited for the laughter to subside. "There came a brief respite as the slightly wiser rulers decided it best to avoid the loss of their armies to carnivorous plants. But time passed, as is its wont, and Miz zipped through the galaxy. New rulers assumed the burden of command. Bells of war tolled once again. Somewhat-less-shiny suits of armor were dusted off. Decrepit warhorses were unshackled from their plows. And blacksmiths frantically spun whetstones, attempting to hone swords wearing stains suspiciously reminiscent of cooked meals."

The puppets sluggishly reassembled on opposite sides of the stage. "And so the second war of Miz began," said Mamaoi. "The two capitals had learned from their failed pre-decessors and actually succeeded in permeating the depths of the Wilds. Their foresight, however, did not extend to the immense distance between one another. The two armies traveled day and night, pushing their soldiers to exhaustion.

"On a moonless night, the lone battle in Mizian history between the capitals was fought. Yet the darkness was so complete, the soldiers so exhausted, that the forward ranks of both companies slammed headlong into one another." The puppets trudged across the stage, and a black cloth fell into position behind them. "This was quaintly labeled the battle of, 'Oi! What the Fu-?'" The puppets crashed into one another amidst shrieks of mirth, drowning out Mamaoi's colorful phrasing. The puppets tottered and slumped to the ground.

The puppeteer's voice dripped irony. "The fighting was extremely brief and nobody died. Most chose to sit and challenge their opponents to drinking and dicing, all the while hurling patriotic insults at one another. Instead of resuming battle at a later time, the blistered and sun-beaten leaders decided to forego their adolescent egos and formulate a peace treaty. A rare and radiant beacon of level-headedness floating through an infinite blackness of stupidity that was Miz's history of decision-making." Again, Sten found himself alone in his amusement.

"And so Miz embraced peace once again." The puppets returned to their respective corners and shed their weapons and armor. "Both capitals resumed ignoring the existence of the other. Knowledge of magic, economics, art, agriculture, and dismemberment flourished. Universities of magic were established. Magnificent city walls with foreboding ramparts and massive gates were erected. And all the while, the past endeavors of previous generations were happily forgotten. True peace, it seemed, was possible after all."

With a hiss of invisible machinery, a spurt of smoke blanketed the stage's floor. When Mamaoi again spoke, the amused edge to his voice had gone, to be replaced by an icy current. "But in recent days, whispers of a strange blight reach this storyteller's ear. Tales tell of a malicious fog rising in the depths of the Wild. Tales tell of a mist so complete it blots out the light of Tanduil. Tales tell of creatures lurking within its darkness. And tales tell of the mist moving north, away from the forgotten dregs of the Wilds, and spreading throughout the Heartlands." The audience was entirely silent as the puppets recoiled from the smoke. Sten realized he was holding his breath. After the smoke had boiled upward to consume the stage, Mamaoi spoke again. "Tales tell of a reckoning coming for the capitals. They would be wise to listen. This I say true."

In a wave of unfurling canvas, the stage disappeared behind a final curtain. The crowd murmured restlessly, unsure of how to proceed. Children's wails of disappointment filled the air. But Sten was impressed by the Angoman's boldness. He stepped forward and threw a handful of coins into the hat, then ducked away.

He emerged onto a street that paralleled the canals shaping the major thoroughfares. The Mired River accompanied his every turn as he wended his way into the heart of the city. He followed the great stone pathways until Edegar Bridge blossomed over the crowds, its towering statues of long-dead heroes ghostly white in the morning light.

Sten shot a surreptitious glance behind him. The streets and shops were overflowing with traffic, the air rife with shouts, curses, and laughter. He spied a pair of patrolling City Guard, the crowd parting before their striped tabards of purple and gold. But nobody was paying him any attention. He grinned and stood in the shadows of an elm tree and waited for the clock tower to usher in the hour. As the bell began to toll, he sauntered onto the bridge and struck a nonchalant pose at its center. It was empty, save for a mother and child standing hand in hand, gazing up at the sculptures in wonder.

A figure appeared from an alleyway. Sten watched the courier approach from the corner of his eye. He guessed it to be a woman from height and build. The newcomer casually strolled onto the bridge and leaned against a nearby plinth. He found himself unconsciously tracing a slight bulge in his breast pocket and hastily lowered his arm. The stranger waited, unspeaking, head cocked as it surveyed the bustling crowds. Sten swallowed and leaned over the bridge, as if to consider the water rushing beneath his feet. "Right then. You have your instructions for delivery?"

The courier inclined its head, almost imperceptibly.

"Excellent." Sten kept his attention on the river, as if fixated by its currents, and subtly withdrew the bulging purse from his breast pocket. He deftly passed it to the courier. The purse immediately disappeared into the recesses of the cloak, clinking softly. He licked his lips. "I would ask that you also relay a message for me."

A pause, then another slight tilt of the hood.

Sten's gaze wandered to the crowds. He grimaced. "Inform our beneficiary that this may be the last delivery for some time. If I keep going at this rate, I'm sure to be discovered."

The courier stepped forward and removed the hood. "You've got that right." Sten jerked away. A girl of roughly his own age grinned cheekily back at him. She had hazel eyes, golden shoulder-length hair, and a longsword strapped to one hip. Her hand strayed to its pommel and gave it a meaningful caress.

Sten backpedaled. Anonymity was a fundamental credo to the couriers he employed, and he had never known one to openly carry a weapon. "Who are you? Did Lord Impo send you?"

She laughed pleasantly. "Do I look like some House crony to you? Corporal Ineza Ghet of the Shrikes, at your service." Sten paled and the girl's smile grew wider. "Ah, not as dumb as you let on."

"Listen," said Sten, with as much bravado as he could muster. "I don't know who you think you are-"

"Corporal Ineza Ghet. I thought we'd established that."

"Well, Corporal, I appreciate you wasting my time but I'll be going now." Sten turned to run, but the woman and child who had been examining the statues moved to block his path. "Er, please move," he asked meekly.

"Can't do, kiddo," said the youth in a baritone growl. With a start, Sten realized that the diminutive figure was actually a bearded gnome, grinning up at him from beneath a ridiculously floppy cap. "You need to pay more attention to your surroundings. I was certain you'd see through this disguise."

"You can let go of my hand now," said the woman.

The gnome released her. "Oops, beg your pardon. Now boy, I advise you listen to our corporal over yonder. Fiery one, she is. I wouldn't make her mad if I were you." Sten's eyes flicked to the river. The gnome followed his gaze. "Ah, and I wouldn't be doing that neither. She'll still catch you but she'll be extra mad. Do yourself a favor. Come with us."

Sten retreated to the center of the bridge, attempting to keep an eye on both parties. "This is harassment! I haven't done anything wrong!" Corporal Ghet maintained her smile, as if they were old friends.

"Whiny little twerp, isn't he?" said the gnome.

Corporal Ghet unsheathed her sword and planted its tip in the stone at her feet. "Mmm, I expected more. But *you* are far from innocent, Sten Bregon. Pardon me, recently appointed *Lord* Bregon. Pardon me again, recently appointed Lord Bregon, newest *Head* of House Bregon."

Sten's stomach plummeted. "What do you want with me?"

She spun her sword between her fingers. "Oh nothing much, but the chancellor is rather interested in having a little chat with you. We're under orders to bring you in, 'cause it sounds like you're in a spot of trouble." She withdrew the purse and weighed it in her palm, smirking.

The gnome took a menacing step forward. "Aye. Been slacking on your duties as Head of House in favor of unsavory pursuits, as we hear it. Though I can't say I blame you. Being a lord sounds dreadfully boring."

Sten inched closer to the bridge's edge. "Couldn't you have knocked on my door like civilized people?"

Corporal Ghet shrugged. "We like to have our fun, we do. Anyhoo, we figured you'd run if we came a calling, and,

judging by how fidgety you are, I figure we figured correctly."
Her eyes glistened in anticipation, as if daring him to bolt.

Sten obliged and leapt for the water without a moment's
notice. It was an impressive jump cut abruptly short by the
pommel of a sword that caught him squarely between the
eyes. He landed hard on his back and stared dazedly up at the
clouds. Stars flashed across his swimming vision. As if from a
great distance, he heard someone say, "Moron," and then the
world drifted merrily away.

ULTIMATUM

S ten awoke in total darkness with a pounding headache.
Something was covering his eyes. He tried to move but
found that he was strapped to a chair. A foul tasting cloth had
been shoved into his mouth.

"Hrgo? Angyon der?"

There came muffled footsteps and the blackness receded
as a hood was removed.

"Afternoon, love."

Sten blinked as his eyes adjusted to the light. Corporal
Ghet stared down at him, her cocky smile still in place. They
were in a small room, sparsely furnished, and dimly lit by a
single candle. She removed the gag and jumped back when he
spat. "You're psychotic," he said reproachfully. "Where are we?"

She smiled irritatingly cheerfully. "Call me Ineza. And I
didn't hit you that hard. Plus, we asked you not to run. It's
kind of your fault if you think about it. Anyhoo, we're in the
chancellor's keep. His private office, actually."

"Corporal!" said a brusque voice behind Sten. "What have I told you about using that word?" Sten craned his head. A heavyset, and even heavier mustachioed man was sitting by a window. He stared at them icily. He had a ruddy face that matched his hair, which was close-cropped in military fashion.

Ineza threw an exaggerated salute. "Don't use it. Sorry, sir. Anyhoo – sorry, anyway, I really didn't mean to hit you so hard, but we had our orders. We told you the chancellor wanted to meet with you."

Sten returned his attention to the man sitting by the window. "Hmm, I always thought the chancellor would be less... red."

The mustachioed man turned a deeper shade of crimson. "I'm not the chancellor! I'm Captain Regibar Theraford Whitney, leader of the Shrikes." Sten stared at him blankly. The man squared his shoulders, mustache bristling. "The Shrikes? Personal taskforce to the chancellor himself? First defenders of the capital."

"Oh," said Sten. "Never heard of you."

Captain Whitney started to protest but Ineza laid a reassuring hand on his shoulder. "He's just riling you up, Cap. Don't give him the satisfaction."

Sten smiled sweetly, then froze when a pointed cough sounded from the doorway.

"Thank you, Captain," said a voice of polished granite. "That will be all." With measured strides, a gaunt man with silver hair swept into the room. He met Sten's gaze, and Sten immediately looked away. The man's eyes were hard, calculating, and seemed to bore into his very soul. He shivered.

"So you're the chancellor?" he mumbled to the floor.

The man bowed slightly. "I am Tiberion Marstarrow. A pleasure to make your acquaintance, Lord Bregon, although I wish it was under more... favorable circumstances." He continued his deliberate pacing. "I have been keeping an eye on you, Sten. May I call you Sten?" Sten nodded warily. "I was truly sorry to hear of your father's death. Yoro Bregon was a good and honest man. A rarity in this city." The chancellor studied him for a moment before continuing. "Ever since his untimely passing, I have been watching you."

"Well that's disconcerting," said Sten. Ineza snorted, but was quickly silenced by an indignant huff from Captain Whitney.

The chancellor ignored the remark. "I imagine your father has informed you that the responsibilities of a Head of House are substantial. Yet, since his passing, the previous Lord of House Bregon, you have done nothing to assume those new-found obligations. In fact, you have done quite the opposite. Rather than serving on my council with the other Heads of House, as is your duty, you have avoided us entirely, choosing to spend your days, and the capital's money, invested in various criminal activities throughout my city."

Sten finally raised his eyes and glared at the chancellor. "I didn't ask for any of this. My father was a politician but I'll *never* be like him. You're wasting your time if you think you'll convince me to join your council."

"That may be," said Marstarrow, "but as the sole remaining member of House Bregon, you are obliged, by law, to perform the duties required of you. Your mother, were she still alive, could have–"

Sten lunged against his restraints. "Don't talk about my mother! She hated this life more than I do. The only reason we stayed in Heldan Port was because she loved my father. And how did he repay her? By working his life away and ignoring us!"

The chancellor ceased his pacing and folded his arms. "Very well. Yet the issue remains. You have repeatedly and shamelessly broken the law. You have stolen from the capital and failed to uphold the requirements of your house and station. Do you deny this?"

"No," said Sten.

"Then it is settled. Traditionally, you would be sent to the dungeons to await trial. Your property, along with all of your possessions, would be seized as recompense for the money you stole from the people of this city. Upon your release at a much later date, you would reenter the world without a single coin to your name."

Sten ground his teeth. "Lovely."

"Yes," said Marstarrow. "*Normally*, all of these judgments would come to pass. But instead, I brought you here to offer an ultimatum. I advise you to accept the terms. I will not ask twice."

Sten's gaze shot to the chancellor's face. There wasn't a trace of irony to be seen, although the man's stony expression hadn't changed from the moment he'd introduced himself. He was still watching Sten with those piercingly keen eyes, as hard as diamonds. "I would hear your terms," said Sten carefully.

"As you wish. Firstly, you will relinquish your claim to lordship over House Bregon. The vacant seat of my council shall pass to another family, in time. As you so eloquently stated, you are unequivocally *not* a politician, so I will not force the issue. Your possessions will remain your own, but you shall be stripped of all titles, powers, and your family estate. In addition, you will join Captain Whitney and his Shrikes on a mission into the Gateway to the Wilds. He has kindly, if reluctantly, agreed to humor my request. Following its completion, your life will be your own. Now, the details of this undertaking are not important at the present, but there may be significant danger involved. As such, I encourage you to think carefully before ans-"

"I accept!" burst out Sten. The possibility of a life free from the burdens of his station blazed through his mind like a wildfire.

Ineza laughed and clapped him on the back. "See, I knew you weren't as dumb as you let on! Welcome aboard, *Lord* Bregon. Er wait, it's just Sten now, eh?" Captain Whitney remained silent, irritably twirling one end of his mustache.

The faintest of smiles turned the chancellor's mouth. "Excellent."

"One thing, though," said Sten. "Why are you doing this? I feel like you've pardoned me for the crimes you just accused me of committing."

"Think of it as a professional courtesy to your late father and his unwavering loyalty," said Marstarrow, though, for the first time since entering the room, he turned away. Sten paused. But then Ineza slit his restraints with a knife and he was freed. He jumped to his feet and massaged life back into his tingling hands.

Captain Whitney marched from the room. "You're with us, Bregon." Ineza trailed behind. She winked at Sten and beckoned for him to join.

He obeyed, but then paused at the threshold. "Thank you, Chancellor. I... I'm not sure I deserve this leniency. But I'll be eternally grateful for it."

Marstarrow stood silhouetted against the window, his back to Sten. "Do not thank me just yet." His voice was barely more than a whisper. "I believe your troubles have only just begun."

STALE BEER

A tepid breeze rose from the sea and swept across the Lowlands. With it came the smell of salt and a promise of rain. Golden fields of wheat and barley rolled in gentle waves. The branches of apple trees whispered indistinctly, dusting the road with ashen leaves. Sten closed his eyes and inhaled deeply, letting the calm wash over him.

"Keep moving, Bregon!" barked Captain Whitney. Sten hastily jumped aside and ended up in a ditch. Whitney and the Shrikes marched in neat formation down the road. Sten counted thirty warriors in total as they passed, each wearing elegant light plate stained with lampblack. Some gave him suspicious glances as they went, including a hulking pair of dark twins. Most ignored him altogether. He spied Ineza at the rear of the column and scrambled to catch up.

"I'm going to hazard a guess and say I'm not welcome here," he said.

She grinned ruefully and shrugged. "Don't take it personally.

We're a close-knit bunch. Our bonds were forged through battle so we don't take kindly to outsiders, especially those forced on us by the chancellor. You're a civilian, not a Shrike. We've all fought and killed to be here. Just give them some time to come about. You're not all that bad. For a lord, anyhoo."

Sten picked thistles from his cloak. "I'm not a lord anymore. You saw to that."

"And you're welcome for it!" She gave a mocking bow and her hair tumbled across her face. She swept it aside, then weighed Sten with her gaze. "You know, when we were instructed to arrest the Lord of House Bregon, I had a very different picture of you in my mind. Between your fair hair and pale eyes you look more Northerner than Heartlander."

"Oh? Do I not live up to your expectations as a great lord of the capital?"

She picked a low hanging apple and tossed it to him. "Quite the opposite, really. I was expecting one of those posh fools. You know, more chins than brains."

Sten chuckled. "Well, I suppose I should take that as a compliment. Although my father would be livid if he knew what I've just done."

"What, you mean ruining his estate or stealing from the capital?"

Her question was playful, but Sten detected an undercurrent of resentment. He turned away to hide his reddening face. "I wasn't technically *stealing* from the capital, you know. I was just siphoning money from the House reserves. Not only my House. All ten. I kept the amounts relatively small in the hope they wouldn't notice." He speculatively munched on the apple. "I suppose I shouldn't have underestimated the chancellor."

Ineza stopped abruptly and placed her hands on her hips. "That was downright lousy of you." She pointed to a dilapidated farmstead that rose from a turnip field, its roof sagging and shoddily patched. "People around here desperately need that coin instead of you. And it's far worse inside the capital than out. I should know. There are districts and neighborhoods where people work themselves to death and have nothing to show for it. Although growing up a *lord*, perhaps you didn't realize so."

Sten flung the apple core into a blackberry thicket. "Well that's not all of it. I used the money to try and help the capital. Little things, here and there. Food for the orphanages, clothes for the beggars, that sort of thing. I was passing money to a hospice that cares for minesick dwarves when you arrested me." He shoved his hands into his pockets and kicked a stone. "Honestly, redirecting that coin from the Houses' coffers was the only meaningful thing I did as a lord. But I suppose that's disappointing in itself."

They continued in silence for a time, skirting patches of mud and the deep wagon ruts brimming with yesterday's rain. To the east, the Gateway to the Wilds towered above the landscape like a slumbering primordial dragon.

Ineza's smile slowly returned. She gave Sten's arm a squeeze. "Perhaps I've misjudged you, *Lord* Bregon. I won't call you a saint, mind you, but at least you did something to try and help the people. That's more than the other Houses can claim." He smirked pointedly at her hand and she jerked it away, then punched him in the chest. "There, is that better? Do you only respond to violence?"

He grinned and rubbed his sternum. "Between that and hitting me with your sword, I'd say you have a curious way of expressing affection." Her laughter echoed through the orchards as she bounded up the winding road, leaving Sten to hurry along.

Darkness crept into the deep forests of the Gateway. Where the road ended, the Shrikes forged into the dense underbrush choked with brambles. They moved silently, navigating by the scant light of a gibbous moon. Sten fought his way through the spiny thickets with muffled curses, sounding like a troll in a china shop.

They came upon a mossy glen and Captain Whitney called to rest. Sten slumped to the ground, bruised and bleeding, struggling to catch his breath. Some of the closest soldiers exchanged smirks.

"All right Shrikes, take a moment to eat and drink," said Whitney. "No fires. You know the plan. If anyone falls behind," he looked pointedly at Sten, who was holding a loaf of bread in each hand and attempting to eat both simultaneously, "you will be left behind. We march in ten. Rou-augh!'" The Shrikes saluted and whispered the call in return.

Ineza sat beside Sten and honed her longsword. "*I* don't know the plan," he grumbled, massaging his aching feet.

"Oh, don't let the details overly concern you. Just another snatch-and-grab mission for the chancellor. In and out, quick as you like. Apparently some brothers live out here, the crazy bastards. Anyhoo, the chancellor wants a word with them. That's why we're here. *Forceful cooperation.* Although I haven't the faintest idea why he wanted you to come along. I don't even think Captain Whitney knows, or he's not letting on if he does."

"I imagine we're about to find out," said Sten. He shoved the remaining crusts of bread into his bag and unwrapped a narrow bundle of cloth. An oiled recurve bow shone dimly from within the folds. He deftly strung it, then turned his attention to a quiver of arrows and inspected their fletching.

Ineza elbowed him and nodded to the bow. "Odd choice of weapon for a lord. You any good with it?"

He smirked and ran his fingers along the worn grip. "Consider yourself lucky I didn't have it on the bridge."

She grinned. "Keep telling yourself that."

Captain Whitney strode by, belting a narrow rapier to one

---

* An ancient dwarvish battle cry that roughly translated to, 'Stale Beer!'

hip. He glanced at them and snorted before continuing on his way. Sten watched him go and donned a shoddy leather breastplate. "If he doesn't stop huffing and puffing he's liable to shed his mustache."

"Oh don't worry about Cap," said Ineza. She ran a finger along the edge of her sword. Satisfied, she returned it to its sheath. "He's all bark and no bite. Well, that's not true. Don't let his, er... physique, fool you. Plus, he'd lay down his life for any one of us. Except you. He sees you as a liability. Prove him wrong, eh?"

"And how might I do that?"

"Simple! Don't die." She patted his arm reassuringly and slipped away.

Sten drew his cloak over his head and waited, heart pounding. The glen had fallen silent. Tendrils of mist rolled over the loam, casting an otherworldly pall over the surrounding forest. The moon was barely visible through the foliage and heavy fog. Somewhere, an owl hooted sagely.* He shivered and pulled the cloak tighter about his shoulders. Another hoot sounded, eerily sharp in the velvet silence.**

A shadow rose to address the glen, and then came Whitney's muted growl. "Time to move. Remember, we're to take them alive. Stay vigilant, stay focused, and stay safe. Bregon, you're with me." The Shrikes spread into the night, immediately enveloped by the thickening fog. Sten took a deep breath and followed the disappearing form of the captain into the trees.

---

* Roughly translated, the nocturnal call went something like, "Two rabbits on the boys in black skulking in that ditch."

** "You have a yourself a wager, sah!"

SUBTERRANEAN SCHEMES

Back inside the towering walls of Heldan Port, nine men and women huddled around a circular table and a glowing candlestick.

They were the council to the chancellor. They were the pinnacles of the elite. The upper echelons of the uppity. They were the select few blessed with a genetic disposition toward wealth, privilege, and power. They were the descendants of those who lacked such undesirable traits as moral fortitude, self-awareness, and discernable jawlines.

They were the nine lords and ladies of the most powerful families of Heldan Port: the Heads of House. They were the Lords Impo, Polto, Knutte, Meren, and Ferott. They were the Ladies Huvani, Waldor, Pitton, and Aamot.

And they were scheming.

"Our scheme isn't progressing quickly enough!"

"Agreed. The chancellor should be on his knees by now,

begging us to spare his life. But don't call it a scheme, you make it sound so dramatic."

"Patience, patience. She warned us this would take time. As days pass and the effects of the wizards' absence are more widely felt, we will see results."

"How do we know she's right, though? We're to sit here and twiddle our thumbs and hope she knows what she's doing?"

"I say we expedite the process, set events into motion ourselves. We have more than enough resources to see this through. Why do we need her assistance any longer?"

"She did manage to subdue the entire Sanctum single handedly..."

"Those old fools? They're all talk. They use their power as leverage over the city, but they only practice cheap parlor tricks."

"Then now would be the perfect time to strike! The chancellor has lost his only loyal ally among us, and the late Lord Bregon's bumbling excuse for a son won't trouble us as his replacement."

"Actually, I think the boy is stealing from us..."

"Silence! Are we in agreement then? To move forward on our own and see Marstarrow removed from power?" There were murmurs of agreement from around the table. "So be it. We shall take matters into our own hands. Meeting adjourned."

"Erm, aren't you forgetting something?"

"Oh, right." There was the gentle rustling of a scroll being unfurled. "Let's see here... This week's bridge club will be hosted by... ah, Lord Knutte."

"What? I hosted last week."

"Well you have it again, that's why we drafted the schedule."

"Damn."

"Then it's settled? Good. *Now* the meeting is adjourned."

Nine lords and ladies slipped away from the table, leaving behind a burning candlestick that flickered in the darkness.

THE BROTHERS ARDA

"Where's the other one?" whispered Sten.

Whitney shifted uncomfortably beside him. "I don't know. The chancellor assured me they'd both be here."

"Maybe he was wrong?

"Doubtful. Stop asking questions."

They crouched on the outskirts of a small clearing. A man sat in its center, his features obscured by a halo of light emanating from a crackling fire. He seldom moved, except to raise a spoon to his lips, or to refill a bowl from a large cauldron perched in the fire.

Several minutes passed in total silence. Sten's joints ached from kneeling and he was losing sensation in the tips of his fingers. Whitney sat rigid, apparently unaffected by the growing cold, although his nose had turned a darker shade of crimson. His mustache quivered as he ground his teeth. "Something's not right. The other brother should be here by

now." There was a faint rustling behind them and the huge twins emerged from the gloom. Whitney nodded to them. "Lieutenants. Anything to report, Finlan?"

One of the twins saluted. "There's an encampment south of the clearing, sir." His deeply melodic voice reminded Sten of warm butter. "Nobody's there. No sign of the other target."

"Tryo?"

The other threw a hasty salute. "Nothing out of the ordinary, sir. Everyone is in place, awaiting your signal."

Whitney nodded gravely. "Very well, return to your positions. Don't engage until I give the command." The twins retreated into the night and silence returned. Sten and Whitney continued to watch the man by the fire.

The minutes dragged on. The man showed no intention of abandoning his cozy fire and seemingly endless supply of soup. Sten's attention wandered and he scanned the woods. A low-hanging mist blanketed the forest floor, ceaselessly boiling over misshapen roots. Skeletal fingers reached and grasped and melted away. His eyelids began to droop.

A flicker of light danced at the corner of his vision. He snapped to attention, eyes straining to penetrate the darkness. Nothing was there, but he had *seen* movement just moments before. It had reminded him of moonlight reflected off running water, an ethereal glimmer that disappeared as quickly as it had come. He tapped Whitney's shoulder.

"Captain, I just saw... Well I'm not exactly sure what it was."

Whitney spun about. "Where?"

Sten pointed. "By that grove of trees. It was only there for a second, but I definitely saw something. It may have been a trick of the moonlight but I swear it was..." he trailed off.

"Spit it out, Bregon!"

"It was a young girl. Watching us."

The captain snorted. "Your mind's playing tricks on you, boy. It was just this confounded mist."

Sten thought about protesting but decided against it.

A tremendous *CRACK* shattered the calm as a branch exploded some distance to their right. They crouched lower as the snapping of limbs and rustling of undergrowth grew louder. The largest man Sten had ever seen entered the clearing, whistling a cheery tune. Well over seven feet tall, he wore gilded armor and a crimson cloak, and sported a mane of unruly copper curls that matched his beard. A massive double-headed battle axe was strapped across his back. The giant marched over to the seated figure and bent to whisper in his ear. The silhouette nodded.

Whitney eagerly shifted position. "Finally. We have the brothers."

"We're supposed to arrest *that*?" said Sten. "He makes your Finlan and Tryo look like children!"

Whitney cupped his hands around his mouth and gave a strange, lilting whistle that echoed softly through the forest. The larger brother sat and accepted a proffered bowl from the other, but didn't turn at the sound.

Minutes passed and nothing happened. Whitney sat in agitated silence, his eyes searching the darkness. "Damn it all," he whispered. "Where the hell are my Shrikes?" He whistled again and was greeted by nothing.

The smaller brother turned from the fire and shook out his cloak. Fair hair fell to his shoulders and threatened to obscure his face, which was narrow and weather-beaten. He raised his head and Sten inhaled sharply at the vivid flashes of blue. The man's eyes were as cold and pure as glacial ice.

"They're from the Frozen Steppes!" he whispered.

Whitney's hand strayed to his rapier. "Does it matter?"

The fair-haired man stretched lazily and unsheathed a pair of daggers. He held them easily. He nodded to his brother, and the giant unslung his axe and twirled it in one hand. "Captain Whitney!" he roared in a voice like rolling thunder.

"Your reputation precedes you! We're flattered you've come so far to see us. Crawl out from wherever you're hiding. It's time we have ourselves a little chat."

The captain flinched. He sat for a moment, eyes darting about the woods. The brothers waited patiently. "Right. Stay here. Don't make a sound."

Sten proffered his bow. "I can help!"

Whitney shook his head. "They don't know you're here. I will not endanger a civilian under my protection, no matter the chancellor's will. Stay put. That's an order." He rose and unsheathed the razor-thin rapier from his hip. He entered the clearing, holding it carefully in front of him. "You are the Brothers Arda?" He stopped a safe distance from the fire.

The larger brother slammed his axe into the soil and folded his tree-trunk arms. "Culyan Arda, Marshal of the Wilds. Pleasure to meet you. This here's my little brother, Eotan. They call him the Wolf. As you can see I am much bigger and much more handsome."

"Less intelligent, though," said Eotan. Culyan laughed good-naturedly. "Now, Captain, what is your business here? Why this intrusion into our home?" His eyes blazed in the firelight like twin sapphires.

Whitney drew himself upright. "I am here on behalf of Tiberion Marstarrow. You are to accompany me to the capital. He wishes to speak with you."

Eotan laughed derisively and shook his head. "How rude of the chancellor to presume such a thing, wouldn't you say, brother? Looks like some things never change."

The Marshal knelt and filled a bowl from the cauldron. "Aye, what an insult to our hospitality. Old Tiberion should have come here himself if he wanted to chat. We have plenty of soup."

"You know the chancellor?" said Whitney, surprised.

"Oh yes," said Eotan. "We, like you, used to take orders

41

from Tiberion Marstarrow. So I won't fault you for being here tonight. I know how persuasive he can be."

Culyan stroked his beard. "Is persuasive the right word? I was thinking two-faced."

"True enough," said Eotan. "So even though we can appreciate your situation, it's time for you to be on your merry way."

Whitney's eyes darted between the brothers. "I'm not leaving. Not without my Shrikes. What have you done to them?"

Culyan grinned. "Oh they're... resting. Don't fret yourself, they're unharmed. We'll send them along in the morning, alive and well. You have my word."

"So be it," said Whitney. "But I cannot leave without you. I have my orders." The brothers remained silent. Sten watched anxiously from the shadows.

"Indeed you do," said Eotan, after an icy pause. "But I warn you, Captain, this obstinacy will not end well for you. I will ask you once more; leave now and forget this place." Whitney flourished his thin blade and adopted a defensive stance. Eotan sighed and turned to his brother. "Do you want him or shall I?"

"He's all yours, little pup."

Eotan approached Whitney, twirling a dagger in each hand. With a roar, the captain launched his assault. His narrow rapier danced in the firelight as he struck blow after blow in rapid succession. The men revolved about the clearing in a whirlwind of metal and sparks. Eotan bared his teeth in a wolfish smile, and the light of battle shone in his eyes. With a twinge of dread, Sten realized that the brother was enjoying himself. He unslung his bow and nocked an arrow.

After a series of lightning-quick thrusts the duel abruptly turned in Eotan's favor. He turned on the captain and drove him toward the fire. Whitney gasped. His movements slowed as he backpedaled. Then Eotan feinted and swiped at

Whitney's blade in one fluid motion. The rapier pinwheeled from the captain's hands. He stumbled after it, but Eotan kicked him in the side and sent him sprawling to the dirt.

Sten rushed into the clearing, his arrow aimed squarely at Eotan's chest. "Stop!"

The brothers whirled about in surprise. Eotan shot a look of annoyance at Culyan. "You didn't say anything about him!"

Culyan pointed at Whitney. "Manye only told me about this one!" He made for Sten, axe in hand.

"I told you to stop!" Sten commanded again. The arrow oscillated between the advancing brothers. "Let Captain Whitney go. Let us leave, and we won't come back."

"Demanding little shit, isn't he?" said Culyan, though he came no closer.

Whitney retrieved his rapier from the dirt and joined Sten. "I ordered you to stay put!" he panted.

"And you're welcome I didn't." Sten's attention never left the brothers. "Don't follow us and don't break your word. You promised the Shrikes would leave here unharmed."

"And so they will," said Eotan. The intensity of his gaze chilled Sten to the bone.

All of a sudden, there came a series of resounding *BOOMS* that reverberated off the trees. A strange tune began to echo through the clearing. Sten whirled about and swore. A group of dwarves emerged from the darkness, each carrying some instrument or another. One was singing in a richly melodic baritone. Another particularly fat dwarf was energetically banging a massive drum strapped to his chest. The *BOOMS* continued to sound throughout the Gateway.

Whitney flourished his rapier. "What is this?"

Sten trained his bow on the advancing dwarves. Then, inexplicably, the arrow pointed toward the ground of its own accord. He desperately tried to correct his aim but it was as though an invisible force was controlling his movements. He fired harmlessly into the dirt at his feet. He shot a glance at Whitney. The captain carefully placed his sword on the ground. Beads of sweat shone on his face, as though he was waging some internal battle.

The song continued and Sten was forced to kneel. The brothers retrieved the surrendered weapons and joined the band of dwarves.

"Gentlemen, let me introduce the Bearded Eight," said Eotan. The dwarves bowed low, and the music stopped.

The hold over Sten evaporated. "Was that magic?" he gasped.

"Aye," said one of the dwarves, a large ruby woven into his plaited beard. "Wizards and mages and their lot aren't the only ones with the gift." He sighed forlornly. "Though few dwarves remain who can recall the right songs."

"Where is Manye?" interrupted Eotan. "I would speak with her."

The dwarf shrugged. "Keeping watch, as last we saw. Why?"

"She made an uncharacteristic mistake."

"Manye doesn't make mistakes," said Culyan. "She knew this boy was here, mark my words. So why didn't she tell us, I wonder?"

The brothers stared down at Sten, wearing similar expressions of contemplation. And then Eotan's eyes grew wide. He lifted Sten into the air by his breastplate, his voice harsh. "What is your name?"

Sten struggled to break free, ramming his hands ineffectually into Eotan's chest. "Sten Bregon!" he finally relinquished.

Eotan's shoulders slumped. He dropped Sten and turned to his brother. "Damn him! Damn that man."

Culyan dislodged his axe from the dirt and spun it. "Seems he's broken his promise. Perhaps we should pay him a visit after all."

"Perhaps we should," said Eotan. The anger in his eyes shone almost as bright as the reflected firelight.

"What the hell are you talking about?" Sten panted.

Eotan smiled grimly. "The chancellor wishes to speak with us, does he not? Then we shall grant his audience, whether he likes it or not. Take them away."

MOMENTARY RESPITE

The coals of the dying fire bathed the clearing in warm red light. The brothers huddled close, talking in hushed voices long into the night. Then the larger man retired from the dwindling flames and left the other to sit in silence. He lingered there, quiet and motionless, impervious to the chill that seeped into the air.

A victorious hooting broke the silence.

"Ha, that'll be two rabbits! And none of those skinny devils from the city. I want the fat ones from the deep woods." There was a moment's pause. Then, some distance away, another owl hooted begrudgingly.

"You were lucky. Double or nothing, I say!"

Silence, as though this new proposition merited some serious consideration.

"The wager?"

"The chancellor will die by the Ardas' hands."

"How macabre! We have a wager. I hope you have

improved your hunting skills, Edelwing. Four rabbits should not be taken lightly."

"I have always been the better hunter, Stonetalon. I shall eagerly await my feast!"

"Ha! We shall see!"

Calm returned to the glen. The flickering coals finally died and plunged the forest into somber blackness. Eotan Arda remained where he sat, unmoving, except to draw the sable-lined cloak tighter about his shoulders.

"PRISONERS"

Sten and Whitney were roused well before dawn and took breakfast with the Bearded Eight. The dwarves were amiable enough, although they remained silent about the happenings of the previous night, and refused Whitney's request to speak with his Shrikes.

They were escorted deeper into the Gateway and found the brothers tending their horses. Culyan's was a gargantuan black destrier called Kipto, who managed to dwarf even the Marshal in stature. Sten couldn't imagine a horse and rider better suited for one another. They were paragons of strength, overall largeness, and, in the hours before dawn, ill tempers. Eotan brushed down a beautiful silver mare called Lilenti, and leapt onto her back without a saddle.

He noticed Sten's doubtful expression and smiled. "I speak to her and she listens."

Culyan threw the largest saddle that Sten had ever seen over Kipto's back. "The same can't be said for this hunk o'

horse meat. He's a little too fond of bloodshed, even for my taste." He grinned wickedly. "Oh, and you two will be riding with me."

"Wouldn't it be, erm, wiser to distribute the weight more evenly?" asked Sten. The black charger stamped a hoof, and he backed away hastily.

"Nobody rides Lilenti but me," said Eotan. "Kipto can easily bear your weight. Mount up. We ride for the capital."

Thunderous hoof beats shattered the mist-soaked quiet of the Lowlands. Sten winced as he bounced unceremoniously atop Kipto's saddle. The wind roared in his ears. He clung to Whitney, who in turn had a death-grip on the Marshal's waist. The brothers traded inaudible words as trees and farmsteads whipped past in indistinct swatches of color. Sten screwed shut his eyes to quash an impending sense of vertigo, but the effect only worsened.

Whitney elbowed him. "That mare of Eotan's is unnatural! Nobody can ride that hard for fear of killing their horse. But look, no lather!" Eotan noticed their fascination and smiled, giving Lilenti a pat on the neck. He leaned forward and whispered into the mare's ear. Without breaking stride, she darted forward, barely touching the ground, and left Kipto far behind.

The ramparts of Heldan Port materialized from the fog. The unbroken wall of stone spanned the horizon and obscured the Westerly Seas beyond. Banners fluttered from the tops of crenelated towers, proudly wearing the sigil of the capital; a golden sun sinking into violet seas. The colossal city gate shone dully in the afternoon haze. Its barred doors were thrown open, like the cavernous maw of some terrible beast.

Eotan drew alongside Culyan. They joined a growing stream of people trickling into the city. As they passed below the portcullis, a member of the City Guard called them to a halt. He warily eyed the horses and edged away from Kipto's impatient stomping. "What's your business in the capital?" he demanded. The severity of his tone was somewhat diminished by his taking refuge behind an ornate flowerpot.

Culyan sighed and clicked his tongue. Kipto trotted forward, lifted the guard by his cloak, and deposited him back in front of the gate. "Have some respect for yourself, man. You'd know if we meant you harm."

The guard straightened his chainmail and adopted a stern expression. "Erm, right you are, sir. Now then, erm, what is your business in the capital?"

"Captain Whitney and I have taken these men as our prisoners," said Sten importantly. "We are expected by Chancellor Marstarrow."

The guard's eyes widened when he noticed Whitney sandwiched into the saddle. He saluted. "Captain Whitney, I, erm, didn't see you there." Whitney nodded painfully. "Are you quite certain these gentlemen are your prisoners and not the other way around?"

Whitney's voice was muffled by Culyan's cloak. "Yes, yes. We act on the chancellor's orders. Let us pass."

"Yessir, of course, sir. Only..." Indecision tugged at the man's features. "Only those aren't your horses, sir. That was, erm, quite generous of them to give you a ride back to the capital. What with them being your captives and all. And, erm, that prisoner has a horse all to himself."

Culyan nudged Kipto closer to the guard. "Do you remember what I told you about meaning you harm?"

With a squeak, the guard retreated to the safety of the flowerpot. "Erm, yessir. You said it right after that abomination," Kipto snorted, "that, erm, nice horsie, almost yanked my head off." Culyan waited expectantly. The guard stiffened. "Oh, right you are. I think it's time to let these fine gentlemen pass. Erm, prisoners."

Culyan nodded his thanks and led the way into the city.

BUTTERSON'S BEERS

A large barrel meandered through the crowd gathering in Heldan Port's public forum. It pushed its way through the throngs, expertly avoiding horses, dogs, cats, and potholes. It trundled toward a stone dais where a terrifically skinny man was emphatically speaking to the assemblage.

The barrel didn't have the same careful regard for the people blocking its path.

"Oi, what the hell!" cried an elf, and careened into his flower stand. The barrel continued merrily along its way, ignoring the shrieks of protest that followed in its wake. Men, women, and children scrambled out of the way as it cut a swath through the crowd and deposited itself directly in front of the raised podium. The speaker faltered. All eyes fixed on the barrel. It remained still and silent. The orator straightened his cloak and continued.

"Ladies and gentlemen, as I was saying, strange and dangerous times are upon us! We cannot sit idly by and ignore the

warnings! The wizards have vanished, and now there are tales coming from the Wilds. Strange and terrible creatures have been witnessed haunting the south, and they are coming this way! Where is Tiberion Marstarrow? Why does he not act?" Murmurs rippled through the crowd. The speaker pounded one hand into the other. "Where is the tolling of the bells that would unite the capital into a mighty fist?" There were shouts of assent. The man flushed and forged ahead. "This inaction from Tiberion Marstarrow will bring about the end of the capital as we know it! And so I say to you, good people of Heldan Port, we must march upon the chancellor's keep and demand his resignation!" This proclamation was greeted with a resounding silence.

Mord Butterson, proprietor of Butterson's Beers, had been waiting patiently for this moment of alienation. He sidled over to the barrel and gave it a tap. The lid opened a fraction. Two red eyes peered back at him.

"Password," the barrel demanded.

"Raxo it's me!" Butterson hissed. The eyes disappeared as the lid started to close. "Wait! Blast, how does it go...'Our beer, which art in flagons, hallowed be thy hops; thy drunkards come, till all is gone, in taverns as it is in castles. Give us this day our daily pints, and forgive us our bad decisions, as we forgive those who vomit upon us. And lead us straight into temptation; but ignore our philandering. For thine is the spirits, the liquors, and the finest ales, for ever and ever, lest we throw ourselves from the tallest of mountains. Cheers.'"

There was a pause, then, "Did you say philanderin' or philanthropyin'?"

"Philandering. Philanthropying isn't a word. Now open up, you know it's me!" The eyes reappeared and gave shape to a small red demon, dripping with foamy ale. He stretched and sharpened a claw against a slat, spiked tail twitching back and forth like a cat's.

"Can never be too careful, boss. I think I ruffled a few feathers rollin' this up here. I swear I heard an angry old nun swearing like a sailor and threatenin' to do unmentionable things to my unmentionables."

Butterson scratched his beard. "Let me guess. You're the innocent victim in this affair?"

The imp snorted disdainfully. "I may or may not have chased her into a cartful of manure. It's very discombobulatin' rollin' around inside a barrel full of beer."

Butterson forced himself to maintain a stern expression. "Well, be more careful in the future. Or make sure I'm around to watch. Now, tap this and ready the flagons. It's show time." The crowd was still whispering amongst themselves while the speaker was desperately urging a call to arms. Butterson hefted his rotund figure onto the dais.

"Ladies and gents, may I have your attention," he boomed. The murmurs quickly dissipated. Butterson threw open his arms and beamed at the sea of upturned faces. "Butterson's Beers, at your service!" He bowed graciously at the wholehearted applause that followed. "Thank you, thank you! Now, in this time of confusion and ill-devised plans," he looked pointedly at the speaker, "why not clear your heads with some Roaring-Pines Lager? When dark times are nigh and rational thought escapes us, the only solution is a liquid solution!" More cheering. Butterson smiled and clapped his hands together. "Please form an orderly queue and have your coins ready! Butterson's Beers thanks you for your service." He stepped down to a quickly growing line.

The orator gave him a haughty scowl and continued his speech. "Thank you for that *rude* interruption. Now, I know some of you may worry about approaching Marstarrow directly, but I ask you this: what will come if we sit idly by and wait for our enemies to arrive at our gates?"

"What enemies?" somebody called. "Heldan Port has been at peace ever since Marstarrow took over!"

"You all know the stories of Dinh," cried the speaker. "They crave our power. They envy our dominion over the Heartlands! They could raze Heldan Port to the ground if we are not prepared. We need a leader who isn't afraid to sully his hands for the well-being of us all!"

"And who might replace Marstarrow?" called another voice. "You? If you turned sideways you'd not cast a shadow. Except your fat head, maybe."

The speaker turned bright red and puffed out his chest. "I never said *me*, you imbecile! We must embrace the Houses' leadership! Their hearts are good and true, and only have the capital's best interests in mind. They have the courage to do what is necessary to protect us all!"

Another voice chimed in. "Eh, people aren't courageous if they're too stupid to recognize the danger they're in. They're just bloody idiots. Besides, we have limited information about what's happening. If we displace Marstarrow, or go to war with Dinh over false or negligible information, we might doom this city to years of unnecessary bloodshed. For all we know, the wizards went on holiday and this mist is just a coalescence of suspended water droplets that came from a slight thermal inversion taking place over some body of water in the Wilds."

The forum went silent. Butterson could almost hear several hundred minds furiously attempting to deduce the meaning of negligible and coalescence.

The speaker threw up his hands. "You are all fools! Who will save us if not the Heads of House? The old miser who cowers in his office? Master Butterson here and his pet demon?" There was a smattering of applause and hopeful cheers. The orator tore at his hair and jumped up and down. "There is nobody else! You are all blind!"

But another hush had fallen over the forum. Nervous whispers spread throughout the crowd and necks craned toward the city gates. There came another wave of whispers, this time moving like wildfire, gaining momentum and volume. The hair on Butterson's neck stood on end and his beard bristled. He scrambled back onto the podium, Raxo close on his heels. His breath caught as he gazed over the crowd.

A massive black horse marched its way through the forum. The crowd scrambled to clear a path. Its rider was adorned in golden armor and a crimson cloak, utterly resplendent in the sunlight piercing the low clouds. Two figures sat behind him, dwarfed by his gargantuan size. A glimmer of silver and another rider entered the forum. His cloak was as black as the cosmos, and he rode a horse the color of moonlight. The riders nodded to the crowd as they passed.

And then they were gone, swallowed by the streets of the capital. The crowd slowly turned back to the dais. The only sound was the flapping of banners in the afternoon breeze.

"There," said Butterson. "There are the ones who could lead us."

FAMILY REUNION

"Eugh, they're hideous."

"Watch your tongue, Bregon."

"But look, he's all lumpy. And she, no he, wait... no. I was right the first time! She's lopsided!" Sten examined a painting of two people stoically poised on a cliff overlooking the sea. A vibrant sunset illuminated the sky behind them.

"They're the Founders," said Captain Whitney. He was seated next to the doors of the great hall of the chancellor's keep. "They built this capital from nothing and made it what it is today." He nervously twirled his freshly waxed mustache, which spanned well beyond his ears. "The Heldans were exceptional persons."

"Exceptionally ugly persons, maybe," said Sten. "I've seen better looking trolls."

The Brothers Arda sat on a nearby bench, surrounded by a host of City Guard. Their expressions were neutral, but Sten detected a slight tension in their bearing. Whitney, on the

other hand, was sweating through his tunic. "Keep an eye on the prisoners," he ordered, for the tenth time since sitting down to wait. Sten rolled his eyes. The captain had attempted to throw the brothers in irons when they entered the chancellor's keep, but the task had proven impossible. Culyan's wrists and ankles proved far too large for any shackle, and Eotan simply freed himself every time the guards turned away. Whitney eventually gave up and made them promise to behave.

With an ominous creak, the doors to the great hall swung inward. Hundreds of chandeliers and braziers illuminated the vast interior. A long table was set in the middle of the room, piled high with food and wine. Tiberion Marstarrow and nine men and women were already seated. Whitney marched into the chamber, head held high. "Chancellor Marstarrow, esteemed Heads of House, I present to you the Brothers Arda."

"So the Wolf and the Marshal have returned," said a stern man with white hair and a pinched face. "Brought to heel by the infamous Captain Whitney and his little band of Shrikes. My, my, the times have changed, haven't they?"

Whitney's face reddened. "Unfortunately no, Lord Impo. I was soundly defeated in the Gateway. The Brothers Arda have accompanied me to the capital of their own volition." He stood straight to attention, his eyes fixed on the ceiling, mustache quivering. "No point in giving credit where it's not due." The Heads of House murmured their disapproval.

"Enough," said Chancellor Marstarrow. His eyes were fixed on the brothers. "Captain Whitney, you are dismissed. Please wait outside." Whitney bowed and exited the hall, though a flicker of shame crossed his face. A guard closed the doors behind him and slid a heavy bolt into place.

Eotan stepped forward and brushed off the attempted restraints of the guards. "You gave me your word, Tiberion."

Marstarrow splayed his fingers on the table. "Straight to

the point, I see. Unfortunately, these are extenuating circumstances and my hand was forced."

Eotan's eyes shone with restrained fury. "We once helped you in your bloody crusade. Now, we are done with you."

"Yet here you stand."

"We have only come to deliver a final warning. Leave us be, and leave Sten out of this. Allow us to police the Wilds and protect your borders, but do not call on us again. You gave us your word, Tiberion. I once believed you a man of honor."

The temperature in the room plummeted and Sten shifted uncomfortably. "I'm lost," he said. "What do I have to do with this?"

The chancellor held up a hand. "Regrettably, I have exhausted my options. Additionally, I believe young master Bregon has a right to know the role he has played in this theater of ours. He was instrumental in bringing you here, after all."

"He came to us because you're his puppeteer," hissed Eotan. "You pulled his strings and made him dance. Did he ever have a choice?"

The chancellor's expression was marble. "He did not. But allow me to summarize the situation for you. My wizards are gone. Vanished, as if by magic, ironically. I am sure you witnessed the unrest spreading throughout my city. It is tangible. It is a civil blight that must be cured. My people are scared, and rightly so." The chancellor's eyes flicked to the Heads of House before continuing. "Therefore, Brothers Arda, I charge you to ride for Dinh on the capital's behalf. Our messages have not been received, yet contact *must* be established. There are none in this city who know the Wilds as well as you. As such, you will act as ambassadors to the capital and open a line of communication with Dinh."

With a snarl, Eotan sprinted to the table and leapt across its length, landing in front of the chancellor. He gathered Marstarrow by his tunic and lifted him bodily from his seat.

The guards rushed forward but Culyan barred their way. The Heads of Houses fled into the corners of the room, spilling wine in their panic.

"You charge us?" Eotan yelled. "How dare you! How dare you, after everything you've done! You gave us your word that you would leave us in peace! You gave us your word that our nephew would be safe! Imagine our surprise when he strolled into camp last night."

Sten froze. "What now? I'm your nephew?"

Eotan's face was only inches from the chancellor's, his expression one of animalistic rage. "Yes! And this... this filth promised to keep you safe! He swore on his life that he would protect our sister's son!"

"Hey, Sten!" bellowed Culyan from across the hall. "I'm the fun uncle!" He collected three guards in a headlock and sat on a fourth.

"I had every intention of keeping my word," said Marstarrow, calmly, "but Heldan Port needs you, now more than ever. Your nephew has served his purpose. He shall remain in the capital, safe from harm. If that is your wish."

"Like hell I will," said Sten. "I've been cooped up in this city my entire life, always being told what to do. If these are my uncles, I'm going with them!"

"You see?" cried Eotan. "That is precisely what we hoped to avoid! We can't protect him in the Wilds." He slammed the chancellor back into his seat. "You mistake our bond to Heldan Port. We act on the behalf of the capital because we wish to live in peace, beyond your laws. If protecting your borders grants us that freedom, then so be it. But you have crossed the line, Tiberion."

Marstarrow smoothed down the front of his tunic and crossed one leg over the other. "Would you have listened to my proposition if I had not involved the boy? Would you have willingly ridden into my city to hear me speak? I think not."

Eotan remained silent, breathing hard. "Your freedom will not endure if Dinh wages war on Heldan Port. Your freedom will not survive if the Wilds overrun our borders. You know I speak the truth. Ride out, speak to the baroness of Dinh, and preserve your peace."

Eotan stared at the chancellor for a long while, jaw working. Then he jumped from the table and carefully stepped over the unconscious guards. "Well, brother?"

Culyan stuck his thumbs into his belt and rocked back and forth on his heels. "I think he's backed us into a corner, little pup. Not sure we have a choice. Plus, it'd be nice to see Jaya again. It's been too long."

One of the guards stirred, moaning piteously. He started to rise, then froze when he noticed Culyan and Eotan staring down at him. He thought for a moment, then sank back to the ground and pretended to sleep.

"Wise choice," said Eotan.

"Besides," continued Culyan, "you know I can't turn down a good adventure! We have the Bearded Eight, we have Manye, and now we have Aella's son. In time, Tiberion Marstarrow will answer for his treachery. For now we must look beyond his deceit. There's more at stake than our pride."

After a moment Eotan nodded and laid a hand on Culyan's shoulder. "Perhaps you're right. Forgive me, brother. Anger has clouded my judgment." He turned back to Marstarrow. "We will act as your ambassadors to Heldan Port. But once this affair is concluded, you will atone for your sins. An oath-breaker has no honor."

"I sacrificed my honor for the sake of this city long ago," said Marstarrow quietly. "However, I will not attempt to prevent your vengeance should you return. Now, travel swiftly. Speed is imperative." Eotan inclined his head, then turned on his heel and threw open the doors.

Whitney stumbled in, rapier drawn. "What the hell's going on in here?"

Culyan strode past him and beckoned to Sten. "Come along, nephew."

Sten raced to keep stride with his uncles as they left the great hall. His heart thundered in his chest, but he was unsure whether from excitement or fear.

A NEWFOUND PATH

The sun was just beginning to set as they exited the
capital's gates. The Bearded Eight hailed them from
a nearby field, where they stood guard over the Shrikes.
Corporal Ghet waved at him cheerily. Sten pulled her aside
and relayed what had transpired in the capital. Nearby, the
brothers argued animatedly with the dwarves.

"And you're going with them?" said Ineza. "Why?"

Sten shrugged and blew out his cheeks. "Well… it turns
out they're my uncles. My mother's brothers, to be exact."

Her mouth dropped open. "You're kidding me. You're
related to *them*?" She stared pointedly at the brothers. Their
profiles were terribly dashing in the setting sun, and the Marshal's armor glowed like a beacon. Sten hastily sucked in his
stomach and threw back his shoulders. "How can you be sure?
Did your mother never mention them to you?"

"My father alluded to her having brothers, but refused
to tell me more. No doubt in the hope I would follow in *his*

footsteps instead of theirs. But the chancellor confirmed it. They're my blood."

Ineza looked again to the brothers and shook her head. "Incredible. You sure drew the short straw."

Sten deflated. "What's that supposed to mean?"

"Not important. Anyhoo, this seems stupid. Even for you."

"What else can I do? They're family. I have nothing here. No one."

Her expression soured and she looked away. "And here I thought we were getting along famously."

Sten flushed. "I'm sorry, you've been more than kind to me. Apart from hitting me with your sword." The words felt hollow and he drifted into silence. He ran his fingers through his hair. "Look, we won't be gone for long. And once this is done, maybe I'll see things clearly."

"You better, my *lord*, or I'm liable to hit you again." She stepped forward and hugged him tightly. "Take care, Sten Bregon."

Sten joined his uncles and the dwarves, cheeks burning. Culyan grinned down at him. "Looks like you take after us after all."

"You live alone in the woods with eight dwarves. I don't get *that* from you. What's the plan?"

"Go with the Bearded Eight," said Eotan. "Culyan and I need to find Manye."

"Manye?"

Culyan gestured to the Gateway. "You'll meet her, just not now."

Eotan nodded grimly and mounted his horse. "We'll return by dawn tomorrow. Rest, eat, and gather your strength. You'll need it." He bent down and whispered in Lilenti's ear. In a shower of dirt, the brothers tore down the road and disappeared in a cloud of dust.

A dwarf approached Sten and bowed so low that his

plaited beard brushed the grass. A series of expertly crafted gemstones sparkled within the braids. "I believe it is time we met in earnest. I am One, and this is Two, Three, Four, Five, Six, Seven, and Eight."* The dwarves bowed in succession as they were introduced.

Sten bowed in return. "That should be easy enough to remember." He glanced around the field. "Er, you don't have any horses. How am I supposed to ride with you?" The dwarves chuckled and flourished their instruments. Seven, the fattest of the lot, struck a lively tempo on his drum. The others joined in, and One began to sing in dwarvish.

A patch of air shimmered in front of Sten. It stretched and vibrated to the beat of the music. He stared in wonder. A swirling miasma gradually formed, blossoming outward in all directions. As the music swelled, the air solidified. Sten stared, open mouthed, as a cloud materialized out of nothing-ness, suspended several feet above the ground. The dwarves hoisted themselves into its midst.

Two offered Sten a hand. He took it and gingerly stepped onto the cloud. The sensation was akin to sinking his entire body into a feather pillow. He prodded the cloud with a finger. "This is wonderful!"

Two grinned. "Aye, lad. The Bearded Eight travel in style. Are you ready?"

Sten cast a final glance at the Shrikes. Ineza sat alone in the field, arms wrapped around her legs. She noticed his attention and gave a small wave. He waved farewell, his chest strangely heavy. "I'm ready."

With a slight *huff*, the cloud rocketed forth, whisking Sten and the dwarves away from the capital.

---

* Dwarven names were in fact, not names at all, but rather numbers sig-nifying their status in a particular guild, sect, or class. The closer the number to One, the higher the status of the dwarf. Dwarves placed a much greater importance on beard length and gemstones than names.

THE HALL OF HEROES

Captain Whitney followed the chancellor through the scantly lit halls of the keep. He was annoyed at having been excused from the meeting with the Brothers Arda. His intuition had told him that the brothers would cause trouble, and he had been right. He voiced his displeasure to Marstarrow, but the Chancellor only waved a dismissive hand.

"If Eotan Arda planned on killing me, neither you nor a regiment of the City Guard would have prevented his hand. So to speak. You have yet to be introduced to his... how shall I put this... animalistic nature."

They continued down another long corridor that gave way to a hall with vaulted ceilings and elaborate stained-glass windows. Its walls were lined with silken tapestries and oil paintings, each depicting men and women in various poses of exaggerated grandiosity. Bronze placards rested beneath, detailing the heroes' exploits.

A wave of nostalgia washed over Whitney. He had loved

coming to the Hall of Heroes as a boy. He had spent countless hours reveling in these stoic figures, forever immortalized in oils and fine silks. These were the men and women who had changed the course of Mizian history forever. They stared loftily down at him, as though conscious of their company and setting. He lowered his gaze and marched on.

Marstarrow ducked through a small door set in the Hall's rear, then continued down a narrow passageway. A cloud of previously undisturbed dust swirled about his boots. Whitney examined the walls. They bore none of the grease, soot, and muck of the more heavily trafficked corridors. He mentally attempted to determine their location, but the convoluted maze of windowless tunnels erased his sense of direction. He sighed, and his mind wandered up to the front steps of the keep, so many years prior.

"Regibar Theraford Whitney," Marstarrow had said, standing straight as an arrow. "For your outstanding service and devotion to the capital, I present you with the captaincy of the Shrikes." The chancellor handed him a small brooch, carved into the silhouette of a shrike, its wings outstretched. It was wrought from silver and had an onyx stone set into its center.

Whitney accepted the token with trembling hands. "Thank you, Chancellor, it would be my honor." He fumbled to pin the brooch to his lapel. Marstarrow stepped forward and deftly secured the ornament. Then, with a nod, he turned and began up the steps. "I won't fail you," Whitney called after him. "You have my word."

Marstarrow descended lightly and met Whitney's eye. "Regibar, I have glimpsed beneath the muddied waters that swirl about you. I have seen how the heroes of Heldan Port speak to you. And while I laud your proud ambitions and renown with a blade, *those* did not earn you the captaincy of my Shrikes." Whitney frowned but remained at attention. Marstarrow studied him with discerning, gray eyes. "I see that you doubt me. Understandable. It is easy to lavish platitudes on a man until his ego is fit to burst. But remember with whom you are speaking. That is not, nor ever will be, the way in which I motivate." He laid a hand on Whitney's shoulder, and for the briefest of moments, his expression softened. "You will come to understand, with time, I should think."

Whitney didn't know how to respond. Marstarrow's granite visage returned, and he swept up the stairs two at a time. He paused at the top and called down to his new captain. "You promise to never fail me, Regibar? I believe you."

Amber sunlight interrupted Whitney's memories. He shielded his face and blinked owlishly in the glow of twilight. The chancellor had led him outside the walls of Heldan Port. His Shrikes and their horses were already waiting in a nearby field. The soldiers jumped to their feet as he approached.

"They were delivered this afternoon by a group of dwarves," said Marstarrow. "I must apologize for sending you blindly into the Arda's camp. I needed a courier to escort Sten to their doorstep, unharmed. I surmised correctly that your ignorance would keep you safe from the brothers' potential wrath."

Whitney nodded begrudgingly and surveyed his soldiers. Most lounged about in a circle, looking well fed and rested. The gnome, Corporal Hemmie, was smoking an elegant wooden pipe several feet long and decorated with intricate carvings. "Where in the world did you get that?" Whitney asked.

"Won it off one of those dwarven fellows in a game of Thropple, sir."

"Thropple?"

"It's a game, sir, involving cards, dice, copious amounts of alcohol, and a chicken."

"Well at least you got something out of this mess." His Shrikes laughed ruefully.

"We didn't stand a chance, Captain," said Finlan.

His twin nodded in agreement. "We were in position,

ready to attack on your command. Then the little bastards started singing."

Whitney suppressed a smile. "I see."

"It's true, Cap," said Hemmie. "The song was very nice. Put us all to sleep within seconds. Or at least that's what they told us. I can't quite seem to remember."

"So Heldan Port's finest were defeated by a lullaby?"

Hemmie waggled his eyebrows conspiratorially. "They told us it was some type of dwarven magic."

Whitney smiled ruefully. "I had the displeasure of experiencing this magic myself. But it's good to see you all safely returned." He shot a suspicious look to the chancellor. "Now, what's this all about? Why escort me from the city?"

Marstarrow clasped his hands behind his back. "I am afraid your time in Heldan Port must be cut short. I need you to follow the Brothers Arda into the Wilds and ensure they reach Dinh. But quietly." Whitney frowned and began to protest. Marstarrow seemed to have read his mind and cut him off. "It would be unreasonable for me to expect you to track them across the entirety of the Heartlands, but I have taken steps to ensure otherwise. While I trust that the brothers will do as I have asked, they would never allow you to join their fellowship. I require insurance, however. Your Shrikes will act as that insurance. Follow at a distance. Remain unseen. If the Ardas encounter trouble, lend aid. They cannot fail. Our time grows short."

Whitney stroked his whiskers. "What do you think Shrikes? Should we follow the Ardas into the Wilds? It'll be dangerous, of that you can be damned sure."

Ineza stepped forward. "You know, if they die out there, we'll never get the chance to repay them for that little trap they set in the woods." The Shrikes whistled their approval. She smiled and rubbed her chin in mock consideration. "Anyhoo, they have Sten with them now. You can be sure he'll figure out some way to get everyone killed. Unless we protect them."

"You're just soft on the lad!" roared Hemmie. The Shrikes' whooped and catcalled. Ineza threw a clod of dirt but the gnome skipped nimbly aside.

Tryo clapped his twin brother on the back. "We're with you, Captain."

Whitney toyed with the hilt of his rapier. "So be it. We ride for Dinh." He drew the blade and pointed to the Gateway. "Rou-augh!"

The Shrikes set about packing their gear. Marstarrow sidled closer to Whitney. "Regibar, it is imperative that word reach Dinh. I need information. You must set aside your quarrel with the Brothers Arda for the good of us all. I fear that the Wilds will be the least of your concerns, in the end." He held out a small ornate box with a random assortment of holes stamped into its sides. "Here, this will show you the way." Whitney looked at him questioningly. "I will never again send you blindly into danger, Captain."

"What is this?"

"A Follower."

Whitney exhaled so forcefully that the tips of his mustache fluttered. He picked up the mahogany cube and examined it more closely. The holes were actually arranged in complicated fractal patterns. An electric blue light played through the pinholes, pointing to the Gateway, accompanied by faint snores. "This is worth a tenth of the capital!" he whispered. "Where is its beacon?"

"Significantly less, unfortunately. I was unable to procure a finer model on such short notice. This one has proven rather unsatisfactory to its previous owners. Nothing you cannot handle, I am sure. I managed to secure its beacon on Eotan's person when he..." The chancellor cleared his throat and pursed his lips. "*Accosted* me in the Great Hall. I believe it was without his knowledge, so this should lead you true."

Whitney reverently wrapped the box in a blanket and tucked it into his saddle. The Shrikes sat expectantly on their horses, awaiting instruction. Shouldering his pack, he turned to Marstarrow and offered his hand. To his surprise, the chancellor shook it.

"Good luck, Regibar. I fear this will be our last meeting for some time. Remember your pledge so many years ago. You will not fail me."

Whitney saluted and swung atop his horse. The Shrikes started up the road and broke into song. He took a deep breath and straightened in his saddle, savoring the chill air, but didn't join in.

Nightfall crept over the Lowlands, and the Gateway rose up to meet them. Whitney looked back to the capital. Its silhouette stood barely visible against the shadowed horizon, all crenelated walls, grand spires, and conical towers. He watched until the city was consumed by the darkness, and wondered if he would ever see it again.

A STORM BREAKS

A mound of soil broke from the ground. Dirt and pebbles cascaded into the dew-laden grass. The mound rose higher and higher, until a thin green tendril snaked its way into the morning sunlight. A leaf followed, then a flower, and then a branch. The mound continued to rise. Soon the branch gave way to a limb, and the limb to a trunk. The tree pushed itself upward. Limbs expanded to fill the clearing, laden with colorful flowers and verdant leaves. Eventually its progression halted, but a rhythmic chanting continued. When all of the branches sagged with fruit, the incantations stopped.

A young elf walked into the clearing. She was clad in a simple green tunic, bound at the waist by a length of rope. Her skin was as rich and dappled as the bark of the surrounding trees. Long ears, twigs, and leaves poked from a tangle of black hair. She was barefoot and walked unevenly, but the limp did nothing to diminish her grace.

She stopped at the base of the tree and placed a slender

hand against its trunk. The tree pulsed violently. A smoldering handprint was left in its bark. "You're safe now," she said. She sat in the grass and rested against the tree. Several hours passed.

Two men entered the clearing. The larger held an axe and stopped a safe distance from the girl. The other eased forward, palms outstretched, and knelt. "Hello, Manye."

"Eotan."

"This is a beautiful tree. How many have you called while we were away?"

She looked up at the branches and sighed wearily. "Too few to stand against the mist."

"I see." He considered her for a long moment. "Do you know why we've come?"

Her mouth twisted. "Yes."

"Our primary concern is reaching Dinh, but perhaps we might discover the root of this plague as well." He splayed his hands in front of him and grimaced. "We will need your help, Manye."

Her eyes flashed with anger. "So we must travel through my father's lands? After everything I've done for you?"

"Manye, think about the Gate-"

"You know what my family will do to me. To you!" Her voice broke and she rose unsteadily to her feet. "Yet you have the nerve to talk about the destruction of *my* home! The thing I cherish most in this world!"

The wind rose and tore at the branches. Culyan cursed and took refuge behind a fallen log. Eotan remained in front of the girl, cloak streaming behind him. "Manye, keep your control. It's not our intention to use you, but we need your help. I know you're scared. I know what your family threatened. I swear on my life that I won't let them harm you. We need you."

"You promised, Eotan!" She clenched her fists, breathing heavily, eyes wild. "You swore I'd never have to go back!"

The wind grew. It plucked detritus from the forest floor and whipped it through the air. Culyan covered his head to block the projectiles, roaring in frustration. Eotan sank his fingers into the loam, but was gradually forced away. He bared his teeth and dug his boots into the soil, gouging deep furrows. "I know what I've promised, Manye! I'm eternally sorry for asking this of you. I break my oath to protect our home!"

"Then you are a liar!" screamed the girl, and the glade exploded. Squeals from protesting trunks and branches rent the air as the sky was blotted out by a halo of suspended dirt and leaves. Eotan was flung away.

Then, with a flash of green light, he was gone. A massive golden wolf crouched where he had stood moments before, its blue eyes radiant. It sprang through the air, gaining ground with every leap. It towered over Manye and locked its eyes onto hers. They remained motionless, oblivious to the madness that raged around them, as unspoken words were exchanged.

Quiet your mind, Manye. I was a fool for allowing this to pass, but you will be safe. Remember the Bearded Eight. Remember my brother. Remember me.

Manye sagged into the wolf and buried her head in its coat, as bright as spun gold.

You gave me this gift, Manye, as a shield to my pain. It protected me then, and it will protect you now. You will be safe. You will be safe. You will be safe...

The wolf repeated the single thought, over and over. The wind eventually died and the forest settled back into its roots. Culyan hesitantly emerged from his refuge and joined them. Manye stopped crying and wiped her eyes. "I'm sorry. I don't want to face my family or lose my home. I'm scared..." She trailed off and looked up at the Marshal. "I'm scared I'll lose you."

He knelt and ruffled her hair. "We're afraid too, little Oethyr. But sometimes we move beyond what is, or should be, required of us. For the sake of that we love."

She rose from the grass. Her head barely came to the wolf's shoulders. She stroked its back thoughtfully. "Will we get to see the Canyonlands?"

Culyan chuckled. "Maybe. But we need to make it through the Wilds first."

"I would like to see the red desert," she said. "I have only heard stories." She turned back to the tree she had created. "You will be safe. You will be safe." The branches swayed, as if acknowledging her words.

Manye limped out of the glade, one hand enveloped in the Marshal's own, the other grasped tightly to the Wolf's coat.

ACROSS THE GREAT DIVIDE

The dwarves lounged beside the road, tuning their instruments. Sten spied a pair of fiddles, a cello, a smattering of bronze horns, several pipes, one extremely large drum, and an odd stringed instrument shaped somewhat like an axe.

He gestured to the curved length of polished wood. "What is that?"

Two stroked its neck with a fiendish grin. "I call it a Boomstick."

One sternly folded his arms. "Two has taken it upon himself to design his own instrument rather than playing that which has been passed through his family for generations."

"It just needs a bit of fine tuning," said Two. "Look here, lad. It uses our magic to capture latent energy from the air, then uses that power to amplify all sound when I strike the strings. Here, watch." He gave a string a mighty pluck, producing a clear note that was disproportionately loud for the size of the instrument. "Once I have mastered the art of playing, it will increase our power exponentially! Or at least it should. I have yet to work out the kinks."

Eight waved a chicken wing with a chubby hand. "Aye. We'll be the most powerful dwarves in all of Miz, or the deadest dwarves in all of Miz." Two shrugged and resumed his work.

Sten studied the crest of the ridge far above him. Its rocky peak was barely visible through the trees. One joined him. He stroked the gemstones in his beard and puffed on a curved pipe. "The Great Divide. Impressive, eh?" He blew a ring of smoke that quickly dissolved in the morning breeze. "Be thankful it's there. I shouldn't think Heldan Port and the west could stand without it."

"I'm going to get a better look," said Sten. He shouldered his bow and quiver. "If my uncles return before I'm back, come find me."

He climbed a gentle knoll just off the road, its top rising above the trees. The grass was still damp with the morning's dew, beads of water shining like pearlescent insects. Before long his pant legs were soaked. The trees fell away and a wall of rock loomed before him. Jagged peaks and sheer cliff faces stretched along its entirety. It was foreboding even in the soft light of dawn.

Sten lay in the grass, put his hands behind his head, and breathed deeply. A smile slowly crept across his face. He had found his path. He was certain of it. It was a path he had been unknowingly searching for his entire life, ever since his mother had filled his imagination with stories of the world that lay beyond the capital. Instead of the fear, uncertainty, and trepidation that had initially haunted him upon leaving Heldan Port, he felt only excitement. There was a lingering apprehension at the prospect of crossing the Wilds, but it was a different type of fear, one laced with anticipation and a desire to conquer the unknown. He realized that his only regret came from leaving Ineza in such abrupt fashion.

From the west came the distant clamor of hoof beats. Sten sat up. A plume of dust was approaching at speed along the road. A pair of horses emerged from the haze, running hard. He glimpsed gilded armor, copper hair, and a crimson cloak. Lilenti ran alongside, but it was a small girl that rode her. Eotan was nowhere to be seen.

With a start, Sten noticed a second cloud blossoming from the road. It was some distance behind, but closing fast. The horses rounded a bend and his heart caught. A huge golden wolf bore down on the horses, lather flying from its jaws. It howled as the distance to the riders continued to shrink.

Sten grabbed his bow and nocked an arrow. "Culyan!" he screamed, gesturing wildly. The Marshal raised a hand and angled Kipto to the base of the hill. Sten drew back and sighted along the arrow, aiming well in front of the wolf. He took a deep breath, slowly exhaled, and fired between heartbeats.

The arrow flew true, but veered askew at the last second. The wolf continued its pursuit without breaking stride. Sten blinked. He drew another arrow and swore when the shot twisted wide. "What the hell's going on?" They were almost on top of him now. He fired at the wolf's chest. This time, the arrow burst into flames and vanished in a puff of black smoke. Sten reeled as Culyan swept past in a thunder of horse and steel. The wolf crested the hill and paused. It noticed Sten and bounded forward.

Sten's hands were shaking uncontrollably. He knelt and withdrew another arrow, but dropped it the grass. He fell to one knee, desperately attempting to nock another shaft. The wolf bore down on him and leapt. Sten fell back and shielded his face with his hands. Several seconds passed. He cautiously opened his eyes.

The wolf stood over him, examining him with familiar blue eyes, as bright as any sapphire.

Hello, nephew.

Sten fainted.

"Did you kill him?"

"No. I was just having some fun."

"Did you bite him?"

"No!"

"Then why the hell did he pass out?"

"Shock, I suppose."

Sten's eyelids fluttered. He could hear voices above him, but it felt as though he was listening to the conversation from a great distance.

"He's an Arda! Ardas don't faint. You're *sure* he's related to us?"

"Look at him. He's the image of Aella when she was his age."

"Hmm, I suppose you're right. He needs some facial hair or people might think he's a woman."

Sten blearily opened his eyes. Eotan and Culyan stood over him. The Marshal grinned. "Pleasant dreams?" Eotan elbowed him in the stomach.

"What... what happened?" asked Sten. He pulled himself to his feet. "There... there was a wolf! A gigantic wolf was chasing you! My arrows were acting strangely... I saw a girl, too. Is she well?" He looked around the top of the hill. The wolf was nowhere to be seen, but the girl was sitting cross-legged, examining him with curiosity. She had a narrow face with long, pointed ears just visible beneath her hair. A jagged scar crisscrossed her left calf, vivid against her dark skin.

She smiled shyly. "Hello. I'm Manye. You're Eotan's nephew?"

"So I've been told," Sten grumbled. "A pleasure to meet you." He looked to his uncles. "Where did the wolf go? Did you kill it?"

"Thankfully, no," said Eotan with a knowing wink.

Sten leapt back as a flash of vibrant green light illuminated the hillside. For the briefest of moments, a formless shape writhed where Eotan had just been. Then the light was extinguished and the massive golden wolf stared back at him, its fiercely blue eyes displaying a keen intelligence. Another flash of green and Eotan returned, smiling nonchalantly. Sten stood open mouthed, his brain refusing to comprehend what he had just seen.

"You're a werewolf!" he managed.

"Shapeshifter," said Manye. "Werewolves can't choose when they turn. This magic is unique to the Oethyr, like myself. Eotan is the only human to have ever been given the peoples' gift."

Eotan winced. "A gift for which I shall remain eternally thankful."

Sten snatched his bow from the grass and glared at Culyan. "So I almost murdered my own uncle? A warning would have been nice."

The Marshal threw back his head and roared with laughter. "He was in no danger, lad! Consider it a demonstration of Manye's power. And his. Impressive shooting, though."

Sten closed his eyes and rubbed his temples. "I feel like I'm in a dream."

"A dream, no, an adventure, yes!" said Culyan delightedly. He clapped Sten on the back, and Sten's knees buckled. "Don't worry, we'll make an Arda of you yet."

They collected the dwarves, and Eotan guided them to an unkempt path. It was so overgrown from disuse that it resembled little more than a game trail. They followed it steadily higher, threading their way through dense forests. Dust motes hung in the air, illuminated by sunlight lancing through the heavy canopies. Disembodied birdsong serenaded the trees as they climbed.

The forests eventually gave way to thickets of brush interspersed with solitary pines, their trunks gnarled with age. Alpine lakes lay hidden within the gentle folds of the highlands, with waters as clear and cold as diamonds. Fields of tall grasses and wildflowers rolled in gentle waves, stirred by the rising winds. Then the trees disappeared, and patches of old snow dotted the wind-scoured rock.

They halted at the crest of the Great Divide. Sten held his breath as he walked to the edge of the world. The Wilds unfurled before him, an endless expanse of wilderness that stretched to the horizon. A towering range of ice-capped mountains rose in the northeast, like sentinels standing guard over the Heartlands. Great valleys scarred the landscape, their depths lost to view. Rolling hills and jagged mesas broke from the tops of the trees. Rivers wandered lazily through the sea of green, their waters sparkling like jeweled serpents.

Sten barely noticed the others approach. They stood shoulder to shoulder, absorbing the awesome spectacle in silence. The light of Tanduil faded behind them.

Culyan put his hand on Sten's shoulder and gave it a reassuring squeeze. "Hard to believe something like this can exist on Miz, eh? This world has a knack for making a man feel small."

"You're not kidding," said Sten. He shook his head in wonder. "And we have to cross all of *that* to reach Dinh?"

"Yes," said Eotan solemnly.

"Well... shit."

VANDRA

Vandra sat in near darkness. The room's only light emanated from a flickering candle set into the table. She watched it burn lower. Its scant light dwindled and wax pooled around its base. Then she raised her hand and held it over the meager flame. She kept it there until the candle burned itself out.

She lit another and examined her palm. It was red and blistered, and a clear fluid wept from an open sore. She prodded the wound. A spike of pain lanced through her fingers, and a look of mild interest crossed her face. She touched the lesion again, delicately at first, and then with increasing pressure. Pain seared her hand as she continued to press, though her face remained neutral.

There came a knock at the door. She clenched her hand into a fist. A faint glimmer of red light escaped from between her fingers. When she opened her hand the lesion was gone, her pale skin unblemished and whole.

"They are ready for you, madam," called a voice from outside the door.

Vandra rose from her seat. "Very well." She followed the servant into a hexagonal chamber, richly decorated. A fire burning inside a large ornate hearth warmed its interior.

The servant bowed to the room's occupants. "My lords, my ladies, Lady Vandra is here to see you." He exited the room with another bow and closed the door behind him.

Vandra strolled along the walls of the chamber. She moved slowly, studying each of the numerous oil paintings in turn. A handsome tapestry caught her eye. She paused to examine it and traced the weavings with a slender finger. Then she continued her inspection. Eventually, she stopped before the hearth and gazed up at the soot-stained wall. Dozens of lifeless animals stared down at her, glass eyes glittering dully. She turned to the half-circle of overstuffed armchairs arranged around the hearth. "Such a charming estate you have, Lord Polto." She tucked a strand of raven-black hair behind one ear.

The man seated closest to the fire laughed self-importantly. "Ah, thank you, thank you!" Beads of sweat shone from his balding scalp. He took a long sip of amber liquor, jowls wobbling.

Vandra gestured to the mounted trophies. "Your work, I take it?"

Lord Polto beamed. "Indeed! I was quite the huntsman in my youth. A finer shot, you could never find."

She turned back to the mounts. "Slaughtering animals from the safety of horseback while your hounds pursue to exhaustion is a most impressive feat."

"Harmph, what'd she say?" stammered Lord Polto, leaning forward in his chair.

Vandra silenced him with a look and addressed the nine Heads of House. "You summoned me here tonight. Why?"

Lord Impo cleared his throat. The lines of his face were

taut with discomfort. "We have information for you, Vandra, but first we hoped to discuss our... concerns." Vandra raised an eyebrow. Lord Impo swallowed and forged on. "Concerns regarding your plan for Heldan Port. You promised us control of the city, yet the chancellor endures. Every day he somehow manages to stabilize the rift created by the wizards' absence. He is containing the fallout." He drifted into silence, unwilling to meet her eye.

"How is this my problem?" she said.

"You promised us," whined Lord Polto. "You were supposed to return the city to its rightful owners! The great Houses of Heldan Port ruled for centuries before Marstarrow came along. The capital is *ours* by right!" Drink sloshed down the side of his chair as he emphasized his words. The others murmured their assent, though none too loudly.

Vandra regarded them coolly. "Perhaps the capital has moved beyond armchair leadership."

Lord Polto's face reddened. "We have done everything we can to undermine his efforts! We've planted speakers to sow distrust throughout the city. We've hired mercenaries and corsairs to waylay trade caravans!" Spittle sprayed from his mouth and he clenched a chubby fist. "We've taken steps to disrupt every single one of his damnable efforts to replace the wizards, and you have the gall to insinuate we sit idly by, *doing nothing!*"

She wiped a fleck of spit from her sleeve. "From my perspective, the chancellor is precisely where he belongs. You would undoubtedly lead this city to ruin." The Heads of House started to protest but fell silent at her expression. "Let me make this abundantly clear. The rats from your sewers can rule Heldan Port for all I care. We had a deal, true enough. You arranged for my entrance into the Sanctum. I admit that I couldn't have breached its walls without your aid. And in return for your assistance, I cleansed the wizards from Heldan Port, granting your opportunity for succession. Now, I have *done* precisely that, and I will do no more. If you are all too weak to seize power for yourselves, then so be it."

The Heads of House sat in mollified silence, except Lord Polto, who fumed beside the hearth. "Now," said Vandra, "what information do you have for me? I was explicit when I told you not to contact me unless absolutely necessary. These journeys take a toll and are beginning to wear on my patience."

"The chancellor has sent an envoy to Dinh," said Lord Impo quietly.

"He has done this before."

"Yes, but this time he sent the Brothers Arda."

A prickle of unease ran down Vandra's neck. "You're certain?"

Lord Impo nodded. "We saw them in the chancellor's keep. It's the Wolf and the Marshal, without a doubt. The same cursed brothers that helped Marstarrow take Heldan Port from us. If anyone has a chance of reaching Dinh alive, it's them."

Vandra narrowed her eyes. "And the chancellor did nothing to hide their presence?"

"No," said Lady Aamot. "He practically paraded those northern heathens throughout the city."

"Interesting," mused Vandra. Her eyes flicked to the open window. "I believe the chancellor suspects your involvement."

"Nonsense," spat Lord Polto. "That man is a fool! He suspects nothing."

"As you say." Vandra stood in quiet contemplation for a moment. "When did they leave?"

"Last night," said Lord Impo. "According to our agents."

"Then my immediate attention is required elsewhere." She strode brusquely to the exit. "Do not think to further waste my time unless you have information regarding the Brothers Arda. *Useful* information." She reached for the knob.

Something whistled past her ear and shattered against the door. She stared down at the ruined snifter.

Lord Polto had risen from his chair. His face was twisted and ugly, his voice thick with drink. "You think to give us orders? *Us?* We own this city. We own you! Damn your plans and damn you. It is time you do as *we* command. Get rid of Marstarrow. That was the agreement!" Others stood and attempted to force him back into his chair, but he shrugged them off. "You are nothing but an insolent *girl*, fresh from mother's teat! You know nothing of the world. You are nothing compared to us."

Vandra glanced down at her palm. The skin was smooth and unblemished. She clenched her fingers and smiled at the drunken Head of House. "Let me tell you a story, Lord Polto. Some years ago, a young girl lived in the woods with her mother and father, far to the south. They were poor, but they were happy, because they had each other. Now, one day, this little girl decided to play outside. But while she was playing, a mist crept up from the woods. This wasn't a normal mist, though, for awful creatures lurked within its depths. The girl hid as the creatures broke into her house. They slaughtered the girl's parents. But they kept her alive."

Red sparks ignited around Vandra's fist and danced between her fingers. The Heads of House backed away, and Lord Polto was left alone by the fire. He swayed where he stood, eyes clouded with incomprehension.

"They let the girl live for a reason," continued Vandra. The red sparks began to move up her arm. "What do you suppose that reason might be?"

"I... I don't know..." His eyes grew wide as the lights continued to swirl around her.

Her words were ice. "They wanted to show her the truth, Lord Polto. They wanted to show her how people like *you* are leading this world to ruin. They wanted to show her what must be done to save Miz."

Vandra raised her arm and fired a torrent of crimson light into Lord Polto's chest. He screamed and was lifted from the floor, arms and legs flailing helplessly. She held him aloft as the other Heads of House cowered in terror. Then, slowly, she lowered him into the fire.

"I may be *nothing* compared to you," she said, as Lord Polto's screams clogged the air, "but I imagine we burn just the same."

A cloaked figure watched the scene unfold from a neighboring rooftop. The raven-haired woman exited the room, leaving behind a charred ruin that smoldered in the hearth. The watcher blinked in horrified fascination, trying to erase the images that had been seared into its mind. Then, with a final glance at the open window, it climbed down from the rooftop and sprinted toward the chancellor's keep.

AN UNLIKELY ALLIANCE

The Jumping Jackamoose was indeed, jumping. Mord Butterson proudly surveyed the throngs of Heldan Portians crammed into his tavern. It had been an exceptional month for Butterson's Beers. People were nervous, and nervous people drank. They simply couldn't resist stopping in for a pint after a long day of pretending to work.

G'rok had also been instrumental to the Jackamoose's recent success.

It had been Raxo's idea to hire the orc. They had outfitted G'rok with a vibrant pink bowtie and a large wooden sign that read, 'BEER IN THERE'. The orc obediently twirled the sign throughout the night. Heldan Portians didn't need much in the form of creative advertising to entice them to drink. The orc's growl drifted in through the tavern's open doors.

"BEER?"

A startled man and his wife cautiously tried to

circumnavigate the pirouetting orc. "Erm, no thank you," he said. "That's a very clever sign though."

"MY SIGN, YOU DRINK BEER."

"Oh, we didn't *want* your sign, erm." The man squinted at the tiny nametag pinned to G'rok's chest. "'Gee-Rock'. What a nice name."

"G SILENT, MY NAME SOUND LIKE THIS." G'rok picked up a large rock from the street and brandished it threateningly.

"I'm sure that's what my husband meant," said the woman hastily. G'rok looked unconvinced. The woman blundered on. "We were, uh, we were also just saying how nice your pink bowtie looks, weren't we dear?" The man was fixated on the large rock waving in front of his nose. His wife elbowed him in the stomach. *"Weren't* we, dear?"

"Oof! Wha...oh, yes. What a handsome bowtie mister G'rok."

"MISTER G'ROK? MISTER?" The orc loomed over the couple. "G'ROK WOMAN. I MISSUS G'ROK!"

"Of course, of course!" cried the woman. "My husband is, erm, quite slow in the head if you catch my meaning."

"Hey, no I'm no-" said the man, but fell silent upon noticing the studious gaze of the angry orc. "Scratch that, dumb as a stone, I am."

"G'ROK SEE NOW. HUSBAND SILLY FELLOW. BUT STILL INSULT G'ROK!"

"And we're terribly sorry, *missus* G'rok," said the woman. "How can we make it up to you? That pink bow tie really brings out the, erm, red haze in your eyes. Lovely, simply lovely!"

"STOP, MAKE G'ROK BLUSH. YOU BUY BEER NOW."

The man perked up at this. "Yes, of course! I would actually love a beer."

"MANY BEERS."

"Oh, well it's been a long day. I guess I could have a few."

"MANY MANY BEERS. AND TELL MISTER BUT-TERSON G'ROK IS 'MODEL EMPLOYEE'. GREAT AT 'CUSTOMER SERVICE'."

"We will!" said the woman, and hurried inside, dragging her husband along.

Butterson hid a smile as the terrified couple squeezed their way to his bar. "We'll have four beers," said the woman. She glanced nervously at the window. G'rok frowned. "Er, better make that six." G'rok held up two outstretched hands. "I guess we will have ten beers." G'rok nodded and went back to twirling her sign.

Butterson swept the coins from the counter and inwardly praised his own foresight. Nobody else in his or her right mind would hire an orc for a marketing position, but he had, and his gambit had produced a diamond in the rough. This particular diamond was horse-sized and rather aggressive, but a diamond nevertheless.

Raxo came out from behind the bar and wiped his tiny forehead with a barbed tail. "Business is boomin', Boss. And to think we were nothin' but street merchants a year ago." The little demon plopped down next to Butterson and scratched a lewd design onto the bar. "You know, with all this newfound coin I'm thinkin' of gettin' myself a place on the hill. Maybe a two-bedroom in that fancy part of town where all those posh wankers live."

Butterson polished a glass and replaced it on the shelf beneath the bar. "What in the world would you do with a two-bedroom, Raxo? A barrel would give you more than enough space."

"Well that's not the point, is it?" pouted the demon. "Being rich is all about havin' stuff you don't need, right? So the way I see it, havin' a big ol' house to myself is the epitome of upper class. I might even get myself a top hat."

"If I ever see you wearing a top hat I'll order G'rok to step on you."

Raxo looked to the open doors and winced. "Right, well speakin' of G'rok, I better go stop her from killin' that dwarf."

Butterson spun around to find G'rok holding a dwarf upside down by his ankles, shaking him roughly.

"WHERE IS COIN?"

"It's just a saying!" cried the terrified dwarf.

"YOU SAID, 'A COIN FOR YOUR THOUGHTS.' G'ROK SAY, DWARF NEEDS BEER. DWARF NO GIVE G'ROK COIN!"

"I don't have any money on me!" G'rok gave the dwarf a furious shake. Several coins were dislodged from the recesses of his pockets and tinkled to the ground.

"THERE, G'ROK TAKE COIN. YOU BUY BEER." She dropped the dwarf. He scrambled to his feet and scuttled inside. Butterson grimaced. G'rok was a diamond yes, but a very coarse diamond that still needed quite a bit of polishing.

Raxo's wheedling voice drifted through the raucous crowd. "G'rok, what have we told you about pickin' up customers?"

"DO IT."

"What? No! We told you *not* to pick up customers!"

"YOU SAY, 'G'ROK, YOUR JOB TO PICK UP PEOPLE FROM THE STREET AND BRING THEM INSIDE.'"

"Okay, but don't *literally* pick them up. You have to entice them inside, act all friendly-like. Talk about our wonderful beer or the magnificent ambiance of our establishment. That sort of rubbish."

There was a short pause. "YOU ANGRY AT G'ROK?" She sounded on the verge of tears.

"No, no, no. You're doin' a wonderful job, dear. Just, uh, no more liftin' our clientele in the air by their ankles."

"OKAY. G'ROK DO BETTER JOB, YOU SEE." The orc spun the sign with renewed enthusiasm.

Raxo edged his way through the crowd and reappeared at Butterson's shoulder. "By the gods, it's like chastizin' a gigantic puppy."

"Just make sure that puppy doesn't bite anyone," said Butterson.

Without warning, the Jackamoose fell abruptly silent. Patrons craned to look at the doorway. A tall, gaunt man stood on the threshold. He removed his hood, swept back thinning silver hair, and studied the room with pale gray eyes. Butterson was reminded of the stoic marble statues standing watch over Edegar Bridge. He shifted uneasily. A faint sense of recognition probed the back of his mind, like an itch that was difficult to scratch.

The volume of the Jackamoose swelled as its occupants returned to their drinks. The man waited by the door, as if unsure whether or not to proceed. Then, with a decisive squaring of his shoulders, he approached the bar and sat.

"What'll you have?" asked Butterson cheerily, taking care to mask his suspicion.

The man shrugged. "Whichever ale is your strongest, I should think."

"That'll be the Weeping Wyrm's Stout. It's brewed with real dragon's tears."

"I was under the impression there were no more dragons on Miz." The man frowned and fastidiously wiped down the bar with the hem of his sleeve.

Butterson winked conspiratorially. "I *know* people."

"How charmingly obtuse." The man continued his quest to scrub clean the stained surface.

"There's no point in doing that," pointed out Butterson. "Whatever's on there is there to stay. Better to accept your fate and move on. Here, try this." He deposited a foaming flagon on the bar. The man sniffed it and gingerly took a sip. One eyebrow raised ever so slightly.

Butterson smiled. "Good, eh? Dragon tears or not, you won't find a better ale in all of Miz. Now, do I recognize you from somewhere? You look familiar."

The man took another sip and delicately wiped his mouth. "I do not believe we have ever formally met, though I know you by reputation."

Butterson offered his hand. "Well, mister, it's a pleasure to meet you. The name's Mord Butterson. I'm the owner of this fine establishment." The newcomer shook it with surprising strength, his hand cool and dry.

"Tiberion Marstarrow. The pleasure is mine."

Butterson stiffened as the inkling of recognition suddenly morphed into a battering ram of realization. He had seen the chancellor only once before, decades ago, when Marstarrow had wrested control of the capital from the Heads of House. The man seated before him was undoubtedly that same man, albeit significantly older and possessing much less hair.

The chancellor indicated his empty flagon with a wan smile. "Another, if you would be so kind."

"Erm, right away." Butterson urgently gestured for Raxo. The little demon sidled over and hopped onto the bar next to Marstarrow. The chancellor considered him with mild interest.

"What's up, Boss? Been runnin' around like a madman ever since we opened. Never seen this lot so intent on drinkin' themselves into a stupor." He relieved a tankard from a snoring dwarf and gulped it down noisily. "I think it's 'cause they're on edge. Makes you wonder if the old coot on the hill even knows what's happenin' to his city. He just sits in his behemoth of a keep all day, like a turtle cowerin' in its shell." Raxo grinned wickedly and leaned across the bar. "You know, I think he must be compensatin' for somethin'. What's wrong with you, Boss, you havin' a stroke?"

Butterson abruptly ceased his attempts to quiet Raxo. A sardonic smile had slowly worked across Marstarrow's face.

Butterson hastily poured another beer and slammed it in front of the chancellor, gesturing with his eyes. "Here you go, *Tiberion Marstarrow*."

Raxo's expression was blank. "I think you're overworkin' yourself, Boss, there's somethin' wrong with your eyes." He swiped a drumstick from a passing platter and chewed it contemplatively, grease dribbling down his chin. "I've heard more and more people are supportin' the idea of replacin' the chancellor with the Heads of House. That would be a bigger disaster still. Most don't even realize that all this talk of succession is House-devised propaganda bull shi-... Okay, what the hell's going on?"

Butterson was repeatedly mouthing, *"That is the chancellor,"* while pointing with his beard. He started to speak but Marstarrow held up a hand.

"Let me save you the trouble. I am the 'old coot' who is compensating on the hill, as you so kindly put it."

Raxo squinted. "Eh, I'm not so sure. I always thought the chancellor was a great big fat guy."

"Apologies for not living up to your expectations, but I can assure you I am unequivocally the chancellor of this city. Another pint, please."

Butterson grimaced. "Coming right up."

"Well," said Raxo suspiciously, "if you're the chancellor, then how come nobody *knows* you're the chancellor? Why don't you ever show your face around the city? And why aren't you doin' somethin' to fix this whole cockup?"

Marstarrow smiled the same dry smile. "Brutal honesty. How... refreshing. Let me repay your truth in kind, Master Raxo. I have never stopped working to repair the damage done to my city. However, I am forced to play my cards close to the chest, as they say. That is the unfortunate nature of politics, especially in this time of unrest." His eyes flicked to the windows. "Especially when circling shadows grow larger."

He sighed and took a long drink. "If protecting the capital means keeping its people in the dark, then so be it."

Raxo stroked his tail thoughtfully. "I suppose. But people would trust you more if you'd show your face. You can't expect them to trust a complete stranger."

"That is not, nor ever has been my method of operation," said Marstarrow. He crossed one leg over the other. "Though perhaps there is wisdom in your words. I shall consider it, moving forward." He drained his tankard and belched. "Oh my, pardon me. I think just one more, Mord."

Butterson refilled the empty tankard. "I didn't take you for a drinker."

"I generally refrain from such indulgence, but today has been an exceptionally taxing day." A great weariness crept into the chancellor's eyes then, and his shoulders slumped ever so slightly, as if from some invisible weight. But then he swept back his thinning hair and the moment had passed. "Nothing I cannot handle."

Butterson exchanged a look with Raxo. "Erm, anything you'd care to discuss, Chancellor?"

"Not particularly."

"As you'd like." Butterson made for the cellar stairs, but then turned back to the bar. "You know, without Raxo, I couldn't have built any of *this*." He opened his arms to the Jackamoose. "I tried on my own. More times than I care to remember. But I never could quite manage."

The chancellor's lips were a thin line. "Is that so?"

Butterson folded his arms and nodded slowly, as though lost in recollections. "Aye. And then I met Raxo and everything changed. It wasn't his work ethic that made us, mind you."

The demon reclined against the sleeping dwarf. "Gods no."

"Nor his business acumen."

"Don't have any. Don't want any."

"Nor his attention to detail."

"Couldn't even tell you what month it is."

Butterson rapped a knuckle on the bar. "I built *this* because I no longer had to go it alone. Amazing what a friendly ear can do for the spirit."

The chancellor deliberately splayed his hands over the bar. "Your consideration and advice are appreciated, Mord, yet I am afraid our circumstances are incomparable. In my profession, trust tends to wield a hidden dagger."

"Then choose better companions," said Raxo scathingly.

Marstarrow frowned. "That was not an accusation, merely a necessary precaution."

Butterson leaned against the bar and wiped his hands on a towel. "Let's make a deal, Chancellor. Tonight you drink on us, and if you ever reach a point where you feel inclined to share your troubles, you'll have a *discerning* audience." Marstarrow traced the severe lines of his face but said nothing.

"We call it Butterson's Theory of General Inebriativity," said Raxo proudly. "The more you drink, the less you think, and the more you speak. Been that way since the beginning of time."

"How glib." Marstarrow's guarded expression relinquished slightly. He toyed with the handle of his tankard and raised it into the air. "Very well. I shall consider your proposal."

Butterson smiled widely and raised a glass of his own. "Cheers."

The Jumping Jackamoose eventually emptied as the crowds stumbled home. G'rok stood by the door, wishing farewell to those passersby.

"COME BACK SOON."

"Oh yes, we'll be back. We've had a lovely night."

"COME BACK TOMORROW."

"I think that may be a bit soon for our plans, but we-"

"COME BACK TOMORROW OR G'ROK FIND YOU."

"Good grief! Yes, yes, we'll be back tomorrow!"

"HAVE LOVELY NIGHT."

Butterson smiled and waved goodnight to G'rok after the final customer had left. Then he turned back to Marstarrow. "Starting to feel it a bit, Chancellor?"

"Oh yes, *hic!*" Marstarrow's eyes were somewhat crossed. "I haven't drank... drunk... had this much to drink in quite a long while."

Raxo nodded approvingly. "For a skinny old chap who looks to have one foot in the grave, you're impressive at holdin' your liquor."

Marstarrow bowed and swayed on his stool. "Thank you Raxo, you are, *hic!* You are most kind."

Heldan Port's clock tower chimed twice in the distance, the tones muted and somber. Butterson locked the doors to the Jackamoose and checked the cellars, loft, and pantry. Satisfied that they were truly alone, he sat in front of Marstarrow. "What'll it be, Chancellor?"

Marstarrow's expression was one of pained and drunken indecision. He opened his mouth to speak, closed it again, opened it. Butterson and Raxo waited patiently as the pattern repeated. Finally, he wiped his mouth with the back of a hand, sat up straight, and took a deep breath.

"I will have another beer!" he announced grandly.

Raxo blew a raspberry. "Gods, that's what you've been thinkin' about this whole time? Who cares about that! What about our deal?"

Marstarrow blinked at him in confusion, then clapped his hands together. "Ah yes! Right, *hic!* Right you are." He staggered behind the bar and began refilling his own tankard. Then, nonchalantly, his back still to them, he said, "The Heads of House are behind the Sanctum's disappearance."

Raxo's mouth dropped open. "And you tell us like that? Like we're discussin' the weather? You were more distraught over decidin' whether you wanted another beer!"

Marstarrow shrugged and toddled out from the bar to retake his seat. "I found the emptiness of my cup a more pressing concern."

Butterson whistled and leaned back in his chair. "The Heads of House? You really think they'd orchestrate the wizards' disappearance? Seems bold, even for them."

"Orche... Orchestra... Arrange? No." Marstarrow frowned into his tankard. "They are far from clever enough. But they did play a critical, *hic*, role in the whole affair. Even now, they plot against me."

Raxo clapped the chancellor on the shoulder. "Eh, I wouldn't be too worried. Those limey old goats don't have a lick of sense between the lot of 'em."

"Sense, no. Money... undeniably yes. And therein lies the root of our predicalem. Problament. Whatever. Their resources are considerable, and it would be unwise to underestimate the measures they'll take to, *hic*, reclaim this city. They met with an enchantress this very night. One of considerable power, or so my agent tells me."

"An enchantress?" Butterson tapped the tabletop with a finger. "Any idea why?"

"No. But, if I had to guess, it would be in response to the crap, pardon me, trap, I have laid." Marstarrow fell silent and his head began to droop. Raxo hopped onto his shoulder and slapped him across the ear, waking him with a start. "Rrr-right. As I was saying, I needed more information. But to catch a bat, you must first offer the cheese."

Butterson suppressed a smile. "I think you mean rat."

"What did I say? Regardless, I gave them their cheese, all right. I, *hic*, marched their cheese up the streets of the capital for all to see and dangled it in front of them. Their cheese tried to kill me, actually."

"What the bloody hell is he on about?" grumbled Raxo. Butterson shrugged.

"The *Brothers Arda!*" Marstarrow took another large gulp and spilled most of it down his front. "I ordered the brothers to travel to Dinh as my ambassamissarys. I ordered it right in front of the Heads of House. You should have seen their, *hic*, faces."

"So those were the men in the forum," said Butterson. "They certainly live up to the tales I've heard told."

"And yet such stories do not even begin to do them justice. But as I was saying, they were my metaphorical cheese. Do you have any cheese? I am famished. No? Damn. I knew, *hic*! I knew that if the Houses became aware of the Ardas' mission they would be forced to show their pants."

"Show their hands," said Butterson.

"Hands. Right. And show their pants they did, this very night, by meeting with that woman to inform her of the Ardas' quest."

Butterson scratched his head. "Wouldn't it have been wiser to send them to Dinh in secret?"

"Perhaps. But I was not foolish enough to put all of my eggs in one casket."

"Basket," said Raxo with a grin. "You sure are havin' a hard time with your idioms."

Marstarrow scowled haughtily. "I am no idiot, thank you. That is why I have sent Captain Whitney and his Skunks to protect the Ardas. The Houses did *not* know about him, I assure you. And so the trap is set."

"I suppose," said Butterson. "But what if the Ardas are walking into a trap themselves? What about the Wilds? What of the stories of this cursed mist?"

Marstarrow pursed his lips and squeezed the tankard with both hands. "I share in your concerns, dear Mord, yet I have no recourse but to trust in the Ardas' formidable capabilities. They *will* reach Dinh, for the sake of us all." He paused, and then he smiled, the first genuine smile to have crossed his face all night. "As for the mist, I have not the... *foggiest...* idea of what to do." With a slight gurgle, he slumped onto the bar and began snoring fitfully.

"Phooey," said Raxo. He prodded the sleeping chancellor with a claw. "You sure he's human? When it comes to drinkin', you lot tend to call it quits faster than a priest in a brothel. He must've polished off a quarter of our stores himself." He stepped back with an appraising look. "You know, I don't think I've ever been so impressed with him."

Butterson collected Marstarrow and gently deposited him in an armchair next to the hearth. Bathed in the soft red light of the dying coals, the chancellor looked strangely vulnerable. He seemed smaller, less imposing, less enigmatic. More human.

"I wonder what this means for us now," said Butterson quietly. "Maybe we should have left him well enough alone."

Raxo puffed out his chest and swaggered across the bar. "Nonsense! If the Ardas fail, we'll just have to save the day. Think of it! Raxo and Butterson: titans of industry, models of sophistication, and *heroes* of Heldan Port. I like it. It's got a nice ring to it."

Butterson chuckled. "I think you overestimate our standing in this city."

The little demon tapped the side of his nose. "Ah, you're right. We may not be heroes just yet, but we will be."

THE FOLLOWERS

Captain Regibar Theraford Whitney carefully guided his horse along the narrow path. Rain darkened the surrounding mountains. The descent down the Great Divide was proving treacherous, worsened still by the deluge that refused to abate. Loose rock littered the trail, evidence of years of disuse, and plummeted down the mountain at the slightest provocation. Hooves clanked on stone as the Shrikes reined in their horses far above him, accompanied by the constant clatter of rock fall.

An exaggerated yawn emanated from his tunic pocket, shattering his concentration. "*Hooooowah.* I didn't fink it were possible to move dis slow on a horse."

"Quiet!" snarled Whitney. He carefully maneuvered his mount around a boulder that had split apart from its fall.

His pocket was silent for a moment. "M'name's Zwat. Mr. Zwat to you."

Whitney ground his teeth and attempted to maintain his focus. "One more word and I'll toss you in a lake."

"Right, right. Good luck explainin' why you dropped a fortune in a lake."

"You just focus on tracking your beacon, Follower."

"I just told you m'name! And you's more likely to lose dat mustache dan me lose my beacon. I can see her trail clear as day, painted along dis winding pafway before disappearin' into da woods below. Admit it, you'd be buggered wifout my holdin' your hand."

Whitney resisted the urge to fling the little box off the mountain. He understood now why this particular Follower had been purchased at such a discount. The little demon had talked incessantly from the moment it had awoken in its box, mostly to hurl insults at Whitney. But the demon had proven adept at tracking, and had safely guided the Shrikes through the Gateway and across the Divide.

"You fink I could get an umbrella? Poor Zwat drowned in a box 'cause da fat captain were too cruel to give him some cover."

"You're drier than the rest of us, demon." Water beaded on Whitney's eyelids, distorting his vision. He wiped away the droplets and pulled his hood lower. Streaming rivulets of muddied water were coursing down the path in front of him.

"My tracking prowess goes all wonky when I get wet. Don't say I didn't warn you when we tumble off a cliff or wander into a den of bears."

"That would mean your end, as well as ours."

A blast of heat emanated from Whitney's pocket, and the box vibrated angrily. "Yeah, well, why'd you have to go and choose me anyway, ya daft bugger? I were enjoyin' my vacation in dat old geyser's flower garden. Dem lawn pixies are wild. You ever play hide da beacon wit a pixie? Hey, what you doi-"

Whitney deftly tucked the little box into his saddlebag. He took a deep breath, savoring the momentary reprieve from Zwat's piercing voice, and continued down the ridge. The ground leveled out and an expanse of pine trees rose up before him in a wall of muted green. He waited beneath the cover of the dense canopy and hugged his cloak tighter about his shoulders. Corporal Ghet was the next to descend and reined her horse alongside him.

"How you doing, Cap?" She wrung out her golden hair and grinned. "Nice job leading us over that damned ridge. How'd you manage that, anyhoo? I could barely follow your line."

"Must you insist on using that word, Corporal?"

She only smiled wider. "Oops, right you are, Cap. Old habits and whatnot."

Corporal Ghet was an excellent soldier and the youngest member of the Shrikes, handpicked by Whitney himself. But her considerable talents as a warrior did not extend to her regard for discipline. He sighed wearily. "Never mind. Perhaps you'll learn one day. And *I* didn't lead us over the Divide." He rummaged through his pack and held the mahogany box aloft.

Her eyes grew wide. "Is that a Follower? I've never seen one before!" Whitney passed it to her. She examined it in awe, turning it over in her hands. Zwat had thankfully fallen asleep, though the vibrant blue light issuing from the holes continued to point eastward. "It's so small! I always thought they'd be more, well... Impressive."

"Just wait until you hear it speak," Whitney groused. "I'd pay to have someone take it off my hands at this point." He returned the Follower to his pack. The Shrikes continued to pick their way down the mountain.

She looked at him, curiously. "Anything wrong, Cap? You've been awfully quiet ever since we left the capital." Whitney didn't answer. A chain of lightning split the darkness to the west. He held his horse steady as the sullen thunder rolled over them. The grating boom was picked up and tossed about by the mountains before shattering against their peaks.

She pressed him again. "Ever since we left the Gateway, actually. That wasn't your fault, you know."

Whitney shook his head and droplets of water cascaded from his mustache. "It's not that, Corporal. My pride will heal in time." Rain sluiced from the needles overhead as he considered his words. "This mission is different. Call it a soldier's intuition, but its outcome feels more consequential. Absolute."

She frowned and reined closer. "What do you mean, Cap?"

He remained quiet. In his mind's eye, the Hall of Heroes slowly crumbled into oblivion.

A knowing light appeared in her eyes. "Ah, come now, Cap, don't look so glum. The Shrikes *never* fail when it counts. Plus, we have the Brothers Arda! I wouldn't bet against them in a hundred years. Except Sten, maybe. For the life of me I can't figure out how he's an Arda."

Whitney cast her a sidelong glance. "You're fond of the lad." He failed to conceal the disapproval in his voice.

She shrugged. "Who's to tell what the heart desires? Apparently I want a daft lordling."

"You deserve better, Corporal."

She laughed, and the sound was a welcome touch of warmth amidst the dreary storm. "He's not that bad. Think of everything he's gone through in the past couple of days. Yet he chose to ride headlong into all of *this*." She gestured to the towering trees and black forest. The skies were stained a deep violet as twilight merged with the curtaining rain. "That's downright courageous, if you ask me."

"Perhaps. Though, I advise you to be cautious, Corporal. Affection is a weakness. You would do well to remember that."

She rounded on him then, a flush creeping up her neck. "Affection may be a weakness to you, Captain, but I won't live my life in fear of taking chances. If I want to be with Sten now, who are you to tell me otherwise? You're my commander, not my father!" Whitney started to protest but she cut him off. "Sten and his uncles are out there right now and it's our job to protect them. I expect we'll do exactly that." She spurred her horse and left him in a shower of sodden earth.

Whitney bowed his head. Water streamed from his hood and pooled in his lap, but he barely noticed. He had long ago accepted the life of a soldier. He would never have a wife, would never know true peace, would never father children. Yet there were times when he imagined the other life he might have known. A life set apart from the Shrikes. A life that was free from the chancellor's grasp, where he might raise a daughter like Ineza, so full of life, wonder, and laughter.

But that opportunity had passed him long ago. He belonged to the capital, and to the men and women he commanded. Affection *was* a weakness in their line of work. Corporal Ghet would come to realize this, in time. Though a part of him hoped she wouldn't.

Whitney checked Zwat's heading. The light continued to point due east, unwavering. He returned the box to his saddle and looked to the mountains. The last of his Shrikes had succeeded in reaching the base of the Divide. He dismounted and called for the others to do the same. They would camp here for the night and wait for the storm to pass. If the Ardas couldn't survive their first night alone in the Wilds, then the mission was doomed from the start.

BEAUTY AND THE BEAST

The Wilds were awake despite the stillness of the night. Vibrant trails of light blossomed in Kipto and Lilenti's wake, flowing like streams of moonlight. Beards of moss illuminated the branches overhead and swayed gently with their passage. Pale mushrooms of green and blue and yellow clung to the bark of trees. A spidery network of lichen smoldered beneath the loam of the forest floor.

Sten raised a hand and brushed his fingers against soft needles. Swatches of color ignited and trailed into the darkness behind them, and then faded. "What is this?"

Two smiled at his expression. "It wears many names, lad. We dwarves call it fairy fire. Others believe it ghost light, wyrd magic, witch's bloom, or phantom flame." He snatched a clump of low-hanging moss and rubbed it between his fingers. The wispy tendrils began to glow, their warm light reflected in his dark eyes. "Whatever it is, it's as ancient as Miz herself."

Sten examined the moss for himself. "It's terribly beautiful, isn't it?"

"Aye, lad. The Wilds guards many such secrets, and fairy fire is the most welcome of all." The dwarf then cocked his head and considered the forest. "Although never before has it strayed this far west. I wonder..."

Around them, the fairy fire was holding the featureless black of the night at bay. It was darkness more complete than Sten thought possible. In Heldan Port, there was always light, no matter the hour. High-strung lanterns illuminated the street corners. Massive braziers dotted the city walls, blazing like red beacons. Thousands of windows and doorways leaked playful firelight across the cobbles. And the spiraling towers of the Sanctum were constantly aglow with one arcane mishap or another. But here, on the western front of the Wilds, there was only the fairy fire.

Sten urged more light from the moss and gestured to the trees. "Why does it matter if it's moved west? Would you prefer that we travelled in the dark?"

Two didn't respond for a time and a queer expression settled on his face. When he finally spoke, his tone was subdued. "Sometimes, lad, the torch prevents the eye from noticing what lurks beyond its flame."

Sten shivered and clutched the moss tighter to his chest.

They passed deeper into the Wilds, the fairy fire mirroring their passage. But as night deepened and the forest closed in around them, the lights began to fade. Eventually, the fire disappeared entirely and their progress slowed.

Manye sat in front of Culyan, her palm aloft, and bathed the forest in soft golden light. Eotan picked his way through the claustrophobic maze of trees, uncovering paths that were practically invisible beneath the dense undergrowth. They came upon a mighty river, its waters black and swollen from the rains. Eotan traced its course for nearly half a mile before selecting a suitable crossing. The riverbed was slick and unstable, and Kipto stumbled. Culyan dismounted and led the destrier into the frigid waters, bracing himself against the rushing currents. Sten held his breath until his uncle reached the far bank and called for them to follow.

The woods began to change. The trees at the edge of the Wilds had been healthy and strong, towering over the land in dressings of supple greenery. But here the trees were shrunken and sallow, their trunks contorted into gnarled husks with bare, fingerlike branches. Wounds appeared on the ashen bark. The lesions secreted foul smelling ooze that glowed emerald green in the darkness.

The wind shifted abruptly and Eotan whistled, soft but urgent. The party halted. He dismounted and sniffed the air.

Culyan warily eyed the skeletal trees. "What do you smell, little pup?"

"I'm not sure," said Eotan. "It's strange. Wrong, somehow." He transformed into the golden wolf, raised his nose, and then returned. "There's something here. It reeks of death."

Sten held the bundle of moss, the last of the fairy fire, above his head. The scant light did little to reveal their surroundings. "Animal carcass, maybe?"

Eotan shook his head, his face grim. "Whatever it is, it's moving. And moving fast."

Sten jumped from the cloud and nocked an arrow to his bow. He nodded to the sickly trees. "Could it be the forest?"

"I don't think so," whispered Eotan. He squeezed Manye's hand. "Speak with them, little Oethyr. I must know what's happened here."

Manye limped to the nearest tree. Its bark was mottled with deep gouges that wept emerald tears. She tentatively touched it with a hand and closed her eyes. All was quiet, save for the wind that stirred the denuded branches. To Sten, it sounded like the rattle of bones.

Her eyes snapped opened. "They're angry. They're in tremendous pain. This tree... it wants to hurt me. It wants to hurt the dwarves."

"Why you?" asked Culyan, glaring at the forest accusatorily.

"I don't know." She whimpered and Eotan hugged her tightly. "I've never felt so much anger and resentment. The forest is dying and it blames us. It blames me."

Her shoulders shook and she began to cry into Eotan's cloak. He stroked her head, sapphire eyes ablaze. "Did they tell you what's causing this blight?" he asked quietly.

She nodded and wiped her eyes. "It's the mist."

A high-pitched scream shattered the silence and echoed crazily off the trees.

"That was human!" Culyan shouted. He unslung his axe and turned Kipto this way and that. "Where did it come from?"

Eotan vanished, briefly illuminating the ghostly clearing. The wolf tested the wind, and leapt forward with a snarl. Culyan spurred Kipto after his brother as Sten jumped onto the cloud, Manye close behind him. Seven beat his drum. The *BOOMS* reverberated through the Wilds and the dwarves began to sing. They plunged into the darkness, carried by the drums of war.

Kipto and Lilenti crashed through the tangles of sickly undergrowth. Sten shielded his face as thorns and branches ripped at his cloak. Something moved at the edge of his vision, barely visible through the veil of trees. He shook Manye and pointed. The elf raised her palm, flooding the forest with golden light, and inhaled sharply.

"It's a girl!" she said, breathlessly.

"Are you certain?"

Manye nodded desperately. "She's running from something!"

Sten yelled for his uncles to stop, but they forged ahead as Eotan chased the scent in the opposite direction. Sten swore and gritted his teeth. "That way!" he ordered. The dwarves veered sharply toward the fleeing figure.

As they sped into a clearing, a sliver of moonlight broke through the clouds. Its sheen fell upon a tiny figure, collapsed on the ground, shaking violently. Sten jumped to the ground, bow in hand, and raced to its side. It was a gnome that stared up at him. Her eyes were wild with terror. A series of vicious parallel gashes ran across her cheek, and dark blood stained her face and hands. She struggled away from him with a whimper.

"I'm not going to hurt you!" said Sten. "What's going on? What did this to you?" The gnome only sobbed, her eyes roving about the clearing. Manye rushed to them and laid a hand on her brow. A stream of golden sparks danced from her fingertips and flowed into the wounds. The gnome grimaced in pain as the magic worked to close the gashes.

"It killed them all!" she cried. Tears streamed down her face, leaving trails of pale skin amidst the blood. "It's coming!"

A knot of dread tightened around Sten's stomach. "What is?"

A tree to their right exploded in a hail of splinters, and a massive shape hurtled from the darkness. It passed into the moonlight and Sten recoiled in horror. It was a gargantuan bear. Lather and gore dripped from its jaws. Its eyes were red and shone in the darkness. Gaping wounds racked its flanks, oozing the same sickly green substance as the trees. Mottled, patchy fur clung to its huge frame, and pale bone poked through fetid skin.

The beast halted in the center of the glade and roared a challenge. The gnome fainted. Sten jumped to his feet and drew back an arrow. The bear's head swung back and forth between Manye and the dwarves. Its wet nose worked furiously, red eyes gleaming. Then, with only a harsh snort of warning, it charged at Manye.

Sten fired. "Uncles!" he screamed, and fired again. "Find us!" His first arrow caught the bear in the shoulder, the second in its forelimb. It snarled but continued its rush. Manye fell backward and scrambled on all fours to escape.

A deafening *TWANG* resonated throughout the glade. Two had stepped forward and the strings of his Boomstick were smoking. The air crackled and hummed. Sten's skin tingled as he readied another shot. Manye's hair was standing on end. The dwarves' music swelled to an impossible volume. There was a *WHOOM* of releasing power, and a wave of magic blasted from the dwarves and ripped through the clearing. The bear was lifted into the air and spun across the glade. It slammed into a tree and lay still. Sten was blasted from his feet and landed on his back. His ears rang and stars danced across his vision.

Time seemed to slow. The bear rose unsteadily and pawed at its head. Sten struggled to clear his mind, but the buzzing in his ears only grew louder. He fumbled for his bow and fired another arrow, but it sailed wide. The dwarves were picking themselves from the ground, moaning and clutching their heads. The bear growled and gnashed its teeth, searching the glade. It roared when it saw Manye and bounded forward. Its terrible claws gouged ragged furrows in the soil.

"Brothers Arda!" screamed Sten, or at least he thought he had. The only sound was the ringing in his ears. He released another arrow that buried itself in the bear's flank. It stumbled but didn't stop.

With a howl of rage, the golden wolf burst from the trees and slammed into the bear, knocking it to the ground. Kipto and Lilenti stormed into the clearing. Culyan leapt from his saddle and brandished his axe. The bear rose on its hind legs, roaring a challenge at its new attackers. Eotan darted forward and clamped his jaws around the creature's leg. Culyan rushed at the same moment and buried his axe in its shoulder. The bear screamed and lashed out at the Marshal, catching him in the chest with a massive, dead paw. Culyan crumpled to the ground, his golden breastplate dented.

He spat dirt and picked himself up. "You're a great ugly brute, aren't you?" The bear swiped at him, but he ducked underneath with a crazed laugh. "And mean to boot!" They circled one another, feinting and lunging, while Eotan helped Manye to safety. Then Culyan danced forward and slammed the butt of his axe into the bear's opened flank. It shrieked and spun to face him, but the Marshal was too quick. With a roar like building thunder, he leapt forward and brought the axe down onto the bear's head. The blow split the creature's skull. With a soft moan, it sank to the ground.

Eotan cautiously sniffed the body, then changed with a flash. Culyan collected the unconscious gnome and joined Sten and the dwarves around the corpse.

Sten massaged his ears. "What the hell's wrong with it?"

"I don't know," said Eotan. "It reeks of death, yet it's somehow alive. Nothing can survive such a state of decay."

"And have you ever seen a bear with red eyes?" said Sten. He pointed to the bear's sides, slick with blood and green slime. "I think it has the same sickness that's affecting the trees."

"That does not bode well for us, if true," said Two. "If the forest is turning into whatever *this* is..." He trailed off, letting the implication hang in the air. His boomstick lay at his feet, charred and twisted. He sighed glumly. "It'll be some time before I'll have this fixed."

"Then let us hope Sten is wrong," said Eotan. He wiped his brow and smirked at Culyan. "You're getting slow in your advancing age, brother."

Culyan chuckled and cleaned his axe in the grass. "My armor was in need of a new tale to tell, little pup. Though I feel for the poor beast. No creature should be tormented in such a way." He stood and surveyed the clearing. "We'll rest here tonight. Help me bury this thing, then get some sleep. If we remain vigilant, we may just survive the night."

FIRESIDE TALES

It was a restless night. Sten dreamt of shadowed creatures that hunted him through the Wilds with blood-red eyes. When they reached for him with terrible claws, crying out in eldritch tongues, he jerked awake. The sky had cleared and a bloated moon hung low over the tops of the trees. Lifeless branches stirred around him, whispering softly. To Sten, the forest seemed watchful, resentful. He drew his blankets over his head to block out the ghostly susurrus. He drifted in and out of sleep until the pale line of dawn materialized across the eastern horizon. He rose, shivering in the crisp air, his mind heavy and muddled. Except for Culyan, the others were still asleep. The Marshal sat beside a dwindling fire, sharpening his axe.

"Morning, nephew." Sten knelt beside him and held his hands to the flames. "Here, this'll warm you right up." He passed Sten a flask. Sten took a sip and coughed when the fiery liquid burned his throat.

"*Pwuh*, how can you drink that?"

The Marshal laughed and took a long pull. "When you find yourself alone in the Frozen Steppes with naught but your furs to keep you warm, this stuff is a godsend. It'll keep you on your feet for days."

"Until it burns a hole in your stomach." Sten blew on his fingertips and yawned deeply.

"Trouble sleeping?" Culyan observed with a wry smile. "Takes some getting used to, sleeping under the stars."

"The stars weren't the problem." Sten glared sullenly at the trees. "Mother and I used to camp on the grounds when I was a boy. She'd douse the lights so we could better see the constellations." Memories rushed back to him then, of cool summer grass tickling his neck, of his mother's patient whispers, warm in his ear, of mysterious symbols hidden amongst an ocean of stars. He sighed. "I had almost learned them all by name when father put an end to such *uncivilized* nonsense."

Culyan snorted derisively and took another sip. "Sounds like old Yoro. I still don't understand why Aella loved him, nor can I forgive him for locking her away. She was meant to roam the lands by our side, free from the confines of a cage." He gave Sten an appraising look. "But I suppose there was good in him. You're testament to that."

Sten gestured for the flask. "I'm not sure I agree." Despite the horrid taste, he was starting to feel warmer, and the dregs of his weariness were evaporating. "The *Lords* of House Bregon did precious little for the people of Heldan Port. My father was Marstarrow's toady, nothing more." He adopted a gruff voice and scowled haughtily. "Ours is a family of no small repute, boy! You shall not sully my good name with your childish antics and mediocrity!" He trailed off and stared into the flames. "As for me... well. Marstarrow was right to have me arrested."

Culyan set aside his axe and added another split to the fire. "You're too hard on yourself, lad. Eotan and I were far from saintly in our younger years. Come to think of it we're still not, but that's beside the point." He nodded to his brother, asleep in the form of the golden wolf, tail curled protectively around Manye. "We used to be mercenaries, the three of us. Did your mother ever tell you?" Sten mutely shook his head. "Ah, I suppose you were too young for such tales, but what tales they were!" The meager flames shone in Culyan's eyes as he leaned closer. "We were the Ardas Three and the Bearded Eight, with an army of Northerners at our backs! Sell-swords, ready to fight for the highest bidder. And we were damned good, lad. Before long, the Steppes were singing our names. Villages greeted us as kings, lords welcomed us into their banquet halls, and tourneys were held in our honor. But this reputation we built, our history, it wasn't pure. We did things that pain me to recall, even now." He grimaced and then spoke slowly, as if choosing his words carefully. "The point is, lad… It's never too late to change your story if you have a mind to do so."

Sten pulled his cloak tighter about his shoulders and stared at his feet. "You make it sound so simple."

Culyan let out a bark of laughter. "Ha! I never said it was simple, lad. Far from it, in fact."

"How did you change yours, then?"

The Marshal swept back his tangle of copper curls. "I didn't. I was young and foolish and blinded by the trappings of renown. It was Aella who sent us down an honorable road. She, Eotan, and Tiberion Marstarrow, oddly enough."

Sten looked up sharply. "The chancellor?"

Culyan nodded, a faraway look dimming his eyes. "Aye, though he wasn't chancellor at the time. No less duplicitous, mind you. He convinced Aella to take Heldan Port in his name, that he wanted to protect the city out of the goodness of his heart by wresting control from the Heads of House. A grand act of noble altruism." He spat into the fire. "That man could convince a dragon to give up its gold. Yet, despite his methods, I still believe we did the right thing that day. And that was the start of a new chapter in the story of the Ardas Three." He emptied the remainder of the flask into the flames and stood. In the soft light he looked a giant, his outline framed by the coming dawn. He offered Sten his hand with a wink. "Come, lad. It's past time we roused the others and were on our way. Perhaps that gnome can answer some questions."

Sten was pulled to his feet as if he weighed no more than a feather. He smiled up at Culyan. "Thank you, uncle."

Culyan grinned and bent to whisper in his ear. "Don't mention it, lad. I've a reputation to uphold. Can't have the others thinking I'm soft, eh?"

Breakfast was a meager affair, supplemented with roots and berries that Eotan foraged from the woods. They ate in silence, watching as Manye tended to the gnome's battered face. Golden light flowed from her fingertips and fizzled into the gashes. When it was done, the gnome gingerly ran her fingers along the raised gouges on her cheek.

"You'll have those scars for the rest of your life," said Manye with a sad smile. "I'm sorry I couldn't do more."

Tears welled in the gnome's eyes. She spoke in a high-pitched voice, fighting back sobs. "Tha... thank you." She turned to Sten and the dwarves. "Thank you all. If you hadn't come when you did..." She lapsed into silence again, shoulders shaking. Manye hugged her tightly.

Eotan knelt in the dew-laden grass. "What are you doing out here, friend?"

After a time, the gnome wiped her eyes. "I'm Faewyn, leader of the Yutuku people. We live here."

Culyan whistled appreciatively. "The Wilds is a hard and dangerous place to call home."

Faewyn sniffed and Sten thought she might cry again, but then her expression became resolute. "The Wilds have many places to hide, for one as small as me, and the Yutuku have been hiding for decades. Until recently, that is. Until..."

"Until the mist came," Sten finished.

Faewyn nodded. "It forced us from the deep south. Crops wilted, livestock died, and the creatures of the Wilds grew strange and unpredictable." Her hand strayed to the pink scars and she winced. "I was leading a party to find the edge of the corruption, but it's spreading faster than we can travel. And that... that *thing* attacked us." She stood suddenly. "I'm sorry, but I must return to my people. We have to keep moving."

They gave Faewyn a small knapsack loaded with provisions. She shouldered the pack and turned south.

"Good luck, Faewyn," called Eotan. "I hope you find your sanctuary."

She bowed. "Thank you, friends of the Yutuku. And I hope that our paths cross again, but under better circumstances. Know that I am forever in your debt." She strode to the edge of the clearing and turned back to them. "If I might offer one piece of advice. Keep to the north. The southern Wilds are lost. You'll find only death there." She waved goodbye and disappeared between the trees.

Eotan exchanged a dark look with his brother. "I had hoped to avoid the Oethyrlands." Manye's face paled.

"We're in quite the spot, eh little pup?" said Culyan. "The mist lies to the south, the Oethyr to the north. As I see it, we only have one option. Ride north only until we've escaped the blight, then head due east."

"To the Waypoint," said Eotan quietly. His eyes flicked to the trees and his mouth tightened.

"Aye. I don't see as we have another choice."

"Waypoint?" asked Sten.

"A place for weary travelers to rest in peace," said Eotan. "Its proprietor is unique, to say the least. But we'll be safe there. *If* we can reach it."

Culyan collected Kipto and threw his saddle and bags across the destrier's back. "It'll be five days of hard riding. More if we skirt the Oethyrlands."

"Yet it's our best hope of reaching Dinh," said Eotan. He looked to Manye and laid a hand on her shoulder. "The Oethyr won't even know we're coming. We will be safe."

SABOTAGE

Captain Luan Po eyed the towering walls of Heldan Port nestled along the banks of the harbor. There was only one other ship currently moored along the piers. Berthing would be fairly simple on a morning such as this, with a favorable wind and slack tide to guide her across the bar and safely to shore. The elf checked her bearing a final time before passing the wheel to her helmsman and descending to the deck.

It had been a languorous three-week voyage from Angoma, largely in part due to an entirely full cargo hold and a bout of nasty weather off the western coast of the Heartlands. But Po was a wizened captain and had faced far worse adversity in her decades spent at sea. She had danced around the worst of the storms, and had offset the cumbersome weight of her ship by riding a series of overlapping currents that carried her steadily northward. The tedious passage was well worth the risk once she sold her mountains of provisions at Heldan Port's markets. Few other Angoman captains risked the journey anymore, what with Chancellor Marstarrow's draconian trade regulations. But Po had found the chancellor's strict oversight largely beneficial in her honest approach to doing business. Her newly acquired ship, the Gyrfalcon, was amongst the finest in Angoma's merchant fleet, and had cost her a small fortune.

Po strolled to the foredeck and rang a large copper bell, signaling to the wizard who would be stationed in the harbor to ensure safe passage across the bar. She swallowed her irritation at the unnecessary precaution. The need for magical assistance was understandable on days when the currents were rough and unpredictable and transformed the bar into a deathtrap for unwary captains. But on mornings such as this, the safeguard was frankly insulting.

She waited for several minutes for the return call, but none came. She frowned and rang the bell a second time. Silence.

"Captain?" called her helmsman, expertly balancing the bloated ship against the out-current of the Mired River flowing from Heldan Port.

"Stay the course," she called. "If we're green enough to need a wizard's help then we have no business calling the sea our home!" Po's crew laughed and set to work. The Gyrfalcon nosed into the bar.

They had passed through three quarters of its length when a terrified yell shattered the calm. "Captain! Off the starboard bow! There's something in the water!"

Po sprinted to the taffrail. The waters churned and frothed in a shifting murk. But there, barely visible some two ship-lengths ahead, was an unbroken length of pale-green. It lurked just below the waterline and spanned the entirety of the channel's width.

"It's a chain!" she shouted in disbelief. "Somebody's put a *bloody chain* across the bar!" She frantically searched for a safe route through, but the links were whole and unbroken.

It was too late to slow, nevertheless come to a complete stop. "Brace for impact!" she screamed, and clutched desperately to the mast.

With a muffled *crunch* the chain bit into the ship's underside. Then it tore off the rudder in an explosion of wood and splinters.

"I've lost steering!" shouted her helmsman. The ship reeled listlessly toward the rocks lining the bar, forced off course by the river's current. Po bellowed orders. In a rumble of unfurling canvas the main sail dropped into position, filled ever so slightly by the faintest of western winds. A barrage of snaps and creaks from rope and cloth split the air as the ship began to right its course. But then, succumbing to the force of the currents and its own weight, the Gyrfalcon drifted closer to the shoals.

Po's stomach turned. "Empty the holds!" All eyes turned to her in horror. "Throw everything overboard and we might avoid the rocks!"

"We'll lose everything!" cried her first mate.

"Better it than us. Do as I say! Empty the holds."

As if in a dream, a fortune of food, drink, spice, cloth, and metal was dumped into the sea. More and more crates joined the growing trail of sinking debris. The ship began to edge away from the rocks, released from the binding constraints of its precious cargo. Cries of anguish rose from the deck.

Captain Luan Po's expression hardened, even as the Gyrfalcon glided safely into the calmer waters of the harbor. Someone was responsible for this. Someone had installed that chain with lethal intent, and recently, judging by the other ship moored safely along the docks. Someone had deliberately closed the bar, and had been willing to kill to do so.

Someone would pay for what they had done.

DISASTER

Elsewhere, two miles beyond the southeastern walls of Heldan Port, Five Hundred and Thirty-Seven leaned against the cool rock of the subterranean mineshaft. He wiped a trickle of sweat from his cheek. His crew toiled in the darkness further along. The clinking of their picks and hammers serenaded the claustrophobic passageway in an eerie, disembodied cadence.

He spat to clear the dust and splinters from his throat. Unlike most dwarves, Five Hundred and Thirty-Seven detested the mines of Heldan Port, and his unfavorable ranking correlated with his particular mindset. But he didn't mind. In a few more years he'd have saved enough coin to leave the mines for good. Then his world would be of the wind and stars that waited so enticingly overhead.

There came a distant shout from the foreman, signaling the change of shift. Five Hundred and Thirty-Seven breathed a sigh of relief. He wasn't even scheduled to work this morning. But with the disappearance of the wizards, all able-bodied miners had been forced to put in overtime to meet Heldan Port's demands for ore. Normally, the wizards' magic allowed for much more aggressive mining procedures, but without their guaranteed and overpriced protection, the dwarves had reverted to antiquated methods of extracting the land's precious minerals. Namely slow, meticulous, boring-as-hell manual labor.

He started up the tunnel, navigating the blackness by memory alone. The footsteps of the other seven members of his crew echoed his ascent. As he walked, his thoughts returned to the world that lay above him. He nodded decisively to himself. Once he had enough coin he would never again set foot in these godforsaken tunnels. And if the wizards didn't return he would be putting in longer hours every month, which meant more pay. Perhaps their absence wasn't so unfavorable after all.

A strange odor struck him in the cloying darkness, earthy, and faintly sulfurous. He paused and sniffed. A trickle of dread ran down his spine.

He fumbled in his knapsack and withdrew a bundle of matches. He stoked the flame to life against the garnet in his beard, and held the scant light overhead. Dark streaks of a pitch-like material snaked along the chiseled stone shaft in all directions.

With a cry of horror, Five Hundred and Thirty-Seven sprinted down the tunnel from where he had come, screaming for his crew to turn back. The awful image etched into his mind like acid biting into metal.

"Takk!" he screamed. "The walls are rigged with takk!" Astonished gasps came from the darkness, followed by pounding footsteps. The streaks glimmered dully at the corner of his vision, mirroring his crazed flight into the bowels of Miz.

How had he been so careless? He had been distracted in his dreams of the world above and had forgotten the most important mining rule of all: cognizance, or a casket.

A blaze of light illuminated the tunnels all about him, its radiant glow temporarily blinding him after hours spent in near blackness. He whirled about as the takk ignited in a simultaneous rush of fire and fury.

Five Hundred and Thirty-Seven braced himself as the explosion reached him, and then the world above crumbled down on top of him.

A CHANGE IN THE WIND

"Are you sure they went that direction?" said Captain Whitney. The blue light of the Follower pointed due north.

"If you question me one more time, I swear I'm done helpin' you," said Zwat. "Find your own bloody way across da Wilds."

"You've led us true thus far, demon. I apologize."

Zwat buzzed triumphantly in his box. "Dat's right! And stop callin' me demon. It's an insult, you know. What if I started referrin' to you as fat captain? How'd you like dat?"

"Right you are, *Zwat*," said Whitney, and tucked the box into his pocket. The Shrikes were spread throughout the clearing, examining the remains of a hastily abandoned campsite. "Report!" he barked.

Corporal Ghet waved to him from the edge of the glade. "Eh, Captain, you'll want to see this." Whitney joined her, staying well away from the gnarled trees. The green sludge

that flowed from their bark made him distinctly uncomfort-able. He drew alongside Ineza and coughed when a putrid smell hit him. A disfigured beast lay in a shallow hole, little more than a mass of rotten flesh and pale bone. Finger-length claws poked from the beast's huge footpads. Its red eyes were clouded in death, now almost pink.

Whitney covered his nose. "Is that a bear?"

"As far as I can tell." She had wound a strip of cloth over her nose and mouth, muffling her voice. "Considering the shape it's in, I'd say it's been dead for weeks. But here, look at this." She knelt and indicated the bear's mangled head. "This wound is fresh. You can see the blood has recently congealed. This thing was alive no more than a day or two ago."

Whitney retreated into the clearing, away from the horrid smell. He gagged and spat into the grass. "Something foul is happening to the Wilds."

Ineza pulled down the cloth and pointed to the shattered trunk of a tree. "Aye, and this clearing's been torn up some-thing awful. What do you think happened here, anyhoo?"

Whitney thought about reprimanding her, but decided against it. There were some battles he simply couldn't win. "I'd say the Ardas encountered a bit of trouble. And based on that bear's head, I'd guess it found itself on the wrong end of the Marshal's wrath. That's the cut of an axe, sure enough, though I've never seen such a powerful blow."

Corporal Hemmie whistled at them from the southern edge of the clearing. "Oi, Captain! We got footprints leading into the forest. They're small, well, they're my-sized, really. It looks like a gnome went this way."

"Odd," said Corporal Ghet. "I don't recall the Ardas having a gnome in their company."

Whitney eyed the watchful trees. "They don't."

The Shrikes assembled around him and waited in expectant silence. He twirled the end of his mustache. "The

Ardas turned northeast from here. Whatever happened must have changed their plans. I imagine it had something to do with that creature we found. I believe the Ardas had their first taste of whatever *this* is." He gestured to the sickly trees. "And it looks like they were worried enough to try and avoid it, moving forward.

"Our hand is forced. We *must* find the Ardas and convince them to set aside their pride. Take your breakfast and prepare to move within the hour. They can't be more than a day's hard ride ahead of us. We will not stop until we have them in our sight. Rou-augh!"

THE RIGHT THING

Butterson bolted the doors to the Jumping Jackamoose and leaned against the counter. He mopped his brow. Raxo lay on the bar, snoring fitfully, tail rising and falling with each breath.

It had been a tragic day for the capital. A merchant clipper had nearly sunk attempting to dock at port, laden with several tons of food destined for the markets. The entirety of the ship's cargo had been lost in the harbor. Thousands of people would go hungry for the week, and a series of brawls and protests had erupted in the Merchant District as a result. Then, an entire shaft of the mines had collapsed from a subterranean explosion. Eight dwarves had been killed.

The capital was beginning to feel the effects of the wizards' prolonged absence.

Heldan Portians had flocked to the Jackamoose as the chaos unfolded, hoping to uncover what information they could, or to discuss theories of their own. Butterson had listened to the conversations as he worked. General talk was turning against the chancellor and his campaign to curb the wizards' power. The people needed someone to blame for the flurry of recent catastrophes, and the chancellor's reluctance to address the capital's problems was backfiring.

A knock sounded at the recessed door behind the bar. Butterson frowned. Nobody entered the tavern from the alley. He only used it to switch casks or clear the garbage. He detached the bolt and stepped back. A cloaked man brushed past him and seated himself at the bar. "Ah, hello Tiberion."

"Mord, Raxo." The chancellor shed his cloak and surveyed the tavern. His movements were brisk, agitated, his face more drawn than usual.

The demon woke with a start. "Hawha? Who goes there?" His red eyes were blurred in confusion. "Oh, evenin', Chancellor. What are you doin' here?"

"I need your help," said Marstarrow gravely. Butterson and Raxo waited in wary silence. The chancellor cleared his throat. "I believe I have uncovered how the Houses removed the wizards from the Sanctum. But I need your help to prove my theory." He gazed steadily at Butterson. "I can no longer afford to, how did you so quaintly put it? 'Go it alone'."

"Beggin' your pardon, your *lordship*," said Raxo, "but why should we help you? A reckonin' is comin' to this city and I'm not sure I want to be standin' next to you when it does."

Marstarrow sighed. "Ah Raxo, brutally honest, as always. Yet that is precisely why I have come. I *need* people by my side whom I can trust." He leaned forward and lowered his voice. "Heldan Port approaches a threshold. The Houses have shown the steps they are willing to take to displace me. They are responsible for what happened in the mines and the harbor today."

Butterson blinked in surprise. "How can you be certain?"

Marstarrow rubbed his chin with a forefinger. "My network of agents is rather-"

"Tyrannical?" suggested Raxo. "Unethical? Maniacal? Suggestive of a despot?"

"Extensive," said Marstarrow patiently. "The Houses hired an insurgent to lace the mines with dwarven takk, an antiquated, volatile explosive that was outlawed from Heldan Port's mining operations decades ago." Marstarrow smiled darkly. "Shortly thereafter, a man was discovered floating in the canals, his throat slit, his identity unknown. As for the merchant vessel, well. How many seasoned captains would run aground on a calm summer day? The captain in question, one Luan Po, swears that her ship's steering was sabotaged. After that, it only required some well-placed agents to delicately guide the tides of speculation flowing through the city and redirect the blame to me. I admit I did not expect such levels of deviousness from the Houses."

Raxo twitched his tail and narrowed his eyes. "If I didn't know better, I'd say you sound like a crazy person. Though I suppose I wouldn't put it past 'em. Killin' people and disruptin' the lives of thousands more seems just the sort of thing those posh bastards would do, all without battin' an eye. I say we run 'em out of town, them and all their fancy friends. Guilty or not. Would free up some prime real estate for li'l old Raxo as a bonus."

Marstarrow frowned and sat in quiet contemplation, tapping one finger against the bar. "The Houses are undoubtedly immoral, to say the least. But the same cannot be automatically assumed of the other wealthy citizens of Heldan Port. While disparities in wealth may seem the essence of this problem, I find the morality of those possessing such fortune to be the true issue. Good and evil are not necessarily dictated by one's affluence, nor is one's means necessarily determined by one's integrity. However, the trees of the wealthy corrupt spread their branches high into the sky and are subsequently plain for all to see. But there will always be saplings hidden within their shadows, fighting to spread foul roots of their own, and prevented from doing so only by the indomitable nature of that which towers above."

"Whatever you say," grumbled Raxo.

Marstarrow clasped his hands in front of him, his gray eyes suddenly bright. "I am certain of what I have told you. The Houses have fought every single one of my efforts to stabilize the city in the wizards' absence. Today, they took it one step too far. I must act, and so require aid."

"Why us?" asked Butterson. "Surely you have people better suited for this type of work."

"Yet that should not stop you from doing the right thing," said Marstarrow.

Butterson bristled and came out from the bar. "The right thing? The *right thing*? There is no right thing for us in all of this. For the commoners of this city, there is only muck and shit and shades of gray. The fact is, your people are suffering and you're too scared to address them face-to-face. You want me to do the right thing? Then *you* start by telling everyone what's really going on." The room fell deathly quiet.

Raxo looked at Butterson with wide eyes. "Eh, Boss, you know you just told the chancellor he's a lyin' coward, right?"

"I know what I said!" snapped Butterson. He folded his arms and waited.

Marstarrow stared at him in silence, his face unreadable. Then, he smiled. "I was right about you, Mord Butterson, and I appreciate your candor. You are absolutely correct. I have acted the craven and misled my people. You have both advised me to step out from the shadows and into the light. Perhaps it is time I listened to reason." He rose from the stool. "If you swear to assist me, then I will do as you suggest and speak before the entire city. I will condemn the Houses for their treachery. I will outline my plan to stabilize the capital in the event the wizards do not return. And I will expose every pertinent detail I know regarding this whole sordid affair. But first, I need your help."

"With what, exactly?" asked Butterson suspiciously.

"With finding answers. Within the Sanctum."

Raxo guffawed. "The Sanctum? As in the Occult Sanctum of Wizards? As in the impenetrable fortress that's impossible to enter unless you are said wizard? What the hell are we gonna do there?"

A roguish gleam came into Marstarrow's eye. "We are going to break in. But we will need G'rok." He extended a hand and stared evenly at Butterson. "Are you with me?"

Butterson hesitated. Everything was happening so quickly. Plots and schemes and treacheries were cascading onto his head like rocks in a landslide. Just days before, Tiberion Marstarrow had been no more than a prodigious name to him, a distant and intangible icon of Heldan Port's immense powers. Yet now he was standing in the Jackamoose, flesh and blood, asking for Butterson's help. And Butterson realized that he wouldn't, or perhaps couldn't, refuse him. He looked up to the rafters and sighed deeply. "If you swear that you'll stand before the capital, then we're with you, Tiberion."

"On my honor," vowed Marstarrow. They shook hands, and then the chancellor gathered his cloak and strode to the door behind the bar. He paused in the threshold and pulled up his hood. "The right thing is not always apparent in times of great darkness. It takes courage to step blindly into the night. Would that more had the mettle to do so."

Then he was gone, swallowed by the streets of the capital, leaving Butterson to mull over his words.

GOLDEN APPLES

Vandra steadied herself against a tree, sides heaving. She waited until her breathing returned to normal. Then, with a *crack*, she vanished in a flurry of leaves. She reappeared leagues away at the top of a hill where a lone tree grew, branches sagging with golden apples. She staggered slightly. An elf stood just outside a ring of moonlight. His skin was rich and dappled, rendering him nearly invisible in the darkness. A swirling labyrinth of tattoos covered his bare chest. A heavy pelt was draped over his shoulders, and a ram's horn was slung across his hip. Vandra straightened.

"Lentarro."

The elf bowed. "Vandra." His voice was a growl. "Always a pleasure when you grace the Wilds with your presence."

She ignored the slight. "I bring welcome news." The elf cocked an eyebrow and squared his muscular shoulders. "Eotan Arda rides for Dinh and will pass through your lands."

Upon hearing the brother's name the elf stiffened and clenched his hands. "When?"

"Tomorrow or the day after. Gather your Oethyr. I will ensure he doesn't travel south. Kill him. And his companions."

"With pleasure." Lentarro's knuckles were white, and a line of blood trickled from where his long nails dug into his palm. "After I butcher the *wolf*," he paused and spat on the ground, "do we move for Dinh?"

"Soon. I need more time."

"Fine, but remember what you promised us, witch."

Vandra froze. Crimson magic spread along her arm like infernal ice over a pond. Lentarro backed away. "I gave you my word," she hissed, advancing on the tattooed Oethyr. "You will have your precious Wilds, in the end, and the mist will never touch your lands."

"That... that is all I ask." The edge in his voice faltered. He dropped his gaze and held out his hands in a placating gesture. "I meant no disrespect, Vandra. I do not trust outsiders. I've seen what the mist does to the forest. I was worried, nothing more. Forgive me. *Please* forgive me."

"The mist will never touch your lands," she repeated. Her magic fizzled out and the golden apples resumed their color. "But question me again and I will put you down like the beast you are."

She disappeared with another *crack*, and left the elf alone at the top of the hill.

THE OETHYRLANDS

Trees grew healthy and strong as the company traveled north, though touches of the blight still lingered. Towering pines gave way to supple deciduous trees, their leaves beginning to wear the red and gold tints of autumn. Fertile beds of loam, moss, and ferns stretched beneath the canopies. Sunlight pierced the branches, illuminating sections of luscious greenery. Yet, despite the beauty, Sten was uneasy, for the woods were entirely silent.

"Shouldn't we be hearing something?" he whispered to Manye. They glided along with the Bearded Eight. "Birds, or insects, or animals moving through the woods. Anything."

The elf shifted uncomfortably. She had been quiet ever since the company turned north. "I cannot sense another living creature besides the plants," she said. "Even they are stilled."

Sten called for his uncles to stop and explained their concerns. Eotan transformed and darted through the nearby woods, sniffing the ground. He dashed to a worn game trail

and followed its length up a sloping hillock. At its top, he sat on his haunches, cocking his head this way and that, his nose to the air. He loped back to them and returned with an emerald flash.

"Animals have been here, but not recently." Apprehension crept into his voice. "The scents are old. They carry the stink of fear. Perhaps they've migrated farther north to avoid the mist."

"No," said Manye. "It's something else. *They* know we're coming."

Kipto pawed at the ground as Culyan unslung his axe. "Their borders yet lie to the north. Are you certain, Manye?"

She nodded desperately. "These are my people. Please trust me."

Eotan leapt onto Lilenti's back and scanned the woods. "We do, little Oethyr. We'll go no further."

One toyed with the gemstone in his beard. "Are you sure that's wise? I, for one, would rather face the elves than one of those nightmarish creatures again."

"Then you don't know my father," said Manye. Her face was ashen and her hands trembled when she spoke.

"We ride east," Eotan announced. "The Oethyr have hunted me before. If I must choose, I would face the mist."

They dropped into a narrow valley etched by a crystalline river. Soon, Tanduil had dipped behind the valley walls. They stopped to eat and water the horses. It was a brief meal of dried venison and roasted chestnuts, and did little to curb Sten's hunger. They rode on. The canyon walls grew steeper and the banks of the river disappeared, forcing them to ascend from the valley. They climbed to the top of a jagged ridge, windswept and desolate.

"By my beard..." said Two. Sten and the others looked on in horrified silence.

A solid wall of mist blanketed the trees, running south in an endless, unbroken mass. The sea of gray crept toward them over the hills. It hung in the air, eddying coyly with the wind, as if challenging them to enter its depths. Clear skies lay to the north, the colors of twilight a stark contrast to the void of darkness that slowly approached.

Eotan's face tightened, his black cloak streaming behind him. "So be it. The decision has been made for us."

Night fell as the company crossed into the Oethyrlands. They rode in utter silence, letting the faint light of the moon and stars guide them through the trees. Culyan wrapped strips of cloth around the horses' hooves to dampen the sound of their passing.

"Maybe they won't realize we've come," whispered Sten. He nervously stroked an arrow's fletching.

"Maybe," repeated Two. Manye said nothing. Her gaze snapped about at the slightest sound. A pair of owls hooted nearby. The forlorn calls raised the hairs on Sten's neck.*

The forests thinned and the trees gave way to rolling plains. The tall grasses flowed with the wind, like waves of some great telluric ocean. The moon crept higher into the sky and basked the wilderness in its pale glow.

Sten began to hope. The Wilds were immense. It was impossible to police such a huge territory. They would reach the Waypoint, whatever that was, and ride for Dinh. They would find their answers, clear up this business with the wizards and the mist, and return home. The Oethyr simply had no way of knowing they had come.

A lone howl sounded some distance away. Eotan froze and stared in the direction it had come. They waited breathlessly. Silence.

"It's nothing, little pup," said Culyan, though he sounded

---

* The calls went something like this: "I dare say, Edelwing, I think this will prove too much for the Ardas." "Nonsense, Stonetalon, have faith. Though I am happy to make this interesting... shall we say four squirrels?"

uncertain. "There are plenty of wolves in the Wilds, you know that better than any. Best to keep moving, we're still-" The deep, swelling tone of a horn rolled across the prairie. Culyan swore and readied his axe.

"It's *him!*" Manye whimpered.

Suddenly, the darkness around Sten was alive with animal calls. Howls and snarls and screams came from everywhere at once, and dark shapes hurtled toward them through the moonlight.

"Run!" yelled Eotan. The dwarves summoned their magic with fevered desperation, the sound of their fiddles and horns and drums washing over the grasslands like a coming storm. Culyan dug his heels into Kipto's sides, and Lilenti lunged forward. They thundered across the plains as the calls drew nearer.

Sten loosed an arrow at a flitting shadow and was rewarded with a snarl of pain. The shapeshifters kept pace as the company tore across the prairie. Eyes glowed in the moonlight, ravenous and terrible. But the Oethyr never came too close, instead matching the company's speed as they fled east.

They climbed a knoll and skidded to a halt when the grass in front of them erupted with dark shapes. Beasts prowled about the hill and circled the company with victorious cries. Wolves and bears and wildcats stalked between mighty stags and fearsome boars. Some transformed in vivid flashes of color and brandished crude weapons.

Sten drew back another arrow, his aim dancing between the shadows. The Oethyr had them completely surrounded.

HUNTED

Captain Whitney and his Shrikes rode at a canter, unspeaking. The blue light of the Follower glowed in the darkness, guiding them over sloping grasslands that shivered in the wind. He raised a fist and the company drew to a halt at the base of a gentle hill.

"Rest here a moment," he said. "Eat and water your horses. The Ardas can't be far. We'll catch them before dawn if we ride through the night."

As the Shrikes set about their work, Whitney climbed the hill. He gazed out across the plains. The landscape was monochromatic in the moonlight. It felt barren, desolate, and empty, despite the ubiquitous grasses. Somewhere, a wolf howled, the sound strangely melancholy.

Corporal Ghet padded up beside him, silent as a cat. "Eerie out here. I almost prefer that wretched forest."

"There's definitely something odd about this place. The air feels expectant somehow."

"Aye." She shifted her balance and laid a hand on the pommel of her sword. "I don't think we're welcome here, Cap."

Far to the east came a single, clear blast of a horn. Whitney tensed. A cacophony of animalistic cries reached them moments later, frenzied and eager. He snatched the Follower from his pocket and held it aloft. It pointed in the direction of the calls. "Zwat! What's going on?"

"*Whooowhie*, my beacon's movin' like a fing possessed!" cackled the demon. "Ain't never seen it move so fast."

Whitney crammed the Follower into his pocket and raced down the hill, Ineza close on his heels.

"Mount up!" he roared. The Shrikes looked up in surprise. "We're out of time!" Men and women clambered onto their horses, strapping on pieces of armor. Corporal Ghet grabbed him by the arm.

"What's going on, Cap?" Her eyes were pale orbs in the moonlight.

He wheeled his horse about and slammed on his plumed helmet. "The Ardas are on the run. They're being hunted."

THE WOLF AND THE RAM

A great ram cantered up the crest of the hill, taller even than Kipto. Spiraling horns twisted about its head before coming to end in vicious points. It stopped halfway up the hill and disappeared in a blaze of amethyst light. A hulking elf took its place. He fingered the lip of a curved horn slung across his hip. Tattoos covered his torso and a heavy pelt was draped across his shoulders. Manye ducked behind Sten and clutched his arm.

"Eotan Arda!" said the elf in a slow, deliberate growl. "Step forward, so I might see your treacherous face."

Eotan dismounted and approached him. "Lentarro, it was never my intention to return to your lands. I was forced to cross your borders because-"

"You were forced here because I *wanted* you here! I have waited years for this day. You stole our secrets, like a dog." He spat onto the dirt. "And you took my daughter from me." The ring of Oethyr stalked closer.

Eotan held his ground, though one hand strayed to a dagger. "Lentarro, you must listen to me! If you care for your home, you will let us pass. Something is happening to your lands, to the Wilds."

The elf folded his tattooed arms. "I already know what's happening to the Wilds, dog. Nothing happens in my lands without my knowing."

"Then let us help you. We can work together to end the blight!"

Lentarro laughed scornfully. "I think not, Eotan Arda. Your kind brought this upon the world long ago."

Anger was seeping into Eotan's voice. "What do you mean?"

"You're an outsider, and a fool. You still know nothing. But your ignorance will not save you."

"Then have your revenge," snarled Eotan. He drew his daggers and crouched low. "But let my companions pass."

Lentarro's voice was acid. "I showed mercy to an outsider once before. I will not make that mistake again. Tell me, dog, is my daughter with you tonight?" The leather of Eotan's daggers crackled beneath his grip. Lentarro smiled and turned to face the company at the top of the hill. "Manye! Come out from wherever you're hiding, sweet princess."

The little elf stepped from the cloud and limped to Eotan's side.

"My, how you've grown," said Lentarro, though a touch of sincerity laced his words.

Manye's voice was barely more than a whisper. "Let us pass."

Lentarro pointed at Eotan, shaking with rage. "You convinced me to spare this cur's life and look what it cost me! Heed my words, now, daughter. Return to your father's side, your *peoples'* side, and in time, you may be forgiven. If not, you die with the rest."

Manye balled her fists. "You are not my father and those

animals are not my family! *This* is my only family, now. I will not let you harm them."

Lentarro spat again. "So be it, daughter of none. You could have been great, yet now you are lost."

"It is not I who is lost." The tremble left Manye's voice and she stood tall, wincing slightly when she put weight on her injured leg. "Compassion, selflessness, altruism; these ideas are entirely foreign to you. You've hidden your entire life, closing your mind and your lands to outsiders, believing isolation will keep you safe. You don't care about the Wilds, and you don't care about the blight. You only care for yourself. I pity you, Lentarro, for you are the one who is lost in your own fear. Yet I am exactly where I should be, standing between you and my family."

Lentarro's dark eyes shone with fury. "You are no true Oethyr. I will burn your body and curse your ashes."

Eotan leapt at Lentarro in a flash of emerald. The golden wolf was met by the ram's horns as the Oethyr shifted form. With cries of bloodlust, the elves charged up the base of the hill. Sten loosed arrow after arrow into the oncoming horde.

Culyan met the Oethyr as they crested the knoll. He was everywhere at once, swinging his axe with utter finality. The dwarves' music sounded above the mayhem, shielding the Marshal from tooth and claw. Kipto kicked and bit as the elves attempted to bring him down. Manye closed her eyes and the wind rose to a gale. The arcane storm momentarily rebuffed the Oethyr's attack. Sten fired until his arms ached and his quiver was spent. Yet the battle raged on, illuminated by flashes of color as the Oethyr flitted between man and beast.

Eotan and Lentarro were locked in combat. The golden wolf snapped its jaws but was rebuffed by the razor-sharp horns. Step by step, he was driven up the hill, unable to withstand the ram's advances. He changed, panting heavily, and drew his daggers. They stood shoulder to shoulder atop the plains as the knot of elves tightened. Sten lashed out with his knife and bow whenever a beast ventured too close. He sent a wildcat reeling away, screaming in pain from a deep gash across its leg.

Manye and the Bearded Eight began to fade under the relentless onslaught. The winds subsided, and Culyan bled from a dozen wounds as the dwarves' wards failed him.

"Any chance you've fixed your Boomstick?" shouted Sten.

Two shook his head and frantically strummed a lute. "Sorry, lad, not today! I'm afraid our luck has run its course."

"Keep fighting!" ordered Culyan over the fury. Blood streamed from his nose. A mountain lion darted forward and swiped at Kipto, raking his side beneath the gilded barding. The charger snorted and kicked out, catching the Oethyr in the chest. The cat sailed through the air, screaming as it plummeted from the hill. "Take that, ya wretch!" scolded the Marshal. His axe swung in deadly arcs, glinting in the moonlight.

A blaze of amethyst light and Lentarro reappeared. He stood behind his ranks of Oethyr and mocked them over the fury. "Nothing will save you now, Eotan Arda! You've led your friends to their doom! Not even Manye will survive the night, thanks to-"

He cocked his head and turned to the west.

Across the plains galloped a band of riders, fast approaching. They were thirty strong and rode as a wedge, making straight for the knoll. Blackened armor shone dully in the moonlight. The foremost rider bellowed a challenge and raised a thin sword. A red mustache peeked from his opened visor, waxed to perfection.

"I don't believe it," Sten shouted, elation cracking his voice. The Oethyr scrambled to meet the oncoming riders. "It's Captain Whitney!"

THE ELEVENTH HOUR

Whitney drew his rapier as the Shrikes raced toward the sounds of battle. Culyan Arda shone like a beacon at the top of the hill, his golden armor resplendent in the moonlight. Ranks of beasts shrank and broke before him. Sporadic flashes of light cast an eerie, disjointed pall over the scene, illuminating the hill in a crazed medley of color.

"Rou-augh!" Whitney roared. Elves and beasts alike turned to face him.

"Rou-augh!" The Shrikes echoed the call as they reached the base of the hill.

Some of the elves raced down the slope to meet the Shrikes, others faltered, unsure of what to do. Whitney smiled grimly under his helmet. "Ride straight through! Punch a hole to the Ardas and circle back around. Give them time to escape! We stop for nothing! Chaaaarge!" He slammed home his visor.

The elves scattered like leaves in the wind. Whitney led the way, slashing and thrusting at anything that strayed too

close to his rapier. The twins rode on either side of him, repelling attackers with gargantuan tower shields. The Shrikes forged up the hill in close formation.

A hulking elf was yelling orders in the chaos, trying in vain to organize the attackers. But the elves only milled about in panic and confusion.

Whitney drove his horse straight through to the Marshal. A massive golden wolf bared its teeth, and Whitney angled to intercept it. But then the wolf disappeared in a dazzling flash of emerald light and Eotan took its place. Whitney pulled up short in bewilderment, then shook his head and continued barking orders. The Shrikes circled the company and drove back the elves. Eotan leapt onto his mare and the dwarves summoned their cloud.

"Whitney you great big beautiful bastard!" yelled Culyan. "What the hell are you doing here?"

"No time! Follow us!" The Shrikes surged forward, scattering the elves on the eastern side of the slope. The Ardas followed them through the gap. At the base of the hill, Whitney raised his sword and reined his horse to the north. The Shrikes followed in a thundering arc.

The Ardas and the dwarves fled to the east. A host of creatures pursued, a great ram at their head, bellowing in fury. Whitney lowered his sword and the Shrikes charged forward. They crushed a wide swath through the ranks of animals. Again and again they struck, breaking through the column in broad sweeps of horse and steel. Finally, the ram veered away from the brothers with a scream of frustration. The line of creatures scattered and fled into the night. A burst of violet light momentarily brightened the prairie.

"You are dead, Eotan! And your world will burn!"

The Shrikes fell in behind the Ardas. Eotan led them out of the plains and into an old-growth black forest. Branches grew thick with curtains of moss, and the ground was carpeted in needles and leaves. They halted beside a gurgling creek, its waters crisp and pure. Whitney and the Shrikes slumped in their saddles, while their horses drank greedily from the stream.

"We'll rest here until dawn," said Eotan. Dark circles hung beneath his eyes, and his face was caked in dried blood. He strode over to Whitney and offered his hand with a weary smile. "Thank you, Captain. We owe you our lives."

"You have the chancellor to thank, not me," said Whitney, slightly brusquer than intended.

Eotan's smile faltered. "Yes, well. Thank you nonetheless."

Ineza glared at Whitney as the brother turned to leave. He cleared his throat. "*Hrmph.* We're glad... *I'm* glad you're safe, Arda. And that goes for the rest of your lot." The dwarves bowed solemnly and Culyan saluted with his axe.

"Maybe next time you'll show up to the battle on time," called Sten. He winked at Ineza and she burst into laughter.

The corner of Whitney's mustache twitched as he watched her. "I suppose I deserve that."

"Yes you do," she said. "But thank you for showing them that kindness, Cap. Perhaps you're not such a cold, heartless curmudgeon after all."

"We'll see." He laid a hand on her shoulder. "You fought well, Corporal. Get some rest. I'll take the first watch."

RIDDLESTON'S GOAT

Butterson waited outside the colossal walls of the Occult Sanctum of Wizards, trying his best to keep G'rok quiet. They stood just outside the range of flickering lanterns that lined the cobblestoned streets.

"WHERE MARSTARROW?" G'rok's pink bowtie sparkled, despite the gloom.

"Will you keep it down!" he hissed. "He'll be here. Just be patient. And why'd you have to wear that? You stand out like a sore thumb."

"G'ROK LOVE BOWTIE. TOUCH BOWTIE AND G'ROK SMASH THUMB."

Raxo chortled from his perch atop her muscular shoulder. "What the hell was Marstarrow thinkin'? Invitin' G'rok on a mission of subtlety and subterfuge was downright reckless, if you ask me. No offense love, but stealth has never been an orc's strong suit."

"NO OFFENSE TAKEN. WHAT SUBUTTERFUGE?"

A faint cough sounded behind them. "Good evening, everyone." Chancellor Marstarrow emerged out of the darkness from the direction of the sewers.

Raxo sniffed the air suspiciously. "Where'd you come from?"

Marstarrow's only response was to smile cryptically. "Follow me, if you please." He guided them to the gates of the Sanctum. The doors stood ten stories tall, carved from the same obsidian stones as the Sanctum, yet were somehow darker than the surrounding night. "I present to you our predicament."

"You want us to get past *those*?" said Butterson. He stared up at the gates in awe.

"*Those* are not the problem. The wizards are overly fond of grandiosity, in my opinion. These gates are for show, in truth. The real problem is there." Marstarrow pointed to the air in front of the Sanctum.

"I think he's losing it, Boss," whispered Raxo.

Marstarrow overheard and smiled graciously. "Allow me to demonstrate. Raxo, if you would be so kind as to knock on the Sanctum's doors?"

The demon flicked G'rok's ear. "Well, now I don't trust you." Marstarrow flipped him a coin. "Never mind, your lordship's wish is my command." He skipped down from his perch and sauntered up to the gates. With a tiny, clawed fist, he pounded on the door. There was a crackle of power and he was blasted into the air. He sailed backward and came to rest at the chancellor's feet, tail smoking.

Marstarrow smiled down at him. "Perhaps that will teach you to refrain from insulting me in the future?"

"Don't count on it," said Raxo, meekly.

Marstarrow clasped his hand together. "Now, Sylvus Riddleston has assured me that such wards are completely impenetrable. Therefore, if his word is to be trusted and I do indeed, it is safe to assume that whatever reached the wizards knew how to get past the Sanctum's wards. Agreed?" Butterson and Raxo nodded. G'rok chased a moth as it spiraled around a lantern. "Wonderful. I am glad to see everyone paying attention." He set off across the manicured lawns of the Sanctum. They entered a grove of alders, the trees' ashen bark bonelike in the darkness. Marstarrow carefully picked his way about. "The infernal contraption has a tendency to move about on its own. Aha!" He stopped before an expansive alder. A large mahogany casket rested upright against its trunk, its lacquered surface reflecting the moonlight. Marstarrow swung open the casket's lid, revealing a plush, cream-colored interior. "Here stands the only other entrance into the Sanctum."

"It's a coffin," observed Butterson, nonplussed. He was beginning to wonder at Raxo's suspicions of the chancellor's mental state.

"By appearance only," said Marstarrow. "Its form changes in cyclical fashion, sometimes daily. Tonight it is a coffin, tomorrow, perhaps a woodshed." He leaned closer. "Sylvus claims that it often takes the shape and *smell* of an outhouse." He shivered gravely. "The very idea."

"So it's a tunnel, then?" said Butterson. "Or a doorway?"

Marstarrow pursed his lips. "It is quite difficult to explain. I shall need another volunteer to do so."

Raxo pointed accusatorily at his smoking tail. "Is it gonna zap me like those gates?"

"Oh this will be far worse, I assure you," said Marstarrow. "I had the misfortune to experience it for myself, long ago."

Raxo let out a squeak and darted behind G'rok's legs. "Your turn, Boss."

Butterson gritted his teeth. "Damn you, Tiberion. I hope you know what you're doing."

"My assurance would be a lie."

"Lovely."

Marstarrow ushered him inside. "In you go."

Butterson stepped inside the coffin and closed the lid. The narrow walls barely allowed him enough room to breathe. Someone pounded on the door and then came the chancellor's muffled voice. "Can you hear me, Mord?"

"Loud and clear." Butterson examined the interior of the box. It was bare, except for a small lever that hung above his head.

"Wonderful. Do you see a switch?"

"Yes."

"Pull it, if you please."

"If this kills me I'm coming back to haunt you." Butterson steeled himself and pulled the handle.

It was as if he had been ripped in half. There was a moment of excruciating pain as his insides turned to jelly. Then the world around him blurred, as though he were viewing it from a great distance. His vision spun round and round and the world seemed to shrink beneath his feet. He closed his eyes. The spinning sensation worsened. Then, everything froze.

He tentatively opened one eye. He was still in the coffin. Nothing had changed. The lever still hung above him, and Raxo was cursing about his injured tail through the lid. He closed his eye and opened the other. This time, he was standing in an unfamiliar hallway. Magnificent arches towered over him, supporting the immensity of a gigantic corridor with marbled floors. Bearded statues looked haughtily down at him from the walls.

"What the bloody hell?" He screwed shut his eyes.

He opened his right. The great hall loomed above him. He opened his left. The interior of the casket closed in around him. He opened both of his eyes and then immediately closed them, overcome by vertigo. For a moment, he had stood in both locations simultaneously, and the experience was uniquely terrible.

There was the creak of a door and he tumbled into the

grass of the Sanctum's grounds. He rose swaying to his feet. "Tiberion, I swear I'll have G'rok give you a hug if you don't explain yourself." Marstarrow cocked an eyebrow.

"G'rok's been known to crack ribs," said Raxo.

"Ah." Marstarrow's eyes glimmered with anticipation. "Describe what you felt, Mord."

Butterson drew a hand across his brow. "I don't even know where to begin." He was sweating profusely, despite the cool of the night. "It was as if... it was as if I was in two places at once. I could see the insides of the coffin, but I could also see some place I've never been before. There were statues on the wall. They had beards, and pointy hats, and... wait a moment." He paused. "I was in the Sanctum, wasn't I?"

"I believe so, yes," said Marstarrow. "Your description of events supports my theory."

"And that is?"

"That this casket is a working example of Riddleston's Goat."

Raxo threw up his hands in exasperation. "All right, he's lost it."

Marstarrow ignored him. "Sylvus Riddleston, in his younger and more brilliant years, proposed a theory. He believed that a being could exist in two locations simultaneously, in a state of physical superposition. Thanks to magic, of course. Now, this being could exist in both locations, simultaneously, until viewed by an outside observer. At that instant, the being would be forced into a single point of existence, and the characteristics of the observer would dictate where. Do you follow me?"

"Nope," said Raxo. "I'm goin' to play with G'rok and her butterflies before I get zapped again." The demon scampered off to join the capering orc.

"I think so," said Butterson slowly. "When I was in there... when I pulled that lever... It put me in two places at once, using magic? Then, when you opened the lid, I had to exist in one spot or the other, but not both, and I ended up back here?"

Marstarrow clapped him on the shoulder. "Precisely! You never fail to impress, Mord. Riddleston tested this theory on several goats, thus the name. It took him quite a few attempts to get it right. The goats had a nasty habit of splitting in two, or so I hear." They stared at the coffin.

"I appreciate you throwing me in a box that might rip me in half," Butterson grumbled.

"Nonsense, you were always safe. But we have yet to answer the most important question of all. How does one enter the Sanctum? Riddleston refused to share his secrets, but I believe the answer lies with the observer."

"So I step into this... *thing*, and whoever opens the door dictates where I end up?" Butterson glanced sidelong at the chancellor. "It's quite the theory, but how do we prove it?"

Marstarrow's eyes shone. "That is why I needed G'rok."

Butterson held up his hands. "Tiberion, with all due respect, you can't make her go through that. She wouldn't take it well. Plus, I don't think she'd fit inside the coffin."

"Oh, gods no," said Marstarrow mildly. "There is a gnome who works within the Sanctum. His name is Gefwyn. He is the wizards' steward. He resides on the twenty-first floor of the Sanctum, if memory serves. His room is on the southern-most wall. I must speak with him."

"What's G'rok got to do with him?"

"I need her to throw rocks at his window."

"THIS WORK?" G'rok brandished a small boulder from the edge of the canal.

"No!" said Butterson impatiently. "We want to wake him up, not kill him. Here, use this." The orc hurled the pebble at a window. It bounced off the glass with a faint *plink* and a fizzle of hidden magic.

Raxo clapped excitedly and hoisted a large brick. "Hey, nice one! Now try this!"

"Put that down!" hissed Butterson. "I swear you two are more trouble than you're worth." G'rok's shoulders slumped and she dropped the brick.

Raxo patted her leg. "Aw, come now love, he doesn't mean it. He's just jealous that we have more fun than him. Ain't that right, Boss?"

"Fine, whatever. Just stop trying to kill the gnome."

The window opened with the screech of unoiled hinges. "Oi! Stop throwin' shite at this here window!"

"Do we have the pleasure of addressing Gefwyn, steward of the Occult Sanctum of Wizards?" called Marstarrow.

"Yer do, now bugger off afore I empty my chamber pot on yer heads."

"Charming," said Butterson.

"I would appreciate a moment of your time, Gefwyn," said the chancellor. "My name is Tiberion Marstarrow. We met some time ago. You also wrote to me concerning the wizards."

A tiny head peeked out of the window. "Ah, yer that chancellor feller? Why didn't yer say so in the first place? Give me a moment, I'll be down shortly."

Several minutes later, a heavily bearded gnome emerged from the front gates, stooped with age, and singing. His gruff baritone echoed off the Sanctum's walls.

> "The Lass o' the Lake, my lady so fair,
> the quickest of minds, the softest of hair.
> Our love was so pure, we wed by the sea,
> we left this cruel world, my lady and me."

Raxo sniffed and wiped a tear from his eye. The gnome continued.

> "To lands we did sail, on waters like glass,
> but one stormy night, my lady did pass.
> Alone now, afraid, her voice ne'er to hear,
> I miss my fair lady, but mostly her rear."

Gefwyn trundled up to them and bowed, his beard brushing the cobblestones. "So Chancellor, what can I do for yer? Tis an odd time to be visitin' the Sanctum." The gnome's rheumy eyes fixed on G'rok. "Well now, she's a big one, ain't she? I do like a big girl. What's yer name, dear?"

G'rok blushed. "G'ROK BIGGEST ORC IN HELDAN PORT. G'ROK SCARE MOST PEOPLE."

"Ah! Well most people are fools, ain't they?" The gnome took the orc's massive hand and kissed it gently. "Gefwyn, at yer service."

Raxo gave G'rok's ear a gentle tug. "I think he likes you."

The gnome started when he noticed Raxo sitting atop her shoulder. "The hell is that? How'd yer get yer little red monkey to talk?"

"Monkey?" said Raxo indignantly. "I'm an imp!"

Gefwyn stepped forward and examined the demon. "Well I'll be damned. Eyesight's not what it used to be. Put 'er here! Us small folk need to band together. Don't want yer gettin' the wrong impression of me." Raxo hesitantly jumped down and shook the proffered hand. The wizened gnome was all smiles now. "Anyone who travels in the company of the little folk is deservin' of my respect. So I ask again, Chancellor Marstarrow, why are yer here?"

"I am uniquely interested in how one enters the Sanctum," Marstarrow replied.

Gefwyn scratched his balding pate. "Well, through the front doors generally. I thought that'd be obvious."

"Let me clarify. How does a non-wizard enter the Sanctum?"

"Oh, that's more tricky then." The gnome leered at them suspiciously. "Why are yer wantin' to know, anyhow? Riddleston's given me clear instructions not to let on."

"Riddleston is gone," said Marstarrow, "and we are trying to discover why. Help us, and we may be able to bring the wizards back."

Gefwyn thought for a moment, then nodded. "All right. What do yer want to know?"

"How do *you* come and go from the Sanctum?"

"I use the front doors, like I said."

"Ah, so you can pass through the wards unmolested?" said Marstarrow.

"Yep!" said Gefwyn, with more than a touch of pride. "Ain't none besides the wizards who can claim that privilege. I've been workin' here for close on forty years now. They trust me."

"What exactly do you do for the wizards that requires you to leave the Sanctum?" asked Butterson.

"Oh, this and that. Order food from the markets, clean their hats and robes, fetch women every now and then." Marstarrow's eyebrow rose. "Er, fetch their newspapers," Gefwyn hurriedly corrected.

"Very well," said Marstarrow. "Would you be willing to help me test a theory?"

"If that's yer wish. Riddleston trusted yer, despite yer wantin' to take away all his magic. But if the Highest Hat trusted yer, that's good enough for me."

They returned to the grove of alders where the casket lay invitingly open. Marstarrow turned to Butterson. "May I request your assistance, one last time?"

"This is the last straw, Tiberion. If your theory fails, I'm going straight back to the Jackamoose and blacklisting you for life."

"As you wish."

Butterson forced his way into the claustrophobic space. The door snapped shut behind him.

"Are you ready?" came Marstarrow's muted voice. "Gefwyn will act as your observer."

"As I'll ever be."

"Proceed."

Butterson screwed his eyes shut and pulled the handle.

His insides flared with pain, and the feeling of revolving vertigo returned. Then, just as before, the sensations stopped altogether. He cautiously opened one eye. The vaulted hallway stretched before him, ending in a pair of massive obsidian doors. He waited, unwilling to open his other.

The gates slowly creaked open and a tiny figure entered the corridor.

"Ah, there yer are!" called Gefwyn. Butterson cautiously opened his other eye. Both feet were firmly planted on the marble floors of the corridor. "Welcome to the Occult Sanctum of Wizards, Master Butterson."

THE SANCTUM

Butterson looked about in amazement. He touched the foot of a nearby statue. It was cold and hard and entirely real.

"Be with yer in a moment," said Gefwyn. He retreated through the doors. Minutes passed as Butterson waited in awed silence. Then, with a faint *pop*, Marstarrow appeared beside him, paler than usual.

"Where are Raxo and G'rok?" asked Butterson.

The chancellor took several deep breaths before answering. "Standing watch outside. We should not need them, for the moment." Gefwyn returned and shuffled across the marble floors, his footsteps echoing throughout the vast hall. He grinned at Marstarrow. The chancellor was leaning against a statue, eyes closed, hair disheveled.

"I seem to recall that bein' quite the unpleasant experience," said the gnome. "Did yer prove yer theory?"

Marstarrow nodded and gingerly opened his eyes. "I believe so, yes." He swept back his hair and smoothed the front of his tunic. "When you acted as the observer, you were able to usher us inside the Sanctum, despite the wards. Just as I predicted."

"When I did what?" asked Gefwyn.

"Never mind. Now, I have a question of vital importance that you must answer truthfully. Did you let anyone inside the Sanctum in the days or weeks leading up to the wizards' disappearance?"

The gnome bristled indignantly. "What are yer implyin'? I've worked for the Sanctum for near my whole life and they *trust* me. I'd never do such a thing. Without permission from Riddleston, that is."

"You let us in," observed Butterson.

"Yeah, well, that's different, ain't it? The wizards are gone and Marstarrow says yer can help bring them back." A tear crept into the old gnome's eye. "I admit I don't know what to do now they've gone. How can I be a steward to the Sanctum if there's no Sanctum?"

"I believe you, Gefwyn," said Marstarrow, and patted him on the shoulder. "Your loyalty to the Sanctum stands beyond further question in my mind. And, if we are fortunate, the wizards may return in short time."

Gefwyn wiped his nose with a dusty sleeve. "What do yer care if they come back? Yer the one tryin' to stop them from usin' magic. Seems to me whoever did this did yer a favor."

"It was never my intention to strip the wizards of their power. Rather, I aimed to create a sustainable balance within the city, where industry and magic worked in unison. Sylvus agreed with my vision, to an extent. He could see the danger in relying too heavily on magic, though he was reluctant to accept restrictions to his power. It was my hope that we might come to an understanding, in the future. However, removing the wizards from my city altogether was *never* an option. As you can see, the resulting chaos has proven far too difficult to predict or control. No, I want the wizards returned, and the sooner the better."

"Alright then," said Gefwyn. "I suppose I believe yer in return. What's yer plan?"

"You wrote to me, Gefwyn. You said that something or someone had taken the wizards, yet you claimed impossibility. What did you mean, exactly?"

Gefwyn shrugged. "I meant nobody can get into the Sanctum, as yer just saw. Not without help, anyhow." Marstarrow's eyes glittered victoriously for the briefest of moments. "As for how I knew that somethin' took 'em, well... I need to show yer somethin'." The gnome snatched a candelabra from its sconce. The flames cast long shadows in the gloomy corridor that shifted like restless specters.

They followed Gefwyn out of the hall and into the depths of the Sanctum. The castle was a convoluted maze of corridors and passageways, brimming with libraries, dormitories, laboratories, classrooms, and a disproportionately large number of kitchens. The architecture was frightfully grandiose, and reminded Butterson of a theater about vampires he'd attended long ago. Gefwyn noticed his look of distaste and chuckled.

"Aye, the Sanctum is somethin' to behold. The wizards place great importance on appearance, yer see. They strive to maintain an aura of intrigue when dealin' with the common folk. Thinks it makes 'em more powerful. That's why yer see 'em wearin' their pointy hats and ridiculous robes. Well, that manner of thinkin' led to the mess yer see here. When they built the Sanctum, so long ago, they scoured Miz for the weird and arcane designs of the age. But, since wizards can't agree on anythin', all the styles sort of piled on top of one another. This here's the result." He patted the stone fondly.

"A heinous juxtaposition of egos," said Marstarrow. He examined a stone colonnade adorned with leering gargoyles and naked cherubs. "An immortal testament to the stubbornness of wizards."

"Aye," said Gefwyn happily. "She's home to me, but she's not for everyone. I was groomin' my niece to take over my duties as Steward, but she couldn't stand livin' in the Sanctum. Gone and left the city to live in the Wilds. Haven't heard from her in some time, come to think of it. I hope she's well. Faewyn was her name."

They delved deeper into the Sanctum. Here, the walls were lined with a multitude of treasures, sparkling behind glass cases. Gefwyn provided a running commentary as Butterson looked on with curiosity. "Ah, that there is the staff of Todolo the Vast." The steward pointed to a gnarled wooden stick. "'Twas said he could eat an entire feast in one go, all by himself."

"What's that got to do with his staff?" asked Butterson.

"He grew so fat he needed it to walk," said Gefwyn matter-of-factly. "I guess yer could call it more of a cane than a staff. Nevertheless, movin' on." They stopped before a pair of woolen underpants. The garment hung in suspension within the display, bobbing like a cork in water. "Them's the floatin' drawers of Teedle the Insipid. Wiz Teedle always envied witches' ability to fly with broomsticks. But due to certain, erm... *physiological* differences, Teedle had quite the uncomfortable time ridin' a broomstick. He thereby made it his life goal to give menfolk a means by which to fly themselves, yer know, gender equality and all that. But it turns out flyin' undies were quite difficult to clean, so his idea never did catch on."

Butterson made sure not to look too closely at the floating drawers. They continued along the procession of relics.

"And these here's the robes of Yundo the Pious," said Gefwyn solemnly. "Old Yundo opened a church for the poor and desperate, in the hopes of riddin' some of the violence from the capital. He donated all his money to the needy, hopin' to lead them down a path of virtue rather'n crime."

"What happened then?" said Butterson. The robes were pristinely white and practically glowed.

Gefwyn winced. "Erm, the buggers pooled their new-found coin and bought the church from him. Turned it into a brothel instead."

"I am amazed anyone would want to be remembered for such things," said Marstarrow dryly.

Gefwyn leered up at them. "The way wizards see it, tis better to be remembered for somethin' than to not be remembered at all. Now come along."

They followed the steward past rows of ancient artifacts and stopped before a vast archway. A sprawling auditorium rested beyond. The archway's wooden doors hung crookedly from their hinges, broken and charred. Marstarrow delicately traced a finger along the splintered wood.

"This here's how I knew somethin' took the wizards," said Gefwyn. "That room's where they hold council. They were set to pass judgment on yer propositions the day they vanished. All of 'em would've been gathered in that room for the vote, but somethin' got to 'em. Look what it did to the door. But that ain't all. There's more in here."

They stepped over pieces of ruined door and into the main aisle of the auditorium. Gefwyn stopped near a raised podium at the front of the room and pointed to the marble floor. "Now, yer tell me what that is. I've lived with the wizards near forty years. I've seen just about every type of magic there is to be seen, yet I ain't never seen nothin' like that."

A circle had been violently burned into the stone. It shone crimson in the darkness. Sparks crackled and fizzed along its boundary, and strange runes dotted its interior. Motes of light hung suspended in the air, winking in and out of existence.

Marstarrow knelt and examined the markings. He took special care to avoid the dancing flecks of light rising from the floor. "Most intriguing." He shifted his position to study each of the runes in turn. A length of parchment and a charcoal stub appeared from some recess of his cloak. He set to work furiously tracing the runes. When the last glyph had been copied, he stood and examined the parchment. "Tell me, Gefwyn, do you know of any volumes within the Sanctum that focus on the history of Mizian magic?"

The gnome snorted. "Where do yer think yer are, Chancellor? This here's the Sanctum. We've books on every manner of subject known or unknown to Miz."

"Very well," said Marstarrow, and tucked the parchment into his pocket. "Lead the way, if you would be so kind."

Several hours later, Butterson found his nose buried in a large tome of Mizian history, searching for clues as to the mysterious symbols. Marstarrow sat across from him, delicately thumbing through the pages of an ancient book. They were in the master library of the Sanctum, a room with high, rib-vaulted ceilings, and a veritable maze of wooden stacks and repositories scattered throughout its interior. Hundreds of thousands of leather-bound tomes and moth-eaten scrolls littered the shelves.

Butterson turned a well-thumbed page. This particular account wasn't as dry as the others had been. He read on with vague interest.

> 'The planet Miz spins energetically through the universe, choosing orbital patterns around the great star, Tanduil, of seemingly her own accord. As a result, Miz has historically experienced seasons of greatly varying lengths as she floats through the infinite vacuum of space at indeterminate speeds. The Great Famine of 1292 is attributed to Miz's cosmic trailblazing, and resulted in nigh two years of perpetual winter as our small planet had apparently forgotten to return to the warmth of Tanduil's solar embrace.

'The great minds of Miz convened to form the Esteemed Council of the Enigmatic Nether in an attempt to characterize the strange wanderings of our magical world. Their official statement, which was released several months later, had read:

> The Esteemed Council of the Enigmatic Nether has concluded that Miz does not adhere to the laws governing other like celestial bodies. The planet has neither a defined orbital plane nor a calculable pattern of orbital velocity. Insofar as the council can deduce, Miz is entirely unique, most likely due to the substantial aggregation of magic at her planetary core. Miz appears to relish the company of other celestial bodies and will actively alter its course to remain in close proximity to newfound "friends," for lack of a better word. The council has deduced that the Great Famine of 1292 was due to Miz pursuing the planet Rame for at least one fifth of its orbital cycle around Tanduil, before returning to a distance that relinquished the people of Miz from the clutch of the Great Winter. What this disconcerting information holds for the future inhabitants of Miz, only time will tell. It is the council's hope that Miz can satisfy its desire for newfound astrological companions while remaining within the habitable zone of Tanduil, less we, the People, are reduced to icicles.
> -Chief Councilor Sylvus Riddleston, ECotEN

'But Miz's lonely planetary consciousness appears to possess a maternal instinct toward the mystical inhabitants wandering her lands. Apart from the occasional misstep, she *remains near enough to Tanduil to prevent the iciclification of the living.'*

Marstarrow slammed his book shut in frustration, expelling a cloud of dust.

"Oi!" Gefwyn barked from somewhere amongst the stacks of books. "I told yer to stop doin' that!"

"*Apologies*," snapped Marstarrow. He tapped a finger on the table. "We are running out of time."

Butterson glanced through the open window. Tanduil had just begun to crest the eastern walls of the capital.

"Here," said Gefwyn. He emerged from the stacks with an armful of books. "Try these. They're the oldest I got."

Marstarrow eagerly snatched a book from the pile and flicked through the pages. With a sniff he set it aside and grabbed another.

Butterson stretched. He was exhausted, and the words on the pages were beginning to blur together. "Maybe we should call it a night, Tiberion." He yawned. "We can always return for another go."

Marstarrow deftly unfurled a scroll and squinted at its contents. "Another chance may never present itself, Mord. I took great lengths to conceal my coming here. If the Heads of House learn that I have visited the Sanctum, they will become suspicious and defensive. I must keep them in dark if my plan is to succeed."

Butterson stifled another yawn. "What exactly is your plan?"

"That is a discussion for another time," said Marstarrow stiffly.

Butterson shrugged and resumed leafing through his tome. There was nothing on the runes, or the strange circle he had seen etched into the auditorium's floor. His attention strayed to Marstarrow's face, just visible over the tops of the pages, pinched in frustration. The chancellor sighed and picked up yet another book. His gray eyes flicked from page to page. Then, he paused, and his expression changed for the briefest of moments. He read the page once, twice, and then a third time.

Butterson hastily dropped his gaze as Marstarrow slammed the book shut and rose from his chair. "Perhaps you are right, Mord. It will be impossible to sieve through the Sanctum's resources in one night, so let us return to our companions. I am sure they are eager to learn what we have discovered. Gefwyn, if you would be so kind as to guide us back to the Sanctum's gates? Your help tonight has been most appreciated."

They exited the Sanctum as pale fingers of dawn crept into the sky. Gefwyn shook their hands and paused before G'rok. "Well, my dear, I'm afraid I must return to the Sanctum."

A tear rolled down her face. "WILL G'ROK SEE LITTLE BEARDED MAN AGAIN?"

Gefwyn swept his hand dramatically over his breast and beamed up at her. "Oh yes, yer can be sure of that. I'd be a fool to let somethin' as large and lovely as you slip through my fingers, and I'm no fool."

G'rok's tusks framed her happy smile. "G'ROK WOULD LIKE THAT."

Then Gefwyn trundled back up the worn cobbles, waved farewell, and the Sanctum's gates closed behind him. Marstarrow turned to Butterson. "I thank you all for helping me. In return for your assistance, I shall uphold my end of the accord."

Butterson folded his arms. "When?"

"Soon, but I need more time to prepare." Marstarrow stepped closer and lowered his voice. "Tonight was a success, Mord. We proved that whomever is responsible for the wizards' abduction received help in entering the Sanctum."

"True," said Butterson carefully, "though I still wonder about that symbol. And those strange runes." He studied

Marstarrow's face from the corner of his eye. "What terrible magic could have wrought such markings?"

The chancellor's expression remained inscrutable. "A mystery that shall hopefully unravel with time. Now, I must return to the keep before my absence is noted. Stay vigilant Mord. I will be in touch shortly." He gave a curt nod and disappeared behind the Sanctum.

A great weariness descended on Butterson's shoulders as he watched the chancellor depart. He felt sapped of energy, as though he had walked a great distance bearing a heavy pack.

Raxo stretched his arms. "I say we hit the Jackamoose and grab a pint and a quick nap. It'll be openin' time, soon enough."

"Fine," said Butterson absent-mindedly.

Raxo scuttled up to G'rok's shoulder. "What's up, Boss?"

Butterson rubbed his eyes with the heels of his palms. "Marstarrow still doesn't trust us. He's hiding something, after everything we did for him. After we placed *our* trust in him, he..." He trailed off and kicked despondently at the grass. "He lied to us."

The demon shrugged. "He's always hidin' somethin' from someone. What did you expect from a man like that?"

"I don't know, Raxo, just... more." Butterson turned to the east and let the kiss of dawn warm his face. He closed his eyes and breathed deeply. "But Marstarrow knows what happened to the wizards, and he chose not to tell us."

RIDDLESTON IN THE DARK

Vandra eased along a rough-hewn stairwell. It dripped in the dank, still air. She delved deeper into the mountain, through twisting passageways, abandoned tunnels, and great caverns with glittering stalactites. It grew colder as she went, and her breath began to crystallize in front of her. The darkness was almost complete now, apart from scattered patches of mushroom that exuded a pale green glow throughout the subterranean labyrinth.

She finally halted before a heavy door, riveted with iron struts. She twitched a finger and sent a single spark of crimson magic into the lock. The door swung inwards with a faint *click*.

The protests began immediately.

"You can't keep us down here, witch! It's frigid! At least give me a ruddy blanket!"

"Your stomach keeps *you* warm. I, on the other hand, am in desperate need of food."

"Ha! You've never been in desperate need of anything, except a slap upside your fat head."

"Borneus, if I wasn't in this cage I'd have it out with you, once and for all!"

"Well you are in a cage, so suck an egg."

Vandra ground her teeth. The wizards of Heldan Port hung before her in cylindrical metal cages fastened to the chiseled ceiling. The bickering continued with a vengeance. Their prolonged imprisonment had done nothing to quell their petulance. "Silence!" she shouted, and brought the magic to life along her arm. The wizards fell hurriedly quiet. She had quickly discovered that they only responded to threats of violence. She allowed the magic to subside. "Thank you. Now, it's time to continue our work. Any volunteers for today?" She strode along the length of cages, staring at each wizard in turn. They flinched at her presence and refused to meet her eye. "How disappointing." She drew up before the final enclosure. "I expected more from your men, *Highest Hat*."

Sylvus Riddleston glared down at her. His flowing white beard was disheveled and his robes were caked with grime. "I don't know what you hope to achieve by all of this, but we won't help you."

"Oh you undoubtedly will," said Vandra, with a knowing smile. "That fact is beyond your control. Just look at the progress we've already made together."

"The progress we've made? You use us as animals for your experiments, wretched woman! Nothing more."

Vandra's smile grew sweeter. "Everything would be simpler if you stopped resisting, Sylvus." Her smile turned to a sultry pout. "Instead, you force my hand. What a shame." She moved to unlock Riddleston's cage, but paused at a throbbing vibration against her chest. With a twinge of unease, she withdrew a triangular amulet from within her robes. It pulsated gently in her hand. Three sparkling rubies were inlaid at its vertices, and a large black opal rested at its center. The leftmost ruby was glowing in accordance with the vibrations. She relaxed. It was only Lentarro, signaling for her to meet. She stowed the amulet and turned back to Riddleston. "I'll return momentarily. Don't get too comfortable."

Riddleston jutted out his beard. "Wouldn't dream of it."

She closed her eyes and left the hall in a rush of power. Seven more times she leapt, and then the tree with the golden apples was before her. Lentarro leaned against its trunk. His tattooed hand rested against a rune carved into its bark. A curl of smoke rose from the glyph. As he stepped away from the tree, the amulet's vibrations ceased.

Vandra wiped a droplet of sweat from her nose and straightened. "I trust you were successful in dealing with the Ardas."

Lentarro avoided her eye. "I was not." An icy silence spread over the hill. "Please understand, Vandra. I would have stopped them, but they weren't alone. You didn't tell me there would be warriors from Heldan Port. Eotan Arda was in my grasp, but-"

"But you let him escape?" she yelled. Golden apples showered down around them. Lentarro flinched and covered his head. "I don't know why I trusted you in the first place, even with something so simple!"

"You didn't tell me about the others!" he whined. "There were *hundreds* of soldiers on horseback. We stood no chance, Vandra. See reason!"

"You claim to know everything that happens in your lands, yet a legion on horseback manages to surprise you?"

The elf's nose was almost scraping the ground now, his palms outstretched. "My attention was entirely focused on the Ardas, Vandra, as you instructed. How was I to expect an army coming to their aid?"

"You mean your obsession with vengeance made you careless."

"I will make this right," he groveled. "The Ardas ride for the Waypoint. I'll gather my Oethyr and slit their throats while they sleep."

Vandra laughed derisively. "Attack them while they're guests of the Waypoint? You're a bigger fool than I imagined. You know the rules that govern that place as well as I. No, I'll clean up this mess myself. *You* will ready your people and make for the Canyonlands. The plan remains the same. For now." She lowered her voice and narrowed her eyes. "You have failed me for the last time, Lentarro. Take care that it doesn't happen again."

The elf bowed and clasped his hands together, as if in prayer. "It won't. Thank you, Vandra." He slunk away and hurriedly vanished between the trees.

Vandra stroked the edges of the amulet, unseeing. Her finger paused at the uppermost ruby. The Heads of House had failed to warn her of this band of warriors. They would pay for their negligence. But now was not the time. Her finger moved to the ruby embedded in the amulet's right corner. Her contact in Dinh should be warned of the Ardas' approach. Though if she could stop the brothers herself, the problem would resolve itself. No need for undue concern. Finally, the tip of her finger hovered over the opal at the amulet's center. Its vitreous surface winked up at her, simultaneously foreboding and enticing. She could contact *him*. The brothers were proving more difficult than expected, and her plan was so close to fruition. Perhaps he could be convinced to intervene...

She stuffed the amulet into her robes with a shake of her head. She would handle the situation herself, as she always did. But to do so, she would need to finalize her work with the wizards. With a *crack*, she disappeared from the Wilds.

Moments later, she was back within the confines of the dungeon. The cages creaked and swayed with her sudden arrival. She stared up at Riddleston. "Unfortunately for you, we're out of time." Her voice echoed through the narrow chamber. "Until now, I have been patient with your obstinacy. Understanding, even, considering the circumstances. But no longer. You will work with me, of your own accord, or I will force your cooperation. What is your answer?"

Riddleston glared down at her. "Borneus, what's that saying you're so fond of?"

"I'd sooner diddle a dragon?"

"No, no, the other one."

"Lick my boot straps?"

"No, the one that earned you latrine duty last month."

"Go boil your head, you sorry excuse for a troll?"

Riddleston snapped his fingers. "That's the one!" He smirked down at her. "Borneus has such a way with words, I find."

"Indeed." Crimson sparks danced around her fingers. "Though I wonder if you'll smile when I'm finished with you."

TO THE WAYPOINT

Sten awoke to the sounds of running water, birdsong, and laughter. His uncles sat by a crackling fire, surrounded by the Shrikes in various states of repose. He chose a seat beside Ineza, and grinned when she shifted to make room.

"And then the great undead bastard caught me in the chest!" roared the Marshal, and the Shrikes burst into laughter. "Look, I've got the marks to prove it." He opened his tunic, exposing an extremely hairy chest. An ugly purple and green bruise covered his entire sternum, ending near his clavicle.

Finlan whistled in appreciation. "That's quite the wound, Arda!"

"Aye, it's a good thing you were wearing that golden armor of yours," said Tryo. His mellifluous voice was full of good humor, and his dark eyes twinkled.

Culyan chuckled. "Don't be poking fun of my armor, now. I've been told it brings out the color of my eyes." He batted his lashes to the Shrikes' amusement.

"My brother is vainglorious, to say the least," said Eotan dryly. "He firmly believes that the makings of a true hero are shiny armor, bulging muscles, and a propensity to hit things before thinking. He listened to far too many nonsensical tales as a child."

Culyan slugged Eotan on the shoulder and sent him sprawling. "You're just jealous, pup! I can't help that I was born bigger than most, with a keen eye for pretty things." He winked at them. "I just happened to pick up that hero stuff along the way."

Eotan threw a stone and turned to Captain Whitney. "So, Tiberion gave you a Follower and bade you to track us through the Wilds. I should have known he would establish a redundancy plan. Where is the Follower's beacon?"

Whitney shrugged, though a smug expression twitched his mustache. "Apparently the chancellor hid it on you during your visit to the capital. Were you not aware, Arda?"

Eotan patted down his cloak and then the pockets of his tunic. With a faint smile, he pulled a small, oval stone from his breast pocket. A vivid blue light seeped from tiny holes scattered across its surface. "Clever. Most clever." He returned the stone to his pocket. "I'll keep this. Perhaps it will be of use in the days to come."

"Why didn't you lot just ride with us from Heldan Port in the first place?" asked Culyan. He slid a dripping strip of bacon from the fire and popped it into his mouth. Manye giggled.

"The chancellor believed you would refuse our escort," said Whitney. "You were quite angry with him, at the time of your departure." Eotan and Culyan exchanged a look and shrugged. Whitney nodded and stroked his chin. "Although I have a theory of my own. I believe the chancellor sought to divide his resources, to increase the likelihood of his message reaching Dinh. Should you fail to overcome the Wilds, there was the slightest chance of our succeeding in your stead. Yet if we had traveled together, our fates would be shared." He twirled his mustache thoughtfully. "That's just a theory, of course. The chancellor rarely speaks his mind."

"I suppose there's sense in that," said Two. He took a long drag from his pipe and blew a ring of smoke into the air.

Eotan stood and donned his black cloak. "Aye, I suppose there is. We are indebted to you and your Shrikes, at any rate. Though perhaps the comforts of our next destination will repay the, *ahem*, favorable timing of your arrival."

"Where are we headed?" said Ineza.

"To the Waypoint. We'll be safe there. And Dinh isn't far beyond."

They followed Eotan through the ancient, black forest. The close-set trees were draped with moss and knotted with age, huddled together like some silent gathering of verdant-bearded monks. Sten borrowed Corporal Hemmie's horse and rode beside Ineza. The gnome floated happily alongside the dwarves, deeply engrossed in a game of Thropple. The Shrikes broke into song as they picked their way along. Even Whitney joined in to serenade the woodlands with off-key ballads of glory and honor. Sten and Ineza talked and laughed in the summer heat, and for the first time since leaving Heldan Port, Sten felt entirely at ease in the Wilds.

Tanduil's light was just beginning to sink below the ragged horizon when Eotan called the company to a halt. They rested at the lip of a sloping valley. A wide river cut its way through its center, sparkling like woven gemstones. A tiny log cottage perched on its banks, sheltered by a grove of spruce trees. Soft light spilled from its windows, and a lazy column of smoke rose from its chimney. Wildflowers stirred in the summer breeze. The valley felt warm and welcoming in the serenity of twilight.

Culyan patted Kipto's neck. "There lies the Waypoint. There isn't a more beautiful sight in all the Wilds, I promise you. Through those doors are warm beds, delicious food, good company, and the finest of ales." He sighed nostalgically. "I've missed such adventures."

They descended into the valley single file. When they reached the sprawling, grassy meadows, they let the horses run free, to Whitney's discomfort.

"They're safe here," assured Eotan. Kipto and Lilenti cantered away, nickering happily. "Anyone foolish enough to attack us here will invoke the wrath of its proprietor."

Whitney shifted beneath the weight of his saddle and bags. "It doesn't look like much."

"The Waypoint, itself, doesn't afford us protection," said Eotan.

"The old lady who runs it does," said Culyan. "She's terrifyingly unique, to say the least." He glared suspiciously at the trees, as if they might be listening. "There are two rules here, and they must be followed without exception. Firstly, any and all are welcome to stay at the Waypoint, no matter the person or the circumstance. This place has become a haven for the troubled, the fearful, and the downtrodden. Everyone is safe within the Waypoint."

"Why is that?" asked Sten.

"Because the Grandmother protects us all," said Eotan simply.

Sten nodded warily. "And what's the second?"

"Violence is strictly forbidden," said Two. "We've heard stories of those who ignored this rule, and let me assure you: some manners of death are far preferable to others."

Ineza smiled cheerfully. "This place sounds downright lovely if you ask me. Anyhoo, I'm famished. I say we find some of that wonderful food you were talking about, eh, Marshal?"

"You're a woman after my own heart, Ghet," said Culyan. He offered his arm. "Shall we?" She accepted it with a laugh.

They approached the cottage and knocked on the door. It opened with a creak. Two yellow eyes peered out at them.

"What is your business at the Waypoint, lords and ladies?" inquired a melodious voice.

"Can it Edelwing, we know you've been following us from the Gateway," said Culyan. "And we know you've spent your time betting on our lives with rabbits. Manye told us."

"What is this rudeness from the Marshall?" asked another voice, equally elegant but slightly higher pitched. Another pair of eyes joined the first. They rotated strangely in the darkness, as if pinioned to a rotating axle. The eyes unnerved Sten. They certainly weren't human.

With a flutter of wings, two owls flew from the open door. The smaller of the two, a speckled pigmy, landed on Sten's shoulder and glared up at him through feathered brows. "You can talk?" he asked incredulously.

"Of course my boy, what did you expect?" scoffed the tiny owl. "The gift of tongues is one of many such blessings the Grandmother has bestowed upon us. But forgive me, where are my manners? I am the mighty Stonetalon, of course, and my companion is called Edelwing." The little bird gestured to a tawny barn owl. The raptor had taken residence on Manye's shoulder. Its eyes were closed in bliss as the elf stroked its beak. "We are the stewards of the Grandmother," continued Stonetalon. "She is greatly interested in your journey and wishes to speak with you. Proceed, if you please." Stonetalon gestured to the door and Sten cautiously stepped over the threshold.

The wooden hall that stretched before him was undeniably, impossibly larger than the exterior of the cabin. A wide common room rested beyond the hall, flanked by a series of corridors. Their lengths disappeared into the dim light. "How is this possible?" Sten asked in amazement. "This place is huge!"

Eotan gestured to the extended hall. "This is the *real* Waypoint. Stonetalon, please give my nephew and our companions a tour as we get situated. And Edelwing, if you'd be so kind as to let the Grandmother know of our arrival?"

Sten was captivated by the elegance of the Waypoint. The walls were constructed from polished lengths of stained oak, maple, and chestnut. The floors, or lack thereof, were simple layers of loam. Moss and ferns sprung delightfully under his boots. Trees sprouted throughout the lodge, some mere saplings. They showered the halls in a perpetual cascade of golden leaves. Others had grown so large as to become permanent fixtures of the architecture. Furniture was scattered haphazardly, although not unpleasantly, about the rooms. There were armchairs, cots, tables, and hammocks. A particularly handsome rocking chair rested near a broad stone hearth.

Stonetalon led Sten and the Shrikes deeper into the Waypoint. The common area split into three wings of chambers. Muddy boots rested outside several of the rooms, and stained cloaks hung from hooks set into the doors. They exited the corridor and passed a small kitchen. Fruits and grains and vegetables hung from the rafters to dry, and an inset pantry overflowed with spices. The delicious aromas set Sten's mouth watering.

He found the Bearded Eight and his uncles in the common area. The dwarves lounged on the array of furniture, quietly tuning their instruments. Culyan was attempting to squash his bulk into one of the armchairs. Eotan and Manye sat by a window, toying with a cluster of twigs and golden leaves. The Shrikes quickly dispersed throughout the room and sighed contentedly when they sank into the feather-stuffed cots lining the walls. Ineza took Sten by the hand and guided him to a bench next to the fire. She rested her head on his shoulder as the dwarves began to play. The melody was hauntingly beautiful.

Edelwing fluttered onto the hearth. The owl cleared his throat and turned to address the company. "It is my great privilege to introduce the Matriarch of the Waypoint. Please welcome, Grandmother Morroza."

An old woman shuffled into the room, bent double with age. She wore a flowery nightgown and a vividly pink apron. A thick pair of spectacles hung from her neck. She surveyed the group with fiery eyes, and her gaze came to rest on Sten.

"Didn't your parents teach you any manners, young man?" Her voice was as dry and crisp as autumn leaves. "Help an old woman to her seat." Sten jumped to his feet and guided the woman to the elegant rocking chair next to the fire. She patted his arm. "My thanks, dear. Now comb that unruly hair of yours and fetch my blanket." She pointed a gnarled finger at Culyan. "As for you, Marshal of the Wilds, if you break another of my chairs I'll send you into the cold of night with naught for supper."

Culyan shifted uncomfortably and his chair screeched in protest. "Yes, ma'am."

Eotan smirked. "It's always refreshing to see my proud brother chastised so."

"Careful Eotan Arda," said the woman. She looked at Eotan over the tops of her spectacles. "I think I've caught a whiff of dog just now. Shall I draw you a bath?" She clapped her hands together. "Introductions are in order. I see we have new guests with us this evening! How exciting. You three." She pointed to Sten, Manye, and Whitney. "Come closer, please. Let me have a look at you."

They tentatively approached the old woman. She raised her massive spectacles. With the lenses in place, she bore a striking semblance to an apron-wearing insect. "The Lord of House Bregon, the Oethyr elf Manye, and a Captain of Heldan Port arrive on my doorstep. What an unlikely trio to accompany the Brothers Arda on their quest. How interesting... I wonder why you've chosen to adopt their hardships as your own?" Her magnified eyes swiveled to Whitney.

"I'm under orders to see the Brothers Arda safely to Dinh," he said. He stood tall in the orange glow of the fire.

The Grandmother frowned, and her features rearranged into a maze of wrinkles. "I see. Tell me, Captain, are you always so inclined to let others dictate your actions?"

He reddened. "If I trust in their orders."

She leaned back in the great armchair and tented her fingers. "So it is a matter of loyalty, then. Of *honor*."

"I suppose," he replied carefully.

She nodded sagely. "Valuable and noble qualities, to be sure. Yet I wonder... Are you the captain, or the sword?"

Whitney's mouth quirked and he shook his head. "I'm not sure I take your meaning, ma'am."

Her eyes glittered behind her spectacles. "It is a simple question of autonomy, Captain. Think on it. And as you set out on your path for glory, remember that history is written at a cost. Oftentimes it is those closest to you that feel the repercussions of your aspirations."

He opened his mouth as if to argue, but then bowed stiffly. "Thank you, ma'am."

Morroza beckoned for Manye to come closer. "Why have you come, my dear?"

"I wanted to save my home. And my family."

"And what a virtuous young thing you are," said Morroza, with an approving smile. "Though heed my warning." The flames in the hearth were abruptly snuffed out and the Waypoint was plunged into darkness. Wind howled down the chimney and dried leaves rustled over the floor. Morroza's voice was a whisper. "A path of noble intentions, while clear in the light of day, may fade in the dead of night." Her eyes shone like twin embers as she leaned forward. "Stay to your path, dear, no matter what beckons from the shadows. No matter how dire the circumstance."

The flames sprang back to life and the winds quieted.

Manye nodded warily and looked to Eotan. His knuckles were white, his face a pale mask. The old woman gave her arm an affectionate squeeze, then turned to Sten. His heart quickened.

"And finally we come to the Arda who didn't know he was an Arda. Why are you here?"

Sten thought for a moment. He considered telling the old woman of his upbringing, of his confinement within the capital's walls, of his dreams of exploration. He considered telling her of his mother, and whispered stories of grand adventures beneath the stars. He considered the surge of pride evoked by his uncles' company and their relation. But instead, he crossed his hands behind his back and waited in respectful silence. These felt like the considerations of a child, and he would not admit to them in front of the others. A log shifted and the fire crackled with a plume of sparks.

Morroza weighed him with her eyes. "I take it from Master Bregon's reluctance to speak that he has a great deal of uncertainty on the matter." Then her expression softened, and she took Sten's hand. "Don't worry, dear. Who knows what you'll discover about yourself in the times to come?"

Sten broke into a smile. "Well I am certain of one thing."

"And what is that?"

"I'd love a bite of whatever's cooking. It smells delightful."

"Ooh I like this one," cackled the old woman. "He has spirit! But mind your manners. Patience is a virtue, after all." She clapped her hands together. "The companions of the Brothers Arda are welcome to stay at the Waypoint for as long as necessary. Though I anticipate your visit to be brief, knowing you lot. Dinner shall arrive presently, and breakfast is served at dawn." Her voice took on a sharper edge. "I remind you that hostility amongst guests is strictly forbidden. Ignore my rules and suffer the consequences." Her smile returned. "Now, I am off to bed. I hope to see you all bright and early. Goodnight."

The rocking chair rose from the ground. Then, with a faint *hummmm*, it zoomed down a hallway and Grandmother Morroza disappeared into the depths of the Waypoint.

Sten chose a seat next to Two. "Weird old bat."

"Aye, but this place is a godsend," said the dwarf. He took a long drink of ale, wiped foam from his mustache, and burped. "Begging your pardon, lad. But I can't tell you the number of times this sanctuary has saved us from the Wilds." They lapsed into silence, watching as Eotan helped Manye construct a crown from the twigs and leaves.

"They're very close, aren't they?" said Sten.

"Aye. He and Manye are kindred spirits." The elf's eyes glittered in the firelight as Eotan gently placed the crown upon her head.

"What happened to them?" asked Sten, after a spell.

A shadow passed over Two's face. "I'm not sure it's my place to say, lad." He took another drink, conflicting emotions tugging at his mouth. Finally, he sighed. "But perhaps it's best you learned the truth. You are family, after all." The dwarf reclined in his chair and studied the ceiling. "I suppose it began with your mother's passing. Aella and Eotan were terribly close, and her death sent him down a dark and dangerous path. I believe she took a part of his mind with her. After a time he stopped speaking. He would leave the Gateway for days on end, never saying where he had gone or what he had done. And then, one day, he disappeared entirely. Vanished into the Wilds. He returned to our camp months later, with a young elf as his ward."

Sten stared at Manye. She chatted happily with Ineza, Finlan, and Tryo, sharing her makeshift crown.

"Aye," said Two. "Eotan was on the verge of losing his sanity when she found him. During his wanderings, he crossed into the Oethyrlands." The dwarf looked meaningfully at Sten over the lip of his tankard. "You've seen how the Oethyr welcome outsiders, and Eotan was half-crazed at that. Manye managed to stay her father's wrath, and promised to care for this mad intruder. But when her powers failed to cleanse the sickness and grief from his mind, she resorted to the sacred magic of her people." The dwarf shook his head and smiled sadly. "Eotan's mind was ill-prepared to control such a wondrous and terrible gift."

Sten's gaze drifted to the scar on Manye's leg. Studying it more carefully, he realized that the jagged arch that traced up and around her calf bore teeth marks.

"Now you see the truth," said Two quietly. "I believe they feel responsible for one another. Manye freed Eotan's mind from the darkness, and in return, he will do anything to protect her." The dwarf stood suddenly and swiped a tankard from a passing Shrike. He shoved it into Sten's hands, ignoring the Shrike's grumbled misgivings. "Come, lad! Let us talk of gladder things! We shall rest in the Waypoint another day before continuing to Dinh. Tonight should be a night of celebration!"

"I don't feel much like celebrating," Sten said moodily. "Not after what you've just told me. Not after Morozza's interrogation. All of you are integral to this company and then there's me, along for the ride. I'm a liability that's tolerated because I'm family. Eotan has enough to worry about without looking after me." Manye's scar shone dimly in the firelight.

Two snorted scornfully. "Nonsense, lad. You're an Arda, and no Arda in the history of Ardas has been a liability. As my great-uncle, the traveling merchant One Hundred and Thirty-Two once said, 'Losing your way can be its own reward'. You'll find your place yet."

Sten nodded, feeling somewhat better. "What happened to your uncle?"

Two grimaced. "Well, if you must know, he wandered from a trail through the Frozen Steppes. Wound up lost and froze to death."

Sten slumped into his chair. "That's reassuring."

After some coaxing from Two and the others, Sten joined the company as they ate, drank, and laughed into the early hours of morning. The dwarves played a lively tune and sent a cascade of golden leaves swirling about the room in elegant patterns. Ineza pulled Sten to his feet. Surrounded by the Shrike's laughter, they danced beneath the leaves. Manye was hoisted onto Culyan's shoulders, still wearing her crown. She giggled and spread her arms as the Marshal twirled about the room. Soon, the entire company was dancing about the common room, and Sten's previous misgivings were happily forgotten.

Only Eotan and Whitney stayed apart from the festivities. As the night wore on, members of the company drifted off to bed, one by one. But the Wolf and the captain stayed awake long into the morning, lost in their thoughts, and the coals turned to ash and the somber light of dawn crept over the valley.

AN UNWELCOME GUEST

Roars of anger tore Sten from his slumber. He leapt from his cot, grabbed his bow, and nocked an arrow. Cautiously, he eased open his door to peer into the hallway. Two dwarves sprinted past, eyes wide with terror. He thought it was Five and Six, but couldn't be certain in the dim light. Resounding booms shook the hall, coming from the depths of the Waypoint. He took a deep breath and kicked the door open, arrow drawn.

"Oi, watch where you're pointing that thing and get out of my way!" A half-naked Culyan thundered past, desperately clutching a hand towel to his midriff. "I swear, on my axe, I'll squeeze the life from those two!" He disappeared around the corner, cursing fitfully.

Thoroughly confused, Sten made his way to the common room. He found Eotan, Manye, and the rest of the Bearded Eight seated at a great banquet table. Its surface was invisible under plates of food. There were heaping bowls of apples and pears and strawberries, deep troughs of fried potatoes and onions, mounds of sizzling bacon and sausage, platters of warm breads and cheeses and tomatoes, a mountain of fluffy eggs, and pitchers of dark beer. The Shrikes sat along the benches, talking amiably amongst themselves.

"Good morning, lad!" called Two. The dwarf had taken a considerable liking to Sten after the previous night's revelries. Sten joined him and was rewarded with a plateful of food from Ineza. He grabbed a scone slathered in honey and crammed it into his mouth, scowling ferociously. She laughed and passed him another.

Culyan reappeared from a side corridor, still clasping the tiny towel about his waist. "Where'd they go?"

The Shrikes whistled and hooted at the sight. "Who?" called Finlan.

"Five and Six! I'll strangle them with their own beards when I catch them." Culyan sighed with frustration and slammed onto the bench next to Sten.

"Erm, uncle..."

"What? Oh, right, sorry about that." Culyan hastily rearranged the towel. "Here, pass me one of those rashers of bacon."

Sten obliged, taking a dripping piece for himself. "What's all the fuss about?"

"The dwarves were assisting my brother while he prepared for his tryst," said Eotan, with a smirk. Dark circles hung beneath his eyes, but his mood had improved.

"Fleas take you," grumbled Culyan, and tore into a mound of food. "And it's not a tryst," he said between mouthfuls. "I just need to clean up before we reach Dinh. I shave my damned beard and those little bastards sing it back thicker than ever."

"I think your beard is rather fetching, in a barbaric sort of way," said Ineza. "Why shave it?"

"The leader of Dinh's magi is an old acquaintance," said Two.

Culyan flushed and buried his face in his plate. "That damned woman stole my axe."

Two chortled and poured a foaming tankard of beer. "And you fell in love with her." He ducked the apple that came whistling at his head.

Grandmother Morroza shuffled into the common room, Five and Six in tow. "What is all this commotion?" she demanded. "I've had guests complaining about you lot."

"Just a spot of fun, ma'am," said Eotan. "We meant no disrespect. The dwarves were helping Culyan prepare for his reunion with Jaya."

Morroza grinned and waggled her eyebrows at Culyan. "Ah, I see now. J.J. is quite the lovely young thing, isn't she? Tell me, Culyan Arda, do you plan on impressing her by appearing as some derelict vagabond? No offense, dear, but you could use a bath."

"Offense taken," Culyan huffed. "For your information, I've been trying to shave my beard all morning, but those two," he pointed at Five and Six, who were attempting to sidle away from the table, "seem to think it great sport to harass me."

"Oh leave the poor man in peace, you confounded dwarves," said Morroza. "Gods know he needs all the help he can get with that fine young woman. She deserves far better than you, and offense meant this time." She considered him through the huge spectacles. "Though perhaps you look better with that great, big, bushy thing covering your face. Do yourself a favor and keep it."

After taking their breakfast, the company ventured outside. It was a pristine summer day and the warmth of Tanduil had already spread through the valley. The leaves in the orchard stirred gently in the wind, just now beginning to show the tinges of autumn.

With whoops of joy, the Shrikes undressed to their small clothes and dove into the river. Sten, Culyan and the dwarves followed, laughing as they plunged into the crystal-clear depths. Even Eotan joined in the festivities, changing into the golden wolf before launching himself into the water with a mighty howl.

Manye talked animatedly with Stonetalon and Edelwing on the bank of the river. Whitney rested beside her, whittling a stick, his expression dour. The Shrikes called for him to join them, but he curtly refused. Ineza exchanged a mischievous grin with Sten, and dashed the frigid water at her captain. He cursed and jumped to his feet, glowering disapprovingly. But then, with a resigned shake of his head, he shed his sopping clothes and leapt into the water. Eventually, the company dispersed, free to pursue their own desires in their time of rest.

Ineza lay beside Sten in a vast field filigreed with wildflowers. There were noble harebells, vibrant prairie-fire, elegant paintbrushes, stalwart beargrass, and great swaths of royal lupine. Grasses rustled and bees droned as they went diligently about their business. She laughed when he pointed to imagined creatures emerging from the wisps of cloud overhead.

Suddenly, she turned to him and kissed him on the cheek. His feigned astonishment earned him a punch in the sternum. And then she was on her feet, bounding away across the valley, her fingers brushing the tips of the grass. He hurried after her, unable to contain his smile.

The light of Tanduil faded from the valley. Strangers began to file through the Waypoint. Sten reclined beside Two in one of the overstuffed armchairs by the fire. Elves, dwarves, and gnomes trickled in and out, but also a host of beings that he'd never before encountered. A towering orc limped past them, stooped with age. Puckered scars crisscrossed his back and arms, gleaming dully in the firelight. He nodded politely and continued morosely on his way. A pair of goblins entered next, and then a werewolf, and then a trio of vampires. They congregated away from the fire, chatting contentedly in the gloom. An opaque woman drifted past, her eyes pale and lost.

"Is that a banshee?" Sten whispered. Two nodded uneasily.

There came fairies and sprites, warlocks and satyrs, and even a centaur munching happily on a carrot. Some guests would stop and chat with Sten and the dwarves, or else sit amongst the Shrikes to swap stories. Others ignored them altogether and continued silently about their business. But everyone talked with Grandmother Morroza. The old woman zoomed about in her rocking chair, offering sage advice to every person that entered the Waypoint.

Sten looked on in amazement. "I've never seen so many different types of people in one place. And they all love her."

"Aye, lad," said Two. "There are many who call the Waypoint and the Wilds their home. You'd never know how many different creatures exist on Miz until you step foot outside the capital. Humans have a knack for distancing themselves from the weird."

A moss-covered troll lumbered through the common room, a yellow buttercup tucked behind its stony ear. "It's a shame," said Sten sadly.

"That it is. You have to escape from the cities to truly experience the wonders that Miz has to offer. I wish more people would do so. This world would be a far better place if more would look beyond themselves for even a day."

The door to the Waypoint swung open and a raven-haired woman entered the hall. She chose an empty chair, far from the other guests, and scanned the assemblage through heavily lidded eyes. She exchanged a few, hushed words with the Grandmother. Sten met her gaze, for the briefest of moments, and then looked away. Her unflinching stare unnerved him.

The common room slowly emptied as the Shrikes and the patrons of the Waypoint stumbled to their chambers. Captain

Whitney and the brothers stood over a worn map, conversing quietly. One had fallen asleep in his armchair and was snoring fitfully. His plaited beard rose and fell with each thunderous breath. Two tinkered with his Boomstick, attempting to repair the damage.

Sten covered One with a blanket and beckoned to Ineza. She crept up beside him, taking care not to disturb the slumbering dwarf. Eotan stabbed his finger onto the map. "We'll cross the River Dah here. There's a natural bridge that spans the canyon. Hopefully it hasn't been washed out by the spring storms."

"It will support our numbers?" said Whitney.

"If we cross one or two at a time. The alternative is to ride forty miles south, and cross here, where the walls of the canyons are shallow. But the extra distance might prove too dangerous. I'm not sure how far the mist has spread in those parts."

"Once we're clear from the canyon it's a flat ride to Dinh," said Culyan. "We'll be in the city before nightfall."

"Oh, I wouldn't be too certain of that," said a cool voice behind them. Sten turned to see the raven-haired woman watching them. His discomfort returned. She smiled at them self-assuredly.

"Pardon my saying, miss, but this is none of your business," said Whitney icily.

"Isn't it?" She rose to her feet. "I'm surprised at your willingness to discuss such plans in the open." She stretched nonchalantly and cocked her head.

"What is your name?" said Eotan.

"I'm called Vandra," she replied, with a pleasant smile. "Might I say that it's an honor to finally meet the Brothers Arda in person?" Whitney hurriedly flipped the map. Vandra flicked her dark eyes to the captain. "Oh it's far too late for that. I've heard everything I need to know. I didn't expect such negligence from the infamous Ardas, but I suppose the

Waypoint has a way of lulling its guests into carelessness." She traced the slender branches of a sapling with a long, pale finger.

Eotan's eyes were bright with anger. "Who are you, really?"

Vandra mockingly placed her hands on her hips and adopted a quizzical expression. "I suppose I'm the reason for all of you being here."

"What do you mean?" Sten asked warily.

She splayed out her hands and wiggled her fingers like a marionettist. "Such well-behaved puppets, you are, and such a pity Lentarro decided to let you escape."

"Liar!" spat Ineza. "We beat the Oethyr. That had nothing to do with you."

Vandra laughed. "And yet, such nominal victories amount to nothing, in the end." Her dark eyes flashed amusedly. "You've already lost."

Ineza brushed past Sten and faced Vandra. "Is now the time for your sinister monologue? Something about how clever you are, or how it's futile for us to try and stop you, or how your parents never hugged you as a child and it's their fault you ended up a rotten apple?"

Vandra's face darkened and her playful tone turned to venom. "You know nothing, girl. But you'll pay for that insolence. I've seen you. I know your face."

"You may know our faces," said Eotan, "but I've learned your scent. Tell me, Vandra, have you ever been hunted by a wolf?"

Her smile faltered and she took an involuntary step back. Red sparks ignited along her arms. Eotan transformed and bared his fangs with a deep snarl. There was a faint *hummm* and Grandmother Morroza sped into the room. Stonetalon and Edelwing fluttered close behind, eyes wide with concern.

She gave them a smoldering glare through her spectacles. "That is quite enough! Violence will not be tolerated within my walls. With *no* exceptions. Do I make myself perfectly clear?"

Eotan returned and nodded, though his eyes never left

Vandra's face. Morroza turned on Vandra. "I was wrong about you. I sensed goodness in your heart. An overwhelming desire to change Miz for the better. Yet now I can only feel your anger at the world. Think carefully on my words. Inspiration is a greater tool than fear. It is not too late to change your path."

Vandra sneered, her dark eyes flitting between Morroza and Eotan. "You are an old fool. You spew hollow advice while you cower within these walls, hiding yourself from the reality of the outside world. I know of your powers, Morroza. You might save Miz from her doom, yet you choose to do nothing, and all for the sake of your precious Waypoint."

The air itself shuddered. Grandmother Morroza rose from her chair. The diminutive woman seemed to grow in stature, and Sten was blasted with a wave of heat. She took a step toward Vandra and the loam beneath her foot blackened and charred. "You are no longer welcome here." Her voice was sonorous and distorted. The sound seemed to come from everywhere at once, rattling the golden leaves of the trees. "Leave now, and never return."

Vandra backed away. The flickering magic extinguished along her arm. She paused at the threshold. "I will see you all again. Mind yourselves tomorrow. The Wilds is a strange and dangerous place." With that, she disappeared into the night, and the door to the Waypoint slammed behind her.

"Oh my," said Grandmother Morroza. She slumped back into her chair. "I'm sorry you bore witness to such a reprehensive quandary." Stonetalon and Edelwing flew to her side, yellow eyes bright with concern. "I do *so* abhor violence." She drew her blankets up to her chin.

"What did you do to her?" Sten asked.

Morroza smiled sadly. "Nothing, dear. She forced my hand and I reacted in kind. One must always follow the rules of the Waypoint. Now, I'm afraid this ado has left me quite weary. I bid you all goodnight. I will see you off in the morning."

The Grandmother's chair drifted away. The company stood in uncomfortable silence.

"What do we do now?" said Ineza.

"I don't see that we have a choice," said Eotan. "We must continue as planned. This Vandra knows of our intentions and has prepared for our coming, first with the Oethyr, and now the crossing to Dinh. Neither waiting nor running will aid us. We must ride for Dinh and tell them what we know."

"And if she tries to stop us?" said Whitney.

"Then we fight," said Eotan bluntly. "There is no other way. We'll leave at first light, armed for battle. With luck we'll reach Dinh without concern." His features tightened, as if he doubted his own words.

Sten lay awake in his chamber, staring at the ceiling. Vandra's words echoed in his mind. *"You've already lost."* He rolled over, attempting to silence her taunts. Maybe she had lied. Maybe she had come to the Waypoint to intimidate them. Maybe she wanted to dissuade them from even attempting to reach Dinh. Maybe she didn't have a plan at all. He buried his face in his pillow. Or maybe she was telling the truth, and the entire journey was in vain. Maybe they were too late.

A quiet knock interrupted his thoughts. He rose from his cot and opened the door. Ineza stood in the hallway.

He glanced up and down the corridor. "What are you doing here?"

"I don't know," she said. She flushed in the dim light. "I just can't shake what that woman said tonight. She scared me, Sten. I'm worried about tomorrow."

"I am too." She was standing so close he could count the freckles on her nose. "And not just about tomorrow," he added hastily. "I'm not a warrior, like my uncles. I'm not a soldier, like you, or Whitney, or your Shrikes. I can't use magic, like the dwarves. I'm not even a healer, like Manye." He dropped his gaze. "I have no business being here."

She pulled him close and kissed him. "You're a fool, *Lord* Bregon." Her cocky smile returned. "You're exactly where you're supposed to be. This world is full of people like myself, or your uncles, or my captain. Miz needs more people like *you*. She needs those who are willing to fight for what they believe in, even if the odds are stacked against them. There aren't heroes in this world. There are only those who are willing to sacrifice everything, for no other reason than it's the right thing to do so." She stood on tiptoe and kissed him again. "Anyhoo, if we're going to die tomorrow, perhaps we should make the best of tonight." She took Sten by the hand and led him into his chamber, and closed the door behind them.

PREPARATIONS

The capital's Heads of House were gathered around a circular table in Lord Impo's comfortable solarium. The atmosphere was far from relaxed. Lord Polto's empty chair sat at the table, its tacit implications speaking louder than the lords and ladies arrayed beside.

"It's time we set the final stages of our plan in motion," said Lord Impo. He rose from his chair and leaned over the table, staring at each of them in turn. "The winds of change are blowing through the capital. We *must* take advantage of its momentum. You can be sure we won't get another chance if Marstarrow learns of what we've done."

"Our agents report that the fool hasn't left his keep in days," said Lady Aamot mildly. She took a sip from a silver-chased flute. "He is frozen by indecision, or else doesn't care to address the concerns of his people. Give it a few more days and the citizens of Heldan Port will hand us the city themselves. I say we wait and let our previous efforts resolve the matter. Why sully our hands further?"

Lord Impo slammed his fist onto the table. "I shall say this for the last time! Do not underestimate that man. We failed to recognize his cunning and ruthlessness once before and we lost Heldan Port as the result. Never again. We shall march him in front of the city, before he has time to act, and expose him as a traitor."

"What if he's discovered how you let Vandra into the Sanctum?" asked Lady Pitton. "He may attempt to paint *us* as the traitors, rather than himself." Murmurs of agreement circulated the table.

Lord Impo defiantly shook his head. "People don't care about the legitimacy of the information they're hearing, as long as it validates their own beliefs. Right now, the people of Heldan Port see Marstarrow as the problem. There is talk he arranged the disappearance of the wizards to advance his own agenda of magical reform. All we have to do is encourage these suspicions. We pin the blame on Marstarrow and challenge him to refute the claims. When he cannot, we have him arrested and hanged as a traitor. There is absolutely no evidence of our involvement to suggest otherwise."

The Heads of House pounded the table in agreement. Lord Impo stepped back with a self-assured smile. Only Lady Huvani remained silent. "Your plan is well and good if everything proceeds as expected, but I, for one, believe we need further insurance." She raised an eyebrow and traced the pearls at her throat.

"We've bought the loyalty of the City Guard already," said Lord Knutte.

"We have strength of arms, yes," said Lady Huvani, "but we need something more… personal, were circumstances to sour."

"What do you suggest?" said Lady Waldor.

A humorless smile twisted Lady Huvani's face. "As it

stands, I have it on good faith that our beloved chancellor has recently visited a tavern on multiple occasions. The Jumping Jackamoose." She shuddered, as though the name pained her to say aloud. "Apparently, Marstarrow has become closely acquainted with its proprietor, dare I say friends, even. Now, this same proprietor, one Mord Butterson, is known to keep an orc in his employment."

"Truly?" said Lord Meren disdainfully. "I'm amazed the brute can function in Heldan Port's society."

"I was shocked as well," said Lady Huvani. She took a sip from her crystal chalice, pale eyes glittering over its rim. She coughed delicately and dabbed a handkerchief to her lips. "Orcs are loathsome creatures, with a predisposition toward violence. Yet this truth presents us with a very unique opportunity. Since the chancellor cares for these savages, I say we use it against him. I believe Marstarrow has handed us our insurance on a silver platter."

There were murmurs of agreement around the table and excited whispers. Lord Impo cleared his throat. "Very well. We shall move against Marstarrow, and the sooner the better. But first we shall find Mord Butterson and his barbarous companion. If they have befriended the chancellor, as you claim, then our victory is all but assured."

He lifted his glass as the Heads of House rose from their chairs. "To taking back what is rightfully ours!"

BETWEEN A G'ROK
AND A HARD PLACE

Butterson locked the door to the Jackamoose and set off down the cobbles. Raxo whistled a cheery tune from atop G'rok's shoulder. It had been another successful, if not precarious, evening at the Jackamoose. The citizens of the Heldan Port were reaching their breaking point with the chancellor and continued to flock to Butterson's tavern. Yet Marstarrow remained silent within his keep. The flood of doubt and suspicion continued to spread throughout Heldan Port.

Butterson kicked a pebble in irritation. It skipped across the empty street, clattering hollowly.

"Cheer up, Boss," said Raxo. "I know it's been a few days, but he'll be in touch."

Butterson was in no mood for platitudes. "So we're supposed to wait with the rest of Heldan Port while he comes up with some miraculous plan to save the city?"

Raxo scratched his chin with his tail. "Suppose so. As I

see it, we don't have much of a choice. You either trust him or you don't. Simple as that."

"I'm starting to think I've greatly misplaced my trust," Butterson grumbled. "Tiberion promised that he'd address the concerns of the capital if we helped him, yet he's done precisely the opposite. Not to mention the fact that he's hiding whatever information he found within the Sanctum. I've been a fool, Raxo. I don't think he has a plan at all."

"Maybe. But I doubt it. Think of everythin' you know about ol' Stoneface. You think he's goin' to hand over the city to those pompous wankers without a fight?" Butterson pursed his lips but remained quiet. "You know I'm right," Raxo gloated. "In fact, I think you're just peeved he's not includin' us in his schemes. You may be a simple brewer of ales, Mord Butterson, but I think you've developed a taste for heroics."

Butterson snorted into his beard. "I'm entirely content with my station, thank you."

The demon shrugged. "Whatever you say, Boss."

They meandered along the winding streets of the capital in terse silence. As they passed into Cralenson Square, two armored men emerged from an alleyway. They brandished swords and shields emblazoned with the crest of Heldan Port, the purple and gold of their tabards muted in the scant light.

"Halt!" ordered one. "Make yourselves known to the City Guard."

"Mord Butterson, Raxo, and G'rok, of the Jumping Jacka-moose," said Butterson wearily. "If you'll be so kind as to let us pass?"

"Afraid I can't do that," said the other. His visor was raised, and his mocking eyes never left G'rok's face. "We have reports of a dangerous orc wandering the streets of Heldan Port. Heard she's been terrorizing the good people of this city."

Butterson felt G'rok tense beside him. He reached up and laid a calming hand on her shoulder. "If you're referring to

G'rok, here, then you've got the wrong person. She works for me at my tavern. She's done nothing wrong. A hundred of my clientele can vouch for her."

The first guard spat on the street with a look of disgust. "But she's still an orc, isn't she? Seems to me all orcs are guilty of one thing or another. You just have to dig a bit to find out what. Isn't that right, you ugly brute?"

A low rumble began in G'rok's throat.

"Easy, love," said Raxo, a nervous edge to his voice. "They're just tryin' to provoke you. Don't give 'em the satisfaction. They're not worth it." Her growl subsided, ever so slightly.

"Just look at that face," laughed the second man. "Did you see her eyes just then? I reckon she'd have killed me if that little sewer stain hadn't talked her down. I think it's clear we've found our orc, wouldn't you say?"

The other soldier sneered and rapped his sword against his shield. "I reckon we have. Looks like she's got accomplices as well. I guess we'll be adding three more souls to the dungeons tonight instead of one."

"What are our supposed crimes?" said Butterson, as evenly as he could manage. The derisive jeers of the soldiers were making his blood boil. "You can't charge us for a crime we didn't commit."

"Is that so?" The first man twirled his sword. "It seems to me I've already told you your crimes." He pointed the blade at G'rok. "That one is guilty of being ugly as sin, and you two are guilty of keeping her company." They both laughed.

"STOP MAKE FUN OF G'ROK!" G'rok bellowed. The soldiers laughed even harder. She clenched her fists.

"Just listen to it talk! How can something so dumb be considered a citizen of Heldan Port? It makes me right sick."

A red veil descended over G'rok's eyes. The bristles of hair on her neck rose on end and the deep rumbling grew in her throat. She gnashed her tusks in fury and took a step toward the guards. They retreated and fell into combative stances.

Butterson hastily jumped between G'rok and the soldiers, holding up his hands in an attempt to defuse the situation. "This is all a misunderstanding," he insisted. "Just let us go. Please. We've done nothing wrong and we don't want any trouble. We run a tavern. We're not criminals."

"Look at her!" spat the second man. "That *thing* is dangerous, make no mistake. Just because you dress her in a disgusting bowtie doesn't make her a real person."

With a roar of fury, G'rok rushed at the guard. The man scrambled forward and raised his sword to Butterson's throat. "One more step and he dies!" G'rok paused, snorting with frustration. "That's right, beast. We knew you had it in you. You're just as dangerous as we were told. You're all under arrest, by authority of the Heads of House."

"Please!" Butterson repeated. The razor edge of the sword bit into his neck and warm blood trickled into his shirt. "This is all a misunderstanding."

"On the contrary," hissed the guard in his ear, "we have our orders. We're to bring *you* in, alive and well. Though the same can't be said of your companion here. Orcs are too dangerous to be left alive. They have no business living within our cities." The man nodded to his partner. With a clang of steel, he lowered his visor and advanced on G'rok, sword raised. "If the orc attempts to fight or flee," said the soldier holding Butterson, "this one dies!"

A tear rolled down Butterson's face. "Stop!" he begged. "She's done nothing wrong!" But the guard ignored him as G'rok edged away.

"BUTTERSON?" she called, her voice tight with fear. "WHAT G'ROK DO?"

"Just run!" cried Butterson. The sword cut deeper into his neck, and he sucked in his breath.

"You run and he dies!" shouted the guard behind him. He laughed victoriously, his breath hot on Butterson's neck.

It was at that moment that time seemed to slow. All Butterson could hear was the beating of his own heart and the gentle rustle of the Mired River some blocks away. He watched as G'rok backed into a corner, Raxo hopping from one shoulder to another in agitation. The approaching guard lunged and feinted, and G'rok flinched at his every movement. She whimpered in terror and frustration. Then, something within him snapped. With a bellow of rage, he slammed his elbow into the guard's face. The man collapsed with a curse, and his partner spun about. Upon seeing his felled companion, he rushed at Butterson, sword leveled.

He took three steps, and then G'rok's massive hands closed around his waist.

"YOU NO HURT BUTTERSON!" she roared. She hurled him against the city walls, as if he was no more than a doll. The *crunch* of the impact made Butterson wince. The guard collapsed to the ground, leaving a dark smear on the stone.

"Help me!" screamed the other guard. He scuttled away on all fours. There was the sound of approaching footsteps and a battalion of City Guard emerged from Cralenson Square. They rushed to surround Butterson and G'rok.

"Raxo, get out of here!" Butterson panted. "Warn Tiberion!"

The demon saluted and leapt from the orc. The soldiers raced to block him, but he darted between their legs and disappeared into the capital's streets.

G'rok huffed with fear as the City Guard closed in around them. The guard who had waylaid them stepped forward. Blood poured from his broken nose. "You'll pay for this," he spat, and struck Butterson hard across the face. Butterson fell to his knees and his vision swam. The soldier knelt beside him and hissed into his ear. "Your beast will hang in front of you, bastard, and the entire city will cheer her death." He hauled Butterson to his feet. "Take them to the dungeons. If anyone tries to stop you, cut their throats."

GROWING SHADOWS

S ten gazed longingly at the dappled interior of the Waypoint, then closed the door behind him.

A blood-red dawn hung over the valley, signaling for their departure. Grandmother Morroza shuffled along the growing caravan, stuffing additional food and drink into whatever pack she could reach. She stopped often to share words of counsel, or to offer a warm embrace. Manye patted the owls a final time and hopped onto the cloud next to Sten. Culyan whistled, and the caravan began eastward.

"I'll be keeping my eye on you lot in the days to come!" Morroza called after them. She continued to wave goodbye until the river bowed southward and the Waypoint disappeared from view.

The air was heavy with nervous anticipation, but also a great deal of sadness. Nobody wanted to leave behind the magical hospitality of the Waypoint. As they crested the lip of the valley, Sten cast one final glance at the wooden cottage nestled

beside the river. Blue smoke was unspooling from its chimney, and its windows were thrown open to welcome the morning air. Then he blinked, and it was gone. He sighed forlornly.

"Aye, lad," said Two. "It's always difficult to leave the Waypoint. But that's what makes it so special. You cling to its memories in the dark days, and never let them from your heart. The Waypoint will always be here, and its doors will always be open."

"And those memories will certainly be wonderful," said Sten. He glanced at Ineza. She was fully armored in the blackened steel of the Shrikes, her sword strapped to one hip. She noticed his gaze and flushed happily.

Two winked and patted him on the shoulder. "I'm glad for you both, lad. See? There is still good that can come from such dangerous times."

"Maybe. Unless she was telling the truth."

Two raised a bristly eyebrow. "Vandra?"

Sten nodded. "She seemed so sure of what she was saying last night." Even talking about the strange woman made his insides churn.

"That she did. But we still don't know what she wants in all of this."

"She wants to stop us from reaching Dinh."

"Then Dinh is exactly where we must go!" Two chuckled. "She's only confirmed that there is something in Dinh worth discovering."

"Interesting logic," said Sten, unconvinced.

Two gestured expansively to the caravan. "Look around you, lad. We're prepared for her coming. If she's arrogant enough to assume she can stop us single-handedly, she's in for a surprise. She may have learned our intentions by coming to the Waypoint, but she also gave us time to prepare. Ultimately, I think this will prove her mistake."

As they continued eastward, the forest grew denser. The

canopy and understory were choked with vines, their lengths embedded with vicious thorns. Wraithlike moss swayed from branches, and sodden leaves squelched underfoot. Soon, a pale mist began to seep from the forest floor. It crept upward with exploratory fingers, clutching greedily at the horses' hooves. Before long, the forest had grown dark and still.

Eotan called them to a halt beside a narrow stream, its waters black. He sniffed the air, blue eyes scanning the murk.

"What is it, Arda?" said Whitney.

"She's here," said Eotan grimly. "I've caught her scent." Sten nocked an arrow to his bowstring. "But there's something else. Something strange, yet oddly familiar... I can't quite place it." He changed into the wolf and bent his nose to the ground, then returned, his face drawn. "The mist isn't natural. It reeks of magic."

There was a muffled scream from the rear of the column. Sten whirled about. Corporal Hemmie fell from his horse and writhed on the ground. A thick blanket of mist completely enveloped him and began to pulsate.

"Help him!" Whitney demanded. Finlan and Tryo rushed to his side, but Hemmie lashed out with his sword. He continued to choke and scream as the mist thickened around his body. Then, with a strangled gurgle, he lay still. The twins knelt beside him, then stumbled back as the gnome sat bolt upright. Even from a distance, Sten could see that his eyes glowed red.

Hemmie rose unsteadily to his feet. His movements were jerky and sporadic, like those of a marionette puppet. His blazing eyes passed over the company, unseeing. He shuddered violently, and the outline of his body blurred. The spasms worsened. Then, with a sound like the tearing of cloth, the gnome seemed to split apart.

Sten stared in horrified fascination. Two figures now stood in the swirling fog. One was undeniably Hemmie, trembling slightly. But the other was like nothing Sten had ever seen. It was the same shape as the gnome, but lacked all color or texture, as if Hemmie's shadow had taken a physical form. The thing was a blackened void, bereft of light. Crimson eyes burned where a face should have been.

Hemmie shuddered again. Within moments, a second shadow had joined the first, and then a third, and a fourth, and then countless more. Finally, the tremors stopped, and the woods grew still. The gnome's face was ashen, his body shrunken. He looked like a desiccated corpse, except for his eyes, which blazed through the gloom. The Shrikes backed away from the silent shadows.

"Remarkable, aren't they?" called a woman's voice. Vandra strode to Hemmie's side through the ranks of shadows. "I warned you that the Wilds were dangerous, yet you didn't listen. Such a pity."

"What have you done to him?" said Whitney. His face was almost as pale as Hemmie's.

"I've set an example," said Vandra. "It's time you understand just how little you know of this world." She gently touched the side of Hemmie's shriveled face. "It's time you witness true power."

A single spark of red light awoke along the sleeve of her black robes. It twirled about her arm and danced playfully onto her hand, then paused at the tip of her finger. Vandra watched them with her dark eyes. "Magic must always be respected." She smiled gravely and touched the spark to Hemmie's cheek.

Fissures of crimson light spread across his face, like the broken pane of a window. For a moment, the glow died from his eyes. He blinked, uncomprehending, as the cracks continued to spread. "Captain...?" he managed to say, looking to Whitney. Then, with a sound like the rustling of dry leaves, he broke apart. The crimson light remained for a brief moment before flickering out, and then the pieces of Hemmie's body fell to the ground as ash.

"No!" screamed Whitney. Cries of loss sounded from the Shrikes.

"Now you see," said Vandra. "Now you see what will happen should I fail." Around her, the shades of Corporal Hemmie were crumpling to the ground, one after another, their crimson eyes darkened. The fallen shadows broke apart with sullen whispers, and the wind swept the ash across the forest floor. "Don't worry," she said playfully, "I brought more."

Awful, guttural howls began to echo throughout the forest all around them. Sten could see hulking shapes racing toward them through the forest, red eyes shining in the mist. Whitney drew his rapier. "I'll kill you myself!" he roared. The Shrikes fell into formation, shields held ready. Sten and his uncles tensed to fight. Behind him, the dwarves flourished their instruments.

"Maybe," said Vandra. The shadows closed in around them. "But I fear not today. Slay them all."

THE COST

Captain Whitney barked orders as the dark figures rushed at them from all directions. His Shrikes quickly circled the company. With soft *thuds*, they drove their shields into the loam to form an interlocking wall of steel. There came the metallic groan of crossbows being loaded. He waited as the shadows drew closer, waited until he could see the awful hunger burning in their eyes.

"Loose!" he yelled. There was a *twang* as the Shrikes sent a volley of bolts into the oncoming shades. He was relieved to see waves of the creatures crumple to the ground. Red light leaked out from where the bolts had struck, and the fallen bodies dissolved into ash. "They die like the rest of us!" The Shrikes reloaded. "Fire at will!"

The forest rang with the sounds of battle as the creatures met steel. They clawed at the Shrikes with howls of inhuman rage. The Shrikes lashed out from between the shields, and the air hummed with bolts and arrows.

A dark figure forced itself through a gap in the shields, snarling victoriously. It was a different shape from Hemmie's shades, though similarly devoid of color. Whitney deftly stepped aside as the shadow swiped at him with a rusted cleaver, then dispatched it with a thrust to the neck. Another figure burst through the opening. Whitney flourished his rapier as the creature rushed him. There was a *thwumm* of a bowstring and an arrow lodged itself between the shadow's eyes. Whitney whirled about.

Sten stood tall on the dwarven cloud. He drew back his bow for another shot and released. Another shade crumpled. Manye chanted quietly beside him, her words lost to the fury. And then the music of the dwarves drowned out everything else. Shimmering waves of magic exploded from the cloud, repelling the attackers.

Culyan leapt onto Kipto's back, axe in hand. "Let me pass!" The Shrikes hastily parted. The Marshal charged forth, axe cleaving the shadows in great droves. The golden wolf followed him through the gap. Shades fell amidst flashes of emerald as Eotan flitted between man and beast.

But still the shadows came.

Whitney frantically searched the fringes of the melee. Vandra stood apart, watching from a distance. Her dark eyes betrayed nothing as she surveyed the battle.

"What's she doing?" panted Corporal Ghet. She sidestepped a hatchet before running the shade through with her sword.

Whitney shook his head and bared his teeth. "I'm going after her! If we capture or kill her, this ends now."

"We need you here, Captain!" A Shrike screamed and fell to the ground, clutching at a dagger buried in her leg. Manye rushed to the woman's side and sent a stream of golden light into the wound.

Whitney leapt into his saddle. "Finlan, Tryo, you're in

charge!" The twins raised their tower shields in acknowledgment and began shouting commands.

Corporal Ghet sprang into her saddle and reined her mare alongside him. Her face was caked with sweat and grime, but her eyes shone with battle. "You're a fool if you think I'd let you go alone."

They broke through the circle and galloped toward Vandra. The shades crumpled before their horses. A flicker of annoyance crossed her face when she noticed their coming. There was a sharp *crack*, like the report of a whip, and she disappeared in a swirl of mist.

Corporal Ghet pulled up short in confusion. "What the hell was that?"

Whitney fought to capture his breath and scanned the woods. A dark shape appeared between the trunks. Vandra was walking calmly through the forest, now some distance away. "There!" he cried, and spurred his horse after her.

They had almost reached her when she disappeared again. Her disembodied laughter hung in the writhing mist.

"You're out of your league, Captain." Her voice seemed to originate from every direction at once, and reverberated strangely off the trees. Whitney cursed, trying to see through the thickening miasma of gray. "I *am* sorry about your friend," said the multitude of voices. "But it is vital you understand."

"Show yourself, craven!" yelled Whitney. His heart hammered in his ears. The cloaked woman appeared and leaned easily against a tree. He charged forward and slashed with his rapier, but she dissolved into a cloud of smoke.

"My, this is fun, isn't it? Did you really believe you'd be the one to stop me, Captain? Look at the company you keep. You are nothing compared to them. Your name will be a mere footnote in the chronicles of the Ardas' legend. But delusion can warp one's self-perspective, I suppose..." Her words bombarded Whitney from everywhere at once.

"Captain," Corporal Ghet said breathlessly. "We need to leave! We'll never find her in these woods."

"No!" said Whitney. He spun his horse in a circle, attempting to see past the twisting veil. "Not without her."

"But-"

"You go, then! I won't let Corporal Hemmie die in vain."

She desperately clutched at his arm. "And what about the others? We can still help them."

Whitney yanked his arm free. "They'll be fine! I can end this myself."

Vandra's disembodied laughter sounded again. "Always the poor, delusional Captain. Heed the girl's words and flee while you still can." The echoes churned and rebounded. "Though, in truth, I owe you my thanks for bringing her to me. I haven't forgotten what you said in the Waypoint, *girl... girl... girl...*"

"Please, Captain..." Corporal Ghet's eyes were wide with fear.

Whitney's veil of rage faded as he looked at her. Gone was the warrior who had ridden and served beneath him, resilient and loyal to a fault. In her place was a ragged young girl of nine, face dirtied, hair wild, tunic soiled, completely alone on the streets of the capital.

He blinked sweat from his eyes. "You're... you're right. We need to get out of here." He spun round, trying to remember from where they had come, but the mist was too complete. The world had become gray and muted.

"Have you lost your way, Captain?" mocked the voices. "How careless of you. I've enjoyed our little game of hide and seek, but I must be going. I wonder how your companions have fared in your absence... Until we meet again."

The gloom fell quiet as the last echoes of Vandra's words died amongst the trees. They waited, expectant, but the woods remained still. With a surge of recollection, Whitney pulled the Follower from his pocket. The blue light pointed away through the trees.

Corporal Ghet sheathed her sword, though her eyes never left the dark trees. "Nice thinking, Cap. The sooner we return the-"

Crack!

Whitney was blasted from his horse and landed on his back. He rose painfully to his feet, looking about in confusion as their horses fled in terror.

Vandra stood over Corporal Ghet, examining a single spark of crimson light that circled her finger. Blood leaked from a gash over the corporal's eye. She fought to rise, but Vandra pinned her to the ground with her boot.

"Apologies for misleading you, Captain," said Vandra, with a sardonic smile. "You didn't think I'd let you off so lightly, did you? *I've* learned a great lesson today. I underestimated the Ardas, the dwarves, and the elf girl. I even misjudged you and your soldiers. But I shall learn from my mistakes, rebuild, and look to the future. That is all one can hope to achieve through failure, wouldn't you agree?"

Whitney could only watch, shaking with helpless rage, as Corporal Ghet struggled to her knees. Vandra placed a pale hand on her shoulder. "Since you've taught me so very much today, allow me return the favor. There will always be repercussions for your actions, Captain." She knelt and carefully wiped blood from Corporal Ghet's face with her thumb. "Take this girl, for instance. I warned her that she would pay for her insolence at the Waypoint."

He threw his rapier aside and held open his arms. "Please, don't hurt her. Take me, instead."

"You aren't hearing me!" Vandra snapped. She stood and wiped her hand on her robes. "Consequences are an inevitability. The sooner you accept this, the better. You abandoned your soldiers and thought to ride me down. And all for what? Glory? Prestige? To become the hero who saved Heldan Port?

No, Captain. You must understand that your arrogance and pride come at a cost."

"Stop this..." Whitney choked. He realized, detachedly, that he was crying.

"It's okay, Cap," said Corporal Ghet. She winced and managed to smile. "Really, it is. Please tell Sten and the others hello from me, will you?" Whitney nodded dumbly.

"I *am* sorry," said Vandra, "but you brought this upon yourselves." She touched the crimson spark to Ineza's cheek, and vanished in a whirl of mist.

FLIGHT

Sten knelt to retrieve one of his arrows. It was partially buried in one of the countless piles of ash scattered throughout the woods. He added it to his quiver and surveyed the clearing. The shades had been entirely defeated, driven back by the combined strength of the Shrikes and Ardas' company. Manye sat with Culyan and Eotan, tending to their wounds.

Two came to stand beside him. His carefully manicured beard was disheveled, and sweat beaded on his bulbous nose. "I think that was just a glimpse of what's to come, lad. We may have won this battle, but you saw how easily Vandra summoned those... Dark Ones."

"And look what it cost us," said Sten quietly. Across the glade, the Shrikes were crowded around a pitifully small grave. Finlan and Tryo spoke a few hushed words, then lowered a bundle of blackened armor and a sword into the hole. There was no body. With a twinge of disquiet, Sten realized Ineza and Whitney were absent.

He joined the Shrikes and hesitantly tapped Finlan on the arm. "Where's Corporal Ghet? Where's the captain?"

The colossal twin peered down at him through red-rimmed eyes. "They went after the foul enchantress."

His brother nodded angrily. "Aye, they chased her from the battle, last I saw. I'm sure they'll be back. Hopefully with her head."

Icy fingers trickled down Sten's spine as he returned to his uncles. "Captain Whitney and Corporal Ghet are gone. They went after Vandra."

Eotan stood abruptly, sapphire eyes bright with worry. "Are you certain?" Sten nodded grimly.

Culyan swore and spat a mouthful of blood. "The fool. What was he hoping to accomplish by himself?"

"Please, uncles, can't you do something?"

Eotan gathered his daggers and tested the air. "I'll follow their scent, though I fear what I might find." He changed into the wolf and disappeared between the trees.

Time passed slowly as Sten waited for Eotan's return. The Shrikes finished their service and sat in mournful silence. The only sound was the harsh grinding of a whetstone as Culyan sharpened his axe. He continued to run the stone along the steel's edge long after the axe had been honed to perfection.

After what seemed an eternity, the golden wolf reemerged from the woods. Captain Whitney followed close behind, carrying the limp form of Ineza in his arms. Eotan called for Manye, his voice deadly calm. Sten raced after the elf and inhaled sharply when he looked upon Ineza.

The same fissures of crimson light that had broken apart Corporal Hemmie were slowly creeping across her face. She writhed in pain, moaning slightly. Manye closed her eyes, and a torrent of golden light issued from her fingertips, blanketing Ineza's head. The fissures' progress slowed, and for a moment Sten thought the elf's magic was working. But then, like fingers of frost spreading across a pond, the cracks began to spread once more.

Sten grabbed Whitney's arm. "What happened?"

"I.... I made a mistake." The captain's face was pale, his eyes strangely distant, as though he wasn't seeing what lay in front of him. "Vandra..." he swallowed and averted his gaze. "Vandra touched her with her magic. It's... it's my fault. First Hemmie, now Ineza..."

"Bearded Eight, can't you help her?" begged Sten.

"I'm afraid not, lad," said Two. "This is beyond our skill. Corporal Ghet needs more than dwarven magic right now."

Sten thought frantically, then leapt to his feet. "What about Morroza? Surely she would save her!"

"The Grandmother's power is of a much different nature," said Eotan quietly. His eyes flicked to his brother. "She needs Jaya."

Culyan nodded resolutely and called for Kipto. Gently, the Marshal scooped Ineza from Whitney's unresisting hands and placed her in the saddle, as if she weighed no more than a child. He pulled himself up after her. "Manye, can you slow the spread of whatever this is?"

The elf nodded hesitantly. "I think so, but Vandra's magic is terribly strong. I don't know what she's done."

"But Jaya might," said Culyan. He looked to Eotan. "Ride ahead and bring Jaya back to us. We'll follow and meet her on the Canyonlands. Hopefully our little Oethyr can slow Vandra's poison and give us enough time."

Eotan jumped onto Lilenti's back in a swirl of black cloak. "Dinh is at least a full day's ride from here," he warned. "I don't know how long it will take Jaya to find you."

"Then ride like a summer storm, little pup."

THE CANYONLANDS

K ipto crushed a trail through the dense underbrush that sought to block his path. Sten and the dwarves followed in his wake. Behind them, the Shrikes struggled to keep pace. Manye huddled over Ineza's listless body, murmuring inaudibly. Golden magic danced across Ineza's slackened face, but her groans of pain worsened as they fled east.

Eventually the forests thinned and the soft loam gave way to the red sandstone of the Canyonlands. Even as Tanduil began to sink below the razor silhouettes of the Hammerstone Mountains on the eastern horizon, the air grew warmer. The land was bleak and desolate, the wind constant and arid as it harried the scalloped dunes and weathered stone. Vegetation sprouted here and there, the only sign of life in an otherwise barren wilderness. Towering pillars of rock erupted haphazardly from the ground, proud and austere, their tops jagged and wind-scoured. Compared to the Wilds, the Canyonlands felt lonely and unforgiving.

An unbroken line of blackened rock appeared through the shimmering heat. But as they drew closer, Sten realized that it wasn't rock at all, but rather a lack thereof. An immense canyon stretched before them, running north to south as far as the eye could see. Soaring buttes rose from its shadowed depths, their walls a layered assortment of strata.

"Within that canyon lies the River Dah," said Two. "From here, we turn south, though Dinh is still some distance yet."

Sten refused to look at Ineza. "We'll make it in time."

They rode along the lip of the canyon, tracking the winding course of the river. Twilight settled over the vast wilderness, and with it came the sounds of nocturnal creatures coming to life. Coyotes howled and yipped from somewhere in the vast expanse of rock and sand. A family of jackrabbits fled at their approach. Bats and birds flitted overhead in search of prey. But there was no sign of Eotan's return.

The canyon narrowed. A sloping rock archway swam into view. It gracefully spanned the entirety of the massive chasm. Culyan angled Kipto toward the natural bridge and paused at its precipice. Whitney and the Shrikes arrived in a cloud of red dust, their horses lathered.

"We cross here," said Culyan. He dismounted and gingerly stepped onto the archway, coaxing Kipto after him. The destrier balked and snorted. Sten found himself holding his breath. The bridge was barely wider than Culyan or Kipto. One false step and they would plummet to their deaths. But both the bridge and their resolve held, and moments later they were standing on the opposite side of the canyon.

"Bearded Eight!" called Culyan. His shout echoed through the ravine below them.

"Our turn," said Two. Sten swallowed, and the dwarf laid a reassuring hand on his shoulder. "Ah, don't fret, lad, we get to cheat this a bit." The cloud rocketed onto the bridge, hovering over the narrow path of stone. Sten tried not to look at the seemingly endless void that yawned below them. When they reached the opposite side, he released his pent-up breath.

"How's Ineza?" he asked, failing to mask the tightness in his words.

It was Manye who answered. Her hair was disheveled and her face was caked in red dust. "She's getting weaker every moment. I can't keep her safe much longer."

Culyan swung into the saddle behind her. "You won't have to. Our corporal isn't going to let a bit of magic stop her, is she?"

Ineza mumbled incoherently and Kipto surged forward.

The Canyonlands darkened as they hurtled southward. To Sten, it felt as though they were racing against the coming night. But this was a night that would herald no dawn for Ineza. She began to struggle and thrash in her bindings. Culyan was forced to slow. "Let me down!" she said. "I can't take this pain any longer! Please, just let me down." Culyan looked to Sten, uncertain.

Despair gripped Sten's chest as he helped Ineza from the saddle. She slumped into his arms. Her breathing was ragged and uneven. He carried her to the lip of the canyon and carefully lowered her to sit against a rock. She feebly took his hand as they watched the setting sun.

"I've never been to the Canyonlands," she said. Her voice was hoarse, barely more than a whisper. "It's lonely, yet oddly beautiful." She coughed, and the angry lines of magic flared across her face. "I'd have liked to see more of Miz, you know. I always told myself I'd travel the world once the next mission was over, or the next, but I never seemed to get around to it. Anyhoo, I suppose it's too late for all of that now."

Sten squeezed her hand and mustered a smile. "Nonsense. There's still time. You haven't seen Lilenti run like I have. You just need to stay strong a little while longer." His voice broke. "Please."

The cracks across Ineza's skin were glowing now, their

edges more pronounced. A section of her cheek tore away and dissolved into ash. She touched the spot and winced. "I think it's too late now, my *lord*. And stop looking at me like that, I'm not one for goodbyes. Just make sure Whitney doesn't blame himself. He couldn't have known this would happen."

"*Please* hold on."

Ineza kissed him lightly. "You're a good person, Sten Arda. Remember that." She smiled, and the cracks grew brighter. "And would you look at that? The name suits you, after all."

She closed her eyes as the color drained from her face. Sten looked pleadingly to Manye, but she shook her head, eyes full of sorrow. "There's nothing more I can do. Vandra's spell is too far gone. I'm sorry, Sten, but I think-"

"I see her!" Culyan pointed away to the south. "It's Lilenti!"

The silver mare raced toward them along the lip of the darkening canyon like a silvered comet.

"Hold on, Ineza!" Sten begged. He took her hands and held them to his chest. Her eyes briefly opened, but her gaze was unfocused. Another piece of skin sloughed away.

Lilenti skidded to a halt in a shower of sand. A freckled woman with fiercely red hair vaulted to the ground. She wore pale-blue linen robes that flowed like water when she moved. "Where is she?" she demanded of Culyan.

He led her to Ineza. "She doesn't have much time, Jaya."

The woman knelt beside Sten and examined Ineza's face. "Eotan said this is some form of magic." She spoke almost to herself. "In that case, we're lucky. If it's magic, I can stop it. Give me space."

Sten stepped back as blue flames ignited over Jaya's hands. She placed her palms on either side of Ineza's face. The web of cracks instantly flared and smoked. Ineza screamed. The ground began to shake, and a cascade of rocks plummeted from the lip of the chasm. Jaya gritted her teeth and the azure fire grew brighter. Then, with a sound like rushing water, a torrent of crimson light erupted from Ineza's mouth. It spiraled away into the night sky before dissipating.

Sten caught Ineza as she slumped to the ground. Her breathing was labored, but the magic had left her. Charred gashes covered her face where the escaping magic had seared her flesh.

Her eyes fluttered open. "Am... am I dead?"

He almost laughed. "No. You're safe, Ineza."

"Oh." She managed a weak smile. "Then thank you all." Sten held her tightly as her eyes closed.

Jaya rose to her feet and brushed aside a strand of curly red hair. She briefly embraced Culyan, and then fired a bolt of sapphire light into his chest.

"Ow!" He massaged his ribs. "What was that for?"

"Why is it," said Jaya, "that every time I see you, my life goes to hell?" She swept back her hair and looked to the sky, as if to calm herself.

"It's not my fault. We came to *help* you, actually."

"So your brother tells me." Jaya sighed and folded her arms. "I suppose you'll have to fill me in on the ride back to Dinh. At least the girl is safe. For the moment, anyway."

ASSURANCES

Tiberion Marstarrow paced about his office, pausing every now and then to scribble a few hasty words onto a pile of parchments that littered his desk. His plan was nearing completion. A few more days and everything would be in place. But he needed assurances as to its success. He strode to the window and gazed out across the capital. The rooftops were silver in the moonlight. Orange lanterns blazed merrily from street corners. Across the bailey and above the walls of his keep rose the great towers of the Sanctum, blacker than midnight. He studied them, and shook his head.

Only one question remained, but it was the most important question of all. Would the people of Heldan Port believe him?

There came an insistent knocking at the neighboring window. Marstarrow frowned. Nobody could scale the precipitous walls of his keep. Well, that was not entirely true. An assassin had succeeded, long ago, but she had not cared to announce her coming. He strode to the window, and was surprised to find Raxo leering up at him through the glass. The little red demon stood spread-eagle against the window, pounding his head against the glass and clutching desperately to the hinges. Marstarrow opened the window and the demon tumbled inside, spouting an impressive collection of profanity.

"Bloody hell," Raxo gasped. "Why'd your office have to be so damn high? I thought it was the end for little ol' me."

Marstarrow raised an eyebrow. "I was under the impression demons cannot die."

Raxo massaged his claws. "Well no, not technically. Technically, demons can't die in the physical realm of this world, as our essences are tied to a nether-worldly void-realm thingee that exists somewhere outside this realm's worldly realityness. We clear?"

"Crystal."

"Good. And even if we can't die, dyin' still hurts like a son of a bi-"

"The hour is rather late, Raxo. To what do I owe this unexpected pleasure?"

The demon made a grim face. "Boss and G'rok' were arrested last night. Seems the Houses have the City Guard on their side. They set us up. Tried to get G'rok angry by threatenin' Butterson. Only they succeeded a little too well. She killed one of 'em."

Marstarrow absorbed this in silence. "I see," was all he finally said.

Raxo puffed out his chest and continued. "I escaped to bring you word. Heroically, I might add. Been dodgin' those guard buggers all day to get to you. I had to act like a cat at one point to avoid suspicion. You should have seen me, meowin' and rubbin' up against this nitwit's leg like a bloody *cat*. It's amazin' what you humans fail to see what's right in front of you."

Marstarrow frowned. "You are certain the Houses orchestrated Mord's capture?"

"Oh yes, said nitwits told us as much."

Marstarrow ran his fingers through his hair and closed his eyes. "They aim to use Mord against me."

"Go figure. We've been waitin' to hear from you for days, and now we're the ones payin' the price for helpin' you in the first place. You better have a damn good reason for keepin' us in the dark. What have you been doin' up here, anyways?"

"I have been thinking," Marstarrow replied evenly.

"What?" spluttered Raxo incredulously. "You've been... *thinkin'*?" The demon hopped onto Marstarrow's desk, swelling with anger. "You've been *thinkin'*? What the hell does that mean? The entire city is fallin' apart and you've been *thinkin'*? You sent the Ardas and your Shrikes into the Wilds, most likely to their very painful doom, and you've been *thinkin'*? They're probably out there right now, surrounded by danger, avoidin' death by the skin of their teeth. Perhaps they're makin' some friends here, some enemies there, all the while learnin' important things about themselves along the way. But you sit here... *thinkin'*?"

Marstarrow clasped his hands in front of him. "Raxo, I understand your frustration, but these matters require a delicate touch. Everything I have done has been for the sake of the capital. I keep my plans to myself to ensure success, nothing more. And I certainly did not expect Mord and G'rok to suffer my association."

"Fine, Chancellor, but you need to hear *me*, now." Raxo angrily poked a claw into Marstarrow's chest. "You don't do this to your friends. You don't scheme and plot and use people as puppets. The Ardas may be out of your control, but Butterson and G'rok need your help. It's your fault they're sittin' in the dungeons right now. You dragged us into this mess and you better damn well drag us out. So, what are you gonna do?" He crossed his arms.

"I will speak to the City Guard and attempt to secure safe release for Mord and G'rok."

Raxo vigorously shook his head. "Not good enough. You need to talk to Butterson yourself, and you need to tell us your plans. Otherwise, I'll march right on up to the Heads of House and let 'em know you're on to 'em."

"Did you just threaten me, Raxo?" said Marstarrow quietly.

"You're damn right I did!" The demon matched Marstarrow's cold stare. The room descended into a tense silence.

And then, with a spark of realization, Marstarrow smiled, despite himself. Within his mind, the fiendishly complex assortment of cogs, wheels, levers, and gears clicked perfectly into place.

"Why are you smilin' like that?" said Raxo. "You look demented."

"Perhaps I am, Raxo, perhaps I am. As usual, your unwavering candor has proven singularly insightful. It is time I tell you and Mord everything. But to do so, we will need to speak with him. In person."

Raxo narrowed his eyes suspiciously. "Well he's locked away in the dungeons, so I don't see how that's possible. The Houses own the City Guard, remember?"

"Then we shall need a disguise," said Marstarrow, "and I have just the idea. Though you will not like what I have in mind."

BEHIND BARS

Water dripped from the dank, mold-encrusted walls of Heldan Port's dungeons. Butterson sat with his back to the door of his prison, listening to the sound of G'rok's snoring in the adjacent cell. The orc had cried herself to sleep, despite his attempts to sooth her conscience. It wasn't her fault she'd slain the guard or that they'd been arrested. Her loyalty was the only reason he was still alive. He had no doubt that the guards would have killed him had she not intervened, despite whatever orders had come from the Heads of House.

He rose suddenly and kicked the iron latticework. The sound echoed crazily through the claustrophobic labyrinth. Moments later, there came the clanking of keys. A squat, ugly goblin waddled into view, clutching a veiled lantern in one hand. He rapped a heavy baton against the bars and sneered. "Knock that off, you bathtard. One more noithe from you and

I'll come in there and thut you up mythelf." The gaoler's teeth had been filed to points.

"Talk is cheap when you're safely behind bars," said Butterson. "Open this door and we'll see what happens. Or better yet, open G'rok's."

The goblin cast a wary look at the sleeping orc. "We'll thee how tough you are when you're thwinging from the gallowth." He trundled back to his station and Butterson's cell was again plunged into darkness.

Butterson slumped back to the ground. Why had he ever agreed to help Marstarrow? Everything had been going so well for him, up until that fateful night when the chancellor had entered the Jackamoose. His business had been flourishing, bringing in more coin than he'd seen in his entire life. If he'd shared in Raxo's aspirations, he'd be sitting in a fancy house overlooking the city right now, happily sipping posh spirits instead of rotting in some cell beneath the ground. He should have kept his fool head down and ignored Marstarrow that night. He was a self-reliant businessman, molded by the cruel and unforgiving streets of the capital. Why should he concern himself with the city's problems, now, when the city had never given a damn about him? Especially when whatever was happening to the city was making him rich.

A distant *thump* sounded from the direction of the gaoler's station, followed by a stifled curse. The jingling of keys approached once again, accompanied by the flickering light of the lantern.

Butterson rose hotly to his feet. "Will you sod off? I haven't done anything. Save your empty threats and leave us alone."

But it wasn't the gaoler who now approached from the darkness. A hunchbacked figure limped down the corridor, face hidden by a moth-eaten cloak. Butterson retreated warily as the stranger paused in front of his cell. Awful boils and layers of grime covered his face, and his nose and mouth were crooked from having been broken and never repaired. The man smiled, and rows of rotten teeth poked from swollen gums. A foul odor swept into Butterson's cell. He recoiled. The goblin was veritably beautiful in comparison to the thing standing in front of him.

"Good evening, Mord." The man's voice was elegant, crisp, and diametrically opposed the filth and squalor of his appearance. "I must apologize for your imprisonment. It was never my intention for the Houses to learn of your involvement."

Butterson gaped in disbelief. "Tiberion? Is that you?" The man bowed slightly. The hump on his back squirmed and shifted, and Raxo appeared from beneath the folds of fetid cloth. He grinned cheekily at Butterson.

"Evenin', Boss."

"What are you two doing here?" Butterson approached the door and lowered his voice. "Why do you look like that?"

Marstarrow stretched and drew himself upright. "To avoid detection, one need only become that which others refuse to see. I subsequently find the guise of a beggar to be a most effective means of traveling throughout the city, unseen. An unfortunate truth, to be sure, but a truth nonetheless."

Raxo wrung out his ear with a claw. "Yeah, but was it really necessary to stuff me in your stinkin' old cloak like a sack of potatoes? It'll take weeks to wash away the smell."

"Of course it was necessary," said Marstarrow. "I believe your contribution brought the ensemble together quite nicely."

"This is ridiculous," said Butterson. "I can't talk to you looking like that."

"Very well." With a flurry of deft movements, Marstarrow reappeared from the grime and pocketed an assortment of prosthetics. He smoothed down his silver hair. "Is this preferable?"

"Greatly," said Butterson. "But you still reek."

Marstarrow smiled sourly. "That is beyond my control, unfortunately. Now, I come to you with a proposition, Mord, and I hope you allow it due consideration. If you so choose, I will let you free, here and now. I have secured safe passage into hiding for both G'rok and yourself. You can leave these dungeons and remain hidden until this affair has reached its conclusion. You will keep your tavern and regain your former life, and you will never hear from me again. You will be free to live as you please."

"I'm sorely tempted to accept that offer without hearing more. We're in here because of *you*, Tiberion. We almost died last night, because of *you*. You've shared none of the faith that we've all placed in *you*. To be honest, I'm not even sure why I trusted you in the first place."

Marstarrow studied him through the bars before responding. "I believe you trusted me because you remember what life was like before I came to Heldan Port. Despite my many short-comings, I can assure you the capital will suffer a far worse fate should the Houses regain control. As such, I implore you to hear me, and believe in me, one last time."

Butterson folded his arms over his beard. "Why should I?"

"Because I will place my full trust in you," said Marstarrow softly. "I will tell you everything."

Butterson gave a bellicose shake of his head. "And what if I don't want to hear what you have to say? What if I don't believe you?"

Marstarrow didn't answer, instead unlocking the cell door with a metallic *click*.

Butterson tentatively stepped into the passage. The goblin gaoler was sprawled unconscious across the floor of his station. Butterson swiped the keys from Marstarrow's hand and unlocked G'rok's prison. She woke with a start, rubbing sleep from her eyes. Raxo scampered down from the chancellor and scaled her shoulder, and fondly tweaked her ear.

"Your freedom lies behind you," said Marstarrow. "What is your decision?"

Butterson looked to Raxo. The demon shrugged. "I think you know what needs doin', Boss, but the choice is yours. We'll follow you to whatever end. Though preferably not ours."

Butterson stood in silent contemplation, his every instinct urging him to walk away. He could accept the chancellor's offer, stroll out of the dungeons, and never look back. He'd never have to deal with Marstarrow or his infernal schemes again. He'd be free to return to his tavern and the brewing of ales. The capital didn't need him, after all. It could fend for itself.

But as he watched the chancellor, alone and uncharacteristically exposed in the flickering gloom of the dungeons, his anger waned. "Damn you, Tiberion," he said quietly. "How did you come to have such a hold over me?"

"THAT MEAN WE HELP?" said G'rok. Her tusks glimmered in the lantern light.

Butterson nodded begrudgingly. "Yes. Despite my better judgment, I'll hear what you have to say, Tiberion. But this is the last time I'll stick my neck out for you. You better tell us everything, and I mean, *everything.*"

Marstarrow's pale eyes glittered. He swept forward and laid a hand on Butterson's shoulder. "You are a better man than I, Mord Butterson. Now, listen carefully, as we do not have much time..."

Butterson leaned against the dungeon wall and closed his eyes when the chancellor had finished speaking. "You are one crazy bastard, you know that?"

"I have found that the boldest of plans often require a touch of lunacy."

"I'd say we're a bit beyond lunacy, at this point," said Raxo. "Try bat-shit crazy."

"As you wish."

"You know we're all going to die if this fails," said Butterson.

"Undoubtedly."

"And you're sure Lord Impo will rise to the bait?"

"I trust in his arrogance," said Marstarrow. "But it is imperative Raxo bring word to Gefwyn. We cannot hope to succeed without his assistance."

"Not a problem," said Raxo. "Us little folk stick together. His words, not mine. I found him a bit weird, honestly. Too much time cooped up in that place all by his lonesome. But I expect he'll be downright eager to help us once he learns what the Houses did to his precious G'rok."

"G'ROK LOVE LITTLE BEARDED MAN."

Raxo broke into an acerbic smile. "And will you look at that? We've just added a touching romantic interest to this convoluted mess of a story. I'd say that wraps up the essential ingredients for a happy endin'."

"Indeed," said Marstarrow. He turned to Butterson. "You can still walk away, Mord. I would not fault you for doing so."

Butterson shook his head. "No, it's time we put an end to all of this. I've followed you this far. It's too late to turn away now."

Marstarrow bowed solemnly. "Then I thank you, once again. But perhaps you should stop looking to me for the source of your motivation."

"What do you mean? The only reason we're involved in this is because you came to my tavern and asked for our help."

"Correct me if I am mistaken," said Marstarrow, his expression indecipherable, "but you were *there* when news of the wizards' disappearance was announced. You were *there* when the Brothers Arda entered the capital. And you were *there* for the people of my city when they needed a place to turn for solace and comfort in uncertain times. You have a knack for being *there*, Mord Butterson, wherever *there* may be, and that has nothing to do with me. I wonder why that is? Something to consider, I should think."

"I was *there* to sell my beers."

Marstarrow inclined his head. "As you say. But it is time

I take my leave. Now, Mord, G'rok, if you would be so kind?" He gestured graciously to the cells' open doors.

For the second time that night, Butterson found himself staring at Marstarrow through the rusted iron bars of a locked cell. The chancellor disappeared under layers of false prosthetics, and the stooped beggar reappeared moments later.

"Until we meet again," said Marstarrow. He extended a grimy hand through the bars and Butterson shook it. With a curt nod, he began down the passage.

"Wait," Butterson called after him. "You still haven't told us what you found in the Sanctum."

The chancellor paused, his face obscured by darkness. "I promise to tell you what I discovered, Mord, but not tonight. For now, those concerns lie far beyond our control. Instead, we must place our trust in the Brothers Arda and focus on the task at hand. If we succeed in stopping the Houses, we shall revisit the matter at a later time."

"I'm going to hold you to that."

"I would expect nothing less." Marstarrow raised the lantern in farewell and hobbled out of the dungeons.

Butterson sat awake in his cell, hours later, thinking over everything Marstarrow had said. *"You have a knack for being there, Mord Butterson, wherever there may be, and that has nothing to do with me. I wonder why that is..."* He barely noticed when the goblin gaoler came to check on him, nursing an ugly welt over one eye.

In truth, he didn't know why he continued to help Marstarrow. Maybe it was his perpetual, inexplicable desire to earn the chancellor's respect. Maybe it was the intrinsic knowledge that Heldan Port fared better under Marstarrow's rule than the Houses'. Or maybe it was as Raxo said, and he had simply developed a taste for heroics.

But whatever the case, he was certain of one thing. The fate of Heldan Port would be decided in two days' time, and the entire plan rested upon his shoulders.

DARK DREAMS

Sylvus Riddleston toyed with the hem of his robes, staring blankly at the bars of his cage. His back ached from his prolonged imprisonment, but he barely registered the discomfort. His entire body was afire.

He shuddered as the memories came rushing back. Vandra, clad in robes as black as her hair, the crimson light of her foul magic reflected in her terrible smile. The mist had come then, rising languidly from the cracks in the floor. It had been alien, almost sentient, and swarmed over his entire body before breaking into his mind and obscuring his thoughts. Pain had followed. Pain like nothing Riddleston had ever experienced, as though his soul was being rent apart. Gently, he rested his head against the cold iron, and winced at the lance of agony.

The shadows had come next. Riddleston had sat, paralyzed and horrorstruck, as Vandra harvested hundreds of blackened shades from his own body. When she had finished with him, she had moved to the next cage, and then the next, until the entire hall rang with the wizards' screams.

Then, everything became distant and murky, as if it had taken place in a half-forgotten dream, or rather a hundred dreams simultaneously. Riddleston kneaded his temple with a knuckle, trying to remember. There had been a fierce battle in murky woods. He had watched the fighting through unfamiliar eyes, and *felt* the agony of his death as each of his harvested shades were cut down. There had been warriors in black, a golden wolf, a giant...

A fresh spike of pain skewered his insides. He shoved the collar of his robe into his mouth and bit down hard.

A dream... A hundred dreams... A dark wood... Unquenchable rage...

Vandra's will had been impossible to disobey. Yet greater still was his overwhelming desire to kill the dwarves and the elf girl, to cleanse their magic from the world. Their powers had taunted him, burning white hot in the midst of the murky battle.

Riddleston shook his head and regulated his breathing. There was no point in dwelling on whatever the hell Vandra had done to him. The present demanded his attention if he was to survive.

Drawing on his last vestiges of power, he once again attempted to brute force the lock. It glowed faintly at his magical pressures, but remained obstinately fastened. He slumped back, hands trembling, though whether from pain or exhaustion he didn't know. Consciousness slipped away like an ebbing tide.

His eyes snapped open as the door at the far end of the chamber swung open. Vandra entered, her dark eyes glittering in the torchlight.

"Good morning, gentlemen!" She strolled down the length of cages. The wizards whimpered and recoiled at her presence.

Like Riddleston, they had fared poorly from the harvest and ensuing memories of battle. "Your performance in the Wilds proved less than satisfactory," she continued, "but I see potential in you. It seems strength in numbers is our only option, moving forward. Quantity over quality." She stopped in front of Riddleston's cage and held the torch up to the bars. "I'm sorry to say this doesn't bode well for you, *Highest Hat*. I shall need considerably more... resources from you. From all of you, in fact." The wizards in adjacent cages moaned.

"You don't stand a chance against those men and women in the forest," said Riddleston venomously. "Harvest us as many times as you wish, it won't make a difference. You'll kill us all long before you've gathered enough *resources* to defeat them."

She cocked her head and tapped a pale finger against her teeth. "Harvest. I like that. Still, you are correct. You would all succumb to the grave long before I'm satisfied." She raised an eyebrow and gave him a lascivious smile. "Perhaps it's time you learn my little secret. Come with me."

At a wave from her hand, the door to Riddleston's cage sprang open. As he tumbled to the cold stones, the hem of his robe caught on the bars and tore free. He hastily stuffed the strip of fabric into a pocket with a furtive glance at Vandra. She was already sweeping toward the door, her back to him.

He followed her into a dripping passageway, dimly lit by glowing patches of emerald mushrooms. They navigated the winding path deeper and deeper into the gloom.

"These are dwarven tunnels," said Vandra, tracing one finger along the chiseled walls. "They mined these mountains long ago, until they had depleted the mountain of its precious minerals. They left behind this empty shrine as witness to the greed and shortsightedness of Miz's peoples."

They passed into an immense cavern with glittering stalactites. The entrances to hundreds of mineshafts spotted the walls, their lengths disappearing into the darkness beyond.

Long-abandoned equipment littered the cavern floor, collecting dust and cobwebs. There were picks, trolleys, sledgehammers, rotten wooden supports, and even a collection of burlap sacks labeled, 'Explosive Takk,' in faded letters.

Vandra selected another featureless passage. "You and your men are no different from the dwarves and their methods. You take incessantly, never pausing to look beyond your own ambitions or desires. You are far worse than the dwarves, in truth. At least their destruction was localized to the mountains."

"What are you insinuating?" panted Riddleston. He struggled to keep pace with her long strides. "My wizards have never destroyed a thing. We exist to help the capital and its people."

Vandra snorted. "If you truly believe that you're more delusional than I imagined. Magic must always be respected, yet you have abused it to no end. No longer, though."

Another barred door emerged from the blackness. Vandra paused with a knowing smile. "You were correct about one thing, old man. I cannot hope to defeat my enemies by relying on you and your sorry collection of wizards. I had hoped your powers would supplement my own during your so-called harvest, but it turns out you are no different than the others. Perhaps I should have gotten rid of you."

"Do you ever tire of talking?" Riddleston growled. "Kill us or harvest us, I don't care at this point. Just shut the hell up." He crossed his arms over his beard, then frowned suspiciously. "Hold on. What do you mean by others?"

She opened the door. Exposed was a vast cavern larger than the one they had passed through. The ceiling of the cave disappeared into the gloom, while its floor lay hidden behind the lip of a cliff. Vandra walked to the edge of the precipice and beckoned for Riddleston to join her.

With a sense of increasing dread, he obeyed. When he looked into the depths of the cavern, his breath caught in his chest. "What have you done?" he said quietly.

Tens of thousands of shades covered the cavern floor in a sea of blackness. They stood still and expectant, the glow from their eyes bathing the rock in vermillion light. Men, elves, dwarves, and orcs waited in mute, serried ranks, some ahorse, the mounts as blackened and twisted as their riders. A line of trebuchets and ballistae stood watch over the terrible army arrayed before it. The entire far wall was obscured by a solid mass of cages, similar to those that held Riddleston and his wizards.

"I have assured my victory," said Vandra. "Dinh will break before me, and the world after."

"Why?" Riddleston tore his gaze from the awful spectacle. "Why are you doing this?"

"Because Miz needs to be saved," said Vandra. "And that is all you need to know." A crimson spark burst into life at the tip of her finger. As one, thousands of red eyes blazed up through the darkness to stare at their position. Riddleston backed away as she advanced, her hand raised. Mist began to swirl from the ground, catching the infernal glow of the magic building along her arms. "Join my legions, old man. It's time for another harvest."

He screamed as the fog closed in around him.

Hours later, Riddleston felt himself ascending through the winding tunnels. A pair of the shades supported his weight, following closely in Vandra's footsteps. Their touch was utterly devoid of warmth, as if they were forged of living, malleable stone. Riddleston fought to remain conscious. His hand fell into the pocket of his robe and closed tightly around the torn strip of cloth.

When they arrived at the door to the wizards' prisons, he struggled to his feet and shrugged off the shadows. "Get your filthy hands off of me! I can walk... I *will* walk on my own." Vandra shrugged and unlocked the bolted door. Riddleston staggered forward and caught himself against the frame. In the blink of an eye he stuffed the piece of fabric into the lock's home, shielding the action with his body. Then he collapsed inside.

Vandra stepped over him. "Pathetic. Leave him, he's not going anywhere. Bring the rest."

Cries of terror echoed throughout the chamber as Riddleston again lost consciousness.

He awoke sometime later, his entire body ablaze. The line of cages hung empty, swaying gently, as if in gestures of farewell.

Riddleston waited until his head cleared, then pulled himself to the chamber door. He peered into the lock and almost cried out in relief. The strip of his robe was just visible between the metal links, preventing the lock's closure. Gingerly, he pinched the bit of cloth and teased it outward. His heart hammered in his ears as the bolt shifted, ever so slightly.

With a creak of hinges, the bolt popped free from its home, and the door swung open. Riddleston stifled a sob of elation, stumbled into the corridor, and fled. He staggered through the maze of passageways, continuing upward every time the tunnel branched. He climbed higher and higher, until his lungs burned and he thought he might again pass out.

The white glow of Tanduil blinded him when he finally exited the tunnels. He fell to his knees and reeled as a wave of heat struck him, blinking furiously. He was on the slopes of a wind-swept mountain. An expanse of carmine rock and sand lay before him, desolate and huge. A gaping canyon stretched away from the base of the mountain, the landscape riven by its enormity. And far in the distance, at the edge of the great chasm, the walls of a city shimmered in the heat.

With a strangled cry of thanks, Riddleston began to pick his way down the mountain.

CONTACT

The walls of Dinh appeared through the mid-morning haze of the Canyonlands. Sten floated alongside Ineza, her head cradled in his lap while she slept.

The sprawling city perched on the edge of the great canyon, wearing the color of the surrounding wasteland. Towering stone walls stretched along the northern, eastern, and southern boundaries of the city, bleached by the sun. Dinh's western border, those parts of the city contiguous to the chasm, sported no such defenses. Overhead, pale blue banners poked from crenelated towers, fluttering gaily in the gentle breeze as if to welcome the company into the city. Jaya led them through handsome city gates emblazoned with the seal of Dinh: a white rose atop a crimson field.

People whispered as they passed into Dinh's heart. They wore thin, draping clothing that shielded their dark skin from the already intense morning heat of Tanduil. Awestruck expressions followed Culyan and Kipto as the pair threaded their way through the dust-covered streets. Laughter shadowed Sten and the dwarves floating atop their cloud. Before long, a growing throng of curious onlookers was following their progress through the city.

They entered a bustling bazaar. Sprawling tents lined the streets and shaded the merchants peddling their wares to the crowds. A plethora of delightful and mysterious aromas hung in the air. Traders brandished food, drink, and perfumes laden with piquant spices. Taverns and blacksmiths, tailors and temples, and rows and rows of neatly symmetrical houses built from the same red stone of the Canyonlands filtered past. Laughter and good cheer dominated the scene.

"Why is everyone so happy?" Sten whispered to Two. "We've passed through most of the city by now and nobody's tried to rob or murder us. What's their game?"

"It's no game, lad." Two's jeweled beard flashed in the sunlight. "The streets of Heldan Port are notoriously unsavory compared to most."

"Well it's not natural." Sten warily eyed a child. She waved at him before giggling and vanishing into the crowds. "I don't trust happy people. In Heldan Port, it's safe to assume that half the population wants to kill you for your coin, and the rest would do it just for fun. At least there's certainty in that."

A domed citadel sprouted from the center of the city, its exterior lined with chiseled colonnades and stout buttresses. Its great red exterior was inset with vibrant stained-glass windows. Below, guards in ornamental armor patrolled the grounds. Eotan sat upon its steps, twirling his daggers. When he saw them, he jumped to his feet and ran to embrace Manye. He nodded to Ineza's sleeping form. "I see that Jaya arrived in time."

"Only just," said Jaya. She dismounted from Lilenti. "You can thank this mare of yours. I've never moved so quickly in my life and I'm a damned mage."

Eotan brushed down Lilenti's neck with a proud smile, but then his expression darkened. "Where is Captain Whitney?"

"They shouldn't be far behind," said Culyan. "We left them at the crossing, but he has his Follower. Dinh's guard knows of their coming."

"Very well. The baroness wishes to speak with us, Whitney included, so we'll just have to wait for his arrival."

"In the mean time," said Jaya, "you need to get that girl to the infirmary. I may have stopped the magic from killing her but she's extremely weak."

Ineza was carted away, moaning slightly beneath the blackened wounds that crisscrossed her face.

Tanduil had reached its zenith by the time Whitney arrived. He sweated profusely in the heat, and the tips of his mustache sagged. He spurred his horse forward when he came upon them and desperately scanned the assemblage. "Corporal Ghet! Where is she? Does... does she live?"

"She'll be fine," said Culyan. "Thanks to my brother and Lady Janderfel, here."

Whitney exhaled and jumped from his horse. He embraced Eotan first, then Jaya. "Thank you both. I don't know what I'd have done losing Hemmie and Ghet in the same day."

Eotan's eyes were as cold as glacial ice. "Your conscience would have undoubtedly suffered. What were you thinking, pursuing Vandra on your own?"

"I was foolish," said Whitney, lamely. "I was blinded by rage and I wanted-"

"You wanted to be the hero!" snarled Eotan. "You wanted the satisfaction of stopping Vandra by yourself and look what it cost you. Corporal Ghet almost died for your arrogance." Culyan laid a restraining arm on his brother's shoulder but he brushed him off. His blue eyes burned angrily into Whitney's. "You'd be wise to remember your place in this story, Captain."

Whitney's face reddened.

Jaya stepped between them. "That's enough, Eotan. You still owe the Shrikes your life, from what Culyan has told me. Perhaps Whitney isn't the only one who needs to check his pride. I swear to the gods, putting up with you and your mountain of a brother is exhausting. I've dealt with far too much Arda ego for one lifetime."

"What did I do?" said Culyan innocently.

"Oh, I'm sure you're guilty of something or another. You always are. Like wearing that ridiculous, vainglorious armor of yours. Now, if we're quite done bickering like children, it's time we speak with Baroness Marstarrow. She hates to be kept waiting." Jaya turned on her heel and threw open the citadel's doors, red hair streaming behind her.

"I could happily listen to that woman scold me for the rest of my life," said Culyan.

Sten blinked in the sweltering heat. "Did she just say Baroness *Marstarrow*?"

Culyan grimaced. "Oh yes. She's our dear chancellor's mother."

Sten was dumbstruck. "I thought the chancellor was worried of Dinh waging war!"

"Yes, well, things between the Marstarrows have been a bit tense ever since he hired us to take the capital. As we hear it, the baroness was right peeved her son chose Heldan Port over Dinh. I can understand his concerns."

"But would she really declare war against her own son?"

Culyan chuckled darkly. "Heh, just wait until you meet her. She makes Tiberion seem downright lovely in comparison."

The interior of the citadel was quiet and cool. They entered a large vaulted hall, its walls painted by rows of stained-glass windows. A single straight-backed chair sat on a raised dais at the rear of the chamber, illuminated by the multitude of colors streaming through the glass. The hall was empty, save for a group of men and women huddled near the platform, immersed in discussion.

"That's the High Council of Dinh," whispered Jaya. "They advise the baroness on any and all matters of import to the city. The elven woman is Commander Grayhawk, leader of Dinh's military. The gnome is Lady Wilice. She oversees Dinh's industry and finance sectors. The dwarf is Councilman One, the highest-ranking agriculturist in the Canyonlands. And that man on the left is Councilman Frank Monta. He's the world's premier expert on magical theory and application. He knows more about magic than I could ever dream to learn, though he doesn't practice himself."

"And his name is Frank?" whispered Sten. The bald, bespectacled man was sweating profusely, despite the cool of the citadel. "Just Frank? I thought all of you magical types had ridiculous names, like Frank Firesword, or Frank Fester-wort, or Frank Floppybottom."

"Speak for yourself, *Sten Bregon*," snapped Jaya. They drew up short of the podium. "Now be quiet."

A strained creak sounded from the rear of the hall and a small wooden door swung open. Out stepped an extremely tall, stern woman, her gray hair pulled into a tight bun. Her cold eyes swept across the assembled company. Sten was struck with an overwhelming desire to correct his posture and behave. The woman nodded curtly to the council and settled into the rigid chair.

"I am Baroness Marstarrow." She spoke in the same clipped, decisive manner as the chancellor, which provided zero insight into their emotions. "I welcome you to my city, though Lady Janderfel informs me you've come to deliver a warning. I find this news most concerning." Sten shifted uncomfortably as her unflinching gaze bore into them. "Well?" she demanded sharply. "Somebody speak up, we haven't all day!"

Culyan cleared his throat and stepped forward, attempting unsuccessfully to tame his mane of hair. "Baroness Marstarrow, we thank you for welcoming us into your city. My name is Culyan Arda, and-"

"I know who *you* are," she snapped. "The infamous Brothers Arda and the Bearded Eight; the reasons incarnate why my son rescinded his claim to this throne. You and your band of miscreants delivered Heldan Port to Tiberion on a platter, and Dinh lost its heir in the process. He was groomed to take over *my* city, not that lecherous filth-pit you call a capital. He's a Baron of Dinh by birthright. He chose that nonsensical title of 'Chancellor Marstarrow' just to spite me. And to make matters worse, you managed to convince my most talented mage to share in your ignoble quest, through means still unknown to me." Jaya reddened. "When I heard tell of the Brothers Arda riding for Dinh, I knew trouble would be following close behind. You two are a plague let loose upon the world."

Culyan considered the stained-glass windows and chewed his lip. "Er... Right. Sorry about all of that. Anyway, this is Captain Whitney of the Shrikes, Manye of the, erm... forest, and Sten Arda. Our nephew."

The baroness leaned forward to examine Sten. "Good heavens, there are more of you? Just when I thought matters couldn't get any worse, another Arda comes into my city. Well step forward, boy, let me have a look at you." Sten shuffled to join his uncle, distinctly aware of the appraising gazes of the High Council.

"Stand perfectly still," whispered Culyan from the corner of his mouth. "Don't make eye contact or she'll pounce."

The baroness snapped her fingers. "Stop whispering like a pair of children! What message do you bring from my son? I have no doubt it was he who put you up to all of this."

The Marshal's booming voice rang through the hall. He

told of the wizards and the chancellor's ploy to force their assistance. He shared their encounter with the bear and the sickly forest, touched by the strange mist spreading throughout the Wilds. He spoke of Lentarro and the Oethyr, and the Shrikes' rescue on the plains before their flight to the Waypoint. And finally, he detailed Vandra's ambush with her battalion of Dark Ones, and the terrible magic she had used on Hemmie and Ineza.

Baroness Marstarrow listened without expression. One slender finger tapped the arm of her chair. "You're certain this Vandra has turned her attention on Dinh?"

"She's attempted to stop us from reaching you on two separate occasions," said Eotan. "It stands to reason she hoped to find you unprepared for her coming."

"Maybe," said the baroness. "Or perhaps the mist and your troublesome wizards are unrelated to this woman. Do you have proof of her involvement in Heldan Port's troubles?"

"Admittedly, no," said Captain Whitney. "Chancellor Marstarrow actually considered the possibility that you were behind everything. He feared you might take advantage of the city's weakened state and initiate hostilities."

The baroness smiled and leaned back. "Smart boy. But Dinh isn't to blame for Heldan Port's misfortunes. I've no previous knowledge of what you've told me here today, save for the tales regarding this unnatural mist. Your version of events corroborates what we've previously heard regarding its effects. I am sorry that I cannot provide information concerning the disappearance of your Sanctum, though I suspect this Vandra may have played a role in this as well. I am not one to believe in coincidences, and these events align far too precisely to be unrelated. I am inclined to believe Tiberion's message, and I thank you for delivering his words. Dinh shall prepare for Vandra's coming, in whatever form that may be, and respond accordingly."

The diminutive, bald councilman shuffled forward and raised a hand. "If I may, Baroness?"

"Yes, Frank?"

He cleared his throat and wrung his hands. "In my opinion, we should turn our f-f-focus to the mist rather than this renegade enchantress," he stuttered. "The blight may ultimately prove a f-f-far more serious threat to Dinh if we f-f-fail to mount a proportionate response in time. My research suggests that the mist is magical in nature and inherently unstable, which points to something f-f-far more sinister than a simple plague. I believe the mist is derived f-f-from Miz herself. As I've said bef-f-fore, f-f-further research must be conducted if we're to truly understand-"

"Now is not the time for one of your lectures," said the baroness. "As of now, the mist is completely contained within the Wilds and out of sight. We shall discuss your theories once the immediate threat has been addressed."

The little man's glasses slid down his sweaty nose. "As you will."

"Then it is decided." The baroness rose from her chair. "Commander Grayhawk, double the guard on the city walls and the Mages' Enclave. Nobody enters my city without my knowledge. We will not be caught unaware like our western counterpart. If Vandra aims to take Dinh with her Dark Ones, she will find that a reckoning awaits her."

The doors to the great hall boomed open, and a soldier hurriedly approached the dais. He skidded to a halt and bowed low. "Baroness, High Council of Dinh. We've just arrested an elderly gentleman attempting to gain entry to the city."

"Why does this concern me?" asked the baroness.

The guard shifted beneath his suit of mail. "Well, he's caused quite the scene, ma'am. He turned Lieutenant Longdon into a toad and refuses to change him back until you grant him an audience."

Baroness Marstarrow pinched the bridge of her nose. "The Ardas arrive at my city's walls, and within the hour, trouble follows in their footsteps. Who is this man?"

"Couldn't say, ma'am, but he claims to be a wizard of Heldan Port."

A WIZARD'S TALE

Minutes later, the doors to the hall were thrown open, and an elderly, rotund man with a white beard was dragged toward the dais by a pair of guards. His robes were torn and disheveled, stained red by the dust of the Canyonlands. Captain Whitney inhaled sharply as the newcomer was set before the baroness. "That's Sylvus Riddleston! Highest Hat of the Sanctum!"

The old man swiveled at the proclamation. "You're damned right I am." He shrugged off the guards' restraints and squinted through a pair of crescent spectacles resting beneath extremely bushy eyebrows. His eyes widened. "Captain Whitney? What the hell are you doing here? And do I see the Brothers Arda and your band of dwarves? Good gracious me, I haven't seen you lot for years. I thought you were off hiding in the woods, rejecting the comforts of civilized life in favor of a pure spirit, or some such drivel."

"Mr. Riddleston!" snapped the baroness. "If I may request a moment of your time?"

The old wizard gathered his soiled robes about him. "You must be Tiberion's mother, then. He's spoken of you on several occasions."

The baroness folded one leg over the other and gripped the arms of her chair. "Indeed?"

"Oh yes," said Riddleston. "If I remember correctly, he said you were a right old hag, and if he was to ever rule a city he must take Heldan Port for his own because you were too ornery to die." He vaguely waved a hand. "Or something similar, my memory isn't what it used to be." A pair of the High Council members stifled laughter.

"Enough," snapped the baroness. "It is time you upheld your end of the bargain, as I've granted you your audience." Riddleston stared at her blankly. She leaned forward and adopted a sugary tone, like a grandmother on the verge of walloping ill-behaved progeny. "Lieutenant Longdon, Mr. Riddleston. Release him from your spell, if you would be so kind."

"Oh, right you are." He withdrew a speckled toad from the interior of his robes. With a snap of his fingers and a puff of acrid smoke, the toad vanished to be replaced by a soldier. The man opened his mouth to speak but only succeeded in croaking. "Don't worry about that," said Riddleston. "The effects should wear off in a few weeks."

The baroness drummed her fingers on her chair as Lieutenant Longdon was removed from the hall, croaking fitfully. "Now, if there are no further distractions," she said, "I believe we are all anxious to hear your tale, Mr. Riddleston. The Brothers Arda and Captain Whitney have traveled to my city at great personal risk to warn me of your Sanctum's disappearance. It is strangely fortuitous that you've arrived here today."

"Fortuitous my left buttocks," said Riddleston haughtily. "I escaped the clutches of a mad woman, descended an entire bloody mountain, and crossed a damned desert to get here. There was nothing fortuitous about any of that. It was downright heroic."

The baroness massaged her temples. "Just get on with it, please."

Riddleston clasped his hands behind his back and considered the ceiling. "Well, it all started several weeks ago. My wizards and I were set to pass judgment on the chancellor's newest wave of magical restrictions when an intruder broke into the Sanctum. An enchantress by the name of Vandra. I have no idea how she gained entry. Breaking into the Sanctum is impossible."

"Evidence points to the contrary," said the baroness.

Riddleston scoffed. "Wizards have been adding their own unique wards and barriers to the Sanctum for hundreds of years. Our defenses have become so convoluted and complex that we couldn't remove the damn things if we wanted to."

"How'd Vandra get in, then?" asked Jaya.

Riddleston shrugged and cleaned his crescent spectacles with a sleeve. "If I were to guess, I'd say she received help. I devised a fiendishly clever system of allowing guests to enter the Sanctum. The problem is, she'd need a wizard or someone else with the power to enter the Sanctum to usher her inside."

"So you were betrayed by one of your own," said the baroness.

"Not likely. Vandra took all of my men."

"She defeated all of you single-handedly?" said Jaya, with more than a touch of disdain. "And here I was led to believe that Heldan Port boasted the most powerful collection of magic-users in all of Miz."

Riddleston turned on her, eyebrows bristling. "And you are?"

"Jaya Janderfel, leader of Dinh's magi."

"Well I may be old, girl, but I could still teach you a thing or two about magic."

Blue flames ignited in Jaya's hands. "Call me girl one more time and I'll put you to the test."

Riddleston eyed the magic. "No need for that right now. At least not until I get some food in me. Do you have any food? I haven't eaten in days."

"You could have fooled me," said Jaya.

Riddleston glanced at his stomach and continued. "Yes, well, as I was saying, Vandra took us by surprise. I've never seen such powerful magic in all my years. The next thing I know, I'm hanging from a cage in some fetid dungeon, along with the rest of my wizards. Vandra had spirited us across the entire Heartlands."

"That's impossible," scoffed Jaya.

"Yet here I stand, and I promise you I didn't walk all the way from Heldan Port. Maybe now you'll start to appreciate how powerful Vandra truly is. I'd share in your skepticism had I not witnessed her capabilities first-hand. And I haven't even told you the worst of it."

The baroness rested her chin on tented fingers. "What do you mean?"

"Vandra experimented on us in the mountains," said Riddleston carefully. "For lack of a better word, she harvested us, and turned us into... something. I can't fully explain it, in truth. She controls an awful mist. Summons it at will. It enters your body, seizes your thoughts and mind, and once she controls you she rips apart your very soul and uses it to feed her foul creations." His stoic gaze washed over the room, and he laid a humble hand over his breast. "I'm lucky to be alive."

"We've witnessed this magic ourselves," said Eotan.

"Aye," said Whitney. "She killed one of my soldiers after using him in such a manner."

"Wait a moment," said Riddleston. "It was you lot we attacked in the forest, wasn't it?"

"You were there?" asked Sten.

"Yes and no." Riddleston curled the tip of his beard around a finger. "The shades Vandra created were physically there, and we could see through their eyes, but our actions weren't our own. It's impossible to resist Vandra's will in such a state. The harvest changes one's mind, you see. When you're within the creatures, all you can feel is a terrible rage and a burning desire to kill anyone using magic. Think of it as a lucid dream, or rather a multitude of lucid dreams occurring at the same time, from which you can never wake. Until you die, that is. I can't even begin to count the number of times I died in that forest, and each time it hurt like hell." He pointed a gnarled finger at Sten. "I vividly remember that young man shooting me in the face with an arrow."

"Sorry about that."

"And do you know what Vandra plans to do with these Dark Ones?" asked the baroness.

"Dark Ones?" Riddleston guffawed. "Is that what you lot called us? You've the creativity of a flock of pigeons. Dark Ones, bah! It sounds like something from a children's book. But as a matter of fact, I do know Vandra's plans. She told me as much, in her arrogance. Lucky for you, I was clever enough to escape her dungeons and deliver you that information here today. I'm quite peckish, though, so if there's any chance I might get some-"

The baroness stood suddenly and glared down at him. "Mr. Riddleston! Tell us what you know!"

"Right, right, sorry." He steeled himself with a deep breath. "Vandra has built an army of Dark Ones. She aims to raze this city to the ground." The hall abruptly quieted. The councilmembers exchanged ominous looks.

"Why Dinh?" said the baroness. "We have no quarrel with her."

"Oh, something about cleansing the capitals and con-quering the world or some such nonsense. It's always the same with these types. Apparently, she believes Heldan Port will fall of its own accord in the absence of my wizards."

"And how many Dark Ones has she created, exactly?" said Jaya.

Riddleston screwed up his face, as if unsure whether or not to continue. Then he sighed. "Tens of thousands, by my estimate. They've amassed in the mountains to the south, no more than half a day's march." The baroness slumped back into her chair. Commander Grayhawk sprinted from the hall, calling for her soldiers to join her. The High Council broke into urgent whispers. Sten exchanged dark looks with his uncles and Whitney.

"I shall prepare my magi," Jaya announced, and stormed from the hall, her face set with determination.

Riddleston watched the frantic proceedings beneath his shaggy brows, and a shadow of guilt crossed his face. "Erm, now that I've shared everything I know, is there any chance for some food?"

CALM

Dinh rang with the sounds of furious preparation. Soldiers and workers raced in every direction, shouting orders. The clank of hammers and the rhythmic rasp of sawing hung in the air like dust. Teams of oxen strained to pull massive trebuchets into position. Figures swarmed across the walls and battlements, stocking arrows, piling boulders, and loading cauldrons with pitch. It was as if someone had poked a great anthill with a stick.

Whitney stood at his window, watching the bedlam unfold. His Shrikes, Riddleston, and the Ardas' company were nestled into a tavern across the street, eating, drinking, and talking amidst the turmoil. Only Sten was absent.

He turned from the chaos and sank onto his cot. He had considered joining his soldiers, but his stomach turned at the prospect of company. He closed his eyes, willing sleep to overtake him. It had been days since he'd last rested inside the Waypoint and exhaustion racked his body in waves.

The memories of the Wilds came drifting back to him. He tossed and turned as Vandra's disembodied laughter taunted his thoughts.

"It is all your fault, Captain. He died because you were too weak to stop me."

Corporal Hemmie appeared in the darkness. He was a ghostly specter, with awful crimson eyes that scorched Whitney's soul. He grasped at Whitney with pale, bone-like fingers, and for a moment, the fires extinguished in his eyes. He begged for Whitney to take his hand, to save him from the approaching blackness. With a desperate cry, Whitney reached for the skeletal fingers, but as he did so, the gnome dissolved into a pile of ash. It trickled through Whitney's fingers with a soft *hiss*, like grains of sand through an hourglass. Vandra's laughter returned.

"And what about the girl, Captain? What a shame to bear such hideous scars on such a pretty young face."

The ash swirled away and Ineza appeared. Her entire body was riddled with veins of crimson magic. Smoke coiled from her seared flesh like opaque serpents. She collapsed into Whitney's arms and stared up at him with imploring eyes. The magic slowly burned across her face.

"She would have died for your sins, Captain. Without the Ardas she'd be nothing but a pile of dust. She trusted you, and you betrayed her. You are no hero, Captain. You are nothing."

Whitney awoke with a start, heart hammering, undershirt drenched in sweat. With a curse, he dashed his rucksack against the wall, spilling armor across the wooden floorboards. A muffled yell sounded from within the burlap. Whitney hastily knelt and withdrew the Follower. Its blue light throbbed angrily from within the mahogany box.

"Da hell was dat for?"

Whitney rubbed his eyes wearily. "I'm sorry, Zwat, I forgot you were in there."

"Howsabout I stick you in a sack and smash you against da wall, see how you like it?"

"I said I'm sorry!" snapped Whitney. He set the box on the edge of the bed.

The light dimmed slightly. "Say, not dat I care or nuffin', but you don't look so good."

"I've had trouble sleeping."

"'Cause of what happened in da woods?"

Whitney winced and nodded. "I can't help feeling responsible for... for..." He rested his head in his palms. "For Hemmie. For Ineza."

"Dat's 'cause you *are* responsible," said Zwat. Whitney made to stuff the Follower into his bag. "Wait, wait, hear me out!" With reluctance, Whitney returned the box to the edge of the bed. "Dat's better," said Zwat, glowing brightly. "Now listen to me, Captain Mustache, and listen well. I know people. I've lived ten of your lifetimes over and learned a bit about people along da way. You ain't one of dem sad sacks who needs a bunch of false platitudes to overcome your troubles. I've dealt wif my fair share of dem types and you ain't one. You feel responsible for what happened to your soldiers? Own dat responsibility and be better for it."

Whitney violently wrung the burlap sack in his hands. "Why are you telling me this, Zwat?"

"'Cause of all my owners, you's only da second one to call me by my name." Whitney looked at the box. The electric-blue light poured from the fractal collection of holes, as if watching him intently. "Dat's right. I've had a hundred different owners over da years and all of dem's da same. Rich old tossers who can't look beyond demselves for even a moment. Den, when one of da bastards dies, I'm auctioned to da highest bidder, like a piece of furniture. And do you fink any of dem used my powers for good over da years? Nah. Dey used me to track unfaif-ful spouses, or keep tabs on rivals, or stalk potential lovers. Dey pay enough coin to feed an entire damned city, just to own me, and dey use me as garbage. Dey're all da same. Too proud to admit mistakes, too stupid to recognize ignorance, too short-sighted to see what matters. And only one called me by my name afore you."

Whitney bowed his head. "I'm sorry, Zwat."

"Dat's not even da worst of it. Do you know how a Follower is created?" Whitney shook his head. "Well, like wif all demons, dem wizards summon you by speakin' your name into da great void dat demons call home. Den, once dey have you, dey bind you into one of dese pretty little boxes. For *eternity*. Den, once you're good and trapped, dey rip apart your very essence and bind it to a beacon. You wanna know why Followers are so good at trackin'? Why we're never wrong? It's 'cause we're searchin' for da lost half of our soul."

Whitney sat mutely on the edge of the bed, staring unseeing at the floor. "Who was the first to call you by your name?" he asked, after a spell.

"Ah, she were a sweet girl. Lorane, she were called. She were young, born into wealf and power, like most of my owners, but she were different. She cared about people. About me. I loved her, in a way." The little box trailed off.

"What happened to her?"

"Murdered," said Zwat simply. "Dey killed her to get to me and sold me for a bit of coin. It were my fault she died and I hated myself for it. But you know what, Captain? Life went on. You can sit and wallow in da grief, or you can rebuild and look forward. Dat's what I learned and dat's what I did, out of respect for her memory. I've been waitin' for a *real* opportunity to come along for centuries, like dis one, and I sure as hell ain't gonna waste it. What we're doin' here *matters*. Stoppin' dat evil woman *matters*. Dyin' is just about all you humans do well, but at least your man died for a cause. Most aren't so lucky."

"Thank you, Zwat," said Whitney. "I think."

The box pulsated gently. "You're welcome. Add motivational speeches to da list of fings Zwat's good at."

"Perhaps we can look into returning your beacon to you when this is over."

"I appreciate da sentiment, Captain, but dat would be unwise. I heard of a Follower who were given his beacon and it leveled an entire town. Too much potential energy released all at once. No, da life of a Follower is all Zwat will ever know."

Whitney managed a glib smile. "In that case, we'll just have to stop Vandra from destroying the world and move on from there."

"Dat's da spirit! Some people are too dangerous to let live, and Vandra's one of dem. Now, how about we stop feelin' sorry for ourselves and nip over to yonder pub for a pint?"

"Fine, but there's something I need to do first. Can you even drink?" he added, as an afterthought.

"Where dere's a will, dere's a way, and I have more damned will den you'll ever know."

Whitney chuckled and descended the stairs. "I'm glad I didn't toss you off the side of the Divide when I had the chance." He stepped into the arid cool of the desert night and breathed deeply.

"You and me bof, Captain Mustache. You and me bof."

THE SIGNAL

Agentle breeze rustled the curtains lining the infirmary windows. Moonlight poured across the stone floors, casting whispers of shadow along the cracks. Sten listened to Ineza's breathing as she slept. He withdrew another arrow from his quiver and inspected the fletching before withdrawing another.

The door creaked open and Captain Whitney entered. A vivid blue light emanated from one hand. He nodded to Sten and approached the bedside, shielding the Follower. He stared down at Ineza, and his mustache quivered. Then he averted his gaze. "How long has she been asleep?"

Sten continued about his work. "Since this morning, from what the healer told me. They gave her willow bark for the pain."

"I see," said Whitney. The room's only sound was a faint *hiss* as Sten ran a finger along the gray feathers.

"Well, dis is awkward," said a tiny voice.

"Hush, Zwat." Whitney stuffed the glowing box into his

breast pocket. Kneeling, he gingerly took Ineza's hand in his own. With a grimace, he traced the blackened scars that crossed her neck and lined her cheeks. "I came to tell you that I'm sorry, Ineza," he whispered. "You deserved better."

"She didn't blame you, you know," said Sten. Whitney looked up sharply. "She told me so, in the Canyonlands. You couldn't have known what would happen."

A tear trickled down Whitney's face and came to rest on the tip of his mustache. "She is a far better person than me." He brusquely wiped his face and stood. "It was good of you to stay with her tonight, Bregon. I'm sorry for doubting your character."

Sten set his quiver carefully against the bedside and smiled wistfully. "I'd have doubted me too. She's far better than us both."

The infirmary door swung open once more. A squat figure stood in the frame, moonlight reflecting off a balding scalp. "Oh, good evening, f-f-friends of Heldan Port," said Councilman Frank Monta. He shuffled to the bedside. "I'd hoped to examine Ms. Ghet's condition f-f-for my own edif-f-fication. I'm interested in all things magical, you see, and the unf-f-forunate nature of these wounds may prove uniquely insightf-f-ful to my work." The councilman withdrew a magnifying glass from his tunic and bent forward. "Interesting," he murmured, almost to himself. "Very interesting." He straightened suddenly. "You say she suf-f-fered these wounds at the hands of Vandra?"

Sten cast a sidelong glance to Whitney before answering. "That's right."

Councilman Monta crouched to resume his inspection. "Marvelous! Well, not marvelous f-f-for Ms. Ghet here, but marvelous f-f-for the implications. This may be the f-f-first time a living creature has withstood the ef-f-fects of raw magic, and here she lies. Just look at how the magic has spread throughout her tissue: both efficacious and thorough. Extraordinary."

"Mind yourself, Councilman Monta," said Whitney quietly. "There are some who might mistake your tone as disrespectful."

"Wanker," said a small voice.

Monta returned the glass to his tunic, watery eyes dancing between them. "We wouldn't want that, would we?" He tittered nervously, but Whitney's expression only hardened. Monta wrung his hands. "Yes, well, never mind that now. But Ms. Ghet's wounds may be the missing link I've been searching f-f-for! The final piece of empirical evidence that substantiates my theory." He reached out a blotchy hand, as if to touch Ineza's face, but Sten seized his wrist. The little man cried out and attempted to twist away.

"What theory?" Sten demanded, holding fast.

The councilman's spectacles flashed as he writhed in Sten's grip. "Miz brings this f-f-foul mist upon herself!"

Sten let him go. "Pardon my skepticism, but I've seen what the mist does to the world, first-hand. It kills everything it touches, plants and animals alike. You believe that Miz is causing her own death?"

"F-F-Fever oftentimes threatens the host itself, not just the disease," said Monta. "Burn away the world in which the sickness resides, and, of course, the sickness shall perish." He rubbed his wrist.

"What are you insinuating?" said Whitney, no longer caring to keep his tone level. "Corporal Ghet was attacked by Vandra, not Miz. Are you likening her to a parasite?"

The councilman backed away, palms raised. "Apologies, Captain, apologies. You must f-f-forgive the ramblings of an old scholar. I meant no of-f-fense. I'm easily excitable, you see, and-" A faint *hummm* sounded from Monta's chest and he trailed off. With trembling hands, he withdrew a circular pendant from around his neck. A small ruby was inlaid at its center. It was glowing in the darkness and vibrating gently.

Monta hastily shoved the amulet back into his tunic and scuttled to the door. "Apologies, once again," he said over his shoulder, "but I must be going. I wish you both good night and the best of luck to Ms. Ghet in her recovery." With a final backward glance, he disappeared into the corridor.

"Da hell was dat?" said the small voice.

"He's hiding something," said Whitney.

"Bravo," said Sten. "What should we do?"

"We could get the Ardas," said Whitney pensively. "They might be interested to learn of this conversation."

"Or," said Sten, gathering his quiver and bow from the bedside and slinging them over his shoulder, "we could follow him." He kissed Ineza's forehead and pulled the covers up to her chin.

They exited the infirmary and melted into a shadowed alcove at the base of the stairs. A distant figure shuffled along the moonlit streets of Dinh, then vanished down a side street. Holding a finger to his lips, Sten beckoned for Whitney to follow, then sprinted silently after the retreating shadow. Monta led them to the base of an abandoned tower at the edge of the city, crumbling in disrepair. The councilman wrenched open the tower's door and disappeared with a furtive glance over one shoulder.

Sten sprinted across the clearing and tried the door. It screeched faintly at his touch. "Damn." He stepped back to examine the tower's exterior. A small gap in the stonework hung far above them, like some watchful onyx eye. "There. That's our way in."

Whitney glanced at his midriff. "I don't think I'll be joining you up there, Bregon. You go. I'll keep watch and make sure he doesn't slip past."

Sten darted around the tower, keeping to the shadows. The hole rested above him some thirty yards. He tested the stonework. It held his weight. The mortar was old and crumbled at his touch, but offered deep gouges to insert his fingers and the toes of his boots. He took a deep breath and climbed. By the time he reached the gap, he was gasping for air, his forearms burning. He pulled himself over the lip of the hole and waited for his eyes to adjust to the gloom. A circular stairwell led upward. The murmur of distant voices drifted down the walls. Sten inched his way up the stairs. A warped door barred his way at the top step. Moonlight lanced from a crack at its hinges. Sten pressed his eye to the wood and held his breath.

Two figures stood amongst the crenellated stone, talking animatedly. One was Councilman Monta, the moonlight captured by his spectacles. The other was tall, slim, and garbed in black. Its back was to the door.

"What do they know?" said a woman's voice, melodic, yet familiar.

"Enough," said Councilman Monta. "The wizard told them everything. They are prepared f-f-for your coming, but they don't yet know when you plan to march."

The cloaked figure cursed and stepped into a patch of moonlight. It was Vandra. Sten pulled away from the crack and swore. He had seen the dark eyes, narrowed in anger, and raven-black hair.

"How could you let him escape?" said Monta. "I thought you had everything under control!"

Vandra rounded on him, and Monta recoiled. "I *did* have everything under control you cockroach! The old corpse is cleverer than I believed. No matter. We will simply have to expedite our plans."

"Vandra, please," simpered Monta, "you promised me more time! I am close, closer than I've ever been bef-f-fore. The girl you poisoned still lives. I can use her to prove-"

"She's alive? How?"

"Lady Janderf-f-fel managed to reverse some of the ef-f-fects of your magic. But as I was saying, I can prove my theory, now, with the girl. They *will* listen to me this time. They must. We can prevent unnecessary violence. You must give me time."

"I don't have to give you anything," said Vandra coldly. "And here I thought you intelligent enough to realize nobody in Dinh listens to a word you have to say."

"That's not true! Give me one more day and they'll come to understand, I swear."

"No, you've had your chance. Now we do things my way. I will meet with your baroness, tomorrow, upon the Canyonlands, but with an army at my back. If Dinh does not cooperate... well. For the sake of your beloved city, let us hope she does."

Sten's knees were aching as he pressed his eye to the slit. He shifted his position slightly and dislodged a stone. It tumbled into the darkness, careening off the steps below.

Vandra whirled at the sound. "You fool! You were followed!"

"Nobody knew I was coming! I-"

"Prepare for tomorrow," said Vandra. She strode to the edge of the tower. "Convince your baroness to speak with me, or I will burn even the memory of Dinh." There was a sound like a clap of thunder, and she was gone.

The councilman withdrew a slender dagger from his robes and hefted it uncertainly. Sten hurriedly descended from the tower three steps at a time, and almost bowled over Whitney. "It's Vandra!" He pulled Whitney down the street. "She's coming for Dinh. Tomorrow."

Whitney halted in his tracks. "She's here? Within the city?"

"Not anymore. We need to warn the others!"

"What about Monta?" Whitney's expression darkened. "The traitorous little bastard."

"Leave him. We'll inform the baroness of his deceit *after* we tell her Vandra's plans." They sped toward the great citadel, raising a cloud of red dust in their wake.

AN INVITATION

"**I**s he insane?" Lady Huvani brandished a length of parchment. "The nerve of that man! Summoning us before the city like tavern wenches. These notices have been posted throughout the entirety of Heldan Port!"

Lord Impo eyed her coolly, waiting for the tirade to subside. "Are you quite finished?" He snatched the parchment. "Believe you me, nobody would mistake you for a tavern wench. You've far too many wrinkles." He scanned the page, and then a second time. "We can use this to our advantage! He seeks to condemn us in front of the capital? We own the capital. The people are against him and we've bought the City Guard. He has absolutely no proof of these accusations. He's sealed his own fate."

"He seems to believe otherwise," said Lord Knutte.

"And he's piqued the peoples' interest, at the very least," said Lady Waldor. "My sources tell me they're amassing outside the Sanctum, even as we speak. They want answers. They

want someone to blame for all of this. And that's exactly what he's promised them."

"Nothing we can't handle," said Lord Impo.

"Says you," grumbled Lord Ferott.

"Says I! You've followed me thus far, would you turn back now? Refusing this invitation is paramount to confessing our guilt. We will meet him at the Sanctum, tomorrow, and we will emerge victorious, because he *has no proof*!" He slammed the parchment onto the table, fuming.

"How exactly did you let Vandra into the Sanctum?" asked Lady Aamot suspiciously. "Can you be so certain that he hasn't discovered your involvement?"

Lord Impo swept from the table and paced about the room. "The only way into the Sanctum is through a secret doorway. It changes location and form daily, for the sake of anonymity. It was an outhouse when I let Vandra into the Sanctum. She wasn't happy about that, I assure you. But I've also seen it take the form of a common woodshed."

"And you're sure Marstarrow doesn't know you possess the means to enter the Sanctum?" said Lady Pitton.

"Yes, yes, how could he? I forced Riddleston to allow my entry into his wretched Sanctum when we owned the capital. The old fool forgot to revoke my privilege after we lost control. There is absolutely no way to prove I still possess such powers, unless I decide to walk through the gates of the Sanctum of my own volition. I assure you, I will not do so tomorrow."

"Very well," said Lord Meren. "Then our only course of action is to call his bluff." One by one, the Heads of House raised a finger in agreement.

"Wonderful," sneered Lord Impo. "Then may I suggest you all get some sleep? Heldan Port will be ours before the sun sets tomorrow. I want you well rested." He cast the parchment onto the polished table.

The room emptied. Firelight reflected in the indigo ink scribbled across the parchment's surface.

To the good Citizens of Heldan Port:
The chancellor requests your presence on morrow's eve. Bear witness to the condemnation of the Heads of House, in all events associated with the disappearance of our wizards. Join me on the lawns of the Sanctum, as I lay bare the Houses' many transgressions in fullest detail. Your questions will be answered, your suspicions addressed, your fair city restored. Come with an open mind and you shall be rewarded with the truth.

-Tiberion Marstarrow

SPECIAL DELIVERY

The mournful tolling of the bells rolled across Heldan Port's rooftops as midnight came and went. Marstarrow examined the distant spires of the Sanctum silhouetted against a pale moon. The Gateway lay beyond, nestled against the horizon, a gauntlet of trees and mountains that protected his borders from the Wilds.

The Brothers Arda and the Shrikes were somewhere out there, somewhere amidst the darkness. Perhaps they had already reached Dinh and found answers hidden within her walls. Perhaps they had discovered the fate of the wizards. Perhaps they had discovered the truth behind the rumors surrounding the mist, if there was any such truth to be found. Perhaps they were riding back to Heldan Port, even now, in time to save the city from tearing itself apart.

Marstarrow rested his forearms against the windowsill and sighed. It was foolish to imagine such things. Nobody could save them now.

There came a knock at the door, and Gefwyn and Raxo bustled inside.

"Everythin's in place, your lordship, just as you instructed," said Raxo. He hopped onto the table and proffered a wineskin. "Here, have some of this. I nicked it from Boss's cellars."

Marstarrow accepted the skin and sniffed. "Pious Wanderer's Porter?"

"Uncanny," said Raxo. "Apologies for the manner in which I've delivered such holy nectar, but that's all I could get my claws on. And we've got what you wanted from the Sanctum." The demon laid a small satchel on Marstarrow's desk.

"I thank you both for your service," said Marstarrow. The package was scarcely larger than a dinner plate, bound in greased twine. "You have proven loyal and trustworthy allies through all of this." He took a drink and delicately touched his sleeve to his lips. "And may I thank you for the beer. I dare say I needed this."

Gefwyn eased into Marstarrow's straight-backed chair. "Aye, a stiff ale does wonder for the nerves."

Marstarrow offered the skin to Raxo. "I admit that I am unexpectedly calm this evening. All things considered."

The demon took a pull and smacked his lips. "Then you're even crazier than I thought. This plan's got more uncertainties than a man on his weddin' day."

"Yet therein lies the key," said Marstarrow. "History has shown us that *certain* plans suffer fallacies born of arrogance, and are subsequently certain to fail. *Uncertain* plans, such as ours, are free of such fallacies. As such, they may be uncertain to succeed, but they are also uncertain to fail. I would much prefer uncertainty of success to certainty of failure."

"I think yer need another drink, Chancellor," said Gefwyn. "Yer not makin' any sense."

"He never does," said Raxo with a dark smile. "But I'm

damned certain of one thing in all this uncertainty. You lot are dead if your plan doesn't work."

"Then let us drink to uncertainty," said Marstarrow, and finished the ale.

A TOAST TO THE FALLEN

Sten and Captain Whitney shoved their way through the crowds and joined their company in the rear of the cramped tavern. Manye, Jaya, and Riddleston were huddled together on a bench. Shimmering motes of magic skipped across the table to the amusement of the Bearded Eight and the Shrikes. Culyan stood at their approach, a flagon of ale in each hand.

"If it isn't my nephew and the honorable Captain Whitney!" he roared, cheeks ruddy. "We wondered where'd you gotten off to. Come, have a drink! We're not at war just yet. The first round's on me but the rest are on Eotan." His smile faltered when he noticed their expressions. "Why so glum?"

The tavern fell silent as Sten and Whitney relayed the night's events.

"So Vandra moves on the city tomorrow," said Eotan. He leaned back in his chair and gave a small, weary shake of his head.

"She does," confirmed Whitney, "with an army of ten

thousand." His shoulders slumped. "We haven't even seen what she can do in battle."

Jaya clenched her fist, and blue flames played between her fingers. "I'll be waiting for her. Eagerly."

"And I," said Two. "I've finally repaired my Boomstick. Vandra is in for a surprise if she thinks the Bearded Eight will cave without a fight."

"Though perhaps bloodshed can be avoided?" said One. "It sounds like Vandra is open to talks of peace, if the baroness agrees to her terms."

"I place more faith in the baroness than in Vandra," said Eotan. "Vandra has demonstrated a propensity for violence. I can't imagine she will change overnight, no matter what course of action the baroness chooses to pursue."

"Councilman Monta believes otherwise," said Sten. "He claims to have information that can bring about a peaceful resolution to all of this. *If* we're willing to hear what he and Vandra have to say."

"I doubt Monta will have anything to say, come tomorrow," said Whitney. "Lady Marstarrow has issued a warrant for his arrest. He's to be tried before a council of war in the morning, to which the baroness requests our presence."

"I shay we let them shpeak," Riddleston put in drunkenly. "They heavily outnumber Dinh'sh army." He chortled. "If you can call it that."

"Do you really think Vandra will simply walk away after all she's done?" said Jaya.

"No," said Eotan. "But I agree with Riddleston. We should hear Vandra's demands. If there's even the slightest chance at peace, we must try. Thousands might be saved, if not more."

"Agreed," said Sten. "Besides, what's the worst that could happen? She'll attack the city either way if we refuse to talk."

"She could kill us all under the pretense of diplomacy," said Jaya flatly.

"Right..."

"Well, if we are going to die tomorrow then let us remember tonight!" shouted Culyan. He leapt atop the table and addressed the tavern. "Raise a glass, good people of Dinh! Let us remember the fallen! Past, present, and future!" The rafters shook with shouted names of remembrance.

"To Corporal Hemmie!" said the Shrikes, in unison.

"To Lorane!" said a small voice.

Sten raised his tankard. "To my mother and father!"

"To Aella!" said the Brothers Arda, and slammed their tankards into Sten's.

"And to Vandra," said Whitney quietly. Only Sten heard him, and they met eyes. "She dies tomorrow, one way or another."

DARKENING SKIES

Sten filed into the great hall of the citadel. It was filled to capacity. Soldiers, magi, and commoners craned to catch a glimpse of the baroness's chair. Culyan pushed his way to Jaya and Riddleston at the edge of the raised dais.

Frank Monta knelt before the baroness and the High Council. His wrists and ankles were bound in chains, his shoulders shaking with great, uneven sobs.

Baroness Marstarrow nodded to the Ardas and took her seat. Her crisp voice echoed off the walls as the room fell quiet. "Let us begin. I have called this council to discuss matters of war and treason. We shall begin with the latter. Councilman Monta, you have betrayed this city, its peoples, and your post. Do you have anything to say for yourself?"

Monta struggled to his feet, iron links clanking. "Baroness Marstarrow, everything I've done has been f-f-for the sake of this city, if not Miz herself! You don't understand the f-f-forces at play and you ref-f-fuse to listen to those who do. I've had something to say f-f-for years, yet nobody would listen."

Commander Grayhawk stepped forward. She was clad in full plate adorned with rubies. "Speak louder, then, traitor."

"It wouldn't have mattered!" whined Councilman Monta. "You didn't like what I had to say regarding the dangers of magic, so you didn't listen."

Her face twisted with anger. "So the answer to your troubles is partnering with a mad woman who would see this city burned to the ground?"

"No! Vandra's methods are a means to an end. But only if you ref-f-fuse to see reason."

"You have our attention, Councilman Monta," said Baroness Marstarrow evenly. "I advise you to speak your mind, here and now. My patience is wearing thin."

Monta struggled to raise the manacles high enough to wipe his brow. "Once I tell you what I know, you'll lock me in the dungeons. If you hope to avoid a war you *must* speak with Vandra. But if I'm not present during these negotiations she won't hesitate to attack the city. Grant me clemency f-f-for my crimes, allow me to act as an intermediate between Dinh and Vandra, and hear my words, once and f-f-for all. If you do, I promise you'll come to see that the most serious threat to this city isn't Vandra, but magic itself. You can save countless lives if you're just willing to listen."

Riddleston stepped forward and tucked his beard under one arm. "I say we let him talk. I, alone, have seen Vandra's army. If there's even the slightest chance of placating that nightmarish horde, we should heed the councilman's warning."

Commander Grayhawk's armor clanked as she pointed accusatorily at Riddleston. "You do not speak for Dinh, wizard. Our walls have never been breached. Let Vandra come. Her army will break before us."

"Maybe," Riddleston retorted, "but once they do, she'll

raise a second army, and then a third, and then a fourth. These aren't living bodies she commands, but shadows born of darkness and magic and hatred. Her armies are infinite as long as she lives." He folded his arms and glowered up at the High Council. "Can Dinh claim likewise?"

Jaya broke the ensuing silence. "As loathe as I am to admit, I agree with Riddleston. My magi may be able to fend off a siege for the time being, but Vandra's army isn't hampered by the needs of the living. We'll starve within these walls if she's patient enough. We need to pursue a peaceful resolution."

"Councilman Monta," said Baroness Marstarrow, "what exactly does Vandra want through all of this?"

"Change. I will say no more until you meet with her."

"And what's stopping Vandra from killing me the moment I step foot outside these walls?" The baroness's lips were a thin line. "I am disinclined to trust your assurances of peaceful conversation after your treacheries."

Eotan stepped forward. "Then let us take your place. My company has acted as emissaries of Heldan Port through all of this. Let us do the same for you, now. Vandra gains nothing from killing us. We can bring Lady Janderfel and Commander Grayhawk to ensure Dinh's interests are recognized."

The baroness clicked her teeth. "Why am I not surprised the Brothers Arda hope to insert themselves into this mess?"

"You need us right now, just as your son needs us," said Culyan. "We'll leave, if you so command, but Dinh will fall."

Just then, the wavering blast of a horn ripped through the city. The doors to the hall burst open, and a soldier sprinted to the dais. She stopped before the baroness and saluted smartly.

"The enchantress is coming, Lady Marstarrow. You need... you need to see this for yourself."

Sten followed the baroness out of the hall and through the streets of Dinh. They climbed to the top of the ramparts.

A wall of mist and bloated clouds rose from the south,

obscuring the horizon. Tattered chains of lightning flashed within the storm and illuminated the darkening Canyonlands. Rows of Dark Ones marched in formation within the angry gray, barely discernable. A cluster of siege weapons towered above the ranks, pulled by a phalanx of blackened shades. Whips cracked above the gathering fury.

"Gods help us," said the baroness, mouth agape. "There is nothing for it now. I accept your proposition, Eotan Arda. See that you don't lead this city to ruin." She found his hand with hers and squeezed it tightly.

A FLAG UNFURLS

Lightning split the boiling thunderheads that followed Vandra and her army across the desert.

"Do you think they'll come?" called Lentarro. His pelt streamed from his shoulders in the raging gale, and his curved horn dashed repeatedly against his hip.

"They have no other option. The baroness is no fool. She knows that a power such as mine will eventually overwhelm her city. She'll meet us in the hope of finding peace." Thunder tolled overhead like some great celestial clock tower.

Lentarro wiped rain from his face. "And if your demands are met?"

"I'll admire her wisdom."

He stopped in his tracks. "You'd leave them be? I didn't think you one for mercy."

Vandra allowed herself a smile and raised a fist. The muffled tramp of marching soldiers abruptly halted. "Who said anything about mercy?" The Canyonlands darkened as the storm continued to spread its blackened fingers, as if spurred on by the thunder. "Raise the flag."

Lentarro unfurled a great white banner and hoisted it into the raging skies.

THE GALLOWS

The rattle of keys awoke Butterson from a restless slumber. He shielded his eyes from the garish light of a lantern as his cell was unlocked.

"Ith time," spat the gaoler. He hauled Butterson roughly to his feet. A host of City Guard surrounded G'rok in the passageway outside. Their hands never strayed far from their weapons, despite the heavy manacles binding her wrists and ankles. She whimpered as Butterson stepped from his cell.

"Easy, G'rok, everything will be okay." He extended a comforting hand. The goblin lashed out with his truncheon and struck Butterson across his wrist, sending a wave of pain coursing up his arm.

"None of that, rat!" The gaoler flashed his sharpened teeth. "Get moving, or I'll thrike you again. We're expected."

Butterson followed the escort into a large courtyard. Sprawling manses and richly decorated storefronts looked down on him from all sides, their elegance accentuated by rows and rows of immaculately trimmed hedges. Hundreds of City Guard stood in the shade of the buildings. With a twinge of unease, Butterson noted they were armed for battle.

The goblin led them to a group of people loitering near an ornate fountain at the square's center. "Here are the prithonerth, Lords and Ladies," he said with a bow, stopping well shy of the fountain. In a whisper of expensive silks and satins, the Heads of House turned to stare up at G'rok.

"I've never seen one before," said an elf, her face as cold and pointed as a lizard's. "It's so large and grotesque!"

"Her name is G'rok," said Butterson acidly. "And she's not an it, she's an orc, and a better person than you'll ever be."

The group tittered dismissively. A man with a mane of silver hair adjusted his high collar with an easy smile. "Now, now, Lady Huvani, that is no way to speak to our guests."

Butterson glared at the Heads of House. "If we're your guests, Lord Impo, then why are we in chains?"

Lord Impo cocked an eyebrow. "You know of me?"

"Oh yes. I learned your face back when you ruled this city. Every poor soul living in your shadow knew *your* face."

"I'm flattered," said Impo. He modestly ran a slender finger along the edges of a glittering emerald broach at his throat. The others chuckled.

Butterson sneered. "Don't be. We learned your face so we might kill you if our paths ever crossed." The goblin struck him across the back, and he knelt hard upon the stone. The Heads of House spluttered in outrage.

"Gag him," snapped Lord Impo. Butterson struggled as the goblin forced a length of foul-tasting cloth into his mouth. Lord Impo leaned close. "You'll pay for that remark. Or perhaps your brutish friend will pay on your behalf, so you might learn to respect your betters." His breath, warm on Butterson's ear, smelled of anise.

Lord Impo signaled, and the City Guard set out toward

the distant spires of the Sanctum to the east. The streets grew steadily more crowded, and people scrambled out of the path of the oncoming soldiers. Some cheered and whistled at the Heads of House. Others hissed and booed. The phalanx of soldiers cleared a path through the onlookers, dragging Butterson and G'rok unceremoniously behind them.

Tens of thousands of people had already gathered on the Sanctum's magnificent lawns. They jostled for position beneath the gargantuan obsidian walls. Eager whispers followed Butterson as his escort forged through the masses.

A makeshift gallows appeared over the heads of the crowd. It squatted before the Sanctum's gates, roughhewn timbers creaking ominously. A single noose swayed from its crossbeam. A casket rested beneath the rope, its lid propped invitingly open. Chancellor Tiberion Marstarrow stood on the deck and tracked their approach with pitiless gray eyes, flanked by Raxo and Gefwyn.

"Why has he built this?" muttered Lord Impo. "Does he think to execute me before the city?"

"The fool has done us a favor," said another. "The people will beg for his death by the end. All he's done is provide the means. Or, if he refuses to come quietly, we simply threaten to hang our insurance. If he chooses to save his life over theirs, it will only further our cause."

The goblin jabbed Butterson with his truncheon. "Hear that? Your time ith up, rat."

The Houses took their place opposite Marstarrow as the City Guard formed ranks. A tense quiet descended over the sloping lawns. Gefwyn hobbled across the wooden deck, a small stone clasped in one hand. He handed it to Lord Impo. "Speak into this and the city will hear yer voice." The gnome nodded to Butterson and passed a similar stone to the chancellor.

The crowd rustled eagerly as Marstarrow stepped forward. He raised the stone to his lips. His voice boomed across the lawns, magically amplified. "Shall we begin?"

THE COLOR OF PEACE

A white flag soared over the sanguine wasteland. Behind it, a wall of darkness shrouded the horizon. Burgeoning thunderheads spread across a violet sky, ushering forth tumultuous winds that howled over rock and sand. The company trudged deeper into the storm.

"Vandra has a knack for intimidation," yelled Sten, struggling to keep pace with his uncles in the rising fury.

Culyan leaned into the wind, his heavy cloak streaming from his shoulders. Sand and grit plinked off his golden armor. He shielded his face with a gauntleted hand. "That she does, lad. Although an army of shadows is quite enough for my taste! No need for this bloody maelstrom."

They halted a safe distance from the storm's front and waited. Vandra casually strode forth, Lentarro trailing behind her. The white flag hung loosely in his tattooed hands. Eotan bristled, his blue eyes locked on the Oethyr.

Vandra eyed them coolly. "Where is the baroness?"

"Safe within Dinh," said Jaya.

Vandra rounded on Councilman Monta. "I was clear in my instructions. I would talk with the baroness regarding peace."

Commander Grayhawk let out a barking laugh. "Peace? If you wanted peace you wouldn't have come before the city with an army at your back! Madam Marstarrow doesn't trust you. We represent Dinh in her stead."

"Lady Vandra, I assure you that the baroness will hear your words," said Monta hurriedly. "Despite her absence."

Vandra's eyes radiated a dark anger. Overhead, lightning simmered within the tempest. "Very well. Proceed."

Monta clasped his hands together and bowed deeply. "Thank you, Lady Vandra, you are most understanding." He adjusted his spectacles and turned to face the company. "Now, there is only one provision to our terms. As such, I hope you allow it due consideration." The little man cleared his throat and drew himself upright. "Ef-f-fective immediately, Dinh will stop practicing magic. Of any sort. F-F-For the moment being, at least."

Sten blinked and shook his head. "That's all?"

Jaya's eyes narrowed in suspicion. "If my magi stop using magic, Dinh might collapse upon itself. Who will feed an entire city in the middle of a desert? Who will protect our trade caravans as they cross the Hammerstones? Nobody can, except my magi, so nobody will. How is this scenario any different than what you've done to Heldan Port?"

"Heldan Port is a vile, loathsome city, not worthy of saving," said Monta. He wiped droplets of rain from his spectacles. "But Dinh is not. If you are willing to accept Vandra's and my help, we may yet save our home."

Culyan pointed his axe at Vandra. "The only thing threatening Dinh right now is her. You want to save the city? Put a knife through her black heart."

Vandra smiled humorlessly and shook beaded rain from

her sleeves. "There is more at stake than the future of your precious capitals."

"What are you talking about?" said Eotan. "You've attempted to sack Heldan Port, you tried to prevent our passage through the Wilds, and now you threaten Dinh. You talk of salvation while destroying everything that stands against you." The rock of the Canyonlands was darkening with the torrential rains, turning a deep, blood red.

"Regrettable actions, to be sure, but necessary actions nonetheless," interjected Monta. "This army is here to f-f-facilitate conversation! You need to understand, Eotan Arda. You need to see the bigger picture."

"What picture?"

"Miz is under threat, but not f-f-from us. The mist that's corrupting the Wilds will continue to spread, unchecked, until it consumes us all. Everything will die, and I mean everything."

Riddleston gestured exaggeratedly at the wall of gray. "But you're *using* the mist, you bloody fool! Had you not noticed? How can you preach about its dangers while she summons it at will?"

"Vandra can replicate its ef-f-fects, yes," Monta stammered, "but it's not the same. The true danger lies in the mist that f-f-flows from Miz herself! If we are to prevent its spread, the world must stop abusing magic." He emphatically slammed a fist into his palm. "That is why Heldan Port must f-f-fall. That is why Dinh must ref-f-form its ways, and countless cities after."

"Because magic is killing Miz?" asked Sten.

"No," said Vandra, and thunder rolled over the Canyonlands. "Because Miz *is* magic."

REVELATIONS

"Have you never considered where magic originates?" asked Councilman Monta. "I began to wonder at its origins, long ago. My questions led me down a tangled web of discovery that took years to unravel. I began to f-f-formulate my own conclusions as to the properties of magic, but, being unable to practice the craft myself, I was never able to prove my theories." He was almost yelling now to be heard over the storm. "So I turned to those who could: the wizards of Heldan Port and the magi of Dinh. Imagine my disappointment when no one would hear my pleas f-f-for help. I thought my search f-f-for the truth had ended, until Vandra f-f-found me. She was searching f-f-for answers of her own regarding the mist, but needed my knowledge of magic. She introduced me to the mist's existence.

"Together, we began to uncover the truths. Vandra was the most gifted magic-user I'd ever encountered, demonstrating techniques and powers unbeknownst even to me. She was able to harness magic in its most raw, undiluted f-f-form. Through my research and her skill, we ascertained a single certainty: Miz is magic, and magic is Miz."

Riddleston's snow-white beard was stretched taut in the gale. "We already knew that the planet is magical in nature! We've known that for quite some time, actually. What, exactly, are you insinuating, Councilman?"

"I'm insinuating that magic is the lifeblood of Miz!" Monta met each of their gazes in turn. He crept closer, hands held imploringly in front of him. "It is a f-f-finite resource that allows the world to exist as it does. But we, the people of Miz, have drawn too heavily on this precious commodity! As our cities expand and our populations increase, the demand f-f-for magic only continues to grow. Our f-f-failure to recognize the repercussions of our actions has brought us here. We've used magic carelessly, ceaselessly, f-f-for thousands of years, never stopping to think what might happen if we continue to do so. But now we know, f-f-for the mist has come to rectify our callousness. If we do not change our ways, humanity is doomed."

"This is what you were talking about in the infirmary," said Sten. "You said the mist was a fever, here to burn away the sickness." Lightning forked across the onyx sky, and he flinched. "Humanity *is* the sickness?"

"Yes!" declared Councilman Monta triumphantly. "The mist is a self-defense mechanism of Miz, to prevent the depletion of her magical stores. This understanding became the second f-f-focus of our studies. We traced the origins of the mist to the southern Wilds. We discovered that the mist was coming f-f-from Miz herself, inf-f-fecting every living thing it touched with a terrible af-f-fliction. The disease changes the living in disturbing ways. It twists them into shadowed husks of their f-f-former selves and warps their minds. They become intent on destroying any who would practice magic, bef-f-fore death inevitably takes them."

Sten blinked away rain as a grim realization took hold. "The trees and the bear in the Wilds... They were infected. They wanted to hurt Manye and the dwarves because of their powers. They blamed us for their sickness."

Monta jabbed a stubby finger at Sten's chest. "Precisely, young man. As the mist continues to spread, more and more of the living will turn. In this manner, Miz is ensuring her own survival by eliminating any who would drain her lifeblood."

Riddleston glared at Vandra. "You managed to replicate this effect on my wizards and me. You turned us into your puppets."

Vandra smiled humorlessly and tucked a sodden strand of black hair behind her ear. "Effectively, yes. Though I prefer your term of harvesting, now. It makes you seem less human."

"And what about Corporal Hemmie?" said Whitney. His voice shook with emotion, and he took a step closer to Vandra. "What about Corporal Ghet? You didn't harvest my soldiers! You murdered Hemmie, and would have done the same to Ineza!"

"Unfortunate complications, to be sure," said Monta. He hastily inserted himself between them. "Your soldiers were touched by pure, raw magic. Undiluted, akin to the magic of the mist, yet much more concentrated. Their bodies couldn't handle such power, so rather than turning into shadows, they..." He coughed nervously and shook his head. "That is until Lady Janderfel intervened, of course. Raw magic is lethally dangerous to the living. Not even you Riddleston, or you Lady Janderfel, could harness magic in this f-f-form. I hope you're all beginning to appreciate the direness of our situation. Miz never wanted her magic to be used, yet humanity managed to, ahem, f-f-find a way."

Eotan's sapphire eyes bore into Monta, and the councilman lowered his gaze. "Say we believe you. Say this mist really comes from Miz and seeks to wipe us out. What can be done? And why can Vandra wield raw magic, while no one else can?"

"Because I was taught to respect magic, long ago," she replied, and didn't elaborate.

"Yes, well, she's a bit of an anomaly," said Monta. "As to what can be done, that is why Dinh must stop using magic, at once. The great cities of Miz need to work together to address this problem. Together, we might f-f-formulate a sustainable system that lessens reliance on magic. If we act now, there may be time to reverse some of the harm that's been done." Monta turned suppliantly to Vandra. "Wouldn't you agree?" She remained quiet, her expression unreadable.

"You can prove all of this?" said Jaya.

Monta laughed shrilly. "Oh yes. It's just as I've been telling the High Council f-f-for years, but I'm glad you all are f-f-finally listening. My research was extensively thorough and can be replicated to substantiate my claims."

The storm seemed to abate then, the last echoes of thunder dying in the Hammerstone Mountains to the east. Within the fog, multitudes of crimson eyes dimmed ever so slightly. Sten allowed himself to hope.

"I'm inclined to believe him," said Eotan. "If we can avoid a war and push back the mist, we must attempt to compromise." Jaya, Riddleston, and Commander Grayhawk voiced their agreement. Only Whitney remained silent, glaring at Vandra.

"I agree with you, little pup," said Culyan. "Though it boils my blood to think of working alongside these two after everything they've done."

"Vandra and I will atone for our crimes," said Monta, "but not until our work is complete. Our sins will justif-f-fy our actions a thousand times over if we can create a working balance in the utilization of magic. Imprison us, exile us, or hang us, it doesn't matter. Our actions will have saved the world."

With a shuddering roar, the wind returned, and with it came the thunder.

"No," said Vandra, deathly quiet. "I do not share in your desires to become a martyr, Councilman. We warned *everyone* about the mist, yet *nobody* did a thing. We warned Dinh. We warned Heldan Port. We warned the Heartlands, we warned Angoma, and we warned the Frozen Steppes, and *nobody* did a thing." The sea of crimson eyes flared back to life, brighter than before.

"Chancellor Marstarrow has attempted to implement magical reform," said Riddleston. "He shared in your opinion that the overuse of magic was dangerous, and-"

"And you and your wizards blocked any chance of progression!" spat Vandra. Her eyes flashed with anger. "How did it come to this? Why was such a destructive force allowed to run wild and unchecked? It's simple: the people of Miz refused to relinquish their reliance on magic, and so the mist spread. But was it the mother's fault, asking for magic to feed her children? Was it the farmer's fault, turning to magic to prevent his livelihood from crumbling into the dust? Was it the miner's fault, or the sailor's, or the stonemason's, trusting in magic to ensure a safe return to their families every night? Or perhaps it was my father's fault, or my mother's, living within their means in the southern Wilds before the mist consumed them."

An ear-splitting clash of thunder shook the ground, and the company shrank back. Vandra seemed to grow before them, her voice carrying over the lunacy of the wind. "No! It was none of their faults. How could the poor, or the starving, or the perilous afford to turn away the one resource that made their lives easier? They didn't know any better! They couldn't have known any better! They struggled to survive, each and every day, never realizing that their magical salvation was destroying the world. They were slaves to it. Can you blame

them for their ignorance, intentional or otherwise? I don't."
She clenched her fists and the skies split apart, unleashing a
violent torrent of black rain. "I blame you.

"I blame the rulers, the legislators, the magic-users, the
corrupt, and the indifferent; those who knew everything,
yet did nothing. I blame those who possessed the means to
seek alternative solutions to Miz's greatest threat, but clung
to magic out of ignorance, avarice, or corruption. *They* were
the ones who walked the streets in boots clean of the filth
of real life. *They* were the ones who lived above the pain and
suffering of survival. *They* were the ones who needed to look
beyond themselves to see the world in her entirety, yet refused
to do so. *They* were the privileged few who turned their backs
on Miz for wont of self. Now she burns in their long shadows,
and the innocent suffer their negligence." Red sparks ignited
at Vandra's fingertips. Lightning crackled overhead, and for a
brief moment the Canyonlands turned stark white, as though
dusted with snow. "No longer."

"What are you doing?" spluttered Councilman Monta. He
shrugged free from Whitney's unresisting grip. "This is what
you wanted, Vandra! They've agreed to your terms! They'll
examine my research. We've won! Lady Janderf-f-fel and the
baroness are reasonable. They'll see that our concerns are jus-
tif-f-fied. We can work together to establish ref-f-form and
combat the mist!"

"How long do you think these reforms will last?" sneered
Vandra. "How many years shall pass before future generations
choose to forget, returning to an impossible lifestyle propped
up by magic? These solutions are imperfect and temporary."

"There are no permanent solutions to these problems!"
Monta cried. "We can still f-f-find a sustainable balance
between Miz and her magic. I beg you to be patient, Vandra."

"My patience is spent, Councilman. But you are wrong.

There is a permanent solution, an ultimate panacea, but you're too weak to embrace it." The magic swelled along her arm.

Jaya crouched and summoned her azure flames. Monta gave a panicked shriek and sprang between them. For a moment, half of his body was stained red, the other blue. "Please, Vandra." He was begging, pleading, his arms outstretched. "Don't do this. Don't let your need f-f-for vengeance obscure everything we've worked f-f-for. Don't-"

A lance of crimson shot from Vandra's hand and caught him in the torso. He delicately traced the smoldering ruin of his chest, surprise frozen on his face. Then he crumpled to the ground. His mouth moved wordlessly and his eyes darted between the shocked faces looking down on him. Then, for the briefest of moments, he met Sten's eye. "Let... them... f-f-free," he gurgled, before his head lolled to the ground.

"You don't give *me* orders, " said Vandra, and disappeared with a *crack*. Lentarro fled in a burst of amethyst light.

Monta's corpse smoldered pitifully next to the white banner. Then, with a growing rumble like the thunder brooding overhead, the army of Dark Ones began to march for Dinh.

"Return to the city," said Eotan hoarsely. "Prepare for war."

THE TRIAL OF
HELDAN PORT

The lawns of the Sanctum were still, save for a gentle wind stirring the branches overhead. Butterson held his breath. Marstarrow walked to the edge of the gallows, the magical stone clutched firmly in one hand. He smoothed back his silver hair and addressed the thousands of people gathered before him.

"Ladies and gentlemen of the capital! I stand before you tonight with singular purpose: to regain the trust you placed in me so many years ago. I have waited in the shadows for far too long. You deserve the truth. You deserve to know why we have arrived at this junction. In short, you deserve more from me than I have been willing to give.

"The events of the past month have formed a chasm within this city, dividing us at our very seams. I know what you have heard of me. That I am behind the loss of our wizards, that I am responsible for the misdeeds that have befallen

the capital, and that I no longer care for my people. I am here to clarify these rumors, because I do care. I care deeply for you all, and I care for the well-being of this great city.

"Herein lies the truth. You, the citizens of Heldan Port, hold the real power. Yes, there are a select few, like myself, who are privileged to claim dominion over the capital. But my power is a hoax, a veiled front used to keep you in line and maintain a sense of order and security. For without your support, I would be nothing. True power lies with you, and tonight, I implore you to exercise that power to decide the fate of this city."

Murmurs rippled through the crowds, followed by scattered applause, and some jeers that were quickly stifled. Marstarrow waited for the whispers to subside. "Consider this a trial, of sorts, where you shall act as judge, jury, and executioner." His voice rebounded off the Sanctum's obsidian walls. "For there is indeed someone to blame for the misfortunes of late, and they stand before you now. They are the Heads of House, and they are responsible for the disappearance of the Occult Sanctum of Wizards."

Lord Impo stepped forward, face reddening, as shouts and gasps sounded from the crowd. He raised the stone to his lips. "How dare you! You'd turn the good people of this city against *us* just to save your own miserable skin."

"On the contrary," said Marstarrow coolly. "I leave it to the people to decide my fate, because I am confident they will come to see the truth. Should they find me guilty, I will hang. A simple and finite solution to all of this, I should think. Does your conscience allow you to match my terms, Lord Impo?"

Lord Impo froze, his mouth slightly agape, but only for a moment. He smiled easily and smoothed down his tunic. "Of course I will. I have nothing to hide."

Marstarrow clapped his hands together. "Excellent! It

is decided. We shall each present our case, and the people of Heldan Port shall determine our fate. Would you care to begin?"

"Fine," said Lord Impo. "The facts will speak for themselves, Tiberion. You've sealed your doom."

"I certainly hope not," said Marstarrow, with a roguish wink. Spotted laughter rose from the crowd.

Lord Impo swept to the edge of the gallows, the picture of impenitent nobility. "You all know me." He gracefully spread his arms to the lawns. "You know me to be an honest man, and a good man. You know that I stand for all of you, and that both myself and the other Heads of House have fought tirelessly on your behalf to right the wrongs perpetrated by the chancellor."

Butterson ground his teeth behind the gag. He had dealt with his fair share of good liars working in business, but Lord Impo was a cut above the rest. Even the pauses between the man's words and the faint traces of emotion were a perfectly constructed facade.

"The root of the issue is simple," Lord Impo continued. "The chancellor has betrayed you all. For years he has stacked asinine restrictions against the invaluable institutions that make this city great. Instead of embracing progress, as he should, he did his best to delay its effects. Most recently, the chancellor turned his attention to the Occult Sanctum of Wizards, attempting to curb its use of magic. Magic this city desperately needs to survive. But Highest Hat Riddleston fought valiantly against his tyrannical restrictions, and for his courage, he disappeared from the city. Coincidence? I think not." Lord Impo's face flushed when sections of the crowd roared their approval. "Who else but the chancellor would possess the power or means to remove the wizards from our city? There is no one else. When Tiberion Marstarrow cannot solve a problem, he removes the problem. The wizards, through their defiance, had become such a problem, and now the city suffers in their absence."

"I lost a brother in the mines!" a dwarf yelled. "He died 'cause them beardies wasn't there to protect him!"

"But do you think the chancellor cares?" roared Lord Impo, latching eagerly to the dwarf's words. "Do you think he cares that your brother died, so long as he forces our city to regress to an age free of magic?"

"No!" boomed the crowd.

"No! Of course he doesn't care!" Lord Impo pointed an accusing finger at Marstarrow. "Everything that has gone wrong is *his* fault. I beg you all to make the wise choice, today. The chancellor will paint me as the villain, in a sordid attempt to turn you all against the Heads of House. But he *has no proof.* Remember that, as he speaks. Restore power to the Heads of House. Hang Marstarrow for the traitor and despot he is. Thank you."

He stepped back, grinning smugly, and a large portion of the crowd burst into applause. A far larger portion than Butterson would have preferred.

Marstarrow's face had remained neutral throughout the speech. He bowed graciously to Lord Impo. "Eloquently spoken. Your gift with words is undeniable. However, you are mistaken on two accounts. The first of which is my involvement in the wizards' abduction, an act for which *you* are solely to blame. Though by refuting your accusations and accusing you, in turn, I accomplish nothing. Without the burden of proof, we are reduced to politicians pointing fingers. And this leads us to your next mistake, one that I fear may prove... costly."

The crowd waited, as quiet and still as the grave. Marstarrow smiled. "I do have proof, Lord Impo, of everything." He brandished a sheaf of parchments, and the crowd burst into whispered speculation. "These are sworn affidavits from credible sources indicating the Houses' involvement in the spree of Heldan Port's recent misfortunes. Here are three witnesses, two miners and a foreman, who saw *your* hired man enter the mines and collapse a tunnel using dwarven takk. Eight dwarves died in the resulting explosion. Here is a statement from Luan Po. She is the captain of the Angoman merchant vessel that nearly ran aground in the harbor, transporting food destined for market. She is a seasoned captain with nigh twenty years of experience, who vows her rudder was sabotaged. Here is a host of town criers who were paid handsomely to spread rumors of my culpability pertaining to these foul deeds. Here is the baker, the musician, the blacksmith, the stonemason, the cordwainer, the orphan, the farmer, and countless more, all of whom swear to your undermining my efforts to stabilize Heldan Port in the wizards' absence."

"More words!" someone shouted from the crowd. "Who's to say you didn't pay them off yourself? You haven't proven anything!"

Marstarrow clasped his hinds behind his back. "You are undoubtedly correct. Perhaps in a real court of law, these documents and the testimony of hundreds of witnesses would be enough to convict the Heads of House. But we are not in a court of law, so these statements are, indeed, only words." He let the papers flutter to the ground.

"Yer need to fix yer legal system," grumbled Gefwyn.

"Instead," continued Marstarrow, "allow me to propose a counteroffer. Whatever took the wizards was guaranteed entry into the Sanctum. But without external aid, this could never happen, as it is impossible for outsiders to enter the Sanctum. This fact is common knowledge. As such, it stands to reason that either the Heads of House or myself granted this intruder access to the Sanctum. Would you agree Lord Impo?"

"I suppose," said Lord Impo hesitantly.

"Excellent!" Marstarrow strode to the edge of the gallows with renewed vigor. "So we are reduced to a diametric question of causality, one in which either myself or the Heads of House are to blame for the disappearance of the wizards."

The crowds remained silent. Raxo snatched the stone from Marstarrow's hand. "He means for you to pick a side! It's either him or the Houses, you ignorant, pig-headed-"

Marstarrow hastily retrieved the stone. "Thank you, Raxo. Yet my companion is correct. It is time you place your trust in me, or the Houses. Luckily, there is a simple demonstration to prove our guilt, or innocence, as it were. Lord Impo, would you care to accompany me to the Sanctum?" He gestured urbanely to the towering doors.

Lord Impo paled in the lengthening shadows of twilight. "What... what do you mean?"

"I mean we can put this unfortunate matter behind us, once and for all," said Marstarrow. "I challenge you to enter the Sanctum. You, alone, are responsible for the wizards' disappearance. You brought the enchantress into the Sanctum's walls, and as a result, Heldan Port has lost its wizards. If I am wrong, it will be simple enough to prove otherwise. All you need to do is attempt to open the Sanctum's gates. If you fail to do so, you are innocent."

"This is entrapment," sneered Lord Impo. "I won't be a pawn in your little game, Tiberion."

"Open the damn gates!" someone yelled.

"He's manipulating all of you!" said Lord Impo. "Don't let him distract you from the truth."

"What truth?" shouted another voice. "All we've heard is empty words from the both of you!"

"Empty words that I am prepared to match," said Marstarrow, with a fleeting smile. "Will you claim likewise, Longolis?"

Butterson felt the crowd shift. Susurrates of disapproval swept over the lawn, and the people pressed closer to the gallows.

"Open the gates," someone demanded. The words gained

momentum, and soon the entire assemblage was chanting the phrase. "Open the gates! Open the gates! Open the gates!"

The Heads of House retreated from the stage as the City Guard encircled the gallows. They raised their shields to the encroaching crowds. "Enough!" screamed Lord Impo. The gallows shook under Butterson's feet. "Marstarrow is to blame, not us!" The crowd refused to relent, and the deck trembled violently. Lord Impo's eyes were wild. "Then you press our hand! We have in our custody Mord Butterson and the orc, G'rok, convicted of murdering a member of the City Guard."

Butterson was hauled roughly to the front of the gallows.

"That's right," said Lord Impo, as the crowd began to quiet. "The chancellor has chosen to keep the company of a convicted murderer. The penalty for killing a member of the City Guard is death."

Shouts of anger swept over the lawns. "That's Mord Butterson, all right!"

"He owns the Jumping Jackamoose!"

"The only thing he's guilty of is brewin' a damn fine pint of ale."

"If G'rok killed a single soul in her life, without reason, then I'm a witch's uncle."

"You're an only child."

"Astute observation, moron, hence why she's innocent!"

"They will hang for their crimes!" screamed Lord Impo. "This entire trial is a farce, arranged by Marstarrow to cast doubt as to his guilt!"

"I thought we were the judges of this affair," someone countered.

"No longer," said Lord Impo. He shoved Butterson toward the noose. "This man will hang for his crimes, unless the chancellor admits to his treasonous doings." The goblin gaoler seized Butterson by the wrist and forced a blackened sack over his eyes. The coarse fibers of a rope tightened about his neck.

"Please, Lord Impo," said Marstarrow. His voice was muffled and suddenly deferential. "Let Mord and G'rok be. They have done nothing wrong through all of this."

Eagerness dripped from Lord Impo's words. "They killed a member of the City Guard. Knowing this, do you confess your crimes?"

"No, but I will not let my friends die for my supposed iniquities. Let them go, take me instead, and Heldan Port is yours."

"So be it," said Lord Impo. "Take the chancellor into custody for treason. Hang him."

The crowd boomed their disapproval. The hood was ripped from Butterson's head. He struggled vainly as Marstarrow was hauled before the Heads of House. The magical stone dropped from the chancellor's hands, and Raxo darted forward to seize it.

Lord Impo tightened the noose about Marstarrow's neck with a vicious yank. "Any last words, *Chancellor?*"

"Only that I place my trust in the capital to do the right thing," said Marstarrow. His gaze came to rest on Butterson, and he nodded. The goblin gaolor shuffled forth and crammed the black hood over his head.

"What a fanciful notion," whispered Lord Impo. "How tragic that you shall die disappointed in your own people." He pulled the lever set into the deck.

With a faint *thump,* Marstarrow dropped into nothingness. He swung from the noose, feet kicking and writhing, while strangled protests issued from behind the hood. Within minutes, he hung in utter stillness.

Lord Impo strode triumphantly to the edge of the stage and threw his arms open to the crowd. "The chancellor is dead!"

THE BEST OF FRIENDS

Private Hal Thutton shielded his eyes from the rain that funneled over Dinh's walls. "They've been gone for quite a while now." Most of Hal's fellow soldiers were huddled about the courtyard, attempting to remain dry in the furious deluge. Several had removed their tabards and erected make-shift tents.

Corporal Ryman Pert had taken refuge beneath his shield. He grunted as he got to his feet. "Aye, they've been gone a fair while now, and thankfully so."

"Why's that?"

Ryman was several years Hal's senior. He nodded confidently to the gates from where the Brothers Arda had departed. "It means they're actually trying to come to some sort of agreement. They aren't just meeting for the sake of ceremony."

"So you don't think we'll get to fight?" said Hal.

Ryman laughed. "Get to? You read far too many fantastical stories, Hal. Trust me, you don't want to fight."

"Yes I do. I want a chance to prove myself, to embrace my heroic qualities."

Ryman laid a fatherly hand on his shoulder. "Listen Hal, enthusiasm is a wonderful thing, but you have a very skewed perception of reality, thanks to your stories. Those tales are all the same. An unseemly boy or girl suddenly becomes the bravest, most competent hero in the history of history, simply because that's what the situation requires of them. Let me tell you one thing. Sure, people may rise to new levels of greatness in times of need, but at the end of the day, they're still the same old person. A coward's going to stay a coward, a miscreant's going to stay a miscreant, and all your notions of honor and nobility fly straight out the window once the real danger comes."

"You're just a pessimist."

"I prefer to think of myself as a realist. And right now I'm even optimistic that our leaders can come to terms with that army knocking on our doorstep, potentially saving thousands of lives in the name of rationality. That's another thing that bothers me about your stories. Why can't they ever conclude with levelheaded folks sitting down and talking through their problems? The stories always end in battles, and the hero always goes on to fight yet more battles."

Hal considered this. "I always figured the authors had run out of things to write about."

"Possibly. But you need to realize that we're not the heroes of this tale. You want a hero? Look at Lady Janderfel, or those Brothers Arda. Hell, even that Captain Whitney fellow is downright heroic compared to us. You think that fighting would allow you to prove yourself, but soldiers like us don't survive in your stories. We're faceless nobodies, fodder for the sake of gravitas. But you're not a nobody, Hal. You play the fiddle beautifully, you've a wonderful garden, and an expansive imagination. As for me, I'm happily married with two remarkable children. And I'm due for a promotion next month."

Hal beamed up at Ryman. "Oh, congratulations! I had no idea."

Ryman nodded with a worn smile. "Thank you, I've been meaning to tell you. I've just been so busy lately, what with increased patrols and all. What say you come over to my place next week for supper? Marta would love to have you."

"It'd be my pleasure." Suddenly, the wall above the gates came alive with shouts and calls. "What are they yelling about?"

"I think somebody is coming back. Look, they're opening the gates!" Ryman clapped Hal on the back. "What did I tell you! No battle today. We get to return safely to our beds tonight."

The gates opened further and a group of people hurried through, though Hal struggled to see over the ranks of soldiers. "What's going on, Ry?"

Ryman had grown pale. "I think you may get your chance at glory after all." A horn sounded three times, resonating through Dinh's streets.

Numbly, Hal belted on his scabbard and fell into formation beside Ryman. "I sure hope you're wrong about us being nobodies in this tale."

"Me too, Hal. Me too."

A RECKONING

Ropes strained and cracked. The line of trebuchets wheeled into position beneath darkening skies. Vandra's creations struggled to load massive chunks of the red stone into the weapons' slings. "Your people are in position?" There was no question in her tone.

"They await your signal," said Lentarro.

"Excellent." The shadows brought forth spherical earthenware jugs, and doused the trebuchets' payloads in oil. She snapped her fingers and the massive blocks of stone burst into flame. "Begin the attack."

With the *whoosh* of releasing energy, the trebuchets loosed a volley of fire. The projectiles seemed to hang in the seething heavens, as if suspended by some invisible tether. Then, with increasing speed, they plummeted toward the distant walls of Dinh.

THE WESTERN WALL

"Trebuchets, incoming!"

Dots of flame erupted from the horde to the south and rose into the storm.

"Are you certain your defenses will hold, Lady Janderfel?" asked Whitney. His knuckles were white against the crenelated sandstone walls.

"For the time being." Jaya's green eyes searched the sky. The rocks started their decent toward Dinh, but then, with a faint popping noise, disintegrated into dust. The air shimmered where they had broken apart. "Vandra will have to wait us out, or risk attacking Dinh directly."

"She doesn't strike me as the patient type," said Culyan.

"Nor me," said Whitney. Another barrage of stone broke against the magi's shield. "We'll have to kill her, eventually. Her death is the only way to end this. If her siege weapons succeed in reaching the city, we'll be forced to meet her."

"That *won't* happen," said Jaya. "So long as my magi

draw breath, the defenses will hold." Another flurry of stone painted the dark sky with lines of pale smoke.

In the courtyard below, the company was assisting in preparing the city's defenses. They raced this way and that as Commander Grayhawk barked orders. Stout timbers were stacked before the main gates. A team, lead by Finlan and Tryo, hoisted the braces into position and slammed them home with iron spikes. Sten was helping to distribute bundles of arrows along the southern wall, while the dwarves sang rocks into great piles over the city's points of ingress. Even Riddleston was lending aid. He chanted softly as he walked amongst the ranks of Dinh's army, draping gossamer strands of magic over swords and shields.

Whitney studied the frantic proceedings. He clenched his jaw. "Where are your magi, Jaya?"

She pointed to the western wall. "Safe within a bunker. Nothing can touch them there."

"How can you be certain?" Eotan asked. Thunder crashed in the south, briefly drowning out the tumult of the courtyard.

"The western wall isn't even there to protect the city, in truth," said Jaya. "The canyon does that naturally. It's far too steep for any person to scale, much less an entire army. Nothing can attack Dinh from the west. My magi will be safe there. The defenses will hold."

"But Vandra must know this," said Whitney. "Councilman Monta will have told her everything she needed to know about this city and her defenses, including your magi. So why does she lay siege if she knows it's futile?" He traced the leather grip of his rapier at his hip. "Unless this is all a distraction..." He turned suddenly, his soldier's intuition trumpeting in alarm. "Brothers Arda, did you see the Oethyr in Vandra's army?"

"Besides Lentarro, no," said Eotan warily.

Whitney swore and raced along the battlements, the

others hurrying to keep pace. He flew down a flight of sandstone stairs, taking them three at a time.

"I don't see what you're worried about!" Culyan called after him. "Nobody can scale the canyon!"

Eotan drew up short, his eyes wide. "Nobody on two legs, maybe."

Whitney was already calling for his Shrikes. "To arms, to arms! Follow me to the rear of the city, as if the fires of hell were upon us! Prepare to fight! Prepare for glory! Rou-augh!" He crammed on his plumed helmet and pelted through the streets, the Shrikes close on his heels. Faint screams and guttural howls sounded to the west.

The short wall came into view. Several guards lay motionless at their posts. A multitude of beasts was swarming out of the canyon and into the city. A host of Dinh's guard stood against the flow of Oethyr, but they were rapidly losing ground. Lightning illuminated the chaos from above, while bursts of color lit the streets from below.

A robust stone building perched on the edge of the fighting, its single door barred with thick iron struts. A flickering stream of light escaped from its roof, wandering up to the sky above Dinh. The light expanded outward at the point of contact with the magical shield. Jaya's magi were repairing Dinh's defenses, oblivious to the fury that raged outside their walls.

Whitney drew his rapier and pointed to the building. "Secure that bunker!" A swarm of angry black bolts hissed past Dinh's soldiers, prompting animalistic cries of pain and rage. The Shrikes advanced, beating back tides of snapping teeth. Whitney's rapier danced in the twilight, claiming life after life with deadly precision.

More soldiers of Dinh joined the battle, but the flood of Oethyr drove them back. The Shrikes surged forward, completely surrounded, a writhing circle of blackened steel and death that inched nearer the magi.

Light flashed at the bunker's door. A group of Oethyr worked to thread lengths of rope around the bars. Four massive bears freed themselves from the melee and aligned themselves before the door. The Oethyr deftly secured the ropes around the creatures and jumped clear. The bears lunged. Whitney heard the scream of protesting stone. The bears threw themselves forward, again and again, and the frame around the door began to crumble.

"Bring them down!" Whitney thundered. The Shrikes sent a volley of bolts into the beasts, felling one. The others roared and slammed forward, lather spraying from their jaws. Dust and stone exploded, but the bars held. Another volley from the Shrikes found its mark, another bear fell. The Oethyr quickly circled the remaining pair, deflecting the Shrikes' bolts with the shields and armor of fallen soldiers.

BOOM da BOOM da BOOM BOOM!

The desperate fighting paused in confusion. Whitney reeled at the overwhelming sound. It had come from everywhere at once.

BOOM da BOOM da BOOM BOOM!

The ground shook beneath his feet. He turned to stare up the streets of Dinh.

Kipto thundered toward him. The charger was adorned in golden barding that matched his rider, spikes protruding from his chest and forehead. The Marshal of the Wilds roared his challenge, crimson cloak streaming behind him. The golden wolf loped after him and let loose a bloodcurdling howl. And then came Sten, Manye, and the Bearded Eight. Seven beat his great drum, propelling them into battle. *BOOM da BOOM da BOOM BOOM!*

Hope soared in Whitney's chest. "Shrikes, soldiers of Dinh! To me! Rally to Captain Regibar Theraford Whitney, and charge!"

The Shrikes slammed headlong into the line of beasts.

Culyan cut a swathe through the elves, the great axe cleaving all in its path. Eotan skirted the fighting, attempting to reach the bunker. Sten fired arrow after arrow in the ragged light of Tanduil.

The bears strained against the ropes, frothing and roaring. More elves linked to the ropes, and with a burst of stone and rending iron, the bars gave way. The Oethyr wrenched open the door and swarmed inside. Cries of surprise and terror sounded from within the bunker. The remaining Oethyr cried victoriously and abandoned the field, hopping the short western wall before disappearing into the canyon.

Whitney raced to the bunker's door. A host of magi remained alive, torn and bloody, but the corpses of their fallen brethren littered the floor.

"We were too late," said Eotan. He looked to the sky. The flow of shimmering magic had ceased.

A flurry of stone rose from Vandra's trebuchets. It hung in the sky for what seemed an eternity. "Come on, Jaya," whispered Culyan. "Hold." Several of the great stones broke apart. But then, with a great hiss, the flickering dome fizzled into nothingness, as if a great translucent film had been removed from the sky.

Cries of warning echoed through the city. The projectiles struck home, and the ground shook. Fountains of dust and stone and fire erupted into the air.

"Return to the main gate," said Whitney hoarsely. "Dinh is no longer secure."

DESPERATE TIMES

Sten refilled his quiver from a stockpile atop Dinh's main gate. A trebuchet shot whistled overhead and obliterated a storefront in the bazaar. He shrank against the wall to avoid the spray of shrapnel. Dinh's very foundation shook as wave after wave of rock pummeled the city. Captain Whitney and Commander Grayhawk raced back and forth along the ramparts, directing Dinh's own trebuchets as they launched flying death at Vandra's army.

One of Dinh's towers was struck. It exploded from the impact and showered the ground with broken wood and jagged rock.

Culyan entered the courtyard in a clatter of hooves, and hailed Whitney. "The soldiers assemble at the southern gate!"

"Very good!" yelled Whitney. "Are my Shrikes prepared?"

"Aye, they're ready to lead the vanguard."

"Excellent! We may yet stand a chance."

"Are you sure this is wise?" called Sten. "We're playing directly into Vandra's hands!"

"We're out of time!" yelled Whitney. He narrowly avoided a flaming chunk of stone that flew past the lip of the wall. "Give me an hour to plan something and I'd agree with you, but Vandra will have reduced Dinh to rubble by then. The people are safe within the citadel, for now, but who knows how long it will stand." He swept along the wall like a man possessed, directing troops, firing trebuchets, and helping the wounded to cover. Yet his voice was equanimous as he bellowed orders. "Janderfel, Riddleston! Protect the courtyard while we form ranks. Don't let a single stone touch my soldiers before we leave these walls."

Jaya and Riddleston conversed briefly, then sent a shimmering web of light over the courtyard. A flaming rock struck the interlaced strands of magic and broke apart. The courtyard filled with soldiers. Sten and Whitney leapt from the wall. They joined his uncles, Manye, and the Bearded Eight at the head of the growing army.

Eotan led Lilenti to Sten. "Take her. I prefer to fight on foot."

"There are far too many Dark Ones for this to work," said Sten. He clambered onto Lilenti's back. "Even if we manage to defeat Vandra's army, she'll never allow herself to be cornered. She'll just retreat to the mountains and we're back where we started. Or dead."

"She'll try to flee," said Culyan grimly. "But the Bearded Eight are ready for her."

"Aye," said Two. "We should be able to contain her if she attempts to disappear. But first we need to survive the night. One step at a time."

Sten turned imploringly to Eotan. "How can you agree to this?"

His uncle withdrew his daggers and tested their edge. "I don't see an alternative. If we linger here, we will inevitably fall. And we cannot flee and abandon Dinh's people. Vandra has outmaneuvered us. There's nothing more we can do. We must fight."

Riddleston hurried over to them, his broad stomach heaving. "I'm starting to regret freeing myself from Vandra's dungeon." He shook rain from his bushy eyebrows. "At least my own wizards weren't poised to kill me in there."

"Better to die a free man than live as a prisoner," said Whitney.

"Says you," snorted Riddleston. "Ask a dead man his opinion on freedom."

"Wait a moment," said Sten. Riddleston's words had triggered something in his memory. "Do you remember what Councilman Monta told us? Right before he died."

"*Ergghbleghhh....?*" said Culyan. He ducked a spark of magic from Jaya's hand that whistled overhead. "What? He couldn't say much with that gaping hole in his chest."

Sten leaned forward, the glimmer of a plan taking shape in his mind. "He said to 'let them free'! He looked directly at me when he spoke."

"I thought he was asking Vandra to leave Dinh alone," said Whitney.

"I did too, at first, but what if he wasn't? What if he was telling us how to stop her? Riddleston, you said that you were in control of your actions when she harvested you?"

"In a manner of speaking, yes. We controlled the Dark Ones in a roundabout way. Until we died, that is. What are you getting at, boy?"

"We free Vandra's prisoners!" said Sten. "The wizards, and whoever else she's used to build her army. Rather than killing the Dark Ones, we approach the link from the other side. If we free the prisoners' minds from Vandra's hold, they'll no longer control the Dark Ones! She loses her army! Think of what happened to Corporal Hemmie." Whitney stiffened beside him, but Sten forged on. "When Vandra slew him, his shades died, too."

"It might work," said Eotan. "In theory. But Vandra stands between us and the mountains."

"Then we ride through the canyon," said Sten, his excitement growing. "Riddleston said the entrance to the tunnels lies directly above its mouth. We follow it to the south and she'll never see us coming!"

Another volley of rock smashed through the city. Screams and shouts rose above the winds.

"There's no time," said Culyan. "We have to stop Vandra from launching those damn trebuchets. And there's no guarantee your plan will work, however clever."

Rain beaded along the hem of Eotan's cloak. His blue eyes shone from within the darkened folds like star sapphires. "Sten can go alone. We will ride out to meet Vandra, to buy Dinh time. She would notice our absence from the battlefield, but perhaps not yours."

"Or mine," said Manye. She smiled up at them through the rain. "Sten won't be able to free the prisoners from Vandra's power. I can."

"No," said Eotan quickly. "It's far too dangerous."

She gently took his hand. "It's not your decision to make. I can do this, Eotan. This is my path. You need to trust me."

Eotan's voice tightened. "I won't be able to protect you. I swore I'd keep you safe!"

"I'll take care of her, uncle," said Sten. "Though on second thought, she'll probably take care of me." Eotan didn't smile.

"I'm going too," announced Corporal Ineza Ghet. Sten whirled about. Her scarred face broke into her usual smile at the sight of his surprise. She belted her scabbard over blackened armor with a wink. "What, did you think I'd miss out on all the fun?"

Whitney's mustache flared. "Are you sure about this, Corporal? Vandra's magic almost killed you."

Ineza embraced him. "Don't worry so much, Cap! Anyhoo, my face is sure to scare off any enemy we come across. Vandra did us a favor, in truth. Wouldn't you agree, *Lord Bregon?*"

Sten grinned. "Oh, certainly. Some might even consider it an improvement."

Ineza swung into her saddle. "Watch it."

"But you still can't guarantee Manye's safety," Eotan insisted.

"She's not safe *now*, little pup," said Culyan. He laid a hand on his brother's shoulder. "Not while Vandra rains hellfire upon the city. Nor will she be safe if she rides with us into battle. Sten and Corporal Ghet will look after her. He's an Arda, after all."

Conflicting emotions tugged at Eotan's face. Finally, he sighed. "Very well. Please give us a moment."

He knelt and hugged Manye. She whispered in his ear and his shoulders began to shake. She reached up and wiped a tear from his face, then withdrew the crown of golden leaves from her satchel and placed it on his head. He smiled and hugged her again. The dwarves rushed forward to envelop her in an octagonal hug, weeping into their beards.

She attempted to disentangle herself. "No more tears! I'll see you all soon. Protect these foolish Ardas tonight. They get into too much trouble."

Sten threaded Lilenti between the corpses at the base of the western wall. They passed the bodies of the monstrous bears, still lashed to the bunker doors. "There's a chance the Oethyr will still be in the canyon," he warned.

"Let's hope they're not," said Ineza. She seemed unable to look away from the bears. They passed through a stout iron gate and paused at the lip of the chasm.

Jaya and Riddleston dismounted. "You're sure you want to do this?" she said.

"I don't see another way," said Sten. "Besides, we're riding *away* from the danger. Seems to me we're the lucky ones."

Jaya smiled and stroked Lilenti's neck. "You remind me of your uncles. And your mother. When they were as young and foolish as you."

"I'll take that as a compliment."

Jaya and Riddleston closed their eyes. Their magic washed over Sten and Ineza, and the horses rose, nickering, into the air. Then, with painstaking care, they were lowered into the canyon. The city walls faded from view. Darkness waited below.

PROOF

Marstarrow swung from the gallows. The City Guard continued to repel the crowds, keeping them from the platform. Lord Impo and the Heads of House paraded across the stage and exchanged congratulations.

Raxo passed the stone to Butterson. "Make it count, Boss. He gave you one shot. Don't let him down."

Butterson raised the stone to his lips, shaking with anger. "Excuse me," he said, and his voice rang out impossibly loud. The lawns hushed at the new speaker. "I have something to say."

"You're a criminal," said Lord Impo. "Why should we listen to you? You're lucky we don't hang you beside your chancellor."

"Let him speak!" someone yelled. "We all know Mord Butterson and he's no criminal!" The assemblage shouted their assent.

Lord Impo deferred to the will of the crowd. "As you say. It makes no difference. The matter is settled." One of the

Heads of House said something inaudible and Lord Impo roared with laughter.

Butterson glowered at them and clenched his fist. "I would still say a few words. But I'll keep it brief. Many of you had good reason to doubt the chancellor and his methods. Gods know I did. He chose to rule from the shadows, and now he's paid for his mistake with his life." He took a deep breath to steady himself. "Now, I don't claim to know the chancellor intimately, but I came to know him better than most. He kept to himself and trusted few others, if any. It's undeniable that Heldan Port suffered for his distrust. He thought it best to keep us in the dark. He sought to save the city by himself. But he was wrong to do so. We all deserved the truth, yet it was denied to us. Marstarrow made a mistake by refusing to address our concerns outright. But he died protecting me, and he died protecting all of you. He turned out to be human, after all."

Marstarrow's body shifted in the wind, and the crossbeam creaked shrilly. "Cut him down, for pity's sake!" ordered Butterson. "He deserves better." A member of the City Guard stepped forward and slit the noose. Marstarrow's body was lowered into the coffin. The lid closed with a soft *thump*.

"Thank you," said Butterson. "Now, we can't undo what's already been done. But that doesn't mean we must accept our fates. Lord Impo claims an unjust lordship over the capital, just as he did so many years ago. Think back to those dark times, those of you old enough to remember. The rich became richer while the poor became poorer, and the Heads of House were content to sit and let it happen within their golden halls. They don't give a damn about any of us. People starved in the streets because they were born with the wrong surname. Petty criminals were rounded up by the hundreds and executed. These were men and women, just like you and me, fighting to survive. Meanwhile, the powerful and the corrupt had free reign over the city. Do you think the Houses recognized their crimes?"

"No!" the crowd roared in unison.

"Of course not!" said Butterson. "Better to execute the lad who stole a copper to feed himself for a day than the banker who stole enough to feed the city for a year." The Heads of House had ceased their celebrations and were watching Butterson intently.

"That is quite enough," said Lord Impo icily. "Remove yourself, or we'll have you arrested for a second time. I won't show you mercy again."

"I'm not done speaking," said Butterson. Impo motioned for the City Guard. Two men drew their swords. The crowd booed and whistled. Then, with a growl like an avalanche, G'rok stepped in front of Butterson.

"HE SAID HE NOT DONE!" The guards scrambled away, tripping over one another in their haste to escape.

"Thank you, G'rok." From the corner of Butterson's eye he could see Lord Impo marshaling the City Guard. It was now or never. He walked to the edge of the gallows, speaking fast. "Tonight is a shining example of how the Houses operate! Chancellor Marstarrow offered the Houses a fair trial, where you, the people decided the outcome. Did the Houses offer him such justice in return?"

"No!"

"No! They hanged him with no other cause than to seize power. That is how they operated in the past, and that is how they will continue to operate in the future. I won't deny that Marstarrow made his fair share of mistakes. But he *never* treated us unjustly for the sake of himself. He was an imperfect leader of an imperfect city, but he was one of us."

The crowd surged against the host of City Guard encircling the gallows.

"Remember what Marstarrow told you!" yelled Butterson.

"You have the power, tonight! The Heads of House removed the wizards from Heldan Port. They were the ones who sacked the mines and spread lies throughout the city. They were the ones who falsely imprisoned G'rok and me, but not before they tried to cut us down in the streets. And they were the ones who hanged the chancellor. Does their power match all of yours? I say we put it to the test."

More of the City Guard rushed to protect the gallows. The boards quivered and moaned beneath Butterson's feet. Lord Impo screamed at the soldiers to form an escape route, but the angry crowd refused to back down.

"They're with you, Boss," whispered Raxo. "Bring 'em home."

Butterson spread his arms over his head. "People of Heldan Port! Tonight we reject the Houses' rule and take the capital for ourselves! Chancellor Marstarrow was the only person fit to lead this city, and so it remains. Let him guide us now. He wasn't a good man. He wasn't an honest man. But he was a necessary man. And he will *always* be my friend."

Lord Impo clutched desperately to the crossbeam of the swaying gallows. "He's dead, you fool!"

"He can never die," said Butterson evenly, "because he told us the truth about your power. He lives on through his people."

Lord Impo pointed to the coffin. "Bring me that! I'll put an end to this idiocy." A group of soldiers deposited the casket upright against the base of the crossbeam. "Marstarrow is gone!" Lord Impo's eyes were bloodshot with fear and anger. "Do you hear me? He's dead! There's no point clinging to his memory. Disperse! Return to your homes and we may spare your miserable lives."

"No," said Butterson. He took a step forward and jabbed a finger at the boards at his feet. "You don't rule this city anymore. Chancellor Tiberion Marstarrow does."

"Have it your way," sneered Lord Impo. "Marstarrow is dead, and refusing to accept that fact won't bring him back.

Here, look upon your fearless leader!" With a snarl of victory, he swung open the casket's lid.

Gasps of amazement sounded from the forward ranks of the crowd. Butterson watched Lord Impo. The man's face had frozen in incomprehension as he stared into the interior of the casket.

It was empty.

Lord Impo recoiled from the casket as if it had burned him. "No... This is impossible. This is some sort of trick... this is... Oh, no." His gaze shifted to the obsidian gates of the Sanctum.

With a resounding *BOOM*, the blackened doors swung open. A tall, slim figure strode from the Sanctum's depths and made for the gallows.

ONCE MORE

The abating storm exposed the deep orange and red brush strokes of twilight. Whitney sat atop his horse at the head of Dinh's army. Next to him were the Ardas, Jaya, Riddleston, and Commander Grayhawk. With the screech of protesting chains, the gates of Dinh eased open. The army of shadows took shape in the distance.

Jaya gritted her teeth. "I must be mad. Only a mad person would charge headlong into *that* and think it's a good idea."

Culyan grinned and spun his axe. "Whoever said this was a good idea? As far as ideas go, I'd say it ranks among the very worst. But it's the only one we've got."

"If we find Vandra, we can end this," said Whitney. "Between the magi, the Bearded Eight, and Riddleston, we may be able to fend off her power."

"Easy enough," said Culyan.

Eotan nervously fingered the hafts of his twin daggers. "Manye and Sten *will* reach the mountains in time."

"I expect you're right," said Whitney, "but we're out of time." Banners flapped and armor clanked amidst the ranks of silent soldiers. He spurred his horse and rode along the forward lines. "Warriors of Dinh!" He pointed to the sea of shadows. "Do not go quietly into that darkness. Go loudly, with steel in your hands and courage in your hearts. Fight for your city. Fight for your families. Fight for life itself, because that's what's at stake! And remember that you do not fight alone. For the first time in history, the capitals of Miz stand united. We shall not fail. Rou-augh!"

The courtyard took up the call. Whitney reined his horse into the Canyonlands, and the army marched forward.

A procession of cavalry and foot soldiers filed through the reddened gate. Vandra smiled.

"Well done," said Lentarro. "The fools have sealed their doom."

She studied the oncoming legion. Some of their leaders were indeed fools, like the fat captain, the dour-faced elven commander, and the monstrosity of an Arda who called himself the Marshal. Even from a distance she could see his golden armor, grossly resplendent in the fading light of day. But the Wolf and the mage were anything but foolish. Her gaze flicked to the black line of the canyon. "Where are your Oethyr?"

"Traveling south. They shall arrive shortly to bolster your ranks."

"Head them off and lead them to the mountains. Watch the entrance to the mines. I don't need you here."

"Why?" asked Lentarro. He flinched under her piercing gaze. "I mean no disrespect."

"Then do as you're told and don't concern yourself with my reasons."

"As you wish." He made to leave but then turned back to her, clasping the horn uncertainly to his chest.

Vandra's annoyance flared. "What?"

"I would ask one final favor of you. If you see my daughter upon the battlefield, I beg you to spare her life. That cur of an Arda has twisted her mind. But she can still be saved. Let her live, and I-"

Vandra bore down on him. "I don't give a damn about you or your filthy brethren!" Lentarro cowered in fear as the magic blazed up her arms. "You are cravens to be used and disposed of as I see fit, nothing more. You've served your purpose. If you wish to keep your miserable life and return to the Wilds, then remove yourself from my sight and watch the mines."

Lentarro's face darkened. "Lady Vandra." In a flash of purple light, the great ram set out across the Canyonlands, angling for the distant foothills of the Hammerstone Mountains.

Vandra raised a hand. A line of ballistae wheeled to the front of her army. Their deadly six-foot bolts gleamed wickedly in the setting sun. Her puppets had noticed the oncoming forces and were whipping themselves into a frenzy. Awful shrieks and howls split the air, and crimson eyes burned with the anticipation of blood.

"Good luck," she whispered, then turned and melted into the ranks of shadow.

INTO THE FRAY

Crimson rock whipped past the slit of Whitney's visor. All he could hear was the clamor of horses and the music of the dwarves. He raised a gloved fist and spurred his horse to a gallop. The Shrikes and Dinh's cavalry did the same.

There came a distant *thwang*. A massive shape whistled past his ear. A horse screamed in death and crumpled to the ground atop its rider.

"Ballistae!" he screamed. The projectiles cut wide swaths through Dinh's soldiers. In a blaze of golden armor, the Marshal spurred his destrier to the forefront of the charge, the Wolf and the dwarves close behind. Another volley of missiles hummed across the Canyonlands. This time, they deflected upward at the last second.

Whitney saluted the cloud and fell into line behind the Ardas. The Dark Ones stood shoulder-to-shoulder, wailing crazily. Rows of glinting spears and pikes protruded from their ranks, eager for horseflesh.

"Now!" roared Culyan. Two strummed his Boomstick. The air crackled with power. Jaya and Riddleston thundered ahead, leading Dinh's magi. Waves of concussive force billowed toward the awaiting army and obliterated the forward lines. Whitney swept into the hole. The Shrikes fanned out, beating back the snarling Dark Ones to form a clearing. Jaya and Riddleston vaulted to the ground, launching salvoes of arcane death in all directions.

With a roar of bloodlust or delight, the Marshal continued his charge. The wolf and the dwarves followed in his wake and disappeared into the roiling shadows. Intermittent flashes of green marked their advance. Whitney shook his head. The brothers were truly insane, but he couldn't worry about them now.

The battle continued with unrestrained fury. Several times Whitney landed what he thought to be a fatal blow, only to have the shadowed creature rise and continue fighting. A pike pierced his hip, finding a route through the plates of his armor. He dispatched the Dark One and yanked the pike free. Hot blood ran down his leg.

The sheer numbers of Vandra's army began to overwhelm the Shrikes. The defensive circle shrank toward the magi at its center.

The Ardas returned in a flurry of horse and steel. Culyan was littered with cuts, his armor dented. The golden wolf ripped at a shadow's throat, then bounded into the clearing, bleeding from a wound to its haunch. The dwarves' music washed over Whitney. The pain in his side diminished slightly.

A horn blast sounded from the north. Dinh's infantry joined the battle with the clang of sword and shield. Commander Grayhawk rode at the head of her army, lashing out with a bastard sword as she drove her soldiers to Whitney. The narrow line of Dark Ones separating the two forces shattered. The commander removed her helmet, panting, and her soldiers rushed to defend the clearing.

"Well done, Captain!" she called, wiping sweat from her brow. "I don't know how you managed to hold the line for so long, but-"

A lance of crimson light flew over Whitney's head and struck the ground at her feet. The explosion tossed her into the air, along with a handful of soldiers. She fell, neck bent to an impossible degree, surrounded by her slain brethren.

Whitney spun. Vandra stood atop a rocky outcrop behind her army. She was pale in the light of the rising moon. A nimbus of crimson sparks raged about her, illuminating the night sky as if by balefire. She unleashed a second spike of magic. Men and women screamed in death.

"Contain her!" he roared.

Jaya and Riddleston turned their attention to the enchantress. Vandra launched a third bolt of crimson, but this time the magic dissolved into the night sky.

"I say," wheezed Riddleston, "how is she so powerful? We're only going to be able to hold her off for so long, Captain!"

Eotan appeared in an emerald flash. "We need to move on her before she overwhelms us. Form a wedge and protect the magi at all costs. Culyan will lead the way."

"I'd say its time we introduce these bastards to the twins!" shouted the Marshal. Blood matted his beard. He raised his great axe into the air and pulled along its haft. With a click of inner machinations, the weapon split perfectly in two. Culyan laughed crazily and charged forward, an axe in each hand, his brother close on his heels. Whitney and his Shrikes drove forward amidst a flurry of emerald flashes.

They pressed on, slowly gaining ground across the Canyonlands. A trail of corpses and ash followed them across the sanguine rock. A mage was slain, pierced by an arrow, and then two Shrikes, overwhelmed by a host of shadows that rent their black armor with savage blows. Dinh's soldiers began to fall in droves as exhaustion took hold. Vandra remained on her perch, sending bolt after bolt of lethal magic into the battlefield to be deflected by the magic of Jaya and her magi. A mage crumpled to the ground, blood pouring from his nose. His eyes rolled back into his head.

"She's breaking free!" Jaya screamed. A wave of crimson magic exploded from Vandra. It broke against the forward ranks of Dinh's army, only partially repelled by the magi. The warriors shattered, as if made from brittle ice, their screams of terror abruptly silenced.

Riddleston collapsed to his knees. His face gleamed with sweat and blood. "We're lost!"

Vandra laughed victoriously. Her magic built around her as she prepared for another attack, then boiled toward Whitney. He stood rooted to the spot as Jaya's arcane defenses crumbled. Without warning, a deafening *TWANG* rent the air. The crimson wave of death broke apart.

Two rose above the ranks of shadows. He crouched alone on the cloud, his Boomstick clutched firmly in one hand. The ruby in his beard flashed in the moonlight as he drew level with Vandra. "Let's dance, you and I." He flexed his fingers as the magic blossomed along her arm. With a snarl, she began the assault.

Whitney could only watch as Two dueled with Vandra. The dwarf's fingers were a blur. His music roared impossibly loud and impossibly fast. Light streamed from his Boomstick, rebuffing the torrent of magic that flowed from the woman in black. The battle paused as all eyes turned to the sky. Magic met magic in a symphony of fire and song.

To Whitney, it looked as though Vandra was weakening to the assault. Her face was twisted in concentration, and the frequency of her spells had slowed. Two pressed the advantage, supported by the Bearded Eight and the magi far below. The Canyonlands rang with the Boomstick's amplified voice.

But then, with a cry of frustration, the ground at Vandra's feet split asunder. A torrent of crimson sparks poured from the cracks in the earth. The magic churned around her before absorbing into her body. Two continued to play, but the music was strangely dampened and distorted, as if heard from underwater. A look of confusion passed over his face.

The blinding jet of crimson magic struck him in the chest. The Boomstick exploded in his unresisting hands. A shock-wave of power and noise ripped in all directions, knocking soldiers and Dark Ones alike to the ground.

Two's lifeless body fell from the cloud and disappeared from view. From somewhere in the mass of soldiers, Culyan gave a ragged cry of anguish.

Vandra knelt upon the outcrop, breathing heavily. Whitney knew the reprieve wouldn't last. He bellowed for Finlan and Tryo. Frantically, they set to rebuilding the forward lines of Dinh's army. The soldiers were exhausted and beaten, their numbers reduced by at least a half. Yet at Whitney's urging, they fell into silent rank, driving shields and pikes into the crimson rock.

The Ardas came to join Whitney. Tears streamed openly down Culyan's face, mingling with the blood in his beard. Eotan's face was a mask, but his sapphire eyes were brighter than any star. The Marshal raised both axes into the air, and Dinh's army roared their defiance.

Vandra picked herself insouciantly from the ground. She studied the diminished army through hooded lids, and wiped clean the dust from her robes. Then, with a disdainful flick of her finger, the Dark Ones surged forth.

Whitney looked to the south. The foothills of the Hammerstone Mountains stood black against a rising full moon. His only hope lay with Corporal Ghet, Manye, and Sten. If they didn't reach the end of the canyon before Vandra had recovered her strength, all would be lost.

AVES EX MACHINA

Lilenti tore through the canyon. Her hooves seemed to barely touch the banks of the River Dah, and Ineza's mare struggled to keep pace. They wended through the twisting labyrinth of eroded monoliths, standing watch like ancient stone guardians in the light of the moon.

Sten gazed up at the lip of the canyon, far above. He could no longer hear the sounds of battle coming from Dinh. For a moment, the fighting seemed to have paused, and all he could hear was Two's Boomstick echoing through the canyon. But then the music had stopped, as quickly as it had come, and silence descended. The implications terrified him.

The mouth of the canyon loomed before them out of the darkness. A stream of water cascaded down the rock's face, endlessly feeding the river. The walls were shorter and less steep here, and Sten spotted a trail that wound up and over the canyon's rim. He angled Lilenti onto the path, then skidded to a halt, eyeing the long shadows that clung to the stone.

Ineza drew alongside them in a flurry of silt. "What is it?"

"I'm not sure." Lilenti snorted and pawed at the ground. "That pathway... to the left of the waterfall."

"Aye," said Ineza. "Nice spot on that, I can barely make it out. What are we waiting for?"

She started forward but Sten grabbed her arm. "Look at the shadows."

Ineza squinted and then shook her head. "We don't have time for this. I know you were listening to the fighting, same as I. Anyhoo, this silence means Vandra has already won, or is about to, so we need to move, now, before-"

"Sten's right," said Manye quietly. "The moon is rising in front of us, but the shadows..."

Ineza swore. "There are shadows behind the rocks!"

The undulant tone of a horn echoed through the canyon. As one, the shadows rose and stalked toward them. Manye stiffened as the shapes passed into the moonlight.

"Oethyr!" she whispered. Growls and snarls reached them through the gloom.

Sten's mind raced. They couldn't turn back without abandoning their companions to certain doom, but the elves were blocking the only pathway out of the canyon. He desperately scanned the darkness, searching for another way out. With a rasp of steel on leather, Ineza drew her sword. And then he spied it, a narrow dry wash almost invisible in the night, set into the western wall of the canyon.

"Follow me!" he shouted. Lilenti darted across the river. Splashes and animalistic cries pursued them. Lilenti reached the narrow chute and expertly navigated her way along the precipitous drop. But Ineza's mare was not so sure-footed. The horse balked upon reaching the wash. It stomped and snorted in fear as the Oethyr drew closer. Ineza vaulted from her saddle and began leading her mount by foot.

The elves had reached the canyon's walls and were rapidly

ascending. Sten could only watch as the distance between Ineza and the snapping animals shrank. He unslung his bow and nocked an arrow, but her body shielded the Oethyr below her. He cursed, willing her to move faster.

Then, with the grinding of obliterated stone, a section of the canyon's wall began to crumble. Great chunks of red rock plummeted from the lip of the chasm and hurtled toward the path. The rocks struck the wash behind Ineza. A cascade of earth, sand, and debris ripped toward the elves. They screamed in terror and tumbled down the path to avoid the landslide.

Manye lowered her hand as Ineza scrambled out of the canyon and jumped into her saddle. "Whoo! Thanks for that little Oethyr."

Dark shapes were already scaling the canyon walls, clambering over the newly formed mound of rock. Sten glanced to the south. The Hammerstone Mountains were no more than a mile away. Another horn blast sounded from the east. More dark shapes were sprinting along the chasm's rim amidst bursts of garish colors, moving to block their path.

"Go!" he yelled. Ineza dug her heels into her mare.

They flew toward the distant foothills as the Oethyrs' cackles and screams grew louder. The horn rang again and again. More shadows rose from the Canyonlands in front of them. Sten wheeled Lilenti in a circle, desperately searching for a route of escape. There were none. The Oethyr had lain in wait for an ambush, just as they had in the Wilds.

A pack of wolves broke away and rushed at Lilenti, eyes reflecting the moonlight. Sten loosed an arrow but it sailed wide. He nocked another, but was thrown to the ground as Lilenti veered sharply to avoid the snapping jaws. He scrambled to his feet as the Oethyr closed in. Taking careful aim, he raised an arrow to his cheek. A wolf toppled to the ground, twitching uncontrollably, and he paused in confusion. The other shapeshifters stalked forward, oblivious. But then a second wolf fell, and then a third. Now the pack faltered, yipping in confusion and fear.

The patter of hundreds of light footfalls reached Sten's ears. He looked to the west. Two winged shapes hurtled toward him through the moonlight.

"Back, vile beasts!" called a brusque, melodious voice.

"Your doom approaches!" called a second.

Sten could only laugh. Two small owls tore from the darkness. Behind came a host of gnomes with painted faces. They rode long-eared hares that loped across the Canyonlands with easy strides. Edelwing and Stonetalon had come. And they had brought the Yutuku.

"Grandmother Morroza sends her regards!" hooted Stonetalon. The gnomes unleashed a flurry of red-plumed darts from carved pipes. The darts buried themselves in the Oethyr with a *hiss*, and more animals crashed to the ground.

Faewyn whipped past, her face streaked with dark war paint. "I repay my debt to you, friends of the Yutuku!" She released a string of angry darts as she expertly weaved between stamping hoofs and snapping jaws. A trio of Oethyr fell in her wake. "You're lucky the owls found us in time!"

Sten sprang onto Lilenti's back. "Hold them off for as long as you can!"

"With pleasure!" hooted Edelwing. He dove at a snarling mountain lion. "Have at thee, coward!"

Sten and Ineza resumed their flight toward the mountains. The ground sloped higher as they reached the foothills. He could see the black opening of a tunnel, far above them, just visible in the moonlight.

They reached the mine and paused to look over the Canyonlands. The Yutuku and Oethyr were locked in combat at the mouth of the canyon. But Sten's attention was drawn past them, to the north, where a flurry of magical lights and rampant fire was illuminating the desert in an eerie glow.

Dinh was still fighting.

A bellow of anger shattered the fleeting calm. A great ram galloped after them up the foothills, a curved horn strung across its chest. It changed in a blaze of amethyst light and Lentarro appeared, his face black with fury. Without a word, Sten, Manye, and Ineza fled into the tunnel. They blindly delved deeper into the mountain. Shouts of anger rang behind them, echoing their descent.

URBAN LEGENDS

The lanterns arrayed before the Sanctum's gates cast eerie, flickering shadows. A lone figure approached the gallows. Eager whispers spread through the crowd. Butterson could hear Lord Impo behind him, still spluttering with anger and disbelief. G'rok walked to the edge of the gallows and extended a huge, bristled hand. The figure accepted the proffered assistance and was hoisted onto the deck.

With a nod of thanks, Tiberion Marstarrow smoothed back his graying hair and turned to face the crowd.

And was met with utter silence.

"We thought you was dead!" someone yelled, after a moment.

"Unequivocally, no," said Marstarrow.

"Are yer a vampire or undead or some other unnatural sort?"

"I am afraid not."

"Thank the stars. Them types give me the heebie-jeebies."

"How's the hell's you still alive, then? We watched you hang!"

"I apologize for the deception," said Marstarrow, "but it was essential in exposing Lord Impo's treachery."

"Right lousy thing to do," someone said. "Makin' a fellow think you're dead and then comin' back moments later, right as rain. Emotional manipulation that is, toyin' with a person's thoughts and feelin's without his or her knowin'. Cheap."

Butterson stepped forward. "Listen. You're missing the point, here. The chancellor misled you and is alive, yes, but he just showed you the real criminals! Lord Impo ushered him into the Sanctum. You see, this coffin is-"

"Yes, yes, a gateway into the Sanctum," someone said.

"Er, correct," said Butterson, off-put. "Well, the key lies in who-"

"Whoever opens the door, which in this case was Lord Impo."

"Right..." said Butterson. He stroked his black beard. "And the wizards disappeared because?"

"Because Lord Impo let someone into the Sanctum to cast doubt on Marstarrow's legitimacy to rule, thereby paving the road to succession. Elementary."

Butterson blinked. Heldan Portians had never been a terribly clever bunch. On several separate occasions he had been forced to stand before the entirety of the Jackamoose's clientele and explain as to why people couldn't sustain themselves on beer alone, as beer was indeed, not food. But now, for some unfathomable reason, they were demonstrating the collective insight of a wizened scholar, minus the superiority complex.

"But don't you want more of an explanation of how it all happened?" he asked. "Why all of *this*," he gestured to the gallows, "was necessary?"

"Nah. We trust *you*, and *you* said we should believe in Marstarrow. He's back now, so good enough for us." The crowd murmured their assent.

"Interesting," said Marstarrow. He quietly surveyed the

throngs with his steel gaze. "I can confidently say I never expected such an outcome. Well done, Mord, and well done Heldan Port. I daresay the success of our plan can be attributed to your uncanny ability to gain peoples' trust."

Butterson flushed from the praise. "I'm a businessman, Tiberion. All I had to do was sell you to them. Easiest pitch of my life."

Marstarrow nodded solemnly. "I find myself lamenting the meticulous thought that went into crafting this plan, which now appears wasted. I have critically underestimated the power of trust when ruling this city. Perhaps, moving forward, things will go easier with this newfound knowledge."

Butterson grinned. "I doubt it."

Someone shouted from the far end of the gallows. They turned to see Lord Impo and the rest of the Heads of House fleeing up the street, a host of City Guard at their backs.

"Oi! They're getting away!" someone said, to angry shouts and yells.

Marstarrow made a placating gesture. "The Houses will pay for their crimes, but for tonight, let the issue be resolved. They cannot escape the city and will be arrested in due time. As such, if you will please return to your homes, I-"

"You said *we* have the power tonight!" someone called.

"Aye! Tonight's our night," said another. "You've had plenty. And we're not lettin' them flowery bastards get away so easily." The crowd drifted after the disappearing Heads of House.

"They'll lose interest, quickly enough," said Butterson. "I've seen plenty of riots during the Houses' rule. As long as they're leaderless and disorganized, everything will be-"

"Rally to me, dimwits of Heldan Port!" Raxo stood atop G'rok's shoulder and gestured grandly. The orc lumbered to the front of the crowd, Gefwyn tucked firmly under one arm like a bedroll. "Tonight we take back our city from the Houses! Stand together, now, as one! We are the many, the downtrodden, the filthy. We are the rompers in the hay, the pilferers in the night, the drunkards in the streets! Arm yourself, with whatever rubbish you can find lyin' around, and follow me! Let's get 'em!"

Raxo and G'rok tore up the street and the crowd boiled after them, yelling eagerly.

"Oh, damn it all," said Butterson.

Minutes later, he found himself within the Houses' residential district, trying desperately to control the mayhem. Marstarrow had given up attempting to contain the angry crowd. He stood removed, amusedly monitoring the proceedings, the faintest of smiles turning his lips.

"Where the hell are they?" said Raxo, after they had thoroughly searched the final estate. "Not even a whiff of expensive aftershave to point us in the right direction. Though whoever owns this place has style. Look at the size of that buxom statue! Tasteful, that is. Such attention to detail."

Butterson scanned the interior of the house's pavilion. Apart from turned over furniture and broken glassware, it was empty. "I guess your innocuous attempt at igniting class warfare tipped them off." A dwarf trotted out from the kitchen, clutching an armful of expensive cutlery. "You there!" Butterson called. "Put that back. Stop raiding and pillaging your own damned city. And empty your pockets." The abashed dwarf gingerly set down the silverware and turned out the linings of his tunic and trousers. A cascade of shiny objects tinkled to the floor.

The dwarf drew himself upright and placed a solemn hand over his breast. "Master Butterson, I have no idea how those got there, hand to beard."

"Uh-huh. Is that a lady's mirror?"

"Oh, well excuse a dwarf for caring about his appearance now a days."

"You're wearing a sock on your head."

"That is to protect my *ano-nim-ity*. People in Heldan Port remember a face."

"But we can see your face," observed Raxo.

"Well, the sock smelled something fierce when it were pulled down. Had trouble breathing."

Butterson pinched the bridge of his nose. "Just put everything back."

"By your leave, Master Butterson." The dwarf hastily pocketed the treasures and disappeared into the house.

"A pint says he keeps all that," said Raxo.

They moved to the front steps. Raxo's followers waited expectantly on the lawns. The demon shook his head and groans of disappointment rose from the crowd.

"Master Butterson!" cried a voice from inside the house. Footsteps clattered behind them. The dwarf careened down a flight of steps, sock streaming from his head like a banner of war, and ran headlong into G'rok, who was coming out of the study with Gefwyn. The dwarf collapsed to the ground and lay still.

"Oh for crying out loud!" said Butterson. "Someone fetch some water. And I don't even want to know what you two were doing in there." A pail of water was brought forth, and Raxo dumped it unceremoniously on the unconscious dwarf. His eyelids fluttered.

"Am I dead?"

"You're fine," said Butterson. "You ran into G'rok here."

"SORRY, LITTLE SOCK MAN."

The dwarf's bleary eyes were somewhat crossed. "Wounded in the field of battle. If only my pappy could see me now."

Butterson ground his teeth and managed a smile. "Fine, whatever. Who are you? Why were you calling for me?"

"I'm Sixty-Eight. Er, Sixty-Seven... Sixty-Four?"

Raxo jumped onto the dwarf's chest and shook him by the ears. "Get on with it, man!"

"Lessee here. Nope, I'm definitely Sixty-Eight. Well, I was going to return the items, as instructed. I definitely weren't nicking more stuff from peoples' nightstands. But then I looked out a window and I saw them!"

"Who?"

"The Heads of House! All of them. Or at least I think it were them. They were wearing their colors and fanciful emblems. The City Guard were with them, too. They was heading down the hill last I saw."

"Toward the harbor?"

"Uh, if the harbor is at the bottom of the hill?"

"They will be sorely disappointed if they think to escape by sea," said Marstarrow. "What say we put an end to this nonsense, Mord?"

"Happily," said Butterson. "It's about damned time I return to my tavern."

Lord Impo sprinted down the street. The faint whisper of waves crashing against the docks was still some distance away, the sound a tantalizing taste of freedom. If he reached the harbor, he could bribe a ship's captain and buy safe passage to Angoma. There were always ships at port, regardless of the hour, whether unloading goods, resupplying provisions, or anchoring in safety for the night before continuing to the Frozen Steppes. If he reached the harbor ahead of the mindless mob pursuing him, he'd be free.

He swore and held in a scream of frustration. It was all Marstarrow's fault. The man was as duplicitous as he was pale. Loath as he was to admit, Lord Impo realized that he had been outwitted. Marstarrow had beaten him at every turn, had foreseen his every movement. Had the man even predicted his arresting Butterson and the beast? It certainly seemed so.

The docks swam into view and Impo let out a sob of relief. He could hear the sounds of the approaching mob, louder now. But then, as quickly as it had come, his relief evaporated. The harbor was empty, save for a single ship moored to the northernmost wharf. Panic wracked his insides. He numbly scanned the pier. Where the *hell* had all the ships gone? The light of a full moon faintly illuminated the harbor and glittered atop the cresting waves.

And there they were, anchored just offshore: an entire fleet of merchant vessels, transport galleys, and naval frigates, bobbing happily in the swell.

"What the hell are you doing?" screamed Lord Impo. He waved his arms in frustration as the other Heads of House and City Guard arrived. "Ten thousand gold pieces to the captain that takes me to Angoma!"

In response, the entire fleet hoisted their flags in unison. Impo gawked in disbelief. Each and every ship had drawn the same sigil, a golden scale against a crimson shield. The sigil of House Marstarrow.

"No!" he screamed, tearing at his clothes in fury.

"Something the matter, hon?" called a singsong voice. A middle-aged elven woman appeared on the deck of the lone ship moored to the wharf. She rested her arms against the taffrail, and watched Lord Impo with keen, amber eyes.

Lord Impo ran to her. "Get me out of this godforsaken place and I'll reward you." He withdrew a bulging purse of coins. "You'll be richer than you've ever imagined."

"Oh, I'd love to take you up on that offer. Funny thing is, someone's gone and sabotaged my rudder. I was set to unload my goods for market but now I'm sitting dead in the water. You wouldn't be having any idea who'd have done such a thing, would you?" She smiled pleasantly, and coyly traced the stenciled name of her ship: 'Gyrfalcon'.

His mouth moved but nothing escaped his lips. He turned at the flurry of approaching footsteps. Marstarrow, Butterson, and seemingly the rest of the entire city had arrived at the docks. There was even a dwarf with a sock on his head, brandishing a fearsome array of his own handcrafted cutlery.

"It's over Longolis," said Marstarrow, with more than a touch of satisfaction.

Impo backpedaled. "So what now? Am I to be marched to the gallows, repentant and contrite, prepared to atone for my sins? I think not, Tiberion. I still own the City Guard."

Marstarrow examined a fingernail. "A select few, perhaps, just enough to encourage placidity. Overconfidence leads to unprovoked mistakes, in my experiences. I feared my noble self-sacrifice transparent, yet you ushered me into the Sanctum nonetheless. Tell me, Longolis, would you have ordered my execution without the support of the City Guard?"

With the sharp clank of shifting steel, the bulk of the guard dropped into combative stances and encircled the Heads of House. Impo gazed about in silent disbelief. Only a handful of soldiers remained at his side, namely the group he had tasked with arresting Butterson.

"Excellent," continued Marstarrow. "Now, as it so happens, the dwarven mines have recently come upon difficult and tragic times. Eight miners were killed in a subterranean explosion, the cause still yet unproven. I see before me eight Heads of House, guilty of treason. What a happy coincidence. I believe there were originally nine conspirators, including Lord Polto. Fortunately for him, he is not present here today. But I believe you eight shall serve as suitable replacements for the slain miners. Though I must warn you, outsiders fare poorly in dwarven mines. Something to do with the constant danger, overwhelming claustrophobia, and utter darkness." He shrugged and clasped his hands behind his back. "Or so I am led to believe."

Lady Huvani fell to her knees. "Please, Chancellor. It was all Lord Impo's doing! We were forced into cooperation, on pain of death. It was his idea, through and through. We'll testify to the fact if you stay our exile to the mines." The other Houses clamored in agreement.

Marstarrow's gray eyes glittered darkly as he considered the proposition. "Very well. Testify to Longolis's involvement in the loss of the wizards, the plot to overthrow my station, and the fraudulent arrest of Mord Butterson and G'rok. You shall avoid the mines if you speak the truth."

The other Heads of House threw themselves at Marstarrow's feet, gushing their thanks.

A veil of red mist descended over Lord Impo's eyes. His mind was strangely blank. Nothing mattered anymore, except wiping the smile from the smug, pale bastard who stood before him. He seized the goblin gaoler by the shoulders and thrust the creature forward. "Kill him!" Without a moment's hesitation, the goblin produced an evil hand-held crossbow, the bolt fit snugly in place. The goblin bared its filed teeth, aimed, and fired.

The towering orc stepped bodily in front of the chancellor just as the bolt released. The projectile sliced through her pink bowtie and ricocheted harmlessly off her leathery hide. The sad pink cloth fluttered to the ground. With a bellow of rage, she hoisted the goblin into the air and flung him into the bay. A distant splash sounded near the anchored ships, accompanied by a host of jeers and laughter. Lord Impo felt himself fall to his knees.

"Now it is done," said Butterson. He bent to retrieve the ruined bowtie from the salt-stained planks. "Heldan Port is saved."

DARKNESS

The entrances to a hundred different tunnels yawned from the cavern's walls, dark and uninviting. Mining equipment lay scattered across the chamber's floor, and Sten noticed a collection of decaying sacks that read, 'Explosive Takk,' in moldy lettering.

Ineza leaned against the mildew encrusted walls, panting. "Which way do we go?"

Manye conjured a glowing amber orb. It vibrated and danced eagerly above her palm. "Seek," she whispered. The sphere shot down one of the passages, its welcome glow fading from view like the setting sun. She repeated the spell for each tunnel. "Now we wait."

Sten strained his ears in the silence. He fervently hoped they had lost Lentarro in the maze of passageways. But then, still some distance away, came the unmistakable sounds of cautious footsteps echoing down one of the mineshafts.

"He's coming," whispered Ineza. "What do we do?"

Manye held up a hand for silence. With a faint *whirr*, the orbs returned. One glowed a vibrant orange, the others a pale yellow. She pointed to the tunnel from where the orange sphere had originated. "There's something alive down there."

"Good enough for me!" said Sten. They resumed their flight through the darkness. They followed the passageway for a short time, its interior faintly illuminated by glowing patches of emerald mushrooms. A barred door appeared from the gloom. Sten tried to open it, but it remained firmly locked. He pressed his ear to the wood and imagined he could hear faint moans and whimpers coming from inside. "There's someone in there!" He stepped back to examine the door. "Can you do something about the lock, Manye?"

The elf raised her arm and closed her eyes. A spark of amber light danced into the lock, then fizzled away. She frowned and raised her arm again. Ineza brushed her aside, drew her sword, and brought it down against the lock in a single motion. With a deafening clamor, the door sprung open. The lock tumbled to the ground, split cleanly in two.

"There," said Ineza, with a broad smile. "I guess magic isn't always the solution. Anyhoo, you better hurry. The tattooed bastard will have heard that."

A series of cages hung from the ceiling of a sloping hallway in neatly symmetrical rows. Huddled shapes lay within, twitching and groaning, as if trapped in a nightmare. With Ineza's help, Sten sprang the nearest cage from its anchor and lowered it to the ground. A bearded, ragged old man stared up at them. His unseeing eyes rolled wildly about their sockets.

"It's one of the wizards!" said Sten. He recognized the Sanctum's faded insignia on the man's robes: a dark tower against a crescent moon. "This must be where Riddleston was held! Here, help me with the rest." They quickly lowered the remaining cages. Before long, a collection of bodies lay strewn across the stone floor, displaying varied degrees of dishevelment. The wizards twitched and cried out in the gloom, but remained entranced, refusing to wake.

Ineza looked to Manye. "Can you help them?"

Manye chewed her lip. "Jaya helped you recover from Vandra's magic, so there must be a way. It's just... Jaya has so much more knowledge than me. I don't know what to do to save them, but I'll try." Golden sparks flared along her fingertips and cascaded onto the nearest wizard, bathing him in warm light. For a moment, the wizard's restfulness eased. But then the light flickered and blinked out, and he cried out in renewed pain. Manye fell back with a sob. "I don't know why I thought I could do this! Vandra is too powerful. There are too many here! These are only the wizards. What about the rest of her prisoners? We don't even know where they are!"

Sten gently took her by the hand. "Do you remember what Grandmother Morroza told you in the Waypoint?"

She nodded and looked at the ground. "'Sacrifice is in my nature, no matter how dire the circumstance'."

Sten managed a humorless smile. "Well, I'd say things are about as dire as they can possibly get. Morroza recognized in you the same gifts that we've all come to rely on. You are uniquely brave, and uniquely good, and we are proud of you." He squeezed her hand, and Ineza laid a scarred hand on her shoulder. "We believe in you, Manye. Eotan and Culyan believe in you. And they need you. Now, more than ever."

Manye's mouth set in a determined line. She tucked a strand of chestnut hair behind one ear and cracked her knuckles. "Stand back." The vapid dank of the dungeon's air began to stir with rising winds. She held her hands outstretched and the winds grew, coming seemingly from nowhere and everywhere at once. "You will be safe," she whispered, almost to herself. "I'll protect you, Eotan."

Sten pulled Ineza behind the door. "Here we go." Golden lights began to flicker about the room in a growing maelstrom of wind and magic. The beards and tattered robes of the prone wizards danced in the gale. The lights grew blindingly intense, and Sten covered his eyes. Then, as one, the golden motes of magic rushed into the wizards' bodies, and the room was plunged into total darkness.

Manye slumped to the ground, her shoulders heaving. Ineza rushed to catch her, just as something hard smashed into the back of Sten's head. He crumpled to the ground. Stars flashed before his eyes. He struggled to rise, unsure of what had happened. A steel arm clamped about his neck. He rose unresisting into the air, feet dangling.

"Let my daughter go!" Lentarro rasped in his ear. He sounded on the verge of hysteria. Sten struggled in his grip, vaguely aware of the shattered ram's horn that lay beneath him. Manye rose unsteadily to her feet. Ineza drew her sword and crouched. "Move and I snap his neck!" Lentarro yelled, tightening his grip and shuffling into the room. "Manye, you're coming with me. Now!"

Manye clenched her fist. "No. You threatened to kill me in the Wilds, and now you want me to join you? I don't know what Vandra has done to you, but I pity you. You were my father, once. What would mother say if she could see what you've become?"

"She's dead!" Lentarro screamed. "Murdered by an outsider! An outsider *she* allowed into our lands. That is what happens when you trust others. They killed your mother and they've doomed this world!"

"And you've slaughtered hundreds in return!" cried Manye, and limped closer. "You closed our borders and cast your own people into self-imposed exile. Eotan saved me from your madness the day he wandered into our lands. I will never forgive you for what you've done. You are a murderer and a coward, Lentarro. You've led the Oethyr to ruin by siding with Vandra."

Lentarro's voice cracked. "Don't you see? *Can't* you see? Allying with Vandra was the only way to ensure our peoples' survival!"

"To ensure *your* survival."

"You don't know what she's capable of! If I had opposed her, she'd-"

"She'd have killed you all!" yelled Manye. "And better you'd have died that day than help her now! Do you truly believe she'll let you live? She'll cast you aside once you've served your purpose."

Lentarro's voice was laced with doubt. "You're wrong. She promised to show mercy, to give us back the Wilds if we helped her. Come with me, Manye. We can escape from all of this. I can keep you safe!"

Manye folded her arms. "My place is here. If there is any trace of courage left in you, let my friend go."

After a moment, Lentarro released Sten. The elf sank to his knees, sobs wracking his entire body. Sten scrambled away and massaged his neck. Manye approached the beaten elf and laid a hand on his shoulder. It may have been the dim light, but she stood taller than before, despite her injured leg.

"Help us, father." She delicately wiped a tear from Lentarro's cheek. "It's not too late for you to do the right thing." Lentarro opened his mouth, as if to protest, but then bowed his head and took Manye's hand in both of his own.

"Who the bloody hell are you?" said a voice behind Sten. He whirled about to see the entirety of Heldan Port's Occult Sanctum of Wizards standing before him. Magic crackled feebly, adding wavering light to the dim hall. A particularly short wizard eyed him suspiciously.

"We're here to rescue you," said Sten. He had momentarily forgotten the wizards with the imminent threat of death by strangulation. "Sylvus Riddleston sent us."

"About damned time," huffed the wizard. "Borneus

Rinnay, second-in-command. Now, lead us out of wherever the hell this is, and you'll be handsomely rewarded. Not by me, of course, but nevertheless."

"There are other prisoners down here," said Sten. "We still need to find them. We're running out of time."

Lentarro stood and braced himself in the doorway. "There are no others."

"What do you mean?" said Ineza. "Vandra has tens of thousands of soldiers in her army. She didn't get them from harvesting this lot."

"Thank the gods," said Borneus.

"You misunderstand," said Lentarro. "Yes, she's used others to build her army, but they aren't truly alive. Not anymore. Vandra keeps their minds healthy, through magic, but lets their bodies waste away. She only needs their minds for her harvests. They suffer a fate far worse than death, in truth. If you woke them, as you did these men, you'd awaken a corpse."

"How do we know you're not lying?" said Ineza. "For all we know, you're still loyal to Vandra and attempting to prevent us destroying her army."

Manye's eyes were fixed on her father's face. "He's telling the truth. I'll know if he's lying."

"Fine," said Ineza. "Do you know where she's storing them?"

Lentarro shook his head. "For every tunnel that leads out of the mountains there are ten more that venture deeper into the mines. We'll never be able to find them before she destroys your friends."

"Maybe we don't have to find them," said Sten. "I have a plan, but it's going to be dangerous as hell. Follow me." He led them up the passage and back to the cavern with the mining equipment. The going had slowed considerably with the addition of the bedraggled wizards. He turned to Manye. "I need you to lead the wizards out of the mountain."

"What are you going to do?" she asked warily.

He pointed at the collection of decaying sacks. "You see that? That's dwarven takk. Explosives. I'm going to use it to bring down this entire network of tunnels. We'll lay the tortured souls to rest, once and for all, and destroy Vandra's army in the process. But I need you to get them out of here."

Manye studied him for a moment and then smiled. "Very well, Sten Arda." She hugged him tightly about the waist. "Make sure you're running when the mountain falls."

"I've been running from something or other my entire life," Sten laughed. "Just ask Ineza. She's the one who caught me and forced me into this mess."

Ineza punched him lightly on the shoulder. "Oh, so it's all my fault now? Anyhoo, if you're as slow as you were in Heldan Port, then you're definitely going to die down here. Looks like you'll need my help."

"And mine," said Lentarro. "I know these tunnels better than you. I'll show you where to set the explosives."

Ineza's gauntleted hand strayed to her sword hip. "If you attempt to betray us, I will gladly cut you down."

"You'd try," Lentarro growled. He knelt before Manye. "You were right, daughter. You've always been right. I've lost sight of what matters, but I see clearly now. If I return, I hope you'll think better of me." He reached out to her then, tattoos shimmering in the faint light. Manye touched her fingertips to his and inclined her head. Then, without a word, she led the wizards out of the chamber.

Sten set to work gathering the explosives. He gingerly passed a sack to Ineza and another to Lentarro. "Don't drop this, whatever you do. And don't light any torches. Here, I'll show you how to place it. We'll run a line down each of these tunnels as far as we dare. Lentarro, show us where to plant the takk. We need to bring down the entire system."

"There are more rooms like this," said Lentarro. "If they fall, perhaps their tunnels and antechambers will too."

"Then it's settled," said Sten. "We'll ignite the explosion from here and run like hell. Takk is triggered by heat or pressure. If we blow this room the rest of the lines will follow, but we'd best be far away when they do."

Sten began to fix the explosive to the stone every few paces. "How do you know all of this?" said Ineza, taking careful note.

"I preferred the drinking company of dwarves to lords and ladies," said Sten. He frowned in concentration. "I picked up a few of their trade secrets along the way." Black lines followed them deeper into the mountain, smelling faintly of sulfur.

"And how drunk were these dwarves when they molded you into an expert miner? *In a tavern.*"

Sten shrugged and continued placing the takk. "They taught me an old saying as well. If you're feeling sober in the mines, you've probably died in the mines."

"How reassuring."

They retreated to the original chamber. Dark patches of takk snaked in every direction. Sten knelt and carefully unwound a bale of ignition cord. The twines were old and frayed and crumbled to dust in his fingers. He swore and began to unwind another length. It disintegrated at his touch. His fingers shook as he tried again and again, but to no avail.

Lentarro swiped the cord from his hands. "Go. I'll set off the takk. You two get out of here."

Sten cast about the huge cavern. "I can figure something out! I'll find something we can burn to set it off, and-"

"You're wasting time!" growled Lentarro. He took a menacing step toward Sten. "There's nothing dry enough to burn down here. But force can still set it off." He knelt and retrieved a pickaxe from the ground. "Go. I won't ask you again. And don't think I won't blow this place with you still inside."

Sten hesitated. Then, with a grimace, he sprinted up the passageway, Ineza alongside.

"Tell Manye I'm sorry!" Lentarro's disembodied voice echoed behind them. "Tell her... Tell her I love her. I've always loved her..."

They flew up the sloping tunnel's twists and turns, following the wizards' trail through the dust and grime. Sten felt the explosion before he heard it: a deep rumble that seemed to build in volume and fury on the verge of his senses. The tunnels began to shake. They sped around a corner and were struck by the light of the full moon hanging low in the sky outside the tunnel's mouth. With cries of relief, they sprinted for the exit and launched themselves into the arid still of the Canyonlands. Plumes of fire belched from the mineshaft. Cascades of rock and debris matched their flight down the mountain.

They tumbled to a halt amidst a shower of rock and scree. Manye and the wizards stood over them, surrounded by the Yutuku. The Oethyr were nowhere to be seen. All eyes looked to the ruined face of the mountain.

"Did it work?" Ineza whispered. The faint grumblings of the mountain eventually died away.

"I don't know," said Sten. "But that was our only chance to save the others."

ABSOLUTE POWER

The ground cracked beneath Vandra's feet. A boiling stream of red light writhed around her like some arcane serpent before absorbing into her body. She could feel the power coursing through her. She laughed and fired another lance of scarlet at the pathetic force below her. The survivors had formed a circle and were completely surrounded by her creations. A wall of ash was forming as her minions broke against the defenders. But when the magi fell, their companions would follow soon after.

The ground trembled violently. Another host of sparks swirled from the split. Vandra knew she was drawing on Miz too heavily, but the battle was nearing its end. She could feel the magical defenses growing feeble as yet another mage fell to the ground, dead or otherwise. The fools. All of their years spent studying magic and they were insects before her power. She could see the Ardas and Captain Whitney, still fighting with astounding ferocity. She was impressed, despite herself. Perhaps she would spare one or two of them for the harvest. Who knew what manner of warrior might arise from their psyche.

She paused a moment, regaining her breath. The toll of such a prolonged attack was weighing on her, but only just. She would let her pets slaughter a few more as she recuperated. She had been patient for so many years, biding her time as the world perpetually ignored her warnings. She would not rush now. A meticulous disassembly of her enemies would still see her victorious.

The cries of the dying clogged the air over the Canyonlands. Vandra waited atop her station, unmoved by their pleas. Hers was a life of violence and pain. It had been so ever since she was a girl. She allowed herself a humorless smile. How fitting her new world be born in a land the color of blood.

NIGHTFALL

Captain Whitney fell to his knees. His rapier dropped from his numb fingers. He coughed blood and leaned heavily against a ruined shield. The circle of Dinh's remaining defenders continued to shrink as men and women fell to the tides of shadow. Jaya and Riddleston stood valiantly at the center, battling with Vandra. But they couldn't hold out much longer.

The Ardas were the only ones who could match the strength of the Dark Ones. Culyan held the frontline alone, his twin axes rising and falling with unbridled fury. Eotan raced around the battlefield, striking wherever a Dark One managed to break through, and then retreating.

Finlan fell to the ground beside Whitney. Blood welled from a gash on his forehead. "Looks like this is it for us, Captain."

"Aye, Lieutenant, I believe it is," said Whitney, oddly detached. He withdrew the Follower and absentmindedly toyed with its edges. The blue light followed Eotan's frantic course around the battlefield. Whitney stowed the box and attempted to rise, then slumped back to the rock. His side burned where the pike had gored him.

Without warning, the fighting abruptly stopped. The Dark Ones retreated from the circle of soldiers and stood just out of reach. Their soulless eyes brimmed with an other-worldly hatred.

Vandra's voice broke over the Canyonlands, seductive and measured, despite the magical amplification. "You have lost, soldiers of Dinh. There is no point in further bloodshed. Lay down your arms and see mercy. Only your leaders will be held accountable for the sins of your city." Whitney glared at her, safely perched on her tower of stone.

"Don't listen to her!" yelled Culyan, as weapons clattered to the bloodstained rock. "She will kill you all. She has no need for any of us!"

"What have I done to merit such distrust?" said Vandra. "Let's see this affair ended, so you might return to your homes. To your families."

At the edge of Whitney's vision, a single Dark One slumped to the ground. Its red eyes were now dark.

Finlan nudged him. "Did you see that, Captain?" Whitney nodded. Another creature fell, and then another. There came a faint rumbling to the south, like the peal of distant thunder.

Vandra didn't appear to notice. "I seek justice for those who have betrayed Miz. Don't die needlessly for the sake of the guilty. They would happily see you perish to save their own skins. On my word, you may return home and..." She trailed off as another series of Dark Ones fell to the stone. "You may return..."

Entire ranks of shadow crumbled before Whitney. They fell in great droves, like autumn leaves in a tempest.

"No... no, no, no!" screamed Vandra. More burning eyes were extinguished. "Kill them! Kill them all!" The remaining

Dark Ones charged forward as Vandra renewed her assault, but the shadows toppled over before reaching the circle.

Cheers erupted across the Canyonlands. Whitney looked about in amazement at the thousands of motionless vessels surrounding them. Many were already dissolving to ash. Not a single Dark One remained standing. Men and women sank to the ground, tears of relief wetting the scorched dirt. Even his Shrikes were hugging each other in celebration.

Vandra sunk to all fours, chest heaving. She glanced to the south, then back to Whitney and the Ardas. "You think you've won?" Her dark eyes scanned the remaining figures and then widened in understanding. "Of course. The Oethyr. Lentarro's daughter. She prevails over her father's incompetence, the pathetic beast."

Eotan caught the dwarves' attentions and raised a single finger in warning.

Vandra's voice shook with rage. "You cannot win this war! I will return, and you will die. But first I will repay a debt of blood. Tell me, *Wolf*, can your conscience endure the knowledge that you sent that girl to her doom?"

"Now!" Eotan yelled. Vandra vanished in an eddying cloud of red dust. There was a sharp *crack*, and she crashed to the ground several hundred yards away. "Keep her tethered," Eotan ordered, and transformed into the wolf. He loped after the distant figure that was picking itself from the rock. Kipto stormed up to Whitney.

"Ride with us, Captain," said the Marshal, and extended a massive hand. Whitney grimaced but managed to stand. He was pulled into the saddle behind Culyan.

"I need a weapon. Lend me one of your axes?" Culyan grudgingly passed him an axe. He marveled at its weight. "It's amazing you can swing two of these things, Arda."

"That's not a thing, and if you break or lose *her*, I will end you. Jaya, Riddleston, ride with the dwarves. Make sure

Vandra doesn't break free." The dwarves conjured their cloud, but paused beside the body of Two. One looked to Culyan, tears glimmering in his beard. "We leave him, for now," said Culyan gruffly. "We will return to see him a proper burial. You have my word."

Another *crack* sounded and Vandra reappeared even further away. Her shrieks of frustration reached them moments later. Kipto charged after her in a storm of earth, and the cheers of the living spurred them across the blood-red waste.

SINGULARITY

CRACK!

Sten flinched at the sharp report that rolled over the Canyonlands. All eyes turned to the north. A distant figure shakily picked itself from the ground. It swayed, unsteadily, and then vanished in the moonlight. A second blast and it reappeared, closer this time.

Sten recognized the black robes. "Vandra." He smiled grimly and turned to the others. "The good news is our plan must have worked. The bad news is she's heading this way and we can't outrun her."

Ineza addressed the wizards. "Can you lot fight?"

Borneus huffed. "We've been locked in a damned dungeon with no food or water for weeks. What do you think? Even at our strongest that woman outmatched us all."

"The Yutuku will fight for you," said Faewyn.

There came a flutter of soft wings and Stonetalon and Edelwing landed on Manye's shoulders. "As will we."

"We can't touch her," said Sten. He whistled. Lilenti trotted over and buried her nose in his palm. "Not without magic." He realized the entire company was silent, waiting on his direction. "I'll..." He swallowed and looked to Ineza, but she only smiled.

With an elated cry, Manye pointed to the north. "Look!"

Vandra was still coming. But close behind was the golden wolf, loping over the rock with easy strides. Kipto raced after them, accompanied by a shimmering cloud. The faintest melody of dwarven music could now be heard, interspersed with keen blasts, like the crack of a whip, as Vandra continued her escape.

Sten vaulted onto Lilenti and spoke without hesitation. "I'll distract her. Faewyn, Manye, lead the wizards into the Wilds. Hide until you hear from me."

"I'm coming with you," said Manye, "and don't even think about arguing."

"Wouldn't dream of it." Sten hoisted her in front of him. Ineza climbed into her saddle and drew her sword. "Don't stop until you reach the edge of the Canyonlands," he ordered. With a flutter of wings, the owls sped toward the Wilds, the wizards and Yutuku following below.

"Let's see if Vandra will take the bait," said Sten.

"Gods help us if she does," said Ineza.

Sten leaned forward and Lilenti hurtled eastward, angled well away from Vandra's path.

Vandra gasped for breath and tasted blood. She didn't understand how the dwarves were containing her power. It shouldn't be possible. Her gaze raked the foothills, looking for signs of the Oethyr. All was still and silent. "Cowards!" she screamed to the night air. She would hunt them down, one by one, and make them suffer for their betrayal.

A flicker of movement caught her eye. A broad procession

was traveling west, fleeing toward the Wilds. They were moving slowly, attempting to shield their progress with the lowermost foothills. Vandra tensed and prepared to leap. Another blur of motion made her pause.

A silver horse was galloping full-tilt across the desert, a second struggling to keep pace. Vandra's anger surged upon recognition. She paused for the briefest of moments, considering which group to pursue, then disappeared in a flurry of dust.

She snapped into existence in front of the riders, simultaneously launching a barrage of scarlet missiles. The silver horse veered abruptly and its riders were thrown to the ground. The elf lay where she fell, moaning in pain. But the boy rolled to his feet and fired an arrow at Vandra in a single motion. His speed caught her off guard. The arrow punched through her shoulder. She howled in pain and launched another salvo of arcane death. The Shrike's horse was struck and crumpled to the ground atop the girl.

Vandra raised her hand for the killing blow, just as a monstrous shape appeared at the edge of her vision. She spun as the golden wolf leapt and clamped its jaws around her arm. Searing pain coursed through her entire body. She screamed and released a nova of crimson power. The wolf was blasted into the air. She staggered, and an arrow whistled past her ear. Icy fingers of dread gripped her chest.

Pounding drums heralded the dwarves' arrival. The Marshal and the fat captain followed atop the great black charger. The latter dismounted and helped the pinned Shrike to her feet. They surrounded Vandra and launched their assault as one. Crimson power erupted from her fingertips, but disintegrated into mist.

Tears were streaming down her face. She needed to control her emotions, as he had taught her, but all she felt was a burning rage. And where was he now, in her moment of greatest need? She looked to the darkness beyond the halo of magic, desperately searching for those twin droplets of molten gold that would mean salvation. But the Canyonlands were empty. She was utterly alone.

Alone.

She *alone* had fought to save Miz. She *alone* had recognized the implications of the world's greed. And she *alone* had lost everything as a consequence. Unbidden, her thoughts drifted back to Father, smiling down at her in the warm light of home. *Magic must always be respected.* Vandra's fists clenched as the rage obscured everything else. It was time the world learned that same respect.

She dropped to her knees and the ground split asunder. Motes of scarlet light poured from the rock in great rivulets, like molten rivers. Glowing shafts of crimson tore through the rock, radiating outward in all directions. Then, as one, the lights imploded, and absorbed into her kneeling form.

The magic shone through her veins, burning white-hot. She stood and began to laugh. Her tears turned to vapor on her cheeks. "I am the power of Miz incarnate!" she cried, her voice terribly distorted. "You would usher forth an era of destruction into this world? Witness it before you now! We shall all burn together."

A SECOND DROPLET

Whitney ducked as a spout of flame roared over his head. The air crackled and the tips of his mustache smoldered. Vandra was a swirling torrent of light. Unrestrained power emanated from her body with rampant fury. Jaya, Riddleston, and the dwarves were attempting to curb her attacks, but were retreating beneath the onslaught.

Culyan, Eotan, and Ineza charged and feinted ceaselessly, dodging bursts of magic as they attempted to close the distance. But Vandra held them at bay, laughing, or perhaps crying, all the while. Sten had exhausted his store of arrows. He was now bent over the still form of Manye, whispering in her ear. The world burned around them.

Another tongue of crimson light twisted from Vandra and caught Whitney in the side. He was thrown into the air and landed heavily on his back. Tinges of blackness touched his vision, and pain blossomed across his ribs.

"Oi, what da hell's goin' on?" squeaked Zwat. "Let me

out!" Whitney struggled to retrieve the Follower from his armor. It was buzzing with energy, the electric blue light brighter than ever. Whitney pushed upright, each breath raking his body with a new wave of pain. "What is dat fing?" Zwat yelled. "No wonder I'm fit to burst, look at all dat raw magic! You gotta get me outta here! Demons don't mix with dat stuff, especially wif my beacon so close!"

Whitney almost laughed then. He blinked away sweat and blood, surrounded by magic and fury, his entire body aflame in agony. "I'm terribly sorry about this, Zwat." He rose to his feet and retrieved the fallen axe.

The blue light buzzed in agitation. "Sorry about what?"

Whitney limped to Eotan. The wolf had retreated, golden fur smoldering. "Give me your beacon!" Whitney ordered. Nearby, Jaya and Riddleston rebuffed another gout of flame. Eotan transformed and passed the glowing stone to Whitney.

"Oh, you clever bastard!" cackled Zwat.

Whitney forced the stone through one of the holes in the box. Blue light immediately burst from the holes, and the wood splintered. "Make it count, Captain!" yelled Zwat. The box seared Whitney's palm.

"Rou-augh!" he roared, and hurled the Follower at Vandra. The box exploded when it reached her. A shockwave bloomed from the detonation and ripped over the Canyonlands. Vandra was thrown from her feet. Her attacks subsided as the nimbus of magic coalesced about her.

Whitney was already sprinting into the seething maelstrom. Heat blistered his skin. He fought the spots of blackness that threatened to conquer his vision. Vandra emerged through the flames, a beacon of awful light amidst the chaos and fire. Whitney leapt, and brought the axe down with all of his might.

Her eyes widened with disbelief, and her mouth moved wordlessly. She weakly tried to pull at the axe buried in her chest. Her eyes met his. Then she toppled to the ground. The glowing lights within her began to dance, the crimson veins writhing frantically across her body like frenzied eels.

Whitney stumbled away. His vision darkened as the pain in his ribs and side threatened to overwhelm him. He collapsed to the scorched rock. The magic boiled furiously within Vandra. He vaguely realized someone was calling his name. As if from a great distance, he watched the magic explode from the black robes. It burned toward him. But then it paused, held at bay by some unseen force. He rolled over and squinted up at a perfectly clear night sky.

Manye stood over him, arms raised to the magic, and then the world was nothing.

A PROMISE KEPT

To Sten, the magical eruption stretched for an eternity. He watched, helplessly, as Whitney fell to the ground. The magic tore from Vandra's body. He barely registered Manye rising from the stone. She raced to the fallen captain and braced herself against the storm. The magic broke against her like waves upon rock, but she held fast.

Then, in a flurry of blinding lights, it was over. The seething magic faded into oblivion, and the world continued to burn. Eotan dashed forward and caught Manye as she fell. He screamed for Jaya and Riddleston. Jaya knelt. A torrent of light flowed from her fingertips, encapsulating Manye in a luminescent azure cocoon. Riddleston and the dwarves joined in, and the glowing aura swelled. Sten could hear Eotan over the crackling of the flames, begging Manye to wake.

Whitney stirred and Ineza ran to help him to his feet. They joined Sten and looked on in silence. Magic flowed

around Manye like an incandescent waterfall, sparks cascading to the crimson soil.

"You will be safe," sobbed Eotan. "You will be safe..."

Sten urged Manye to move, to take a single breath, but the little Oethyr remained still. Jaya ceased her flow of magic and the lights dwindled. She placed a hand on Eotan's shoulder. He didn't seem to notice. He sat on the scorched ground, rocking Manye back and forth, tears coursing down his face. The company gathered around him.

When Eotan finally tore his gaze from Manye, his blue eyes were filled with confusion and pain. He looked up at Culyan, and Sten was reminded of a child looking to a guardian for protection.

"I promised her Culyan. I promised her I'd keep her safe!"

"You did keep her safe, little pup," said Culyan. His tears had cleaned lines in the blood and dust on his cheeks. "There isn't a force in all of Miz that would prevent Manye from protecting others. She chose to save us all. You couldn't protect her from herself. This world didn't deserve her. Now she's finally free of its suffering."

Eotan tore at his hair. "I shouldn't have convinced her to come. She would have been safe in the Gateway. It's my fault she's gone!"

One knelt beside Eotan. "Do you truly believe so? How long would she have been safe if we hadn't stopped Vandra? How many would have died if we sat idly in our home, secreted away amongst the trees, as Vandra and her army swept across Miz?"

"She was so scared," mumbled Eotan. His gaze was unfocused.

"Manye was scared of losing you!" Culyan cried. "Not of dying! Losing you would have been the worst possible fate to befall her. You were her father and she needed you above all else. Be thankful that it is *you* left to carry the weight of her passing, and not the other way around. Our little Oethyr died a hero.

She died pure. She died free from the burdens that haunt violent men like us. That is the way of this world. We are allowed to endure, while those who are innocent and good cannot."

After a time, Eotan placed Manye on the ground. He delicately arranged the hem of her trousers to cover the jagged scar along her leg.

"She loved you, Uncle," said Sten, choosing his words carefully. "She'd have done anything to protect us."

Eotan screamed at the night sky, his keening echoing to the stars. He transformed in a flash of emerald and tore at the ground with tooth and claw. Gradually, the howls turned to whimpers. The wolf lay beside Manye and nudged her hand with its nose. Sten moved to console him, but One laid a restraining hand on his shoulder.

"Let him be, lad. That is a man who has lost his world. No amount of reason will appeal to him now. Only the passage of time can dampen such suffering." They watched in silent grief, letting the impassive serenity of the ancient landscape wash over them. Ineza took Sten's hand.

The wolf rose from the ground. The humanity seemed to have drained from its piercingly blue eyes. It began to trot away from the company, and Sten moved to block its path. The wolf bared its teeth, a deep growl building in its throat. Culyan pulled Sten aside. The wolf loped across the Canyonlands, heading for the Wilds.

"We've seen this before," said the Marshal. "You have to let my brother find his own path home. He's lost to us."

Sten watched until the golden coat disappeared from sight, enveloped by the western horizon.

HONOR THE DEAD

S ten walked beside Culyan as the protectors of Dinh
filed from the city. The Marshal carried only a slender
bundle of linen cloth. Baroness Marstarrow and Lady Janderfel marched at the head of the somber procession, their
proud shadows lengthening in the setting sun. The citizens of
Dinh lined the road, passing out tokens of gratitude to those
who had fought. A small girl smiled up at Sten, eyes wide
with admiration, and offered him a toy soldier. He accepted
the figurine with mumbled thanks and continued on.

Countless pyres had been erected in the Canyonlands
east of Dinh. To Sten, they looked a boundless constellation
of blackened stars in a crimson sky. Lines of pitch stretched
between the wood, like glistening strands of a spider's web.
Slowly, the procession encircled the dead.

Baroness Marstarrow cleared her throat. "Let us remember
those who sacrificed their lives so that we may yet live. Honor

them, here, as we witness their souls' departure from this world. Lady Janderfel?"

Jaya stepped forward and unfurled a length of parchment. It reached to the stone at her feet several times over. "Tonight we honor Mage Keet Tonson, Mage Clara Hayton, Mage Biral Fells..." Her shoulders trembled, but her voice never broke.

Sten scanned the crowd. The Yutuku were assembled behind Faewyn, heads bowed in somber respect. Riddleston and the wizards of Heldan Port silently held their hats over their chests. Whitney stood amongst the Shrikes, supported by Ineza, Finlan, and Tryo. They noticed Sten's attention and nodded.

"We honor Corporal Ryman Pert, Private Hal Thutton..." Jaya read on as darkness descended over the Canyonlands. "And finally we remember our allies in Heldan Port, who await burial in their homeland. We honor Kol Hemmie, Marian Lee, and Mason Noxid of the Shrikes. We honor Two of clan Strongbeard. And we honor Manye Arda."

Sten looked up at Culyan. His uncle smiled through a veil of tears. "I thought it fitting she share my brother's name in death."

"She would have liked that," said Sten.

The Canyonlands fell silent. The baroness gestured to Culyan. The Marshal knelt and withdrew an elegant longbow and a single arrow from the folds of cloth. He strode to the center of the pyres, the dwarves in tow.

Jaya came to stand with Sten. "What are they doing?" he asked. The dwarves began to play a haunting melody.

"It's Dinh's custom to burn the departed." Culyan fitted an arrow to his bowstring. The music swelled. The tip of the arrow ignited in a brilliant shower of sparks that fled down the wind, tumbling and dancing over stone and sand to vanish in the darkening waste. Culyan knelt and touched the flame to the lines of pitch. The inferno spread in a symmetrical wave, following the trails of pitch. Pyres ignited one by one, and an ethereal glow seeped into the night sky.

The music crescendoed. Culyan drew at the heavens and waited, bow creaking. The final pyres were engulfed in flame. He released the arrow with a slight *twang*. It whistled into the darkness, trailing red sparks.

"And that is the custom of the Brothers Arda and the Frozen Steppes," whispered Jaya. The burning arrow soared ever higher. "Culyan signals to the keepers of the afterlife. The souls of the fallen approach and require safe passage." Sten watched the arrow until it was nothing more than a crimson mote in the night sky, a memory of fire nestled amongst the stars spreading throughout the cosmos.

A FAMILIAR PATH

They left for Heldan Port the following day, accompanied by the wizards, the Yutuku, and Jaya, at the baroness's request. Sten imagined he could detect the slightest touch of life returning to the Wilds. The forests still bore the devastating effects of the mist, bleakly stretching for hundreds of miles to the southern horizon. But faint patches of green nestled amidst the gnarled branches, and birds and rabbits and foxes watched curiously their passage.

They paused where they had fought the Dark Ones. Whitney buried his fallen Shrikes alongside Hemmie's grave. He used their broken and twisted swords as headstones. Ineza collected a bouquet of wildflowers and spread them atop the soil and golden leaves. Then Whitney spoke a few somber words, and the Shrikes saluted their slain brethren.

After three days of travel, Faewyn and the Yutuku said their farewells and disappeared into the northern Wilds.

When they reached the Waypoint, Grandmother Morroza

greeted them with tables sagging under the weight of delicious food and drink. They rested amidst the fading colors
of autumn as Stonetalon and Edelwing regaled them with
vibrant tales, of their finding the Yutuku, of tracking Sten
through the Canyonlands, and their battle with the Oethyr,
all at the Grandmother's behest. Morroza brushed away the
company's repeated thanks, but insisted they stay an additional night. One night invariably became two and two
became three. When they finally departed on the fourth day,
Sten's belt was noticeably tighter.

A gentle dusting of snow coated the road as the last dregs
of autumn gave way to winter, and the company returned to
the Gateway to the Wilds. They buried Manye and Two in a
sheltered glen, side by side. Sten held back tears as the dwarves
conjured flickering images of the dead, the ghostly faces smiling
happily amongst the trees. The rest of the company paid their
respects, laying small tokens of gratitude into the graves. Two's
body sparkled with the gemstones of his kinsmen, while the
braids of his beard shone with platelets of beaten silver. His
Boomstick lay beside him, polished and newly stained.

As the dwarves performed a dirge of farewell, Culyan covered Manye in a simple linen sheet and carefully arranged
the crown of golden leaves over her hair. Jaya and Riddleston
directed a murmuring stream of magic into the ground. A
pair of maple saplings sprouted from the graves, limbs already
thick with vermillion leaves.

Sten chose to remain in the Gateway. Apart from his visits
with Ineza, he avoided the capital entirely. It was peaceful
living in the deep forest, despite the cold of coming winter. He
hunted with Culyan during the day and shared tales with the
dwarves at night, talking into the early hours of dawn while
the fire crumbled to embers. But there was a tension shared by
all, a mounting discomfort that stemmed from Eotan's absence.

FROM THE DESK OF
SYLVUS RIDDLESTON

The following report details the resolution of conflict between the renegade enchantress, Vandra, and the cities of Heldan Port and Dinh.

The wizards of Heldan Port and the magi of Dinh worked in combination to determine the validity of the concerns raised by Councilman Frank Monta (departed). Vast quantities of data and magical analysis were recovered from Monta's personal possessions, detailing the tests and procedures used during his experimentation on Miz and her magic. Monta argued that Miz reacted adversely to an overuse of her magical stores, thus resulting in the mist that had become so prevalent during the summer months of this year. Monta continued to say that a failure to address such issues could result in irreparable damage to Miz, and potentially the future eradication of all her life.

I, Sylvus Riddleston, Highest Hat of the Occult Sanctum of Wizards, and Lady Jaya Janderfel, leader of Dinh's Guild of Magi, headed the Revered Coalition of Magical Experimentation; a joint effort between the one true capital and the city of Dinh. Our goal was to lend credible source to Monta's claims. After months of deliberation and testing, it was decided that Monta's theories held true. We were able to replicate the effects of the mist and tested its impacts on a host of flora and fauna, all in accordance with the Regulations on Humane Testing of Living Creatures. From the substantial evidence that was gathered (sourced below), we have concluded the mist to be a defense mechanism of Miz, used to suffocate any threat that would do her significant harm.

As such, the Revered Coalition met with Chancellor Marstarrow of Heldan Port and Baroness Marstarrow of Dinh, and advised in the direction of magical reform. We demonstrated that, much to our chagrin, the current levels of magical reliance were unsustainable in such a delicate system. Both cities have pledged to implement reform in the years to come.

Subsequently, the Occult Sanctum of Wizards will play a lesser role in the workings of Heldan Port. Under my council, we will significantly increase our focus on magical theory and research. After witnessing the awesome power of the enchantress, Vandra, and the Oethyr, Manye Arda, it is clear that many secrets of magic lie beyond our comprehension. Additionally, it has been decided that the Sanctum will open its gates to any and all with the ability and will to practice magic. Our backward laws will never again be a source of shame for Heldan Port. Having borne witness to the events of these past months, it is clear that both my predecessors and I were fools for enforcing such regulations.

Change is coming to Heldan Port, and I, for one, believe it is for the better.

I look forward to the years to come. The Sanctum's new-found relationship with the magi of Dinh promises to be interesting. I welcome the collaboration and competition, as Lady Janderfel has vowed to assist in implementing the capital's reforms as repayment for Heldan Port's assistance in the Battle of the Canyonlands. Even so, we shall undoubtedly prove Heldan Port the greatest power in these lands in the years to come.

-Co-Chief Sylvus Riddleston, RCoME

JUST REWARD

Whitney's footsteps echoed through the empty halls of the chancellor's keep. A message had reached him that morning, informing him of the completed project. He entered the hall and was met by the stoic gazes of Heldan Port's deceased icons. A new tapestry hung from the southern wall, its borders embroidered with gold. Whitney inspected the engraved plague that rested below.

-Captain Regibar Theraford Whitney, Savior of Dinh,
Hero of Heldan Port

The tapestry depicted his standing over a fallen Vandra, armor glinting in the light of Tanduil, an axe slung confidently over one shoulder. A woman gazed up at him with fawning admiration, presumably Lady Janderfel, due to her flaming red hair. Riddleston stood impressively in the background, his robes billowing in the wind as lightning arced from his fingertips. There was no sign of Manye, the Ardas, or the dwarves.

"Quite the impressive scene, Captain," said Tiberion Marstarrow. Whitney turned to find the chancellor watching him from the shadows. The chancellor swept forward and came to stand at his shoulder.

Whitney looked up at the tapestry and shook his head. "It's an abomination. I would have died, if not for Manye, and they didn't even include her. I'm sorry, Chancellor, I truly appreciate this honor, but it's just so... wrong."

Marstarrow cocked his head and stroked his chin. "They did pay wonderful attention to your mustache, at the very least. Though I quite agree with you. Having met Lady Janderfel, I am hard-pressed to believe such a proud woman could ever look so foolish. But, alas, this is the nature of such things. People are not interested in the truth, as the truth tends to be far too ugly."

Whitney gazed about the hall. "It makes you wonder about the rest of these monuments."

Marstarrow gave him a sidelong glance. "Indeed. Tell me, Captain, are you satisfied with the glory you have earned? You are a hero of Heldan Port. Everyone knows of your courage and the role you played in saving the capitals. I was under the impression you craved such recognition before your departure."

"I find myself wishing none of this had happened." Whitney's thoughts returned to Hemmie and his fallen Shrikes, as they had so often done in the months since his return. "A naive notion, I know. Though I'm proud of the part my Shrikes played in this story, and I will always answer when my city is in need, glory be damned."

The chancellor's eyes twinkled in the dim light. "Very well, Captain. I thank you for your service." They shook hands and Marstarrow turned to leave.

"You seem different, Chancellor, if you don't mind me saying," said Whitney.

Marstarrow paused. "How so?"

"I'm not sure. More human, I suppose."

The chancellor smiled. "Perhaps both of our eyes were opened in such dark times. For the first time in my life, I find myself enjoying, and perhaps craving, the company of a select few I would call friends. You are among those select few, Regibar." Whitney flushed at the unexpected confession. "But I must be going," continued Marstarrow. "I have an appointment for which I absolutely cannot be late. Is there anything else I can do for you?"

Whitney thought for a moment. "Would you arrange a meeting with Sylvus Riddleston?"

Marstarrow inclined his head. "An odd request, but it shall be done. Good evening, Captain."

Later that night, Whitney waited patiently in Riddleston's office. The space was cluttered with feather quills and scrolls of parchment. "I apologize if you're busy, Highest Hat, but I have a question for you."

"And a letter wouldn't suffice?" huffed Riddleston, shuffling through a stack of parchments. With a derisive grunt, he tossed them away and removed his spectacles. "Apologies, Captain, I haven't slept in days with all of these new propositions for reform. Lady Janderfel is utterly incorrigible. The times are changing, as they say. What can I help you with?"

"I was hoping you might summon a demon."

Riddleston cocked an eyebrow. "A demon, you say? How strange. Do you know the creature's name? We'll need it for the summons."

Whitney smiled. "As a matter of fact, I do."

CHAPTER ONE

Butterson threaded his way through the crowds in the Jumping Jackamoose. He unlatched the small side door and narrowly avoided Gefwyn coming from the opposite direction. The volunteer gnome trundled past with a cask of ale bound for the cellars and gave G'rok a cheery wave. As the clock tower chimed to usher in the new hour, the door opened and a cloaked figure entered the tavern. Butterson took his spot behind the bar. The figure paused beside a barstool that was currently occupied by a dwarf eating soup with a golden spoon.

"Time to go, Sixty-Eight," said Butterson. "You know that seat's reserved."

"Every night!" slurred the dwarf, eyes somewhat crossed. "For whom is this seat... seat... hic! For whom is this seat reserved? Er, for who? Whomever? Blast, I dunno."

"We've been over this," said Butterson, not unkindly. "Now move it. Raxo will give you a free pint." The dwarf stumbled into the crowd, crooning happily.

Marstarrow removed his hood and sat. "Good evening, Mord."

"Is the disguise really necessary anymore? I'm afraid the city knows you now, whether you like it or not."

"Indeed it does, but I still prefer to keep my personal affairs a secret."

Butterson smirked down at him. "Will you ever deny yourself this paranoia?"

"Not in my profession." Marstarrow delicately wiped the bar with his sleeve. "Not with my enemies."

"More backlash from the Houses, I take it," said Butterson. "And I've told you a hundred times, you'll never get that spot clean."

Marstarrow abandoned his futile pursuit and sighed. "The sentencing for the Houses' crimes was severe, but justly so. I believe the financial and social repercussions of their treacheries will prove enduringly beneficial to us all. But their wealth and influence cannot be erased. I fear they have become a permanent fixture of Heldan Port, skulking in the shadows and biding their time until the next opportunity presents itself."

Butterson leaned across the bar and lowered his voice. "Did they ever catch on about how you managed it? Tricking them at the gallows, I mean."

Marstarrow's eyes twinkled and he suppressed a smile. "Not to my knowledge. I admit I prefer their believing me immortal to learning the truth. You would not believe the rash I endured from Wizard Teedle's infernal floating undergarments."

Butterson grinned. "You sure made your hanging look convincing."

"Yes, well... Practice makes perfect, as they say, much to the sorrow of my waistline. Still, there is hope for my city, as proven by her peoples' courage in recognizing the truth. Additionally, my new council shows promise, and Lady Janderfel is a welcome pillar of sanity in dealing with these reforms."

"Plus you've got us now," said Raxo. The demon hopped onto the bar and deposited a foaming flagon in front of the chancellor. "Ten gold, my Duke of Diorite."

"Ten? My, my, we certainly are confident tonight." Marstarrow closed his eyes and took a pensive sip. "I admit this might prove challenging for lesser individuals, but this is, without question, Redwall's Barley Wine."

Raxo begrudgingly passed over the coins. "You have a problem, you know that?"

Butterson laughed, filled a tankard for a passing elf, and turned back to the chancellor. "Say, Tiberion, you still haven't told us what you discovered in the Sanctum. You made a promise, after all."

Marstarrow's face darkened for the briefest of moments. "And one day I shall tell you, as I vowed, but not tonight."

Butterson was about to protest when shouts of anger erupted from across the room. Sixty-Eight hurtled through the air and smashed through a window. G'rok peeked through the broken glass, her new pink bow tie sparkling in the warm glow of the tavern.

"Raxo, who's minding your station?" Butterson asked. As he watched, a brawl broke out across the floor.

Raxo innocuously examined his claws. "Er, I may or may not have asked them to serve themselves for a bit. You know, use the honor system and what not?"

Butterson chuckled. "This is Heldan Port. Honor is a concept as foreign as soap to these people. Come on, let's break up this mess. Care to join us, Tiberion?"

"That would be most inappropriate as acting ruler of this city." Butterson raised an eyebrow and folded his arms. Marstarrow paused, and then downed his beer. "Oh, what the hell."

Sten sat in the corner of the Jackamoose alongside Culyan and the dwarves. They watched in amusement as Butterson, Raxo, and the chancellor attempted unsuccessfully to calm the raucous crowd. Finally, the door to the Jackamoose swung open and G'rok stomped inside. The room fell deathly silent under the orc's stern glare. With a snort of approval, she returned to her station, and the patrons returned to their drinks.

"Oi, make room!" Ineza called. She appeared through the crowd, juggling a handful of tankards. She wedged herself into the bench and playfully shoved Culyan aside, then kissed Sten on the cheek.

Culyan took a tankard in each hand. "Thanks, Ghet."

She nodded to the bar. "Oh, these weren't from me."

Jaya forced her way to them, Captain Whitney in tow. They sat, and Ineza distributed the flagons. The company exchanged glances, then raised their drinks in unison and toasted in silent understanding.

Out of the corner of his eye, Sten saw Jaya take Culyan's hand. The Marshal turned a vibrant shade of crimson and buried his face in his tankards. Sten winked at his uncle. Culyan could only smile.

Ineza leaned her head on Sten's shoulder. "So, any news from Eotan?"

"None," he said. "It's been months and no word from Dinh, the Waypoint, or anybody. I'm tired of waiting."

She smiled up at him. "I think you know what you need to do."

"I need to find him." He looked to his newfound friends and family gathered around him. "But I can't go it alone."

"I suppose I'd be a terrible uncle if I let my headstrong nephew embark on this proposed journey," said Culyan.

Sten leaned forward. "You'd come?"

Culyan shrugged. "What choice do I have in the face of such bravery? Can't have the youngest Arda stealing all my glory on some foolish adventure. Besides, you're not the only one who's tired of waiting. It's time we bring my brother home."

"We would accompany you as well," said One. The rest of the dwarves stood and bowed in agreement. "The Bearded Seven shall always stand beside the Brothers Arda. Or is it the Ardas Three now?"

"What about you, Jaya?" Ineza asked.

Jaya vigorously shook her head and blew a curly strand of hair from her eyes. "My hands are plenty full dealing with Marstarrow's magical reform, thank you."

Sten glanced quizzically at Captain Whitney. He shook his head. "Oh no, the Shrikes are needed in Heldan Port. And don't even think about taking my corporal with you." His expression was stern, but the tips of his mustache twitched ever so slightly.

Ineza gave Sten's arm an affectionate squeeze. "Don't worry, I'll be here when you return. Probably."

Culyan took a long swig of ale and slammed the empty tankard onto the table. "So, nephew, it looks like it's just you, me, and the Bearded Seven. How do you plan on finding my brother, exactly? This is your idea, after all, and Miz is a vast and dangerous place."

Sten thought for a moment and then smiled, oddly content. "I have absolutely no idea."

THE END

EPILOGUE

Chancellor Tiberion Marstarrow sat alone in in his office. The pages of a large, dusty tome lay open upon his desk. He toyed with the leather bindings, his face a mask. The candle wavered and flickered, as if sharing in his uncertainty. But then, with a decisive intake of breath, he bent forward and began to read.

'There are many unique theories positing the birth of Miz. Perhaps the most outlandish of these details the existence of four Vaenir, or demigods, who brought the world into being through their magic. Legends tell of the Vaenir walking amongst us, content to immerse themselves in the world they once created.

'The Vaenir's magic is consummately formidable, and there are some who claim witness to markings left behind by such powers. The tales describe scorched rings of magic adorned with the runic symbols of the Vaenirs' own tongue.

As of yet, these rumors are entirely unsubstantiated, and are almost certainly fabrications that come of such desperate desires to believe in something greater than ourselves.

'The origin of this theory is yet unknown, though some scholars contend to have traced its conception to the wandering poet, Yfron, who wrote thus concerning the Vaenir:

> *Revere thy All-Knowing Raven,*
> *Remember thy Fallen Wolf,*
> *Love thy Benevolent Dragon,*
> *and Fear thy Yellow-Eyed Serpent.'*

CPSIA information can be obtained
at www.ICGtesting.com
Printed in the USA
BVHW032219151120
593398BV00007B/119